GRIME

GRIME

A NOVEL

SIBYLLE BERG

TRANSLATED FROM THE GERMAN BY

TIM MOHR

ST. MARTIN'S
GRIFFIN
NEW YORK

First published in the United States by St. Martin's Griffin, an imprint of St. Martin's Publishing Group

GRIME. Copyright © 2022 by Sibylle Berg. English translation copyright © 2022 by Tim Mohr. All rights reserved. Printed in the United States of America. For information, address St. Martin's Publishing Group, 120 Broadway, New York, NY 10271.

www.stmartins.com

Designed by Omar Chapa

Library of Congress Cataloging-in-Publication Data

Names: Berg, Sibylle, 1962– author. | Mohr, Tim, translator.
Title: Grime : a novel / Sibylle Berg ; translated from the German by Tim Mohr.
Other titles: GRM. English
Description: First U.S. edition. | New York : St. Martin's Griffin, 2022.
Identifiers: LCCN 2022028671 | ISBN 9781250796516 (trade paperback) |
    ISBN 9781250796523 (ebook)
Subjects: LCGFT: Dystopian fiction. | Novels.
Classification: LCC PT2662.E64 G7613 2022 | DDC 833/.92—
    dc23/eng/20220617
LC record available at https://lccn.loc.gov/2022028671

Our books may be purchased in bulk for promotional, educational, or business use. Please contact your local bookseller or the Macmillan Corporate and Premium Sales Department at 1-800-221-7945, extension 5442, or by email at MacmillanSpecialMarkets@macmillan.com.

First published in the German language as GRM by Sibylle Berg, copyright © 2019 by Verlag Kiepenheuer & Witsch, Cologne, Germany

First U.S. Edition: 2022

10 9 8 7 6 5 4 3 2 1

CONTENTS

GRIME

THE MILLENNIUM

began lousy.

There was no Y2K bug.

There were no fucking catastrophes.

The thing is, the citizens of the Western world had been looking forward to something finally happening after the hopelessly dull 1990s. Something not tied to a financial crisis; those only offered a bit of titillation for investment bankers as their bodies plunged the last few meters toward impact on the pavement and they wondered: Will my super sculpted body splatter on the sidewalk just like some fat, white, loser's body? Or will it bounce back up into the air?

The new millennium had a title. It was. *ADHD*. And beneath the title, in italics, stood: *WE'RE RESTRUCTURING SHIT.*

It was the era when Facebook got big. When a lot of older people thought that idiotic site *was* the internet.

It was the era of mass hoaxes, mass manipulation. Unbelievably quickly, people became addicted to Likes from strangers. Even more quickly, young people got addicted to a kind of excitement made up of a mix of bullying, violence, sex, and bullshit.

It was the era when genuine human cruelty was supplemented virtually.

When the yearning for understanding gave way to the rage of the ignorant.

Never before had there been so many conspiracy theories spreading online like wildfire. The Vatican, the Koch brothers, the Mont Pelerin Society, the Club of Rome, the reptilian elite, the flat-earthers—with the complications of the world seemingly increasing by the day, so too did the population's desire for a god of thunder.

It was the era before something.

It's always the era before something.

Then later, after the new millennium had gotten warmed up a bit, there had indeed been a collective event that united people in a sense of excitement: an airplane flew into the Pentagon and left a large hole in the building that looked like someone had dug a tunnel in a sand castle with a wet hand. Two other planes landed in skyscrapers. The skyscrapers imploded, and again people jumped out of windows.

It was the millennium during which doubt overcame the global population. And it became normal to mistrust the state and intelligence services, the press and academics, the weather, books, vaccines, scientists, and women.

The new millennium brought an array of unbeatable benefits for people lucky enough to have been born just then. All over the globe, people's lives improved. Or so it was said. People lived longer and more happily, more received education, infants survived infancy. Markets had made it all happen. Hooray for markets.

There were a few losers. They'd either been unlucky or hadn't tried hard enough to succeed. Everyone could make something of their life. As long as they wanted to. Brilliant.

They extracted fossil fuels. Natural gas and oil were extracted from the seabed with hydraulic fracking. Stuxnet—the computer virus—slowed down the Iranian nuclear program. Blockchain, which would render banks redundant, was invented. As was the e-bomb. The world was reorganized, the West fought to retain its importance. In the East, China, Russia, Japan, and Korea united to redefine markets.

Voice recognition was introduced for computers. AI wasn't yet a mainstream topic. People had mobile phones. They took pictures of themselves. They had things to do. Nonstop.

This is the story of

DON

THREAT POTENTIAL: *high*

ETHNICITY: *indistinct shades of nonwhite*

INTERESTS: *grime music, karate, sweets*

SEXUALITY: *probable homosexual*

SOCIAL CONDUCT: *unsocial*

FAMILIAL CONNECTIONS: *1 brother, 1 mother, father—occasionally, but mostly not*

It begins in Rochdale.

Fucking Rochdale. A place that needed to be preserved and put on display in a museum as a warning about thoughtless development. A brass plaque: "This is how people live in the new millennium if they are not suitable to market conditions."

A catchment basin for the superfluous. A pool of non–genetically modified rejects.

So, right, Rochdale. A shithole near Manchester. Known for the consistency of its weather. Bad, that is. Rochdale, according to evaluations, had already been the most depressing city in the United Kingdom for five years running. A municipal embodiment of brain damage is definitely not conducive to consumption, so the city had found itself in a fight for its very existence. For decades. Like thousands of cities in the Western world that all resembled each other: brick buildings, crumbling streets and a derelict cinema, shuttered post offices, shuttered supermarkets. Nobody needs those things anymore, because it's the internet era. You can stream any film. And buy all essential foodstuffs, meaning margarine and white bread. Delivered in cardboard boxes. Though the residents might as well have sprinkled wallpaper with salt and devoured that.

Among the relatively limited circle of objectophiles, Rochdale was known for its seven social housing towers. Consequently you'd see them creeping furtively around the towers, excitedly licking the peeling facades. There was always something happening at the Seven Sisters, which was the buildings' unofficial name. And it usually had to do with the demise of a resident. Don envied the people who got to live there. They had more interesting lives. More interesting than hers, which took place in a totally ordinary social housing complex a few minutes away. In the Seven Sisters the drug trade was run on a grand scale, family members killed each other, and time and again people jumped or—let's say—slipped out of upper-story windows. Don had never seen a dead body at that point and was convinced that the sight of one would reveal a great secret. Perhaps it would open its eyes, the corpse, and in the manner of a helmet-haired BBC reporter ask: "So, just what is it like for a young person"—pausing, considering the best way to phrase it—"to grow up in this city?" Don would act as if she were thinking the question over and then say: "You know, people all regard the life they know as normal. You just don't know anything else. I was born here and never questioned the city or its shabbiness. It's just the way it is, like the bad weather, like the boring school holidays, I never gave any thought to the fact that other places exist. Or put it this way: I know that it's claimed online that other places supposedly exist."

The corpse would persist—"Is your manner of speaking really appropriate for a child?"—before reverting to being dead again.

Don was no longer an extension of her parents but an autonomous person. She was no longer scared when her mother wasn't around, no longer searched her face for signs of trouble, no longer asked herself how she could please her mother. In short, Don no longer asked herself what she could do in order to finally feel loved. Don did better without this total emotional dependency.

If she were older and more convinced of her own importance she would have mumbled things like: "I'm perfectly capable of being on my own." But nobody asked her, because Don was so young that adults did not yet see her as a person. Despite the fact that everything was already there. The feelings, the thoughts, the loneliness. There just weren't familiar compartments into which to sort the feelings.

Don didn't regard the early years of her life as having been awful. Maybe a little bleak, though back then she didn't know the right word to express that. Maybe a little dreary and dull, as is normal during the transition from childhood to youth, when you sense that something will change but you're not sure what. Don had music.

Grime seemed to have been invented just for her. Don didn't know who had invented it or from what components—that was the stuff of discussions between young men who were able to project an aura of invincibility by deploying insider terminology—

Don just knew the music sounded the way she wished to feel. Angry and dangerous. Grime stars had the best sneakers, chains, and cars. They were someone. They'd made it. They were heroes.

Grime played all day in the neighborhood. The music suited the attitude toward life. Though children wouldn't talk about having an attitude toward life—it was just their life. When you're grown-up you numb rising feelings with drugs, when you're young you listen to music. And then numb yourself with drugs. Grime was raging, filthy music for children leading filthy lives. Don listened to grime in bed, in the bath, outdoors. The great outdoors.

So—

In front of the window a lamp, rain or something similar, or maybe the window was just dirty. The flat occupied the first and second floors. You could, if you had completely lost your mind, call the whole thing a town house.

A very, very small, shabby town house. It consisted of two small rooms with a view of an outdoor concrete seating area and a metal fence. Once while watching TV it occurred to Don that something was missing from all the foreign movies: metal fences. They existed in such manic frequency only in England. Every few meters. Red, green, blue, whatever, didn't matter as long as it was fencing and it was metal. Every fucking thing was isolated from life by fences—schools, parks, kindergartens, fire alarms. It wasn't clear whether they were supposed to make citizens feel safe, offering a sense of safe harbor in turbulent times, or they were just thrown up as colorful accents amid all the gray. Don wished for a fence around her bed to keep away her brother. To whom she wasn't particularly close.

Beyond the fence, outside, there was a path along which, just a few meters from her window, other residents of the block moved as if they were using imaginary walkers. It was relatively dark, and oddly damp, but Don didn't notice back then. That there was always a draft seemed normal. Her mother was still somewhat together, she did her best to play family, though it was a bit awkward, as if she were building a dollhouse out of mud.

That everything could get worse didn't seem like a possibility at the time. Not to a child, since fear of the future is a pastime of the aged, who don't have any future anyway. Back then Don's world was fine, except for the fact that she didn't have a fence around her bed, or, better yet, a little room in the basement where she could lock up her brother. The brother whined. He was probably pissing the bed again. Don almost thought she could

Hear the urine running out of him and

Don was—

Furious.

Many couldn't manage it. To muster such a righteous rage. Most of the older people who hung around Don's city were numb and tired and squatted in corners and barely had enough energy to lift their heads. Once in a while they'd be fed. But their stomachs couldn't tolerate it, this solid food in an empty existence, and they'd throw up, only to be too weak to lift their heads out of the vomit. Most of the people Don encountered were old. That was no wonder at seven—or nearly seven. Or nearly eight, but, of course, older looking. Or at least believing she looked older. Don's hair grew straight up. Her eyes were crooked and dark, and Don was little, even for a nearly seven- or eight-year-old. She was little and furious. Don's rage was so ever-present in her daily routine that she would never think of saying: "Fucking hell, am I pissed off today." She knew no other condition. She'd been furious since birth. Or at least as early as she could remember. She hated the world where she had to live. Which was a few square meters large.

She hated this world and refused to come to terms with it. She had no relationship with her place in it, or rather the place allotted to her by virtue of her birth, with the preordained path set out for her, that would start with a poor education. In the event she survived that step without accidentally getting caught up in a stabbing, then would follow an attempt to secure an apprenticeship.

Not getting an apprenticeship, sitting around in government agencies and applying for welfare benefits, getting no benefits because some document or other is missing; coming home to find her mother has hung herself, leaving the apartment, landing in some kind of shelter for young women, getting pregnant, getting beat up by someone for getting pregnant, giving up the baby for adoption, or not, it didn't matter. She'd wait for an apartment in a social housing complex, start to drink and smoke crack and watch TV, staring at other people's pseudo lives, aka life as it's supposed to be. Light-skinned people who drink tea in their gardens and do honest work with their skillful hands. They fall in love, the people on TV. And then comes: fucking violin music.

In Don's world nobody fell in love. The people in her city hated each other or clung to each other because of a sense of panic they all felt, though nobody could say where it came from, this unease. They had apartments after all. Most of them. They had food. A kind of food.

Don read a lot, understood little, but still far more than an adult would think possible of a so-called child. Don felt:

Rage.

Are you serious? This pile of shit that you plunked down here? "Watch it! That's what's left. It might not be great, but it's yours. This is the earth that we've eaten bare, this is your neighborhood, your city, which serves the purpose of housing workers so they can produce some useless shit that nobody needs. Got it? It doesn't require anything of the people in your city except to vote for right-wing nationalist idiots who always have an answer to the question of who is to blame."

When people know who's to blame, they feel better, because then divine justice is restored. And there's a target for their hate. In Don's city you hated foreigners. Period. Don's city, that she would never leave, where she would waste away her entire life. Where it would end, though actually it was already over even before it began, because she was born in the wrong place. To the wrong parents, and on top of it all the weather was wretched. Had anyone asked her? Had anyone asked her to take part in these proceedings, run according to rules she had no say in? What human obligation was she fulfilling with her stay here, shitting among the eight billion people—or, by the time the thought was finished, perhaps it was nine billion—who were crawling around looking to see if they could conjure up some sort of advantage somehow. Who all wanted—something.

Life was a gift.

This unbelievably stupid saying hung in the damp kitchens of the slum residents, embroidered on pink wall hangings. What happened if you rejected it? What if you just weren't interested in this gift in the form in which it was intended for you? Nobody escaped their surroundings through work. There was no work anymore anyway.

It was impossible to attain better living conditions, there was simply no space available in a world where the few were intent on keeping the many at bay.

"Why did you do that?" You want to ask the old people. "Why give birth to children you hate because they're loud, because they're losers—from the word go, because you can see yourselves and your miserable childhoods in them, because you know you're going to screw it up, just like your parents did and your parents' parents did, by passing on this hopeless existence?

"What's the point? Leaving the children in their own urine at the foot of the bed where you're passed out drunk or fucking somebody? You get off on their tiny bones that are so easily broken, on the feeling of finally having power over somebody who's scared of you, and then you look at the children, hazily, and hate them for their neediness, that's so much like your own. You were never helped either, not by anyone.

"Your dull brains get some sort of satisfaction from tormenting your children, do they? You'll show them, eh? The people lording over you. The ones who turned you away, pushed you from the city centers where they drive around in elegant electric cars and speak of an ever more prosperous future.

"You could go on strike. But from what, since you don't do anything? Nobody would care. You could start an armed resistance, but—you don't have the energy. Or the weapons. And no idea whom to aim them at. So you just lie there. With your face in your vomit.

"Why are there still men wandering around freely out there who don't want to be fathers, they just want to turn up to fuck or to beat women, beat them to death, before they slump into the corner and say: This isn't what I wanted. You didn't want any of this? It just so happens that it stinks outside and it rains nonstop. And that from the very first moment everyone has to be afraid of everyone else, because they have this so-called survival instinct. Nobody can bear it."

Don couldn't bear it.

And

Refused to accept her preordained role as scum.

And

Wasn't going to wait for love anymore.

Wasn't going to wait for something like a future to sprout in front of her door. Nothing would ever grow here, it was a desert left behind by the elderly, along with these so-called living—living?—conditions. And yes, for fuck's sake, Don was passive-aggressive, she was female, she couldn't do any better. Was she supposed to take testosterone injections just to get more enraged, was she supposed to shoot herself up with hormones to try to convince herself she was smarter than she was, and that she ruled the world?

People like her had been put on display in zoos in the old days. The thought occurred to her randomly.

When people have the opportunity to torture others, they take it. When they have the chance to take something away from others, they do it, this mechanism, or call it: this instinct. That they let guide them, without thinking, that they give free rein to eradicate anything and everything that stands in their way—

Don hated the stupidity, the brutality, the deviousness and deceitfulness, the stench, the hairless, sweating bodies and the slimy fingers that tested everything for commercial potential.

"You want war, you got war."

Said Don. To herself.

This is the story of

HANNAH

ETHNICITY: *Asian?*
SEXUALITY: *heterosexual*
INTERESTS: *self-absorbed*
INTELLIGENCE: *proven*
DISTINGUISHING CHARACTERISTICS: *none*
FAMILIAL CONNECTIONS: *only child, loving parents*

Before she met Karen, Don, and Peter.

When she didn't yet know what Rochdale meant, or tragedy.

To backtrack just a little:

Hannah lived in Liverpool, with two genial parents who were typical of the fading middle class. They'd rented a house with a shabby back garden, owned two bicycles, and were able to pay their electricity bills. Hannah considered love from her parents the normal state of things—that they would throw her in the air and caress her. That they'd hold her hand and be proud of her, that they'd sit with her at bedtime and come to her room to check on her when she was asleep, all this she took for granted. Through the constant affection of her parents Hannah had developed an outsized ego as a child. Hannah didn't doubt herself. She was tall and thin and never looked like a cute little kid. More like a miniature version of an interesting adult. Hannah never wanted long hair or dresses or pink stuff; instead she studied old photos of Katharine Hepburn online. That's how she wanted to look one day. Aloof and instilling a bit of fear. Hannah's home was located in a problematic part of a city that consisted mostly of problematic parts. But her problematic part of town was unequivocally the most problematic. You often heard shootings outside, you rarely heard sirens, the police had long since given up on the area. But Hannah didn't care. Nothing outside could affect her when she was in bed listening to her parents quietly talk to each other.

That sensation of being sheltered and loved would later save her from many things.

From killing herself, for instance—

Something which seemed to

DON

Completely incomprehensible—to be dead, gone, no longer enraged. The fascination Don felt about the dead ended the day of what was called the Massacre. That sort of incident—meaning: a crazed teenager shooting other teenagers—was largely unknown in the country at that point, because there were hardly any fathers with well-stocked gun cabinets, at least if you disregarded the hunting rifles of the upper class. Fathers in Rochdale had beer. If there were fathers at all, since Don's experience with parents, as was true of most children, consisted primarily of contact with overburdened women.

Don hadn't retained much memory of the incident. Just shots, which sounded like New Year's firecrackers, screaming children who sounded like they were under water, and slow-motion images of people running or crawling in every direction. While lying on the floor, Don wondered about the way the killer must have revealed his intentions online. Had he worn a hoodie? Had he sat or stood with a gun and said something that included "system, disrespect, women, never taken seriously, and now I'll show you . . ."? What music had he played in his video? Slipknot? Something more thumping. Pitbull? He probably wasn't the brightest bulb, like most people here. Some of the children lying on the ground took pictures of themselves during the so-called massacre. Some of them had iPhones. The poorer fuckers had crap Chinese phones. The approximately eight hours a day they spent on their devices was supposed to make Don's entire generation into a bunch of unfocused idiots.

Man, oh man, thought Don, who on earth sticks fake plastic nails onto their fingers? Don was lying on the ground next to an older girl, staring at her nails. She'd never seen anything so awful. You could see the yellow horn through the back of the fingernail. The girl was ten or thirteen and looked like a baby hooker. The downside of grime videos. They really didn't offer positive lessons for discourse surrounding gender or queer theory. The women in the videos showed a lot of bust and backside, along with gold jewelry and fake nails. They mostly waltzed over to the passenger seat of some showy car that a gangster rapper had stolen or bought with his mad riches. Money doesn't make you happy, Don thought randomly, and started laughing just as the police commando team came storming in. Then there were more shots. The dull click of the attacker's semiautomatic rifle faded into the rich stew of noise produced by the commandos' proper machine guns. When it was over it was quiet and the shooter was dead. Along with a few girls. Don had finally seen corpses. It was less grandiose than in Don's fantasies. People were just lying there and no longer existed.

This is the story of

KAREN

SEXUALITY: *heterosexual*

INTELLIGENCE: *highly gifted*

CLINICAL PICTURE: *predilection to obsessive behavior (licking light switches)*

CONSUMER BEHAVIOR: *inadequate*

ETHNICITY: *genetic defect*

FAMILIAL CONNECTIONS: *two brothers. Single mother.*

I'm alive, thought Karen. She didn't know whether she should be wildly happy about this. She wasn't the emotional type.

She was injured and had suffered trauma. Said a paramedic. "What's your name?" asked the paramedic while dealing with Karen's head wound. "Karen," said Karen. And the paramedic's glance wandered past her, searching for a more interesting victim, someone with a bullet hole through which he'd have to shove intestines back in, or someone whose leg needed to be sawed off immediately, right there. Without anesthesia, like in the movies. Here, bite down on this, it's going to hurt for a minute. He would have saved a life and then would rise, covered in blood, with the severed leg backlit. The paramedic said: "You probably have trauma." "That's normal," said Karen. "Can I leave?" The paramedic nodded. Karen removed herself without rolling her eyes. All children had trauma. It was a permanent condition. Karen didn't care. Trauma was her middle name. Karen lived with her mother, who was always on the verge of a breakdown, an older brother, who tortured her whenever he felt like it, which was often, and a younger brother, who would die soon, though that didn't keep him from being an evil asshole, all in an apartment that would have been too small for one person. Karen didn't care about that either. She was, as mentioned, not the emotional type. She believed in genetics. Her genes must have jumped generations. There must have been a scientist somewhere in her ancestral line. Because Karen was smarter than her entire family, probably smarter than all the residents of Rochdale put together. Her life took place in books and online. She operated in a wonderful world of microbes, genes, bacteria, viruses, and microorganisms to which she gave names. She dreamed about them. Karen's life became uncomfortable only when she had to leave her own head and do things regarded as normal. Like going to school, eating, washing herself. The only joy Karen took in so-called normal life was the weather. It rained so often in Rochdale that at least on the street she could use an umbrella. Beneath an umbrella Karen was invisible. She tried the trick at home. But it didn't work.

"For the love of god."

Cried the mother of

DON

In the next room. She'd heard about the incident on the news.

There were still news programs on the state television station, rain constantly blowing into the faces of sturdy blonde reporters. Who were always standing with microphones in their hands in front of police tape, commenting on catastrophes.

So Don's mother cried, "For the love of god."

"You kids could have died. You could have died," she cried.

And wrapped her arms around Don's brother euphorically. Her arms trembled with fear. Arms again. It seemed as if English women were made of nothing else. Don stared at her mother's body and was sure that masses of flesh like that could never grow out of her.

"Go on, bring him something to eat," ordered Don's mother—her son pressed to her breast.

So much for family structure.

Mass shootings and misogyny are siblings, Don later read. And it's mostly young men who go crazy. Something in their lives didn't work out the way they'd imagined. Something to do with power. Or penis. Or because everyone didn't fall at their feet as they imagined would happen as a result of the way they were used to being treated by their mothers. Don wasn't surprised. She knew a thing or two about weakness. She had a brother, after all.

And a mother who didn't particularly value any creature that lacked a penis. Nearly all the women in Don's orbit worshipped men and boys and scorned women. They were probably ashamed to belong to the losers, because the only thing lower than women were foreign women. The only thing that linked Don and her mother seemed to be their sense of deficiency. A massive sense of loserdom that expressed itself in everything they did. Don decided very early in her life never to become a woman. At least not the kind Don knew from Rochdale and from the videos. Not the kind who distinguished herself primarily by playing up gender stereotypes with her clothes and painting her fingernails with glitter polish—victims. A man or boy, no matter how weak, would always be valued more than a woman, even if she was a professor or cyberneticist. And speaking of weak, Don's brother had a lot of shortcomings. Beginning with his way of walking. Don's brother always stepped forward with just the front of his foot and lurched after it with every step, giving him the aura of a complete idiot. He breathed too loudly, smacked his lips when he ate, his mouth always hung open—and

Don couldn't remember.

Her mother ever having hugged her. Or touched or patted, or that she had undertaken anything you'd see a movie mom do. But—at some point things not done become embarrassing to even contemplate doing. Perhaps her mother was dying to hold Don close but she'd unfortunately let the moment pass when it was possible to start. And anyway she was busy. She had to constantly run along behind her son to wipe his face, to pinch his cheeks, and to listen rapturously when he talked about his equally idiotic friends. Don's brother needed only to breathe to provoke elation in the mother. Don, on the other hand, she rarely contemplated, and when she did her gaze betrayed the same helplessness with which she regarded herself and her own life.

"I took part in the uprisings," said

DON'S MOTHER

CREDITWORTHINESS: *none*
ETHNICITY: *Black*
INTELLIGENCE: *average*
HOBBIES: *BBC television programs, the royal family, rummaging in thrift shops*
SEXUALITY: *masturbates to photos of Prince Charles*
FAMILIAL CONNECTIONS: *2 children, 1 absent husband*

Often.

Don could never picture her mother as an upstanding Black Panther revolutionary. She probably exaggerated her role in the London street battles. That was supported by the fact that Don's mother used bleaching cream, straightened her hair until it hung from her head like sliced cheese, that the skin color of the supposed father of her children was ambiguous, and that she had no friends from those supposed circles. She preferred to keep company with whites, she rhapsodized about the capital. That her parents left London after the unrest back then was a huge source of humiliation to her, since Rochdale was the brick-and-mortar manifestation of the fact that Don's mother would never nibble scones at an English flower market with white ladies in twinsets. Don's mother had learned a decent trade. She was a trained retail saleswoman, or something equally useless from the 1.0 era of the economy. She'd worked for a transport company, a supermarket, and an appliance store and was always replaced at some point by someone in another country, because the trend was to send jobs abroad, because the trend was that a handful of people wanted to make ever more money to protect themselves from the end of the world. This desire had to be respected.

Don's mother was only able to find temp jobs. At a laundry, as a cashier, at a gas station. And, for long periods, none at all. She was scared during those phases. And she was scared when she had a job that she'd lose it again. She couldn't sleep, could barely eat, barely breathe, and always lost the job. Scared. Always scared of everything. She dreaded winter the most, because that was the time when the children got sick, which meant at least eight hours sitting around the hospital, which meant she'd be out a job once again. Then she'd have to go to the unemployment office, let herself be treated shabbily, and be forced to take a course, like for instance one on how to compose a properly written job application. Which, upon every gas station owner in town, most of whom are illiterate—now, now, let's not be racist—naturally makes a huge impression. When the money from the unemployment office was gone and Don's mother still had no job, she had to go to the Christians and their food banks.

DON

Hated the visits to the Christians. They meant: waiting an hour or two outside. And then standing in front of women whose teeth were too big and who smelled of old, wet kitchen rags, whose red faces had big noses with burst veins and whose yellowish gray hair was always matted down in the back. Letting people like that fill your pockets with canned beans was deeply humiliating. And here's a little something nice for the wee ones. Who were these horrid-looking people, what gave them the right to their condescending charitableness that didn't distinguish between welfare recipients and dogs? Don always imagined going back to see these gracious people, with a machete. She pictured herself, and the Christians in their own blood, their skirts riding up, their legs twisted on the floor. And then Don saw herself leaning over the victims and for a finishing touch shoving tins of beans into their mouths.

Which was completely unfair, of course, since without the Christians who fed and petted the poor, most of them would probably already be dead. The aim of the state was to reduce social services to a minimum in order to foster the strong, hardworking segments of the populace. As well as. Just to save money. As well as. To maintain the country's neoliberal course.

The contempt capitalists held for the poor had become institutionalized. Homeless, unemployed, those with disabilities, the sick, the feeble had to fulfill painstaking, incomprehensible, idiotic bureaucratic requirements just to receive a minimal sum that barely kept their vital functions going. The unusable part of society could lose all assistance because of small technical errors, and then they were just stuck. In their rancid gaffs with no electricity or heat or food. And who helped them then? The Christians helped them then, people who got their serotonin fix by dedicating themselves to the preservation of those unworthy of preservation.

Don started to hate almost everything around her. The police who patted down every kid, every day, who lived in social housing.

Out of habit, for fun, or just because they could. The children had to stand in rows, empty their pockets, pull down their pants, put their hands on their heads. Something about power or respect meant that probably one or two million kids grew up knowing with all certainty that they were not protected by the state.

The police virtually never found any drugs or weapons, because, after all, what kind of children would be so stupid as to carry suspicious things when they knew they were being surveilled. Weapons were stored in empty old factories. Same with the drugs.

Don hated. The worn-out looking people at the agencies who treated her mother as if she was just too lazy and stupid to keep her life in order; she hated the public housing authority's maintenance man who barred children from doing anything, from running, talking, laughing, breathing. She hated her father—

Whose influence on the upbringing of his children was negligible. Occasionally he sent money. Rarely, actually. But when it happened, Mother always gave a long speech about the goodness of this man, she said she'd be lost without him, then she cried. What Don had learned was: women took care of all the never-ending, practical, unpleasant things that were necessary in life. They stood in line at agencies, dragged their children to doctors' offices, and disappeared into their apartments to take care of other women's duties until they eventually became mentally ill, which in their circles always meant depression, which in their circles always meant: Mother laid in bed, cried, and didn't get up anymore. Women didn't accomplish the extraordinary. Extraordinary accomplishments were male things. Interesting activities emanated from men. They stood beneath streetlamps, listened to music, smoked, drank, dealt drugs. Boys made the cool music. Back then there were still no women in the grime scene who were important. Who were as threateningly angry and loud as the men.

Men annoyed

PETER

DIAGNOSIS: *psychologically peculiar*
RISK FACTOR: *unestablished*
SEXUALITY: *heterosexual, maybe*
IQ: *unclear*
ETHNICITY: *white, referred to as Caucasian, right?*
FAMILIAL CONNECTIONS: *no siblings*

It had simply been dumb luck, Peter's birth, and on a day when it didn't even rain. Something had probably gone wrong. It happens more often than you think. On the day of his birth, when his mother saw the face of the midwife and then of this child. Which was luminous and clearly not from her husband, who was also long gone by then. The very dark-haired, very stupid husband. And Poland, yeah, well, in fact, out in the countryside in Poland, do something when you're young, when the country's latent fascism makes you sick, when you already know all there is—the cowardice of the people, the empty shops, the dusty streets, and, first and foremost, the absence of all hope. Do something with a luminous child who barely talks, who never looks anyone in the eye and spends hours staring at the ceiling or having silent conversations with his fingers. Do something if the ten moronic men in the village offer no suitable sexual prospects for you whatsoever. So, England it was. There were already millions of other Poles there, and you rarely heard any complaints. Many of them found on the island something they couldn't find at home. Work. Money. Change. Interesting foreigners and, with time, perhaps a vacation home back in Poland, which was undeniably scenic. That was enough for a new life. And it was possible—if you weren't too discerning; and if folks from the East were anything, they were frugal.

Poor folks from the East, it should be specified. Poor people from the East knew how to get by, they were hungry. They were unsentimental. They could fight and weren't spoiled. Here's to clichés!

In the village where Peter came from, the place his mother wanted to escape, there was a Sand Street. In Peter's mind Sand Street was made of muck and would open up at some point and swallow everything, but there were houses on the street that could seem romantic, at least when they were totally surrounded by snow. Old garden fences, broken windows, sagging doors, holes in the flooring. Of the hundred people in the village, almost all were over fifty and looked over seventy. Helplessness incarnate, people who'd never managed to make it to another city or flee to a foreign country. Scraps of meat staggering down the dusty street as soon as their welfare checks arrived to buy a stockpile of alcohol from the kiosk that, alongside alcohol, also sold pickles in dusty jars, and oatmeal. The stuff alcoholics like.

Peter was hated by the men in the village. He was different. That was enough. He was always near his mother. Which was where the village idiots wanted to be. There were only a few other women in town. Anyone who could, left. And they'd be gone soon, too, Peter's mother often told him. Until then she wanted to have fun. And whatever she meant by that, it always began with her walking down the dusty street of that Polish backwater in a short skirt, looking as if she were going to some sort of casting. Peter knew what casting shows were, he knew everything, because even in the far reaches of Poland they had the internet. Peter found the way his mother conducted herself strange. She laughed too loudly whenever some alcoholic spoke to her, her skirt slid up to her crotch, and she forgot her son, that is Peter himself, as soon as a man showed up. Peter had no idea why she preferred the company of toothless alcoholics to his own company. There was nobody here who could appreciate beauty in any form. It took practice to recognize beauty, training that could never have taken place here. It was ugly in this hole of a town. Flat, no trees, no hills, just fields and houses like ruins. As already mentioned, most of the people had disappeared, Peter was the only one who didn't want to leave. He didn't care about the location. It was familiar. That counted. Peter liked his own company if he didn't have to talk to people or hear noises or squeeze under a gate that had just jangled shut, or if his mother was away. Being with his mother was the norm. When norms were disrupted, Peter panicked. He had no idea why. He only knew it was the way he was. Mostly he felt as if he were sleeping and wanted to wake up. His mother disappeared into their apartment with some alcoholic. Peter didn't like men.

There were too many of them.

Thought

DON

Anywhere things were interesting, they were sitting around. When they showed up in groups it was unpleasant. The group in front of Don's house—well, more like "house"—managed to lure over a little stray dog the other day. The cadaver sat there for several days.

Don didn't know why men did such things. But she knew you had to be scared of them. You couldn't provoke them. They could yell without it sounding like screaming. They talked nonsense in broken sentences. But you wanted them to like you. You wanted to please the coolest gangster. Or serve him. So as not to get beaten up. Like Don's mother. Like all the mothers on the block, who mostly raised kids on their own because the men left as soon as they didn't feel like beating their women anymore. Among women, stress-induced depression was the most common disease in the country. Sort of a disease. Whatever. Women. The suicide rate among women over forty rose to an absurd level, the exact percentage Don had forgotten. A lot of kids with depressed alcoholic mothers lived in constant fear of coming home to find family members lying dead somewhere or hanging or facedown in a bathtub. The coming generation, made up of psychotic former children of poverty, Ritalin-crazed psychotic former children of the dying middle class, and the sadistic former children of the elite, would be well prepared for the new era.

Incidentally—just emerging back then was the movement of

The

LEFT BEHIND.

Men.

Young and middle-aged throughout the Western world who found themselves in homoerotic unity under various names. Alt-right, neo-Nazis, National Action, Aryan Brotherhood, White Nationalist Party, League of St. George, Blood & Honour, Stormfront, Identitäre, Vigrid, Deutsche Heidnische Front— the involuntarily celibate

Groups—

That gave them back a feeling of power that

Women

Had taken from them. Millions of white men had been emasculated. Right. Wrap your head around that.

Fucking hell. They had too much testosterone or not enough, both painful conditions, and found themselves in a world that no longer needed them. Useless and angry. Not loved and not listened to. Doughy around the middle,

Women,

That is—individuals that you could purchase, as so-called policewomen, judges, doctors. Like foreigners with glasses. Like if a dog were to become a politician. Women were something they could all agree upon as responsible for this malaise they felt in a world that was no longer comfortable. Which had never really been comfortable, but at least you weren't confronted with it in the old days, for fuck's sake. In the old days there'd been no internet to tell you how uncomfortable it had become. It could really make you bitter.

Well, it was not proper to wander through the streets of the Western world beating women. So somebody else had to be on the hook. Foreigners. Same as women, just with bigger penises. With which they stole the women away from white men, the women the white men hated. Okay, it was complicated. Fuck it.

The left-behind ironed their shirts, lifted weights, peeked at the penises of men next to them, thought about all those penises in action. If you'd strung them together you could have fucked the world back into order. Linking up around the globe they created a massive shitpile of healthy, armed, radically right-wing fascists hopped up on a fear of fading into insignificance.

In

DON'S

surroundings, there were no Nazi groups or Nazi parties. The men around her were too lazy to gang up together. The sensation of uselessness the third generation had allowed them to become flaccid, the once proud fishermen, construction workers, proud—whatever shit it was—meaning they'd done honest work with their honest hands on some honest bullshit or other that made some other man rich. Whose descendants, now holding government offices, decided on the unemployment benefits for honest workers. That a person who doesn't—let's just say—manufacture wire, is no longer of any value, and will get angry as a result, is understandable. And is, in fact, considered a mitigating circumstance if a man from the area lands in front of a court for beating his wife or child completely or only nearly to death.

When women survived the morbidly predictable, socialized rage, they patched each other's wounds once the sporadically appearing, humiliated men had lost control. Subsequently the men withdrew, confused about the mess they'd created. Then there was peace, the wounds healed, then the men returned and everything started over again: women lost themselves in rapture to the appearance of a toothless man who spent the entire day sitting in front of the TV with his hand on his crotch, until he went to the pub in the evening and sat there instead. Almost all women felt incomplete without a man. Or to put it in formal aesthetic terms: men livened up the scene inside the horrid apartments and in front of the houses.

Speaking of

Don's surroundings.

Eighteen row houses, two stories, brick, fences, nobody expected any trees or plants of the concrete. Here lived: refugees, unemployed, people with missing limbs, bad eyes, alcoholics, junkies, ever more of them arriving from London because their social housing units had been transformed into private owner-occupied flats. Just not owned or occupied by them.

Don had never seen buildings surrounded by whispering treetops, had no experience of high-performance heaters, windows without drafts, clean bathrooms, or fountains, as Rochdale was a very equitable city, where things were equally shitty wherever you went.

If you left her block and went out into the city, which Don often did with Karen, for lack of anything better to do, you found a main thoroughfare. The attractions of this main road were thrift shops, where items donated or found on the side of the road were sold to residents of the thriving community. Aside from various bet shops and one-pound shops there was a shopping center, where half the storefronts were empty, and a Costa Café, where they liked to stand out front and watch the tourists. That is, the three per month who mistakenly strayed into Rochdale because they'd read in a bad online guide about some food-and-drink festival or about Dippy, the dinosaur in the natural history museum. Okay. Those three people who then hustled down the main road petrified and, in desperation, visited the parking garage at the shopping center—they loved to watch those people. The tourists gave off a luster like gold. They could. Just leave after they'd downed their overpriced Costa Café and had a sufficient fright from the pregnant minors and all the young Pakistani men tromping through the shopping center.

They could disappear to places that were definitely better.

On days when there were no tourists to be observed, Don and Karen checked out the old clothes and morbidly sad people trying on old clothes in the thrift shops. Three-quarters of the residents of this city of eternal rain were unemployed. So they had a lot of time to examine the trash their neighbors dragged to the thrift stores and pawn shops in order to put the proceeds toward a bit of lager. Once, it was said, this had been a city bursting with prosperous workers. The empty shells of the formerly grand, bombastic, prosperity-giving factories stood all around, evidence of this distant, wonderful era. They'd been closed because nobody needed the crap they produced. In the new millennium you needed banks, financial services, and IT workers. They called it evolution.

These days the factories were empty and served as adventure playgrounds, as drug and weapons stashes, and as meeting places for sex in exchange for payment. Jobless old men fucked away their monthly benefits there, and young girls fucked there to get a bit of affection. Ditto for a handful of homosexuals. Karen and Don often watched people having sex in the factories, which they found disgusting. When they weren't spending their time on the main road, watching grime videos at a playground, or creeping around factory buildings, they got up to things that involved annoying passersby, stealing things, or fighting with other groups of kids. With the help of YouTube tutorials, Don had from the age of six practiced martial arts in Mandale Park, which was empty aside from a few homeless people who were too drunk to pay her any attention. Wasn't such a brilliant park. More like an indeterminate cluster of scrubby trees and shrubs. Don had really gotten into Krav Maga. A technique

that was very effective and could ensure survival. Like the shooting classes
Don had watched online, the tutorials by FARC rebels on how to kill or
build a shelter. Don found it exciting to look at pictures and videos about
armed resistance. Women who could assemble a machine gun in seconds flat
or finish off an enemy with a quick jerk and turn of the head. She'd found
something that made her burn with desire, something bigger than her. She
trained hard, and her body changed and grew. In width. Compact, like a pit
bull. Thought Don.

This was the period when her brother wasn't just wetting the bed once a
week but daily. Because of his trauma-induced feelings. That he could only
express via urine. Don lay in the stinking little children's room and felt excited.
She knew she'd soon disappear from here. Away from the scent of urine, the
glare of the lamp outside, the shuffle of people waddling behind their invisible
walkers. Don closed her eyes and tried to imagine a future. Though she never
really succeeded at it. She didn't know what it smelled like at the seaside or
in Bangkok, she had no idea what rich people in elegant apartments did. So
she just imagined London. White, gleaming, and modern. And right in the
middle of it, herself. Picturing this unknown world kept her excited until the
following morning. She held on to it until school, where of late Don was no
longer laughed at as gay or cursed as lesbian. The other kids had begun to
fear her. A development she enjoyed. She'd been sneered at and derided for as
long as she could remember. She didn't conform to average specifications. Her
average classmate was white. Or Pakistani. Girls wore dresses or skirts. They
began using makeup at age seven and had sex for the first time at ten. Boys
smoked, drank beer, and wore hoodies, they were white with bags under their
eyes, or they were Pakistani, in which case they had nothing to do with the
others. There was no room for interpretation, no in-between. In between there
was only Karen and Don. The freaks. The ones you could beat up. But that was
in the past. Now when Don set foot in the schoolyard with Karen, everyone
looked at the ground. Like in the animal world, thought Don, as she swaggered
across the yard like a fucking cowboy. Karen walked behind her, or at her feet,
Never fully there.

KAREN

Sat in her room, which was actually a closet, with no windows, but at least
a door. It doesn't take much to satisfy people. She read about Bajos de Haina,

a city in the Dominican Republic that had been contaminated by a battery recycling company. City of freaks. They intrigued Karen, who wondered what it would be like if everyone in Rochdale looked like her. Or if they were all interested in the same things she was. At age five, Karen had found a book on system biology and ever since had been obsessed with microbes, blood, hormones, and computers. Those had become the worlds in which she preferred to live instead of on the shabby surface of this so-called world. Karen ran her hand over the scar on her head—

After the incident, which, we remember, was euphemistically described as a mass shooting, when Karen's superficial wounds were being treated at the hospital, she had tried to imagine how surviving the shooting would fundamentally change the structure of her family. How she'd leave the hospital and her mother and brothers would be standing there, and they'd all hug, and then go together to McDonald's. Tears, hugs, and so on. That didn't happen. Karen didn't like to go out in the street on her own. Even though it was all she had ever known, now it bothered her to be gaped at all the time. It felt as if the stares were boring through her skin and into her organs. Stares. Scornful, disgusted, horrified, disapproving. Karen looked different.

She wore bifocals and could have used braces. Nobody around here had braces. Or good teeth. A lot of people had no teeth at all. Rochdale was a place where nobody sculpted their bodies with plastic surgery or in fitness studios, and there were a thousand forms of neglect to marvel at,

But Karen had really gotten it bad. A recessive genetic inheritance, a glitch in the production of melanin, was responsible for Karen's white, frizzy hair, the light, freckled skin, the colorless eyelashes and eyebrows and the light blue eyes. In politically correct terminology Karen was said to have albinism, but that didn't help her maintain a healthy self-esteem. Her mother and her older brother were dark-skinned and beautiful. At least in Karen's eyes. Everyone else was beautiful, and she looked like a dinner roll that you'd find under a dumpster. Karen had come to terms with being an outsider. At least come to terms with it as well as a young, nearly pubescent kid who's reviled by nearly everyone as extraordinarily hideous can come to terms with it. Reviled by toothless old fat-sacks, by cockeyed foul-smelling women with lopsided heads and by pimply, reeking boys. Karen was the kid who stood alone in the corner during recess. She was the kid smaller kids stared at and adults made comments about. She was the kid with a dysfunctional relationship with her brothers. Even her little brother despised Karen, which was amazing since he had Hutchinson-Gilford syndrome. If anyone knew what that was, it was only by the name progeria. Most people just called her little brother "alien," and though he should have been a tiny, needy person he somehow was a malicious little asshole. Genetically speaking, something had gone wrong in Karen's family. In an English social drama, the cursed little family could have been a haven of warmth, humor, and love. But unfortunately they were just people who happened to live in a social housing unit together and got on each other's nerves. Or beat each other up, like on the day Karen came home from the hospital after the incident, disappeared into her room and then at some point needed to go to the bathroom. Her brothers had partied the night before, meaning hanging out on the street partaking of a mix of drugs and alcohol. Then the little brother would probably be pushed down the baby slide or used as a human shot put. Fun into the wee hours, at least to judge by the babbling voices from the living room.

The apartment was too small to provide even a modicum of privacy. There was the bedroom for the brothers, the living room, where their mother slept, Karen's closet, a tiny bathroom, and a kitchen, all wedged into forty-three square meters. All in ochre. That perhaps had been white at some point in the distant past. Or red. It didn't matter. Everything a bit—run-down. The curtains were closed, the living room reeked of booze. The brothers sat on the sofa looking like a man and his puppet. The larger one good-looking, the little one strange-looking. They were watching YouTube videos of people who glued their foreskin shut with superglue. Their brains were already irrevocably damaged by constant stimulation. The TV was also on, with the sound muted, showing catastrophic reports from Japan, which had just been hit by a massive tsunami. The idiots made jokes and Karen stared, frozen, as old women squatted on a hill and gaped at their wildly romantic coastal town where a container ship had been washed in. The two dumbfucks Karen was supposedly related to squealed with delight. Fatalities. There were fatalities. Maybe they'd show a corpse. It never ceased to amaze Karen how many hours the two of them could waste just staring at something or other. Or drinking alcohol and talking nonsense. And how little time they devoted to things that might have made human beings out of them. Like reading something or even bathing. One of them noticed Karen and yelled at her to get them a snack. Karen knew there was no point in arguing and set bread and margarine out in front of the two morons. The older one kicked her, perhaps because he didn't approve of the quality of the proffered food. Karen fell to the floor. The younger brother screamed with laughter. Poor bastards, Karen thought. The brothers were bored with the emptiness in their heads, with the disastrous effects of the hormones that made them feel like they were the rulers of the world. Testosterone kept them from seeing themselves realistically for what they were, two young men without any prospects for a decent life. If you believed the statistics, one of them would be dead in a few years. The other would probably succumb to a gunshot wound soon enough. Unfortunately the date of their demise wasn't fixed. Until then, they'd hunker down here with the spliffs that were supposed to calm them down.

Karen stood up at the moment her mother arrived home after a double shift. With burning eyes and tired of all the idiocy.

Just die already,

Thought

THE MOTHER

ETHNICITY: *Black*

RELIGION: *Catholic*

ATTRACTIVENESS RATING: *4*

POLITICAL ORIENTATION: *tired*

HOBBIES: *sleeping*

HEALTH STATUS: *abuse of tranquilizers, onset chronic stress-induced depression, cavities, osteoporosis*

As she stood in the entry hall and looked into the living room.

And suddenly remembered. Karen's mother saw herself standing in the entry hall on another night, years before. The big difference was—

She'd still had hopes back then.

The difference was she'd been young back then.

Her youngest son, who was two and looked like a tiny old man, was sitting in a playpen in a puddle of shit. Her daughter, who always seemed like a discarded scrap, was biting her fingernails while the oldest of her children, who was distinguished by a monstrous appetite for destruction, squatted contentedly in front of a pile of broken glass, which had previously been some household item or other. The open doors of the cabinet, the absence of male clothes, and the missing rainy-day jar gave away the fact that it had been too much for her boyfriend, the father of the children. He'd obviously been overwhelmed. One must understand. He was a musician, talented, still young and undiscovered, and couldn't squander his life raising children with various defects.

Karen's mother knew at that moment that the course set out for her life would have been easier to bear if she just let herself fall out a window. She was twenty-six then and had just started a continuing education program to become a surgical nurse, a program she quit the day after she realized she would be alone with three children.

Even if her husband hadn't contributed much to the bottom line, actually nothing at all, at least he had looked after the children.

Karen's mother began working as a night nurse; a retired woman next door looked in on the children every half an hour. Unfortunately she quickly gave up after she was repeatedly hit by thrown projectiles.

Karen's mother paid a babysitter from then on, ended up in arrears on the rent, her hair fell out, she had panic attacks and lost her job. The unbelievable stroke of luck that came of this unpleasant situation was that she was allotted a flat in Rochdale by the social benefits office.

Which is where she was now standing.

In the entryway, years later. And no longer as an actual person. Karen's mother no longer existed as a sexual being with dreams and hopes; she had become something devoted to just one task—keeping herself and her children alive, even if it wasn't clear to her at times why this was a good thing.

Probably due to her chronic fatigue, she had the sensation that nothing was real. The family lived in one of the seven residential towers that looked out over nothing. At her job, she tended to the consequences of boredom in the area. Young men with gunshot and knife wounds, boys whose hands had been blown off by fireworks or whose eyes had been damaged as a result of some dare. Men who'd stuck their genitals in vacuums and doorjambs, in animals or freezer compartments. Men who'd inserted bottles and fruit, drills and hammers into their assholes. Men who'd drunkenly fallen over, run into walls, or plunged into water. Men who'd sawn into a body part or been pinned beneath cars. Children who'd been fucked or beaten half to death or worse. And women after aborted suicide attempts. With half their faces blown off, quadriplegic after jumping from an inadequate height, organs burned after drinking drain cleaner. Sometimes when she came home from the night shift to the apartment she didn't even recognize the three people waiting there. Karen's mother didn't have the time to imagine how her life might look. She just wanted to sleep. And forget.

Everything

Is what

HANNAH

Wanted to do.

She had survived her mother. She would manage the rest. Possibly. Hannah had been born at the seaside. Well. Sort of seaside. In Liverpool, we already mentioned it, proud city of longshoremen, blah, blah, blah. Automated cranes had long since displaced the longshoremen, business was negligible anyway; after the textile and steel mills disappeared people hadn't had work in years and drank, children founded gangs. That's what the city had become known for in the interim: for being an assembly line for armed child criminals who murdered each other in order to bring a bit of intrigue into their boring lives among radical right-wing, nationalist, or just helpless parents. Weapons are infernal things. Though they make it easier to realize the fundamental human desire to eliminate other people. It used to be that children worked as mules for drug kingpins. They flew to Holland or Spain on easyJet, bought drugs, smuggled them in container ships. But. At some point the children realized the only thing keeping the big dealers on top were the weapons. So they got their own—you could get a nice 8mm Luger for just £350. Small fully automatic machine guns cost £500. Whoa, fully automatic machine guns. A dream come true. The children began to shoot people. First the big dealers, then the rest of the adult criminals. Then they terrorized their neighborhoods, shot kids from other gangs, and finally themselves.

Hannah's parents were Indian Jews, the third generation in England. People loved to ask, What, there are Jews in India? when they felt the need to have a conversation to demonstrate their openness, because people loved to show openness in England—at least they did before the situation escalated.

Hannah's parents had run a photo business in Liverpool. Photo business? Yep, that's right. It wasn't a particularly big earner; to be precise, it didn't earn anything at all anymore, and Hannah's father made a little money working by the hour for the Liverpool Jewish council. At least they lived in a house. Well, sort of a house. A cramped, drafty thing. Two stories, downstairs the shopfront and the kitchen, upstairs two little rooms, creaky stairs, tiny dark backyard.

At least they had enough food to eat. Well, sort of food. Hannah didn't care that it consisted almost every day of some form of potatoes or noodles with tomato sauce. She was a kid and loved noodles with tomato sauce, and like most kids she appreciated the predictability. Hannah's parents were very friendly, and so, until the day she would henceforth always think of simply as "*THE* day," her childhood was perfect. That was not a given. Not a week went by when a new kiddie porn ring wasn't exposed, the corpses of children weren't found in flower beds or freezers, badly abused children weren't discovered. Children were the future, it was said. Not many believed in the future anymore. QED.

Hannah had no idea what future meant, but in this term which was meaningless to her, she would always experience pain whenever she thought of "THE day," pain as if someone had stuck a hand into her body and ripped out an organ.

"THE day" consisted of what you could call a confluence of unlucky coincidences.

Hannah's father had taken her to a football match. Like all the male residents of the city, he was crazy about football. Football was an important means of mass distraction to stave off revolution. Almost as important as conspiracy theory websites, filter bubbles, Nazi sites, falsified reports, manipulation, porno sites, and the hobby of flooding the internet with stupid faces and shitty commentary. Alongside all of that, it was football that kept the mass of socially weak, the current and future losers, the second generation of educationally deprived, and the older generation, the rejects of capitalism, from hanging themselves or looting or thinking. The stadium had cost a few hundred million. It floated above the sagging roofs of Norris Green like the wing of a guardian angel. The football club donated tickets to little gangsters or let them practice there some afternoons to keep them off the streets. In a very manly but also authentic display, players hugged kiddie murderers for photos. How sweet. Everyone in the entire country was crazy about football. They could be junkies, homeless, sick; as long as their club won, the world was just fine. The euphoria lasted for a week. Until the next match.

The so-called rebellion of the left-behind would only take place if football were suddenly banned. But why would anyone do something so stupid? It would be like banning smartphones. Or alcohol. Or the royal family. Even the various terrorist groups that through a series of murderous attacks had for years slowly prepared the country for a wave of fear didn't dare touch the stadiums. A terrorist attack on one of the playing fields of the gods would have meant war.

Hannah's father wore a green and red scarf, he was part of a large, strong, not humiliated troop of men if a game was won, and if their club lost, then the men could finally cry about their lives. Football fans were one of the last groups where an individual could briefly muster a feeling of sympathy for someone else. The stadium, a site where men wrapped their arms around each other and cried together. What sort of indomitable power might they generate if they joined together in their directionless misery outside the stadium. But they didn't. They killed each other. After the match. Or threw acid in each other's faces, which was the hot shit this season.

When Hannah and her father arrived home after the game, two police officers were standing in front of the door. Whispers. Unfortunately we have the unfortunate duty to inform you that your spouse.

And so on. It whooshed into Hannah's ears. Mother had strayed into someone's line of fire, probably child gangs, and now lay in the hospital.

It doesn't look good. Said the police, possibly, or maybe Hannah imagined it. Why do they live in this fucked-up neighborhood, they're upstanding people after all? Why do they live in an area the police only dare enter in convoys? And so on. Probably only imagined sentences that didn't add up to anything. Hannah's memory started again only at the hospital. Where she stared blankly at the mass of people crowding the waiting room.

They were waiting for their

Vaccination.

A wave of Japanese encephalitis was threatening that year. Every day there were reports about the horrible threat. Inducing fear of the disease with its expected fatalities in the range of tens of thousands. The government had ordered vaccinations from China. China or Japan, whatever. The vaccination was mandatory. Hannah remembered getting hers. It had been administered directly to her head. Which had been quite horrible. It had been three days before. Hannah had cried, but her mother had been there, as she always was when she cried. Or laughed, or when she was sick or hungry or nervous—her mother had always been there.

And now

Her

Mother

Was somewhere in the bowels of this hospital. At the mercy of people with covered faces. In a hospital that had recently been cited for acquiring rusty cannulas to cut costs, a revelation that caused no uproar in the media. This hospital that had supposedly removed organs without consent in numerous cases. Father, said Hannah, waiting for him to look at her or hold her or do something else that could have contributed to improving the situation. He was an adult, after all. Adults were supposed to know what to do in cases like this.

But

As always happened when Father had a problem, he forgot that Hannah was a child. That a child wasn't so good at solving problems alone. That a child always imagined the world coming to an end if nobody said everything would be fine. Nothing would be fine. Hannah looked with panic at the commotion spilling out into the waiting room from the surgical wing. Activity. Nurses. Blood supplies. Always at the end of a commotion in a hospital stood a young doctor, who with a practiced look of dejection on his face said: We did everything we could. We're still awaiting additional details.

The additional details

DR. BROWN

INTELLIGENCE: *average*
POTENTIAL FOR AGGRESSION: *high*
ETHNICITY: *pink*
HEALTH STATUS: *onset dementia due to chronic fatigue*
CREDITWORTHINESS: *not available*
SEXUALITY: *S&M with tendencies toward rape*

Should have known.

The emergency surgeon had been working for twenty-three hours.

And he knew: it was the universe's punishment for attending the wrong university. And not having connections. The rest was the fault of the system. You know how it is: the system has to shoulder the blame for most botched lives. At Brown's age, parentheses forty-four, you were a head physician, working at a private clinic, had gone into plastic surgery.

Or.

You didn't have any connections and were a failure and worked at a municipal hospital in emergency surgery. Which meant: overtime, modest pay, and a very good chance of having a heart attack. On that particular day there were just two shooting victims laid out on the examination tables. A white man the same age as Brown with a single bullet hole in the lungs, and a nondescript swarthy woman with multiple holes in the chest region. Both were stabilized, and then Brown had to decide, of course. One after the next. He couldn't be both places at the same time, after all. And who does one opt for? The person who resembles oneself, or the one who, in skin color and texture, in gender and most probably in social status, is wholly and completely beneath oneself? One must necessarily be judgmental in a situation like this. But. While the dark-skinned woman died on her table, while Dr. Brown operated on the man who on aggregate resembled him. Nobody noticed Hannah, who was standing in the operating room. She tried to hold her mother's hand. She tried to commit Dr. Brown's face to memory. And at some point was pulled outside by her father.

Unclear is how

HANNAH

And her father got home.

How they survived that first night,

If indeed they did.

Forgotten. Along with the subsequent period, that all muddied together into a blur without a beginning or an end. Following tradition, the funeral took place quickly. A rabbi and a few congregants, the gravestone, and still it wasn't the moment when Hannah broke down and finally cried. She had to comfort her father. They sat shiva at home for a week. A few acquaintances came over with food, then nobody came.

The two who'd been left behind could have helped each other alleviate the feeling of being alone against the world, but they weren't up to it. Hannah didn't realize that the photo business would be definitively closed now or that her father was at first stoned every day and then moved on to other drugs because he still felt too much when he smoked marijuana; she didn't notice that money got tight, that an eviction notice arrived, and that the remnants of the family were allotted transitional accommodation in Rochdale. "It'll be nice," said the father in this new voice that always sounded as if he were under water. "It's a peaceful little city, and there's a lake nearby. They have a Victorian city hall, a dinosaur, and a very good football team. Rochdale AFC." Said Father. Then he cried. Hannah thought it hit her father harder to leave his football team than to leave the house where Hannah had spent her entire life. Hannah hunched over her mother's old clothes, which she had laid out on the bed. In a new city there wouldn't be any places she had been with her mother. She would lose all the paths they had ever followed together. If her mother was still around somewhere, she'd be unhappy because she wouldn't be able to find Hannah anywhere.

The last memory of what Hannah would stash away for many years under the heading of "Home" was a fat woman from the charity shop who looked at the clothes laid out on the floor with slight disgust. Her mother's clothes. That still smelled of her. That she could still see her in. That then disappeared into boxes and were carried out by two men.

Then they moved. They squatted in the bus with two duffel bags and two backpacks, surrounded by people in threadbare suits, who rubbed their dirty plastic shoes on their pant legs as they gave updates via their phones about their location and condition. Almost every single one of them had on a fitness tracker. Almost every single one had a guilty conscience because he or she had invested too little effort into the regeneration and expansion of their own resources. But they were so tired, the people, after long rides to their places of work or to two or three places of work, and the teeth of so many of them were rotted, as bad teeth were the calling card of the losers back then. Everyone on the bus ground their jaws as they sat in the bus. Except for Hannah's father. He was dead. Or looked dead.

Hannah had had enough of adults.

She'd had enough of bus rides through shithole landscapes, enough of situations she'd like to simply disappear from. For the first time Hannah felt how humiliating it was to be a child, and dependent.

When they finally arrived in Rochdale, it didn't look any better than anyplace else. Than Liverpool. Just a smaller version. Just shrouded in rain that apparently never let up. Victorian. Dinosaurs. My ass.

A few weeks earlier Hannah would have thrown herself to the ground and kissed it like the pope, and her parents would have laughed. Now she found herself with a completely absent father and had to motivate him while pretending she knew what to do.

Using Google Maps, they walked down the main street, which was empty and terminated in a residential development that had apparently been expunged of actual residents. Hannah rang the bell of the super.

A fat old man, parentheses thirty-five, opened the door and, if you were to attribute anything to the open fly of his pants, had probably been interrupted while visiting a pedophilia site. The super took them to the lower level of the building—and just look at what they'd been able to do with a simple cellar. The rooms were painted in neon colors, laid with wood-grain linoleum, fitted with Wi-Fi and cable TV. A team of well-compensated city planners had hit on the idea to address overcrowding in the metropolitan area. It had turned out terrific. Windows—well, okay, there were no windows, but what was there to see outside anyway?

"When the furniture arrives . . ." said her father. It didn't seem to matter to him where they were or why. And what furniture, anyway?

"Here's the communal kitchen," said the super, showing them a communal kitchen. There was a refrigerator where each resident could put their lockable food container, a gas stove that could be operated with a cash card. Same for the laundry machine, "here's where you get the cards for warm water, and here," said the super, "are the cards for the TVs," which were already installed next to the beds in each room. "You have to put money on them. Good day." Said the super, then he went back to the people he loved.

"Well at least there's a TV," said the father, dropping himself onto the bed. A dust of old skin particles danced in the fluorescent lighting, and Hannah was too dulled to come up with a way out.

She could try to get the ball rolling. Get flowers, a poster of a horse, and sheets. Or say: "Hey, come on, we'll go register at the welfare office so we can get vouchers for the soup kitchen." Or: "Let's go explore the city. Dinosaur museum, cafés, whatever else. We can hang out and meet friends." Or: "I saw some great thrift shops, we could go check them out."

It didn't matter.

Nothing mattered. "Maybe the agency won't pay the rent," said Hannah, "and we'll be put up in a rubbish dump." In earlier times her father would have answered: "That'll be brilliant. There'll be rats, highly intelligent animals, we can train them. And rubbish dumps are usually quite tranquil. There's food there, old clothes, we can build a house. As for the odor, well, it's just an odor."

But her father didn't talk. He just sat there, staring off, for so long that Hannah got angry. She was the child, for fuck's sake. And rather than say something injudicious, it would be better to explore her new home. Labyrinthine subterranean hallways, on the walls graffiti, fluorescent lights, a few doors standing open, inside faint signs of life. Lots of old men; here and there sat a few single mothers who'd worked in industries that no longer existed, all their functions cranked down to a bare minimum.

And suddenly

DON

Was nervous. Her brother wasn't there, he was probably in the basement playing with decomposing pets. It had just happened. She had just begun to observe herself and her surroundings as if from the outside. Since the vaccination, to be exact. Now she wouldn't get encephalitis, but she'd also never manage to reoccupy her body. From one day to the next, Don had lost all sense of contentment. As if she had needed a pair of glasses that had now been paid for by medical insurance, bit of a joke there, because there were no glasses for people on welfare, which had led to a drastic increase in the number of rear-end collisions and illiterates. Don had also begun to notice the smell—a mix of cheap food, insufficient ventilation, damp clothes, mold, and carelessly washed people. Outside was the absolute emptiness of a Sunday evening. Don felt so utterly bored that her body started to itch.

Don figured it would be easier to die than to live on with this sense of unease.

The problem was

Don had discovered her sexuality. That's how you'd say it if you were a nutter. Don hated everything about herself. Her muscles, the stockiness of her body, which made her look like a little wrestler, her skin, her too-big mouth, her crooked eyes, her too-high forehead. Don walked around the apartment, sat around, went out onto the street, and every activity ended with her flopping down in her bed trying to remember Karen's lecture.

"It's not bad," Karen had explained a few days before. "It's puberty. Hormones. It's like they've swapped you out for an alien. Do you feel like that?"

"Well, let's put it this way, I never used to think, Wow, this is me. But now all I can think is that I'm no longer myself. You know what I mean?" Don had answered.

"I get it. Chemical processes. It would overwhelm you if I described the exact processes. Or do you want me to?" said Karen, full of hope to be able to deliver a long lecture.

"Nah, never mind," Don answered.

"Fine. So," Karen continued. "Puberty is like saying goodbye to a dear friend. To yourself. At some point you'll be healthy again, like after a cold. It just takes a few years. During which time it's essential not to make any mistakes." That in theory Don knew everything about her bodily condition helped very little. She sat on her bed with nervous fidgety legs and began to get interested in the world of pornography. She saw: Man-fucks-woman porn. Many-men-fuck-woman porn. Man-fucks-bound-woman porn. Man-fucks-dog-and-chicken porn. She found the films unsatisfying on various levels, including in the area of language. After the bestiality category, Don landed on hot lesbian sex. Don was fascinated. To put it in a neutral way. She began to fantasize about women. Or more precisely, the illustrations of her awkward imaginings revolved exclusively around

HANNAH

Whom Don had met upstairs in the 1.0 world. The way children get to know each other. Don was standing in the yard, watching the new Stefflon Don video on her phone, Stefflon Don being the person our Don, whose actual name was Donatella, had named herself after. Stefflon Don rapped about diamonds and a Rolls-Royce. Hannah came up to her and said: "That's shit music." Shortly thereafter the two of them fell to the ground fighting.

They'd been friends ever since. It made everything bearable for Hannah, because now she had a daylight life and a cellar life. Speaking of which—whenever Hannah thought she had mastered the layout of residents in the cellar apartments, they'd be swapped out as if overnight. Only her father was always there, like he was stuffed.

Since he'd discovered the internet, he never moved. He showed Hannah cat videos. Just picture it—two people in an English basement which a real estate ad would probably describe as a "charming pied-à-terre with cable TV in the heart of the city," looking at videos of cats in boxes made by people in Asia who were probably also stuck in some basement. The internet—what a magnificent, world-embracing invention. Where people could self-actualize.

Hannah, for example, took dozens of photos of herself every day. Her dark hair fell to her hips, and impressive cheekbones protruded from her face. These things needed to be documented. She let a weather app determine what she wore, she found her way around the city exclusively by Google Maps, tracked her physical activity, her body fat percentage, and sang grime to a playback app. In short, Hannah grew accustomed to the new conditions. She was a child, and they grow accustomed to any kind of shit, because they lack comparisons that would allow them to recognize the wretchedness of their circumstances. Even grief becomes a normal condition. It wasn't always focused and sharp, it just became a background noise, always there, somewhere in their brains. Hannah could laugh and look at grime videos and talk about boys, and yet the grief was still present and made Hannah feel as if nothing was real. A laughing Hannah avatar made its way through the day, but at night it was cold. The nights, when she couldn't sleep, she thought of Dr. Brown. Whom she would someday kill. The nights, when screams came from the cellar.

When

HANNAH'S FATHER

ETHNICITY: *Asian*
HOBBIES: *cat videos*
HEALTH: *endogenic depression after loss*
POLITICAL TENDENCIES: *none*
CONSUMER VIABILITY: *nil*

Couldn't sleep. Like so many. Millions lay in prisons, in dark holes, in shanties, lay next to their decaying mother in bed, in slums where the stench was the most pleasant aspect of the place. Many no longer knew why they should stay alive; they would desperately have liked not to be there anymore, but how did one go about that, how does one die? It's not easy to kill oneself. Where to get the energy when life already feels as if you've taken sleeping pills. You can't just feel your way along the wall blindly. The futility of every motion caused bodily pain. The way to the kitchen through the basement hallways with their flickering lights and the neon-colored walls, and behind the doors always someone sitting there engulfed in madness. Surrounded by promises made by some agency to give them hope. To make them believe they can make it. Which in this social system always involved a yacht.

Life in the cellar was like a halfway point between life and death. There was a marked slowing of thought and increasingly hazy movements, an apathy that gripped every part of the body. This was very helpful for Hannah's father, because in every life-sustaining measure he saw disgust-inducing evidence that he wasn't yet dead. He began to hate even Hannah. Because she was there. He hated himself for his hate, but was too tired to examine it.

He saw his dead wife everywhere. She stood next to him. Sat next to him on the bed. Hannah's

Father knew that he would die here, because he would never again have the strength to transport himself and Hannah anywhere else.

He discovered the

Dream Island Forum

By accident. Well, sort of by accident. It was what happened when you typed "How do I kill myself" into the search engine. Dream Island. Now also available as an app!

Hurrah!

A platform for people like him. Tired of life. Too cowardly to die. He had found friends. They talked together. They cried together. They encouraged each other. Traded tips. They supported each other in their death wishes and accompanied each other down the last path, so to speak. Since Hannah's father had joined the community, a young man had hanged himself. One girl had jumped from a roof, another had overdosed on pills. The group had watched them die online, they'd sung and prayed until the goal of their fellow member had been reached.

After the departure of a Dream Island member there was a moment of silence in the forum. The ones left behind lit a candle and

When

HANNAH

Came home one night her father wasn't there. Nice, she thought, that he seemed to have shaken himself out of his stupor. After an hour Hannah went into the bathroom. Where her father was lying in the bathtub with open eyes and open wrists. He was smiling.

On Dream Island, people cried, hearts flooded the profile picture of Hannah's father.

Hannah knelt beside him.

Now she was

most definitely alone.

Closing the zipper of the body bag did in fact generate the muffled noise like on TV shows. The transporters of the body offered Hannah neither attention nor sympathy. Hannah had stood for a moment in the corridor, looking at the stairs as her father was carried up them. Then she'd packed her things and gone to the playground. There she got from the other children the address of a squatted building. It was on the outskirts of town. Which sounded farther than it really was, because in Rochdale everything was on the outskirts of town. The building itself seemed solid. Thanks to the boarded-up windows. It looked the way you'd imagine a building full of street kids would look if you didn't take American movies as a guide. A bit squalid. From inside and out the building looked rusted and covered in mold. If there is such a thing, then here it was, and the children who lived in these ruins weren't cartoon punks, they were just dirty children. The water had been shut off, so barrels in the back garden collected rainwater. Electricity, stolen. And the twenty homeless youth-slash-children were constantly sick, coughing, lying in the corners like dogs, freezing. Children nobody was looking for, nobody missed. Hannah took up residence on the ground floor and stopped going to school for fear of being remanded to an orphanage. In which case a wonderful future among the majority of society would stand at the ready for her. She could sell shoes in a thrift shop. Or get pregnant and go on unemployment. Or die.

Hannah knew that in theory she had no more parents. And that she was supposed to be sad. But there were no feelings. She believed. What was the point of developing feelings which would inevitably end in sadness, when nobody was there to sympathize? Nobody to comfort you. It didn't make sense even to cry.

Hannah was nearly twelve and looked older because of her build. She had cut her hair to two centimeters in length, her eyes were heavily ringed in black. And of course she'd given herself a few facial piercings; it's what you did back then.

And outside it was summer.

It was too light out.

Which is why

DON

Saw her brother too clearly. He was sitting at the computer. Either he was in school staring with an open mouth at pornos on his device or he was sitting at home looking at it. Don didn't care what he did. Her family didn't matter to her one bit. People didn't matter. She considered them an aberration. What would be the drawback of the planet flying through space pleasantly decorated with rocks instead of this biomass?

Speaking of which, Don's mother took sedatives in order to forget that her life had been completely botched.

And as long as we're talking about the subject of mental illness,

Don's father

Was either still in prison or back in prison. Don had visited him once. The room where relatives meet men they are unfortunate enough to be related to was full of specialists of every criminal stripe. Tattooed, muscle-bound men whose stupidity sent chills down your spine. Don was full of hope that her father would at the very least become a more accomplished criminal during his stay. He was in for the second or fifth time, and at some point he'd just have to become somewhat more sensible. But if that ever happened, the little family would never taste the fruits of his newfound talent, because as soon as he was released he came to move out his things. During a visitation day he'd met a woman. She was fat and blonde and lived a few houses away from Don. "Goodbye, Father," said Don as the uninteresting little man departed. Don's mother took a fistful of pills.

Don's father's fat new woman subsequently gave birth to a fat little child, and Don was indifferent about the whole thing. Once in a while he came for a visit. First there would be fighting, always about the money he had invested in his new family, whereupon the father felt aggrieved, as he'd not managed to become rich, and this, naturally, caused him to become aggressive. Then the parents screamed at each other and drank alcohol; subsequently Don would hear noises from the mother's bedroom that, thanks to porn, she could identify as the sound of fucking. Afterwards the parents screamed at each other again.

And

Don looked out the window at the sky. She wanted so badly to fly away. To a continent free of families. At least the sky looked like home.

PETER

Had arrived a short while before.

It was sometime before sunrise. Had been.

The ride had felt as if it had lasted one hundred days. Peter's mother had managed to make things easy for herself, and whenever she awoke she'd taken a slug from the vodka bottle she'd brought along, quickly looked to make sure Peter was still there and the bus driver hadn't dozed off, then she slumped down again. Peter had stared numbly straight ahead. His pupils didn't move, he wasn't fixed on any point, everything he saw blurred into an amorphous wash. Peter felt watched. And for good reason. The occupants of the bus who weren't sleeping or drunk were staring at Peter. He was one of those people who gets stared at. Uninhibited. He knew he looked like an alien, but he was sure that people stared at him because of his repulsiveness. The way you'd marvel at a particularly disgusting insect.

People had grown accustomed to him back home.

Now there was no more home.

There was just the bus, the night that was coming to an end, his sleeping mother who wanted to get away. Anyone with an ounce of sense wanted to get away. Away from a place that looked like 80 percent of the places in the world where people lived. And all of them yearned for TV cities. Someplace where people sat on stoops in front of town houses, whistling, drinking coffee from paper cups while bent over their devices.

And so, England. It was as good as any other country one didn't know anything about. The English prime minister had welcomed well-educated Polish workers. But for god's sake, not so many!

Now there were more than two million of them, and they were hated. Poles. It was their fault. Along with the Muslims. Or the hedgehogs. Some group of poor idiots had to take the blame so there was a vent for the apoplexy of the masses that resulted from the overestimation of their prospects. Blah, blah, blah. You know how people are.

Peter and his mother had no idea about the attacks on Poles, the imminent Brexit, the Nazis. They had other things to worry about. Used to have. That was then.

Hello, England.

Hello, you idiots, did you really think we were waiting for you? Then have a look around! The area around the bus station, it looked as if a war had just been lost. There were fire pits, campgrounds, plastic tarps, and hundreds of people standing against the walls of buildings and squatting on curbs. Peter had learned that it didn't help things to follow his impulse to throw himself to the ground and scream, so he walked behind his mother, staring at the ground he'd liked to have been lying on.

Peter had wanted out of himself ever since he could remember. He was imprisoned in his own body, and it was impossible to make contact with those outside. The situation made Peter so angry that he occasionally slammed his head into walls or began to scream. He wasn't angry at other people but at himself and his inability to break out of this millimeter of skin that separated him from everyone outside. From people who laughed. For instance. He never laughed about anything beyond the scope of himself, he laughed only at jokes he told himself.

Not long afterwards Peter and his mother arrived in Rochdale, where some acquaintance of some drunk from their village had been living for the past few months. Rochdale was a place that with its bad roads and dilapidated buildings was only marginally different from their village in Poland. Their. Ex-village.

The address they had with them belonged to a former school, or maybe it was an insane asylum, with a large hall where dozens of Poles had spread out their suitcases and bags, their children and clothing, among their mattresses. A mattress cost fifteen pounds per week, and Peter's mother signed a promissory note to a hairy Polish man. Back home his surroundings hadn't mattered to him. They didn't bother him. But this was unbearable. Loud. It smelled of food and people and poverty. Peter couldn't sleep. He listened to his own heartbeat, which didn't calm him. He yearned for someone to hold him, and knew he wouldn't be able to stand being held.

Peter's mother disappeared early in the morning to find work in Manchester; there was a strip where day laborers could cheerfully offer themselves to various idiots. All Peter's mother had said was "Wait here." Before she left. She'd given up talking to Peter. The mother-child bond left a bit to be desired, which was Peter's fault. Like everything. War, poverty, the weather—all his fault. Peter stared at his hand. He ate cookies that his mother brought home each night, and didn't dare at first to go out into the streets. During the first weeks. After a while, when he'd had enough of the stench of the hall, he stood at the door for a few days and stared out at the nonexistent trees. A few days later he made it to the first cross street, and then at some point Peter wandered around the neighborhood. Through which from then on he took the same circular route. Sometimes for nine hours a day to calm himself.

Peter spoke to nobody.

Something wrong with that boy, said the people who needed to know. Who watched him walk past. Who had nothing wrong with them whatsoever, stand-up folks who never thought about the fact that they were freaks of nature, primates who despised each other and fell out of windows, fell down stairs, hung themselves during sex, took pictures of their toenails to post online, who believed in elections and in the queen who loved to wave to them as she rushed around in her gilded carriage.

Speaking of which,

Peter had looked at photos of his new home back at his old home. England. During the '70s of the previous millennium. Filthy children in dark alleyways, garbage in the streets, alcoholics in the streets, and what he saw now resembled the pictures. Just a hint of color and some advertisements; otherwise, nothing had changed. The dream of worldwide prosperity for all hadn't been fulfilled. Yeah, well. Still better than in the Middle Ages. Almost everywhere was better than Poland. The Polish men worked at construction sites in ten-hour shifts, they traipsed in groups through the dead city center in the evening just to land in the sleeping hall, where Polish was the only language spoken, where there was Polish food and a comfy mattress. The women worked ten-hour shifts on farms, cleaning streets, working in tailor shops, shoe repair stores, bakeries, supermarkets—they commuted up to three hours every day, to London, Edinburgh, and whatever all the various holes were called, in order to sell their limited abilities at market. All hail the markets.

It was the time when the majority of the biologically British population sat paralyzed, awaiting the downfall, too tired to think. They had devices, they were busy, and Peter could watch them undisturbed. It made no sense to him why millions from his old home had come here—back there after a workless day they'd sit down on a sofa, here after a ten-hour shift they'd sit down on an inner sofa, which is to say on a mattress, WTF. Could the end goal of a life really be to take out a mortgage on a drafty little house in an area that looked like Poland and subsist on the fantasy that somewhere a few hours away the queen lived, yes, that you might meet her on the street with her cute dogs, that you might breathe royal air, so to speak? While Peter walked and thought, his mother was driven to fields where she harvested asparagus stalks and strawberries and then finished her day working at a bar in Manchester.

After some time has elapsed

While his mother was working the night shift, an event took place that had to do with a Pole. The Pole was named

SERGEJ

INTELLIGENCE: *average*
POTENTIAL FOR AGGRESSION: *high*
ETHNICITY: *white*
CREDITWORTHINESS: *not available*
SEXUALITY: *hyperactive*
POLITICAL ORIENTATION: *inclined to right-wing extremism*
FAMILY: *somewhere*

He'd come to England a year before. He was young and had believed that England would be waiting for him. At home in Pila, in that wonderful city with the exquisite manor house, people constantly told fairy tale–like stories of young Poles who'd become millionaires in England. And now here he was sitting in a filthy hole after he'd found no affordable accommodations in London, doing wretched jobs in Manchester. Up and out of the mattress encampment at five, in the bus to the construction site, working in questionable safety conditions (two losses in recent months, three workers severely injured, with no prospects of recovery, with no prospects of being able to pay for a bus ticket home, with poor prospects of receiving a spot in a homeless shelter).

So, days: steelwork. Evenings back. Drink in a pub. Bye-bye. On his free days (two up to now) Sergej had checked out proper life in Manchester. Well-dressed people strolling into the Radisson hotel, limousines driving up. People who shopped in Selfridges, who laughed, who had normal existences. He didn't understand the language or the people, but he wanted a life, too, since the one currently being offered was just simply shite. And he couldn't think of finding a wife. The Poles wanted rich British men, the local girls wanted rich British men. Or women. Or peace and quiet. None of them wanted Sergej. And. That was no way for a young man to live, a young man with job training after all, not partaking in life, feeling invisible. Nobody smiled at him when he walked through the city in his work clothes. Nobody nodded or greeted him or said: "Thanks for doing our dirty work for us, you know our own unemployed are just too depressed to do it. Too tired. They've been told for so long that there's nothing for them to do that they've actually come to believe it. They've been shown for so long that they're not worth anything that they've come to believe that, too. Now they're too tired to get up, to make demands, to get upset."

It didn't comfort Sergej that he was one of a million Poles here on this unfriendly island. What kind of attitude was it, what kind of system was it, that imported workers only to have them sleep on mattresses and never be greeted on the street? Not so much as a thank-you. And going back home is not an option. And going to America is not an option, there's no money for that. His money was too precious to spend on a prostitute. Money. It was the only thing Sergej could think about. The only thing that interested him. That it shouldn't be the most important thing or that it was vulgar to think about was something only people with money said, people who'd never been hungry and who'd never seen life as a choice between just two options—to die in your own filth with your dick in your hand, eaten by a dog, a failure, or to make it. Anything interesting in life took money. The freedom not to have to work or to choose what job you would like to do. Maintaining space between you and other people, traveling to foreign countries, and a proper bed with privacy. For fuck's sake—the moron on the mattress next to him again. Banging his head on the ground for the past half an hour. "Shut up, you idiot," said Sergej. Then again, louder. A few others in the room shushed him, annoyed. Sergej decided to shut the little fucker up. Then he can just whimper and won't have to keep smashing his head.

Then Sergej had grabbed

PETER

with one hand, covering his mouth, and with the other hand pulled Peter's pajama pants down, opened his own pants, and stuck his penis into Peter's backside. Peter didn't know what exactly had happened, he had no idea about sexual things, but it was uncomfortable. It hurt, and elicited in Peter, someone who was always lonely and didn't know how to make contact with others, a new sort of loneliness, one with an added dimension of coldness. He stopped breathing and waited until the man withdrew from him and disappeared into the dark. An old man next to Peter had watched the entire incident—if you wanted to call it that, because you didn't want to try to figure out a better word that fully encapsulated all the brutality that went with penetrating a child's body, ripping things in a child's innards, caring not about the fact that it was a tiny human being that one was rubbing oneself against—the man had watched the incident and jerked off while doing so, then rolled over and gone to sleep. Peter sat swaying in a corner of the bathroom the next day and the day after that.

A few days later

Peter's mother came home from her shift at the bar. Home, such as it was. She was excited because—

She'd been discovered. By a scout for a television production. Movies, TV series, that shit was the last 1.0-based job field where there was still ample work for wetware. People (without jobs) who still had time to watch television didn't want to see avatars being amorous. They wanted to see real people, with human emotions. Content providers were marshaled to replace every aspect of life, including watching TV, with something similar to television, offering series and films by the ton to keep people who were unemployed or marginally employed from having any thoughts at the end of a day of work or while standing for hours in line at the food bank. It didn't work. You had to make decisions on those platforms, which few found themselves in any shape to do. So there was still television, kind of. With wonderful light entertainment. For all these various formats and series and programs, they needed, shall we say, performers. Lots of them. The viewers wanted to see new faces; it was enough to have to live with one's own every day. There were about three million performers on virtual reality shows and movies on the island, all of whom had just one goal: prepare people for their futures. Create habits so that changes in reality wouldn't attract attention. Just as the American dream had, through state-subsidized books and movies, been used to create a desire in people to consume and accept their roles in society, movies and shows like *The Matrix*, *The Walking Dead*, *Terminator*, and *Big Brother* had in the recent past prepared people for what the future held for them.

Almost all British reality shows were set in social housing blocks and concerned the foundering poor or gangs or teen mothers or sex slaves, so that anyone who had not yet landed there at the very bottom felt scared and kept quiet, and anyone already there saw themselves and were pacified. Nearly all scripted television series were set in the country and concerned happy, confident domestic servants, edifying country doctors and police officers, all of them roaming through Oxford because it still looked the way everyone wished England looked, the way England had for the majority of people never been—sophisticated, charming, eccentric. Nearly all movies were set after an apocalypse. There were always EMP bombs set off, which knocked out the power. There were always fires, financial meltdowns, plagues, and people who were very fit, running around, because they were so fit, and managed for that reason to escape the calamity.

Peter reacted to his mother's new career the usual way—not at all. He was occupied for the next few weeks trying to understand what had happened that night on the mattress. He couldn't figure it out. So he erased the memory of the incident. And filled the gap in his mind by thinking up the solutions to unusual problems. Time and again he developed approaches that could save the world by for instance promulgating bicycles capable of flying. Such ideas were the sort of thing one had during the night. Only most people woke up the next day and realized they'd dreamed up nonsense while half asleep. Peter never woke up. He grew. He'd gotten at least twenty centimeters taller during the months in Rochdale. Thanks to his savant syndrome he could already read and understand English perfectly, though his speech suffered from the fact that he barely spoke, even in the school where he now had to go every day, where he sat alone in the last row. The extra twenty centimeters protected him from the bodily attacks he would have normally been subjected to as a freak.

Otherwise the life of the little immigrant family progressed brilliantly.

With the advance for her first role—a Polish cleaning woman being made redundant by robots—the two were able to move to a new little apartment which had its own bathroom and kitchen and a window onto the street, where Peter could sit after school. He stared at the street, at the goddamn Poles sauntering to their construction sites and back again from their construction sites, and he waited for his mother. Who came home later and later.

Like on this day.

When Peter awoke, he saw her packing her suitcase. That's how you said it. Nobody had suitcases anymore, but whatever the it was she was packing it, quietly, as if not to wake Peter. The thoughtful

MOTHER

INTELLIGENCE: *okay*
SEXUALITY: *asexual*
HOBBIES: *Danielle Steel audio books*
MARKET UTILITY: *below average*
FITNESS LEVEL: *poor, encapsulated TB*

Didn't take much with her, there'd be all new things, bought by her new boyfriend, a rich Russian something or other she'd met a week ago, at exactly the right moment. The jobs weren't coming anymore, the entertainment industry had already had enough of her in a short amount of time, a pretty profile alone wasn't enough to carry the load, her poor English made speaking roles impossible, the offers for Polish performers were limited almost exclusively to porn films, and now she was packing because her new boyfriend wanted her to move into his apartment in London, but unfortunately without

PETER.

Whose head was totally empty. His body was cold. You know, I'm doing this for us, said Peter's mother, stuffing a pair of lace underwear into her bag. She did have feelings for her child, but. Not particularly strong ones. Not so strong as to turn down the Russian. She relished the image of herself in a large apartment in London too much. With staff. With clothes. And Peter would be taken care of. He'd take care of Peter. Perhaps a tidy boarding school soon and then at some point,

but—

THE RUSSIAN

INTELLIGENCE: *excellent*
POTENTIAL FOR AGGRESSION: *high*
ETHNICITY: *white*
CREDITWORTHINESS: *okay*
NET WORTH: *only 8 million left*

planned to have—if at all—a few more children of his own. His interest in a disabled son not made by his own sperm was negligible. The Russian smirked whenever he encountered the prejudices of people from the so-called West toward simple, primitive, corrupt, brutal Russians. He saw their contempt and at the same time the fear in their eyes. He liked it.

He'd grown up in an elegant modern apartment in Moscow, the child of a pair of professors, spoke eight languages, had unfortunately graduated only magna cum laude in economics and psychology, and had never wanted anything else except success. None of the supposedly typical motivations for a desire for power and success applied to him. He was educated, loved, he just had no desire to put up with someone above him, he had no desire to have neighbors, he wanted to sue into oblivion anyone who annoyed him, he wanted to be surrounded by beauty, and he wanted to follow his natural inclinations. Darwinism. Be the tip of the spear, not the spear. The Russian didn't fetishize money in a sexual way. He just wanted enough of it to forget about his mortality. He dreamed about digitalizing himself before his demise. Perhaps, he thought at times, he'd have been less happy if he'd been taller and more handsome. If he'd believed the game was all about muscle definition and pulling the prettiest women. But he was short. And he'd gone bald at twenty. At the beginning of his professional career he'd dedicated himself to the commercial use of the Aral Sea. Which in the meantime had completely disappeared due to the appropriation of water for industry and agriculture and so forth. The enumeration of his business activities bored him. They followed the simple pattern of growth. Unfortunately the Russian and his businesses got in the way of an oligarch with government connections, who for boring reasons feared that the businesses run by the Russian, who had no close contacts in government, would cause a drop in his revenues. His businesses were frozen at the same time he was charged with espionage. He was just barely able to transfer a modicum of capital to Panama and flee the country. Now he was slowly doing better. Now he was doing well enough to fall in love. For the first time in his life.

"It's actually terrific." Said

PETER'S MOTHER

who was finished packing and was gaining momentum as she talked. She stood there with her suitcase, which was a duffel, and wanted to leave.

"It's not for long, I'll leave money for you and I'll come visit every week—What am I saying?—every day, well, every second day. You have everything here. Right." Said Peter's mother to the silent child. Who no longer looked like a child. "The rent is paid. There's food in the fridge." The mother kneeled in front of Peter. She had a tattoo on her shoulder, which identified her as an older person. Young people didn't get tattoos. What would they get them of?

"It's not for long, and you're already . . ." said Peter's mother.

"Twelve," said Peter.

"Right, exactly," said his mother. "When I was that age I was already—" Peter would never learn what his mother had managed by that age, because downstairs in front of the door the Russian's driver honked, and Peter's mother jumped up, took her imaginary suitcase, and left the apartment with a hastiness bordering on rushing. Finally Peter stood up; something seemed to have broken through the leaded glass of his consciousness. Quietly he said: "Don't go." But his mother went, she didn't listen to him, she tried to shut her ears, she hopped down the steps, and Peter followed her, steadily mumbling, "Don't go, don't go." The Russian's Bentley stood on the street and he was seated in the back of the darkened car. Peter's mother opened the door and Peter clung to her sweater. "Don't go. Don't go." This was quite a lot of words, given his condition, but it didn't help. Peter's mother ripped herself free, the Russian gave the order to drive off. Peter ran a few meters after the car, fell down, and remained sitting in the street. He didn't know how he would stand up again or continue to move at all.

Peter was so nervous that it caused his system to shut down completely. Somehow he managed to make it back to the apartment. Somehow he started to breathe again. He sat motionless on the floor for a week in the apartment that was missing a mother. He didn't eat, didn't drink, wet himself. Nobody questioned why Peter wasn't at school. Hey, he was a Pole, he was a loser, he was a freak, so nobody wondered where a loser kid was when he didn't show up for class, where he wasn't going to learn anything anyway. Peter had forgotten school, forgotten himself. He crawled around the apartment. The heat was shut off. Ditto the gas. The water still worked. His mother really had left money. With careful planning it would last for a month's worth of food. Peter ate tinned ravioli, he froze, and he looked out the window. The internet was dead. Nothing to read. Nothing to divert his attention. Peter waited without knowing what for, without missing his old life he waited on a new one. Something would have to happen. Something always happened—for instance, the water was shut off. After a few more days, with the money nearly gone, an eviction notice arrived. Of course, after the previous invoices concerning the rent. An eviction meant the arrival of police. And police would suppose that, in Peter, the situation concerned a child, and then they'd seize upon measures presumed to be appropriate for children. So Peter packed the things he considered essential, a couple of books, an alarm clock, the phones, a sweater, and a pair of pajamas, and closed the door behind himself. Out on the street, as always, indecisive. Peter stood there at a loss, probably like anyone else who for the first time didn't have a home would stand there at a loss. Complicating things was the fact that Peter was not yet an adult and had no friends, because he didn't even understand what the term meant. He would probably hit upon an idea as he walked, so he set off walking. He wasn't frightened, because he

didn't know what to be frightened of. Of the cold, or the night? Of death—
that would be ridiculous. Peter knew everything about so-called death. It was
a condition like before birth. A condition as if he were sitting inside himself
but unable to get out. Except not sitting.

He didn't feel fear, rather a great aversion to having to adjust to a new
situation. One advantage was the fact that he didn't ask himself questions.
Like, what would become of his life now, where he would sleep, what he was
supposed to eat. Peter just walked. At some point after some two hours of
walking, during which he had circled the crappy little town five times, he sat
down at the entrance of the parking garage downtown and waited.

They'd be off any minute

DON

knew.

They had a trip ahead of them. In order to strengthen the mother–child
bond, the little family was going to London. A bus ride. Dreamed up at some
point while the legal guardian was high. It was, as far as Don could remember,
the first trip in her life. Nobody she knew went on vacation. The daily life of
the people in Rochdale was a never-ending celebration of idleness. Don had for
weeks been looking forward to visiting London. She was so excited she could
barely sleep. Just the sound of the name of the capital city made her heart
beat more quickly. She'd wandered the streets via Google, and what she'd seen
was—alive. In contrast to the prevailing sensation that in Rochdale everything
that had ever lived had been boiled to death.

Don's mother laid out a thin dress that she sprinkled with water. Yes, she
sprinkled it. In lieu of an iron, it was a good trick for smoothing out cloth. The
family slept fitfully the night before the trip. Don woke up far too early, jumped
out of bed. While she was in the bathroom trying on muscle shirts, the doorbell
rang. It took a while for Don in her excitement to assign a name to the sad little
figure at the door. It was her father.

He stood there crying. Bracing himself with his arm on the door frame
in order to absorb the trembling of his body. Don's mother came running immediately in her smoothed dress. Father was having difficulties with his new
woman, as his bloodied eyebrow attested. Don's mother was totally out of her
head with happiness at seeing the old bastard again. Like a dog who saw its
master again after a long time, she jumped around the idiot, and the children

stood mutely behind her in the entryway, a feeling of disappointment welling up in them. In short: a little while later they were all sitting on the bus. Don's mother sat on her ex-husband's lap, snogging, while the children sat silently behind them. Don's brother threw up at some point; it was his first bus ride. It was Don's first bus ride, too, but she knew how to control herself. Her mother was so woozy from joy and from drinking from the bottle of liquor her father had brought along that she didn't notice the mishap. Don cleaned the brother up with the stuffed animal he carried with him as a result of infantilism. Don's brother was no longer a child. He, too, was in the midst of puberty and already had fuzz on his upper lip. Don heard him jerking off in the darkness of the children's room. About five times per night. Don couldn't get the noise out of her head when she looked at the moron. Anyway—

Shortly after the family had left the outskirts of Manchester behind, Don's lust for travel had completely evaporated, and when the bus pulled into the bus terminal in London several dull hours later—the moment she'd imagined would be so intense and incredible—she just wanted to go home. She had perhaps never in her life experienced such a feeling of disappointment like that moment, because the part of her that was still a child had hoped that something miraculous would occur. When the bus driver ordered them to exit the vehicle, Don woke her so-called parents. Then they all stood there perplexed in the drizzling rain and the parents began to fight about the map. All around the bus station people lay on the floor with blankets and suitcases. Don saw a woman urinating on the curb and a baby lying on top of a duffel bag as if dead.

The group made it to the nearest pub. The parents drank on. At some point Don's father started to cry again, because nobody was taking care of him or he was alone or he was a failure. Don's mother fell off her stool. The children picked her up. And then they rode back.

When they arrived in Rochdale it was dark. Silently the family shuffled down the main street. Don lagged far behind, yearning. For something unusual that could save the day. For music, something loud, for love or a bank robbery. And then she saw him sitting at the entrance of the parking garage. The most beautiful person she had ever seen. A thousand times more beautiful than Beyoncé. He was slumped there, staring into the distance. Don stopped and looked at him from a few meters away. He looked so unusual here in front of this eyesore of a parking garage. As if a superstar had mistakenly wandered into the little city. Don had only ever seen someone like that in music videos or movies. As if lit from within. So perfect. So blond and thin. The boy looked truly astonishing. Here of all places. In total contrast to Rochdale. A few drunks staggered down the street, the businesses were all closed, the lights were out, no bars nearby, the Costa Café was closed as well. And the boy sat there without moving. Perhaps he was stuffed. Don sat down next to him.

"She's gone," said the boy after a while.

Don wasn't interested in who was gone. In her world someone was always disappearing. Usually it had to do with legal guardians who ended up in jail, psychiatric facilities, or the cemetery. Nobody here talked about their family situation. It was boring, since it was always a variation of the same story: adults who had failed at life.

It occurred to Don that the boy didn't look her in the eyes. He wasn't particularly talkative, either. "Come on." She said, standing up and pulling Peter to his feet. Which unsettled him a bit. She took him to Hannah in the squatted building.

From that night on the group became a foursome.

This is the story of

DON, PETER, HANNAH, AND KAREN

who from now on spent all their time after school and on weekends together. They'd found their family. And with it a space like a portable cave that was always with them. They had recognized each other. As outsiders, as fringe phenomena, as outcasts, and this was astonishing enough because they don't normally recognize each other, those who stand around the edges of the schoolyard. They always look toward the masses, to the weirdos, the geeks, the nutters, the too fat or too thin, the gay or verminous, and they never recognize themselves for what they are: strange. The ones at whom other kids, normal kids, will point to years later while looking at class pictures on their phone and say: "That one—can't remember his name, what a nutter—don't know, he was just weird somehow."

A miracle happened with that little group, or maybe the weather was to blame, a quirk of the surroundings had brought them together, and it was unclear whether they were bound together by something other than the surroundings, other than the fact that the majority found them odd.

Because nobody had told them what was good and what was evil, they'd adopted their own law: nobody will hurt us anymore.

This was nonsense, of course, since humans were disposed to hurt each other. They couldn't do otherwise, humans, though this was not yet known to the foursome, who didn't even reveal weakness in front of the group, like crying once in a while, because they didn't know any better. Because they were still children and sometimes just had no clue how they could manage everything. Establishing a life and reconciling themselves to the idea that nobody is waiting for them. And the daily grind. My goodness, just don't think about the daily grind. Ever longer lines at the soup kitchen, ever more bullshit at the welfare office, ever more knife fights at school, it can be overwhelming as a child.

But—

they'd found each other and were no longer alone.

The four of them were friends and were sure they'd stay together until the end of their lives. Nobody would ever separate them. They thought.

One day after a few weeks,

During which they were so happy with each other it was as if they had just fallen in love, while sitting at the playground, among used heroin needles and some rusty swings, they swore a blood oath. "Any of you have AIDS?" asked Karen, who disinfected her hand after any contact with objects or people. As she considered what infections could be carried by another person's blood, Hannah had already made a cut on her hand. Hannah wasn't scared anymore. She had lost everything that a child could lose, and once in a while she cut her arms with razor blades just to feel something. Then she looked at the wounds and felt ridiculous for engaging in this stereotypically female form of autoaggression. Peter held out his hand silently and let Hannah cut him even though he didn't understand what the oath was supposed to be good for. Still, he was happy in the group. Like all of them. The children who now placed their hands one on top of the next seemed to light up on the little playground. They were no longer the weirdos. They were a unit.

Then it started to rain again, as it always did in Rochdale during the longest days of the year.

It was summer

Which, in the world of

MA WEI

Meant the air quality would deteriorate a little. Otherwise everything was the same as always. Conspiracy theory number 569, to explain the fast-paced change in the world, was as follows:

China—and when we talk of China, we're talking about within the so-called Party—had adopted a forty-year plan thirty years ago. The plan contained the steps necessary to scale to the heights of world power.

First, become the cheapest global producer of everything. Which helped the Chinese population attain modest wealth. And also served to gain access to the technical know-how behind all the products developed abroad, which were produced and copied and finally perfected in China.

Reports about the precarious status of the Chinese labor force originated at that time. Brutality, backwardness, and so forth. The documentation for these reports was all shot in Chinese movie studios in order to spread to the rest of the world an image of a backward third-world empire. Artists loyal to the Party also reported abroad about the inhumane conditions in China. They accused. So to speak. And manifested the reputation of the country. Which in the meantime stabilized the currency. And increased state revenues. And with absurd speed, thanks to the mass of cheap labor and to the dictatorship, restructured the country. Everything old disappeared. New buildings popped up all over the place, shopping malls, cutting-edge factories, infrastructure, ecological and environmental protections were perfected, the air got—better. The Western world outsourced among other things its industry and manufacturing to China. The markets, you know the story. Which led to step 2 of the plan. In coalition with Russia, Korea, Vietnam, Malaysia, the Philippines, and some Arab countries, the weakening of the West was tackled in earnest. Hacking, spying, vote manipulation, the electronic manipulation of the divisions within Western societies proceeded efficiently—also because most phones and the bulk of the software they ran were made in China.

You know the story.

The countries of the West were increasingly ruled by absurd, fatuous dictators. Sad men who reeked of failure, who accelerated the collapse of the Western system.

China bought half the world. Land in Africa, Pakistan, in the East, ports all over the world, businesses, buildings, mines, oil reserves, sites for mining rare earth elements. The domestic population had discovered the joy of consumption;

they wouldn't give it up for anything. They could buy new apartments, cars, and domestically produced Apple devices and Gucci bags. They were

Happy because they could consume.

So much for conspiracy theory number 569. Perhaps there was a bit of truth in it, perhaps not. Mr. Ma Wei was definitely very pleased with the developments of the world at the beginning of this glorious millennium.

It was summer

which meant

THE CHILDREN

Had summer holidays. Which consisted of days that turned to night without any transition after 198 hours. In the yard, withered grass covered with plastic bags as if to admonishingly remind the observer about the plastic waste in the world's oceans. Against the fences leaned bored children with no money to go to a pool. Of which there were none anyway. Days during summer holidays began with a good breakfast—which very few of them received because either their mother was sleeping off her depression or had left for the filthy jobs that you got as a single mother, most of them related to cleaning, prostitution, caring for old people, or the packaging of some machine part or other. Many got white bread. White bread always did the trick if you spread it with mayonnaise. Sometimes that wasn't available. In which case a stout-hearted gulp of water and then to steal something later. From the yard came the constant sound of balls being mindlessly kicked against a wall. The bleakness made it so the body wanted to lie down again almost immediately upon getting up; it couldn't lie down, though, because it was too nervous. At some point the children went out to be with the others, to stand around or to kick balls against the wall. After a few hours, shortly before they smashed their heads against the concrete out of boredom, they left their block to go lean on a fence somewhere else and look at music videos. Their stars came from places that looked similar to Rochdale and had still managed to produce a life. Which meant gold chains, large cars, gold bags, Gucci, and collector's sneakers.

What the children understood as a life had only to do with money. Money was what separated them from those in real cities, meaning Manchester, which they visited once in a while. Riding public transport without a ticket to go look at people strolling around Selfridges. They all dreamed of living in Selfridges, and they hated the people who drank tea there and bought porcelain dogs. The children belonged to the newly defined Generation Z. The end of the alphabet. The end of the food chain, well-researched, in order to better sell them products. They were the second wave of digital natives. Connected physically to digital technology, they'd become a performer generation through lack of perspective. The more crowded the world became and the more interchangeable people became, the more desperate was the desire to be seen. Even though there was no point.

DON, KAREN, HANNAH, AND PETER

Had of late only taken photos of themselves where they were unrecognizable, owing to the idea that they would probably want to become criminals later on.

Since then, only hoodie photos.

Since exceptions had been made to allow the army to take action against demonstrations.

Since there had been discussions about privatizing the police and the army.

Which didn't matter. And which didn't lead to outrage among the populace. The British weren't inclined to public, vulgar displays of protest. Peter had read that in an article. Everything the children knew they'd learned online. They'd been born in the new millennium and didn't know anything else. They didn't consider ADHD a disease, old people were just unbearably slow. And they considered the city where they lived the dreariest city on earth. Ever since algorithms rated areas by their profitability, nothing happened here anymore. The last halfhearted investors had jumped ship when they'd been strongly warned by an investment app about the wayward inhabitants of Rochdale.

Generation Z lived on their devices, where there was always more happening than on the boring streets of their shithole towns. They talked to each other in chat groups, stared at selfie accounts, they spent eight hours a day glued to displays and had no idea what could possibly be wrong with that because the online world consisted of photos, movies, and games while the offline world was made up of bad weather and junkies, dilapidated buildings and boredom.

So online it was.

"Yes." Said

MI5 PIET

"Very nice. The high level of compliance of the general public when it comes to questions of security. Occurs to me randomly. I'll show you the experimental setup now. Would you like the short version, that is, the one everyone can understand?"

THE PROGRAMMER

"That would be great. Though when it comes to understandability, it's not a problem for me. I'm autistic."

MI5 PIET

"Didn't mean to offend you. I'll give it a try. So. For every man, every woman, every child, we have—"

THE PROGRAMMER

"That is, anyone with a device and internet access."

MI5 PIET

"Yes, exactly,

"We've produced an avatar. Based on all the data collected from each person."

THE PROGRAMMER

"Age, gender, sexual orientation, political activities, consumer behavior, clinical history, criminal record, credit and financial profile, political leanings, modes of transport, resource usage, consumer behavior, dietary failures, orthopedic insoles, porn consumption—"

MI5 PIET

"Yes, thanks, we understood, so we've built an electronic avatar for nearly every single person. Algorithms calculate a precise location profile for each person, a threat profile, they calculate voting and buying patterns, determine the anticipated likelihood of criminal activity, the—"

THE PROGRAMMER

"Which in the case of children from a troubled area is very high."

MI5 PIET

"Correct. Additional surveillance . . .

Oh, look, it's summer."

Curious glances outside.

Nothing going on outside, thought

DON

Annoyed from the moment she awoke.

Don wanted. Everything. Immediately. To become an adult. An idea of what she should do with her life. To get out of Rochdale. To grow.

Not to be stuck in this agitated, strange body any longer. Was something else she badly wanted. Don thought about love. Meaning: she watched more pornos—like everyone who thought about love. Everyone Don's age was busy watching porn. Pornos were the basic foundation of sexual education for growing people. Boys learned how women should look and that they were always up for it. That they lounged about, women, and that you had to bang them long and hard to be a good lover. Girls learned that as a woman you had to writhe rapturously if someone kneaded your breasts roughly and prodded your vagina with a penis. As a result girls would mostly wait their entire lives for this wonderfully satisfying sensation when a penis was shoved inside them and their breasts were roughly kneaded, they learned they had to dress like porn stars in order to have the pleasure of a man who would treat them like shit. So all the girls Don's age looked like hookers. They could then take pictures of themselves in their fantastic hooker wear and post on Instagram about what top-notch hooker clothes they had on. When they forgot to photograph themselves, the precautionarily installed cameras took care of it for them. There probably wasn't a nook in the country that wasn't covered by surveillance cameras. At the end of the 1990s the government had begun to install them for the protection of the citizenry. First at every intersection and bridge, every tunnel, then in the lamps of basement entrances, and by now the job was done. There were simply no more places to put cameras. Not a sliver of space between person and device. Nobody got upset about the cameras, because it was good for security. By 2001 at the latest it was because of the Muslims. Everyone understood.

It didn't change anything about Don's situation.

Even after she'd watched porn. And before. And at night. In fact always. Don was afraid of herself. She no longer knew herself or the feelings welling up inside her. Something dark had taken hold in her, something that had to do with life and death. She moved differently, more aggressively. She wanted to brush people away with her demeanor, wanted to see them jump out of her way. Don listened to "Stress" by Justice on repeat. When she wasn't listening to Justice, she listened to Young M.A.: "Them bitches cold as ice, man you swear them chickens frozen / Them pieces maxing out, you would swear those bitches broken."

She moved like Young M.A., boys stared at her, Don stared back, and she felt nothing. Any excitement, like when listening to music or masturbating, she did not feel. She started to box in a neighborhood club that, like all the clubs, was run by an ex-criminal who'd found god. When Don wasn't boxing she practiced martial arts in the park.

But

It didn't calm her down. If Don were suddenly old and, transfigured, wanted to look back at her life, this summer would have been the most intense period of it. The summer when she was alive in a way she was never again to experience.

Sex is probably only that way in the imagination. Quick, dangerous, destructive, and intense. Perhaps sex is only good when you don't actually have sex. When you still believe that sex will change the world or that you can fuck someone to death. For Don there was nothing romantic or tender about puberty. It was about destruction, she just didn't know whose destruction. Don wanted to be a boy. Wanted a cock. And despised boys. She wanted to be around girls, smell them, look at them, but girls embarrassed her. No idea why. There was nobody Don wanted to talk about her situation with. Or could talk to. Because she didn't know what her situation was about. It was probably the same for the others. They were all suddenly grown, their voices and odors had changed. The children were uneasy and bored, they were waiting for the summer to finally pass. All with their smartphones, with dozens of apps that decorated their faces with funny masks and delivered their biometric data, watching grime videos. Rating Tinder photos, looking at snuff films, and laughing at naked classmates who'd been stupid enough to put their genitals on the cloud. A girl had tried to kill herself. With drain cleaner, after too many comments about her uneven-sized breasts had been posted. She'd survived. Well. Kind of.

Most children, no different than adults, were too dumb to understand what they were doing, but back then nobody understood what the internet really was. There was at least a little talk during that hot summer. It was perhaps the hottest on record. Somewhere, constantly, it was the hottest, the wettest, the coldest weather on record, the world outdid itself with superlatives, the oceans rose, ice melted, animals died off, and everyone just continued on as if it was all normal, which perhaps it was. It didn't matter. There were devices. And nobody, not one person, had gotten encephalitis. Or a strange flu. But new lights were put up everywhere.

Don's mother had begun to take sleeping pills. She slumped on the sofa with her mouth hanging open and the TV blaring. Another show about the effectiveness of emojis as a reward system. So-called reward systems were being propagated everywhere, meant to replace the old system of punishment. For a just world and all that. People like to be rewarded. It produces endorphins, it makes them happy, the people. Outside the heat shimmered

And

DON, PETER, HANNAH, AND KAREN

Met up every morning. They sat together outside each of their various homes in turn. Then they went to the old factories, sat around there, then went to the playground.

"Should we beat somebody up?" asked Don on one of these interminable afternoons, on the way to one of the abandoned factories in the hope of watching people in the act of having sex. The others looked up briefly from their devices.

"Beating someone up is not radical enough for me," said Karen. Since the vaccination she'd had headaches more often. And been inclined toward violent fantasies.

"Do you have the feeling they implanted something in our brains when they gave us the vaccination?" she asked.

Peter nodded. "Trackers. They must have implanted trackers."

Don touched her head. "It would be interesting," she said, "if they had injected us with nanosensors that worked their way through our brains and sent all our thoughts to a control center. Of course, you have to wonder who could possibly be interested in our thoughts, but . . ."

Karen said, "Exactly, that's it. A vaccination. Takes a second, don't you guys get it?" None of them got it.

"Everything in the world is determined in seconds," she continued. The others readied themselves for one of Karen's usual rants, which in their most extreme form didn't end in less than an hour.

"I'll put my penis in the vacuum," said Karen. "My hand in the blender. Chain myself to the car and jam a brick on the gas pedal. Send a message to the school director, climb up a ladder, drive across an icy bridge at night. Light the coal oven with the flue closed and go to sleep. I'll push the button that starts a nuclear war.

"Know what I mean?" None of them knew what she meant.

"One false choice," said Karen, "that you can't even call a choice, more like a reflex. And the result is landing in a coma in the hospital, a shattered family, welfare, layoffs, divorce, and ending up on the street, life without a hand, life in a wheelchair. Choices are illusions of holding power. Oh, yeah, power, how cool. And then they think, well, what they call thinking, and write notes full of pros and cons, but in the end everything is decided—in seconds. When they make false choices in fucked-up lives. But they could all just not be made. You understand what I mean?"

"No," said Don. "No idea."

Peter stared glassy-eyed.

Same with Hannah.

"So," said Karen,

"we'll take revenge on everyone who's hurt us. Let's make a hit list. On it goes everyone who has tormented and insulted us. We'll track them down, figure out their weaknesses and give them a second they'll never forget."

Karen looked at the others with a slightly crazed look.

None of the others knew exactly what she meant, but a hit list sounded good, it was a welcome diversion from the last days of the endlessly long, dull summer. And then they all sat alone with their thoughts and recalled moments they wished to forget. That they'd suppressed, so that they could grind them into dust when they were old enough to. They thought of loneliness and humiliation. About being fucked on stinking mattresses, beat up, they thought about death and helplessness.

Peter wrote down his mother, the Russian, and Sergej, the Pole who had raped him. Hannah noted Doctor Brown, her mother's murderer. And Thome Percy. Developer of the site Dream Island.

And Don jotted down Walter, her mother's former boyfriend.

Then they didn't know what to do next. They were suddenly no longer cool, young, and strong. They were children who actually just wanted to cry. And knew that nobody would comfort them.

"I'm waiting."

Said

THOME

INTELLIGENCE: *average*

POTENTIAL FOR AGGRESSION: *high*

ETHNICITY: *pink*

SEXUAL ORIENTATION: *asexual or perhaps homosexual*

FETISH: *sniffing athletic shoes*

POLITICAL CLASSIFIABILITY: *right-wing conservative. But also doesn't really matter*

HEALTH RISKS: *high blood pressure. Fatty liver*

It was the time when his mother was still alive. His real mother. Mother—
Motherrrrr!—

Mother didn't answer. It was midday, she was probably lying on her George
III sofa. Thome hated that piece of furniture, with its brocade cover darkened
at head height by the grease of his mother's hair. Thome's mother considered
frequent hair washing a hobby of the newly wealthy and the lower class. Her
hair was always matted down on the back of her head. It was the color of her
faded cashmere sweater. If she wasn't lying on the sofa she was perhaps outside
with the dogs. Those filthy creatures that looked as if they'd had their legs
sawed off. Good hunting dogs who, on their sawed-off legs, hunted other animals to death. The hunt, a displacement of the lust to kill people on the turf

of the Scottish Highlands. Mother knew a thing or two about that. About killing, scorn, scones, and alcohol. In the community where Thome's family home stood, there was nothing but drunks. Amazing, eh? That the country's upper crust consisted of a giant cirrhotic liver, that alcohol wielded the scepter in this manicured bougainvillea-covered development. Owing to a bit of a stalker quirk, Thome knew what every resident did at every second. He knew them naked, knew what they ate, how they voted, knew their influence in politics, knew which weapons they stored where, which sexual proclivities they harbored, he knew how long their orgasms lasted. Already at a young age Thome laid the foundation for his later passion: observing people. And pondered how he could hurt them.

In the circles Thome's parents moved in, there was no morality. Morality was something with which to occupy the underclass in a contest to curry favor with a higher being.

In the circles where Thome grew up, there was neither political correctness nor organic food, people smoked, drank, whored around; they were the last free people, who had nothing to do with those beyond the bougainvillea bushes. The people here didn't know Netflix, Facebook, they'd never been to McDonald's or on a package holiday. They didn't know there were self-service supermarkets and Google search engines, they didn't know Starbucks or Tinder, except that

Those businesses belonged to them.

On Thome's street there were a few men with pronounced pedophilic tendencies. The enjoyment of being tied up and debased was at home in nearly every building on the street—Thome sensed his thoughts wandering, which was normal in a brilliant, quick mind such as the one he carried.

"Then we should set off, sir. Are you ready?"

The quirk of addressing himself formally was something Thome had affected since his time at boarding school. It gave one a sense of security to know an adult was with you.

So

It was in earlier times that Thome stood with his father and mother behind a bush in the Scottish Highlands waiting for game. It was Thome's first hunt, he was terribly frightened. He had his boning knife attached to his belt;

around him the Scottish Highlands in fog, inside him terror. "We are here to put the animals out of their misery." His father had said. Which could make sense if you considered life misery, as his parents seemed to. Thome froze. He was waiting for

THE RED DEER

OPENNESS: *N/A*

HEALTH RISKS: *depression, hunters*

He was a rather introverted game animal. Amazing that anyone could have had enough of life, thought the game animal, just the way one cannot imagine getting old when one is young. That happened to others. Others, with their embarrassing self-inflicted aging.

It would never happen to him. At least hunters were good for that. And

There it is, the shot to the chest, but. No pain. Thinks the game animal. Did they miss, the complete and utter idiots? Is even that too much for them to manage? Unfortunately no, because I can't manage to keep my eyes open. I'll just close them for a second. What's the meaning of this? The most beautiful moments of life aren't playing back. Inside. No tunnel, no light. Only me. Alone. With the sky, the light, that's going out. And the knowledge that everything, everything, for nothing. Was.

And then the sun goes down—for the last time.

Goodbye, you unspeakable assholes.

Barrel of laughs with you. You complete and utter idiots, thought

THOME

And heard the shot as if from a great distance. When his father brought

him the head of the animal, he threw up. On the deer. On his father's tweed
trousers. And then Thome cried. He couldn't stop. Back then. When his father
began to despise him. And his mother got cancer. Because of him. And died.
His fault. Later things got worse.

The curtains of musty-smelling velvet—outsiders would be shocked if
they were to enter the villas of the upper class and see the run-down, decayed
condition of the furniture, which the upper class considered befitting of their
status—were pulled halfway closed. The father—a Sir, by the way—was sitting with his head resting on his hands in a dark corner of the room. On the
bed where nine generations of relatives had already lain dead now lay Thome's
mother. A stern woman with large breasts. She'd been. And the breasts, which
even now towered toward the ceiling, had been the greatest source of shame
over the course of her life, the low-class bosom which hindered her while
hunting. Contrary to her silent wish, which she included in her drunken evening prayers, she hadn't expired while on a hunt, but from breast cancer. A
disease about which people always whispered: "She fought so bravely." As if
that would interest the cancer cells. Cancer cells were humans in miniature
form. Eat everything that crosses their path with no regard for the damage,
taking for granted, out of greed, that the host will eventually cease to exist.
Thome's mother had chosen an unlucky moment to become ill. Biosensors had
only just been invented. Programmable bacteria that could be read from the
outside. Later they'd track down cancer and set to work right in the middle of
the tumor. But yeah, that was later. Thome stood at the side of the so-called
deathbed and explained away his absence of grief or sympathy with a string
of quirky and absolutely hip mental diseases. Asperger, ADHD, giftedness,
WTF. He felt nothing and could only think: Oh well, gone is gone. Thome
had survived—somehow—his boarding school years at Manchester Grammar
School as the catchment basin for the perversions of his fellow students. Now
it was off to university. His grades were middling, but the contacts of his
parents—sorry, his father—eliminated any misgivings. So it would be Cambridge, and so his way forward would be sketched out. If he didn't completely
screw it up, a comfortable life lay before him. A family villa on a private road
on Holland Park, an influential post somewhere, first in IT, due to his aptitude
for nerdy explanation, later politics, then a stroke. Until then: membership
in a first-class college society, and perhaps he'd get to know a woman who

loved cashmere twinsets and would live out her last few unencumbered years at Cambridge attending group sex parties. And later, as a moderate alcoholic with a weakness for hunting dogs, produce a couple degenerate children for him. Incidentally, the mother had just died of cancer in a region of the body people like her never referred to by name. Amusing detail. An astonishingly inappropriate sigh echoed through the silence of the room.

THOME'S FATHER

SEXUALITY: *S&M fetish, prodigious Viagra consumption*
HOBBIES: *collects medals and used panty liners*
INTOXICANTS: *smokes Havana cigars, opium*
HOBBIES: *loves to work on his back with a back scratcher*
HEALTH RISKS: *high blood pressure, onset cirrhosis*

Sighed. He had to do something to give expression to his sadness. Thome's father was a member of the House of Lords and managed the still handsome fortune of his family, which had roots back to the thirteenth century and which, despite closed factories, was still respectable. He owned pieces of several digital companies that principally dealt in the collection, evaluation, and manipulation of data and, as an old friend of the military, was on the verge of founding the country's first private army. He financed an online newspaper where imaginative students published fake videos, photos, and reports that furthered the so-called division of the populace. At his IT firm some of the employees in the microtargeting division were working successfully on the reinvention of Britain. A lot going on, this old house. You could say that Thome's father along with other billionaires would play a significant role in the collapse and resurrection of the country. Like god. Or Jesus. Whatever. Thome's father was a member of the Hayek Society, an aggregation of free market fundamentalist idiots who were members of the Atlas Network, an aggregation of still more neoliberal idiots who were busy with the abolishment of government, and all of them wanted to quickly reshape the world before they died. Or just get more power. Or money. Or—

Let's take a quick look, for instance, at the plan various old bastards had been executing for some time. When you use the instruments of democracy to completely pulverize trust in democracy—that is, put absolutely rubbish individuals in top positions, instigate civil wars, incite the so-called good against the so-called bad by means of Nudging, by the manipulation of their goddamn brains via devices, social media, false information, when you render the press utterly untrustworthy, when you encourage brutality, Nazis, ignorance, and fascism—in short, when you perpetrate insane chaos, that means in the short-term: diminished profits. But shit happens. You just have to consider the unbelievable easing of the financial system the next step involves. The next step, which was already imminent.

The Earth. It needed to be liberated from humans a bit. Sound crazy? Not at all. If it comes across strange to you then it is only because you can't grasp the magnitude of the vision. Right, well. Let's talk about the family. How it wanted tradition, and how

THOME

Was a disappointment for the noble pedophiles. Thome had gotten accustomed to being despised by his parents. In his circles that was actually a basic principle of family. Mutual disdain was the foundation on which the kingdom had been built. Tradition, boarding school, university, expensive cemetery plots. That's how you could summarize the CV of his people.

His mother's burial at the family grave site was a heady celebration. Even his mother's short-legged hunting dogs attended the ceremony, with astonishing restraint. About a thousand old, rich, white people shuffled along behind the coffin as it left the crown chapel and so forth. Thome was a half-orphan and still waiting for a feeling. Feelings were unseemly in his circles.

Thome had learned that it was unimportant to orient himself to any other subset of the population than white men. Most of them in his milieu were unattractive but well dressed. A standard Thome considered attainable. Most of them despised women and feared them at the same time—something he could again see in himself. Thome was at a sexual age, but it had never been taken to

extremes. He had masturbated. In every corner of the family villa. Most effectively in his parents' bedroom. Formerly, that is. When his mother, god rest her
soul, was out and about. Thome stood at the bedside and wanked. That was
always the most intense discharge. Sometimes in the cellar. Watching the gar-
dener. Not bad either. Before. Now he was bored, stared at the ceiling, stared
out the window into the endless manicured park. He lay on his bed, listened
to electronic music. And wondered whether he should engage a prostitute. So
he'd finally know how youth was supposed to be, which he hadn't lived out up
to now. But. When he pictured going into a brothel where it smelled bad and
then finding the women lined up at the bar, all of whom looked like service
people—in fact maybe one of their own servants would be there earning a
little extra income, and he'd go to a room with the cook he'd known since
he was four, where she would laugh at him because of his penis, which was
unusually crooked and pointed at the end like a dog's. A Corgi. Thome knew
all about that. But not about sex. The time was not yet right. The time—
reminded him. He needed to map out his future. At some point he'd be the
CEO of an internet company whose earnings dwarfed most countries' GDP.
Thome thought of himself as a cross between Peter Thiel and Mercer. An IT
god whose looks didn't matter. Because Thome wasn't good-looking. Pale,
sweaty, with thinning reddish hair and a runny nose. He was about six feet tall
with hips twice as wide as his shoulders and even in his youth the beginnings
of a paunch. But Thome knew that as a result of his social status, his physical
appearance played a decidedly insignificant role. With his name it didn't even
take the family fortune to be able to choose from the most attractive women
in society. Attractive in quotation marks. The best of what comes from generations of incest. Small blue eyes and fat asses. Thome used to worry about
his appearance. Let's just say boarding school was hell. But on the plus side
he could now program and knew that he was sexually confused. Was he into
S&M? Children? Animals? Diapers. He'd tried that once. He'd found adult
diapers in a secret drawer in his parents' room. Along with bestiality porn and
a few snuff films where Polish housewives were fucked to death. There's always
something. So it wasn't diapers, but what was it? Sexuality, lived out openly,
wasn't something that happened in Thome's circles. He would arrange his
sexual life the same way as everyone he knew—marry into a prestigious family and keep everything else private. In dungeons, at sex parties and in clubs,

with prostitute or slaves. He could hardly wait. He could hardly wait to go to university. Computer science at Cambridge. He'd started programming when he was six. Later on he'd achieved some sensational hacks—faking fingerprints and iris scans, for instance. There was a lot of recognition to be had online for something like that. Thome would never found something like Uber or Netflix. His future lay in the intersection of power and technology. And out there. Markets are celebrated. Hurray for markets. One of them was having a birthday. These wonderful free markets. Cheers. Old men rejoiced. They had erections. Men like Thome's father. He knew what was being planned. In the background, invisible to most, the markets—hurray for markets—powered by algorithms, had developed lives of their own. Some of the most important investment firms with dull names like: Gartmore Group and Blackwood, RIT Capital Partners PLC—

Now Thome had forgotten what he was trying to think of; it happened to him ever more frequently and had its origins in his absurdly quick mind, which once again was engaged with multiple topics. It was the moment prior to some financial crisis or other that was supposed to bring the country to collapse again. Before a financial crisis is always, of course, also after one. Markets will straighten everything out. The water supply had just been privatized. Meaning. The price of water had quadrupled, and because as a result the natives began to use less water the new owners made losses which were to be offset by tax money from the natives. Beautiful. On it went. The transport system. In private hands. Which consequently led to a dramatic rise in ticket prices and a simultaneous deterioration in the rail system. Then it was the schools' turn. Which brought with it a wave of mass layoffs of teachers. The social economy. Meaning: the country's populace paid levies for the eventuality that they might need welfare benefits, disability payments, unemployment, sick pay, or old age pension, the state handed this money over to private companies which spent the majority of the money on their supposed infrastructure, allowing them in the end to save on paying for the upkeep of public facilities, medical supplies, those in need of emergency services, and pensions, and to turn a profit for the owners.

It was the last gasp of the European Community, and

The intelligence services consummated their collection of all data, which according to rumor was stored in a vast so-called research facility in Switzerland. The so-called research facility, which nearly every cash-rich country in the world had a stake in, had an autonomous, neutral status not subject to any legal jurisdiction. Aerial photographs showed evidence of heightened electrical activity. Physical experiments. You understand. It was the largest data trove in the Western world. But back then nobody knew about it yet. What good was it supposed to be to intercept billions of emails and save browsing histories? Who would benefit from all the social media Likes and posts? Who was supposed to read it all? People thought. Who all used computers and smartphones. Hardly anyone realized what they were doing. Except Thome. He pictured himself as director of the intelligence service. Or as owner of a powerful cyber army. That's where future wars would take place. Wars that would be won with data. Or with the destruction of security systems. Destruction sounded good. That would be brilliant.

MI5 PIET

"Now, just between us, I laugh, to the best of my abilities, which are more suited to a smirk. When we look at the future of this young man's avatar, his future doesn't look so interesting. Could you say something more specific?"

THE PROGRAMMER

"Of course. My artificial neural network shows—

"There's—

"Nothing.

"But—"

THOME

Was finally where he belonged, at Cambridge. The place that cranked out Nobel Prize winners one after the next. The university that until not too long ago only accepted people who spoke Latin. And who spoke it? Exactly, private school kids. And what did that mean? Exactly, there were no normal people here. Outside of a few scholarship students, everyone here belonged to the same class.

Thome felt as if all the components of his weakly defined sense of self had become congruent with the external conditions. To breathe here in one of the cradles of the Empire was to be part of a grand canvas, something Thome had never experienced before. Thome was a member of the rowing club and lunch club as well as a secret society that was so secret it had yet to hold a single meeting. They grew up here, the future politicians, judges, lawyers, and weapons dealers of the nation, surrounded by marriage material that would

never resort to a career. Thome was possessed by the eager restlessness that
held sway over people when they did the right thing in the right place. When
they followed their purpose. Thome bent over his work after lectures, yes,
he could picture himself from above: an ambitious young cadre who, with a
furrowed brow, devoted himself to the big IT questions of the future. In the
evenings he went to the club, on weekends he rowed. His body was changing
for the better along with his mind, that much he could already tell. When he
gazed out at the campus it was as if he were looking at the family he'd never
had, when he prowled the pubs of the venerable little town he saw people who
looked like him. A few interesting women were also around, surely a good
match would be made here.

The campus was peaceful on that
Sunday.

Thome's happiness at being far removed from his father, from the boredom, the feeling of being insufficient, was only minimally tarnished by the
inconvenience of a few laborers. Cleaning, washing socks, rolling up socks.
Thome imagined for a moment sinking for various reasons into poverty and
having to do all those daily human chores. Grocery shopping. Standing in line.
Cooking things, making the bed. Thome had no idea how other people—
they were people, after all—managed it. All those tedious, time-consuming
activities whose only aim was to keep the human organism alive. Buying toilet
paper was clear evidence of having defecated. He had never seen a single one of
his relatives or acquaintances buying toilet paper. The toilet was never mentioned; it was invisible and silent. Except for sexual uses. He knew of neighbors
who had installed a glass toilet in their bedroom to be able to watch the stool
leave their partner's bodies. Turned them on. Thome knew he had nothing in
common with other "people." This wasn't meant to be arrogant, it was just a
fact. He had tried now and then to engage people in conversation. But he didn't
understand what they were talking about. Raf stopped snoring. Who the fuck
was Raf? Thome shared his room with a young man who was related to somebody from the royal family. But, really, who wasn't? With little effort Thome
could easily establish ten provisional connections to major royal houses via
his family tree. Some promiscuous great-grandfather had found his way into
family trees all over the place. Back to Raf.

Whose hair fell over his only minimally degenerate, aristocratic face.

Thome resisted the impulse to tousle it. He was British. Meaning you didn't tousle, you engaged in conversation. That had to suffice as foreplay. Raf started snoring again. It had been a late one yesterday. The Pakistani drug dealer had invited Raf, Thome, and two other smug idiots from the Cambridge Rowing Club to go to Rochdale to have sex with very young girls. None of the young men had ever been with prostitutes before, and as a result they enthusiastically accepted the invitation straightaway. Anything dirty was alluring, you wanted to be part of it.

An odd calm had held sway during the drive to Rochdale. The young men felt uneasy. Not because they were on their way to stick their genitalia into people who were presumably none too excited about it. None of the young men thought of a prostitute as a human being, because along with the fact that they were women, they would also be those people. The young men couldn't be blamed for the fact that they deemed unimportant any life form born outside the ruling class. One must factor in tradition, education, and people's propensity to place themselves above others, and one must be charitable in the assessment of their state of mind and character.

So.

The unease of these young arseholes was a result of being in an ugly car, with a Pakistani. Breathing the same air as him, aware of the dirty seats beneath them. As repellent as the place they rolled into at some point. On a mattress in a basement apartment, probably called a garden apartment in working-class circles, sat two loaded minors watching music videos on their phones. Right, now what? Asked the men, looking at the girls, not knowing how to proceed. The young Pakistani sensed the insecurity and demonstrated how it worked. He shoved his hand under the skirt of one of the girls—an albino, it appeared—kissed her roughly, opened her top, waved over one of the young men and shoved him into her.

Except for a few psychopaths, everyone has an inner cliff edge. Below, in a dark gorge, lies what humans have learned to recognize as "evil." One small step, come on, said Evil down there in the dark. Let yourself fall, everything'll be easier. The first young man took that step, he left himself and the prison of his sense of decency. He fell onto the albino grunting and fucked himself silly. He'd never had an orgasm like it. A dirty, powerful orgasm. The Paki rubbed cocaine on his gums and the young men followed his lead. They didn't find

it strange to watch each other fuck; on the contrary it made them that much
more horny, it was what they really wanted, to get off with each other without
being gay, and when it was Thome's turn—one of the girls had passed out in the
meantime—his penis wouldn't get hard. Thome felt the way he had that time
when hunting, when he'd thrown up on the stag. Like a failure. He watched Raf,
who was moving around right next to him inside the not-an-albino girl. How
furiously Raf slammed his pelvis against her lower body. Bubbles were coming
out of the girl's mouth. As if she were already dead and her body was leaking
gas. Thome looked at Raf, his thrusts, and suddenly he could do it, too. If he
shut his eyes. So he shut his eyes. He wanted to make a good impression on
Raf. He started to work the albino over. In all holes, until they bled and the
Pakistani had to intervene. And calm Thome, who'd become possessed.

Everyone was silent during the drive home. The memory of their classmates' naked genitals lingering like a dream.

That was just a short while ago. And now it was Sunday, and Thome
looked at Raf's half-naked body, which was provocatively covered with freck-
les. Thome stepped closer. He saw the reddish hair on Raf's legs. Thome was
still in his underwear. As he went toward the dresser he pulled the sheet from
Raf's body, leaving his bottom exposed. Thome stood still, his heartbeat surg-
ing furiously, his mouth opening, and the bulge of an erection formed in his
underwear. So, get going with that bulge, a pair of sweatpants thrown over it
and off into the virginal sublimity of Sunday. Thome looked one last time at
the sleeping Raf, left the dorm, and just then heard the aristocratic crackle of
gravel in the driveway that heralded an approaching visitor. A Bentley—or to
be more precise, his father's Bentley. The combination of father, erection, and
jogging was probably predicated on chaos theory, thought Thome, massaging
his calves and awaiting the appearance of his father. His father exited the vehicle, in the passenger seat of which sat a woman who looked to be barely older
than Thome, in a short skirt and very high heels. The woman climbed out
teeteringly. A new employee? A nanny. Why would father bring a fucking ser-
vant here? Thome's father cleared his throat. "This is Tamara." Said Thome's
father. "We're getting married."

Later

So, after a few weeks, when Thome drove home, he entered the family
villa through the service entrance. He crept through the now unfamiliar house.

Tamara had really outdone herself. The new mother. Who of course wasn't a prostitute but a consultant. She helped Russians newly arrived in London deal with questions concerning real estate, assets, investments, arranged invitations to horse races and the acquisition of valuable diamonds. The business concept was booming. And with Tamara marrying into the ruling class it got an unbelievable boost. She had excitedly redecorated the house. The boxwoods were replaced with modern sculptures by an exiled Russian artist, the old parquet floors torn out. Now marble lay on the floor, and the old furniture had yielded under the direction of an Italian interior designer to furniture made by the hand of the great artist Colani. Tamara loved Italian design.

Now. Unfortunately

THOME'S FATHER

was absent. Late love and political ambitions were a disastrous combination. He needed the support of his friends to become prime minister. It couldn't be allowed to transpire that all his efforts would be rendered futile by the impulses of his old penis. From then on Thome's father took part in every middling hunt he was invited to, revitalized his contacts to the royal family, and hoped that society would forget his wife as long as she was invisible. Society was obstinate, never forgave and forgot. "Oh my dear, what a pleasure to see you," began the conversations conducted with his father. "Will we see you at the Moorhuhn hunt?—Oh excuse me, I need to firm up a few details with Lord Summerburn. We'll have the pleasure later." His spouse was never mentioned. Never. Invited. She roamed around the villa in a bathrobe and was bored, if she didn't happen to be selling oligarch-preferred diamonds or Bentleys or a German-owned company or Rolls-Royces or a German-owned company. The country's IT firms belonged to Russians and Americans, the bulk of the city to Arabs and Russians.

XIANG MAI

"Nothing belongs to the Russians or Arabs anymore, or the Germans. Especially not the Germans."

"Pipe down, you idiots," thought

THOME

that weekend, as he sat in his room and Russians rubbed shoulders downstairs. Women who managed to look cheap despite very expensive clothing, men whose brutality couldn't be hidden by bespoke suits. That's real international understanding, that's globalization, here's to the people. All of them mutter: "Cheers." That people so often operated within the parameters of their own clichés was amazing. Thome went down—at times with utterly no other goal than to bother them—and joined the Russians, who seemed a bit insecure. He watched the lady of the house. Looked at her breasts that pressed out of the neckline of her top. Thome didn't even find the thought objectionable that his father, whom he could only picture in flannel suits, had allowed his penis to be sucked by this woman. It was a brilliant moment. When Thome pictured his father with his pants pulled down and this Versace-bitch in front of him, it was the moment when he lost all respect. It was before hate filled him,

Months later

With hatred for everything. His life. Cambridge. His studies, which Thome had hoped would mark the emergence of his personality from the chrysalis— caterpillar, butterfly, and so on—were a flop. His expectations lagged behind. Same with his intellectual aptitude. Nearly every day Thome ran up against the limits of his comprehension. He watched fellow students pass him by intellectually, he remained seated behind a sign in his mind that read: "Done." Sometimes he beat his head against the wall to loosen the synapses. Success continued to elude him. He got up to the sign, pushed and pressed against it as if constipated, but he could get no further. This is what it's like to grasp one's mediocrity, realized Thome, a destiny he shared with millions of scientists, engineers, artists, and athletes around the world, who all knew that for them it would never come to anything phenomenal but who nonetheless pressed on and kept up hope despite all reason. That a miracle could still occur, a valve would burst, some mental eruption would set their creativity free. Even setting aside his mental failure, Cambridge was also a social disaster. Rumors of his father's misalliance had made their way around the Empire within days. There was barely anything society wouldn't forgive. The love of children, dogs, including sexually, cheating, homosexuality, the loss of wealth, drug addiction, everything seemed pardonable and would be stylishly hushed up— but not fraternization. If there was one thing the upper class disdained more than poverty it was new money. Arabs, Russians. To screw someone from this strata was acceptable, as long as it took place discreetly. But one did not marry such people. Everyone still remembered the last scandal, with Lady Diana

Spencer and her Arab. As well as how this problem had been taken care of. It was the ruling class's worst catastrophe since Edward VIII wanted to marry a divorced American in 1936. Moments that put into question the future of the monarchy were more traumatic than the attacks of 2005. For Thome, his father's late lasciviousness had horrible consequences. He was socially

Dead.

His former roommate was now sleeping with the 6th Earl of Canterbury. Thome's second bed remained empty. The rowing club had kicked him out, ditto the lunch club and secret society. There'd been talk of new bylaws. One didn't ask for details, one accepted one's destiny like a man. A man who no longer had any friends. Nobody wanted to shower with him. Or have him at sex parties. Or speak, smoke, drink, or—let's put it simply—have anything to do with him. Thanks, Father. Thome's life had reached what at the time was its low point. He saw himself as an unattractive, mediocre person for whom suddenly a comfortable upper-class life was no longer waiting. Hate, which had always constituted an indeterminate part of Thome's character, promulgated itself digitally—the future development of the world was for the most part due to frustrated bros like him. Who ruled and shaped 99 percent of the world's knowledge in Wikipedia and Wikimania and Wikileaks and blogs. They coded, they hacked the economy, they wrote algorithms that in their minds would rule the world with artificial intelligence that reflected their own. Cheers! Thome began to create his first platform. He called it: Dream Island.

At some point

DON

Gave

Up.

On the summer. On herself. On the collective pressure to enjoy her youth. Please, how's that supposed to work anyway? How are you supposed to be happy about something you didn't ask for? Should she sit around and drink beer, destroy bus stops, have sex with one or more of the sickly boys from the area just to get it over with? Don stayed in bed. She was young and had what felt like a hundred years to fritter away. From the bathroom the sounds her brother made on his smartphone. Probably honing his sexual competence.

Those endless summer weeks were a catastrophe.

Because Don's mother discovered alcohol. The most vulgar of all drugs.

At first Don didn't know what had changed her mother so much. Made her so moody and aggressive. But at some point she realized the personality change had to do with the bottles always standing in front of her. Gradually she learned to recognize her mother's condition based on her halting gait, her saucer eyes, and the slurred consonants. Don's mother always found a good reason to beat the children. Of course, it's important to know. That bodily pain is not the biggest problem when it comes to getting beaten. It's the outbreak of violence and vulgarity that makes the incident so miserable. The air becomes toxic, objects lose their innocence because they are witness to the humiliation. All of this made the period during which Don's mother drank the most unpleasant of her entire childhood. All of her later memories were exclusively from that year, condensed into bodily pain and mental revulsion.

Sometimes Don went to the pub with her brother to plead with friendly insistence on her return home.

In order to avoid her staggering through the apartment later, screaming. ("Hey Mother, the walls at home are a bit moldy, and we don't have any money to pay for electricity, but we could sit in the damp kitchen and eat bread and margarine.")

Like in some shitty Dickens Christmas movie, the two of them would stand at the bar where their mother was sitting with men who always had something sticking out somewhere and who laughed too loudly. After a while it would become too embarrassing even for the drunks and she would follow her children. At home there were beatings.

One night Don's mother tried to use an ax (where did she get a fucking ax?) to break down the bedroom door behind which the children had locked themselves. Don and her brother rappelled down from the window using sheets and spent the night at a playground. Don consoled her simpering, whining brother and calculated how much longer she had to be a child. Clearly too long. She wondered what alternatives there were. Now. The opportunities for a small child who hadn't finished school to make a living on the free market were limited. All the ideas that quickly popped up—working on a ship (as what, for god's sake?), making child porn, entering the drug trade—were unappealing. The world Don knew consisted of Rochdale, the idiotic family, school, and her friends. She couldn't imagine anything else.

Childhood, with all the diseases it can entail, is probably the most horrid period of life. A child's perception of the seemingly infinite duration of life multiplied the sense of unease. To feel like an independent person but not to be one, dependent on the moods and temper of legal guardians who themselves didn't know any better. Don had no idea that there were childhoods where young people sat in the back of cars on long summer days, looking out the window as their parents navigated toward a holiday spot. Childhoods where if they fell, someone put a bandage on their wound and sat next to their bed and patted their head. Children's misfortune wasn't a result of being able to compare their situation to other children's but rather the result of their inability to know what they needed in order to create a feeling of well-being.

Don's mother started to bring men home. As if she wasn't unpleasant enough on her own. People who slurred, were loud, and with every motion seemed to lay claim to something that they would in case of any doubt take with aggression. The men staggered into the furniture, pinched the children's cheeks, or simply ignored them and shoved their mother toward her bed with glassy eyes. Don always worried about her mother because she didn't know what was going on inside the room, in front of which she sat with a kitchen knife so she could intervene in case of emergency. One of these men became her mother's steady boyfriend, which was discernible by the fact that he came over more often. He was an absurdly big white guy with strange rust-colored hair and a little hump where his neck met his back.

The man moved into the apartment after a few days with two plastic bags. With a serious look on his face, he put out books and writing materials on the kitchen table, as he was doing a distance learning course in theology. He prayed. Nonstop. Before every piece of bread with margarine, after every bowel movement. Mornings when he emerged from the bedroom. He kneeled in front of the sink and thanked god for this and that. "Walter could serve as a role model for you," said Don's mother, looking lovingly at the dirty bastard. "Now we have a man in the house again who will look after us," she said. Don's brother withdrew and pounded his fist into his bed. Even though he saw his father only every few months, he looked up to him greatly.

As if the universe wanted to have some fun with the new family arrangement, Don's mother found a job at a cafeteria in Manchester. She left home every morning at seven. And so the children stayed with the man who was named Walter and who started his day with prayers. He kneeled in front of the kitchenette and spoke to god. One day Don was watching Walter as he prayed and had to quietly giggle. The burst of laughter just came out—at the sight of this strange man in a social housing unit talking to his master. Walter turned, saw Don, and sprang toward her. He punched her in the face. "You laughing at me? You don't laugh at me!" he screamed, flying into a rage.

WALTER

Was just one of millions.

A million Walters, and every day there were more who were. Mad. So very mad because they knew they were right. Because they were a million Walters. And were right, and nobody cared. They hated it when the margarine went off. When women passed them while driving. And when it rained and their shoes got wet. And when dogs barked at them. And when children spoke with those unnaturally high voices that sounded like the voices of porn stars. And when Blacks had better teeth. Walter was never comfortable inside. He could never sit down with a nice cup of, let's say, Thai mountain tea, beneath a Cypress tree, and just let everything slide. There was always a tension that desired something, and never something good. The desire had to do with a release. If Walter wasn't fucking someone or fighting, if he couldn't kick a dog aside or kill a squirrel with a rock, the red-haired swine, then he sat on a chair in the kitchen where he had already destroyed everything that could be destroyed. The chair was made of steel. What kind of an idiot thought of making a chair out of steel? And on that chair he sat, both legs nervously bouncing up and down at a frantic pace he was unable to stop. The windowpane was already shattered. Same with his fist. Walter passed on what he had learned. He had grown up with his father, god rest his soul, in a flat he himself had later taken over. The father had been unemployed and had a badly enlarged liver. His mother was gone, she was a hooker, which is why she was gone, and Walter grew up with the knowledge that nothing in the world mattered except strength and aggression. His father thrashed him with every object in the apartment that was sound, and he was beaten up at school because he smelled bad, because he lied, because he couldn't look anyone in the eye because when he looked his father in the eye he got beaten. Walter wet himself, he chewed his fingernails, he stunk. And why wouldn't he, since the apartment was filthy; fruit flies did their rounds, maggots wriggled in old jam jars, and his father wore underwear he never washed; there was a dried ring of puke around the toilet. When there was dole money his father set out and bought alcohol, then there'd be fighting, then the money would be gone, and Walter would have to go out and steal food. That's how it had been for Walter, and when he was finally grown-up and unemployed like his father, when his father was finally dead and Walter discovered that there were people who were afraid of him—that is, women and children—he began to blossom. To become loud and to find god; indeed he was so happy that there just had to be a superior being who had set him on this path. God, of course.

This god was a man, who gave him an idea of why he was on earth. And Walter finally knew how he could put structure in his life. Then he had met a woman. And then he moved into her place. Shut your mouth. He screamed, and

DON

Was silent, and that made Walter even more upset for some reason. Walter screamed that he would show her what pain was. He grabbed her arm and twisted it out of its joint.

When Don came to, the television was on. Walter had made margarine sandwiches. There's no punch line.

From that day on Walter had made it his mission to make Don into a believer. He locked her in the bathroom. He made her kneel on peas. Learn Bible passages by heart, and he was never happy with the result, which meant punishment. The most memorable punishment involved the toilet, into which Walter shoved Don's head, under water, over and over again under, until Don became panicked and flailed around—and so forth.

If an uninvolved, mentally healthy adult had observed the situation, the person would be afflicted with a total absence of hope for the child. Don trembled, and she knew she was about to die. Die. The concept was pure terror, cold bottomlessness. Don lost control of her bladder. Urine ran down her legs. Walter stepped away from Don, lying on the floor, at the exact moment when Don's mother came home. She pissed herself, said Walter, and Don's mother slapped her face. Then she went into the bedroom with Walter and a bottle she'd brought home with her. Don's brother never rose from the computer.

The next day Don waited for her mother at the bus stop. When she arrived after Don had been waiting there for an hour, when Don told her everything, her mother walked silently with her to their housing estate. She said to Walter, who was cooking something in a pot: "My daughter lied to me. She made up bad things about you." Then Don's mother began to cry and yell at Don that she begrudged her happiness in life, and to Walter she said: "You have to punish her." Walter dragged Don into the bedroom, shoved her onto the bed and ordered her to take down her pants and not to piss herself again. Don heard Walter remove his belt from his pants. Then he hit her. For several minutes. One could withstand being hit, if one distracted oneself. By taking a vow, for instance. Don swore that nobody was going to harm her. Never again. She no longer felt the humiliation, she saw the pitifulness of Walter, of her mother. It was just a question of time until she would get out. Disappear. Walter, however, took care of himself. He met a new woman and moved with her to London.

That was the summer when everything went wrong.

Or something new began.

"Go on, make a face like you're dead,"

Said

HANNAH

The children tried to conjure up dead looks. Dull eyes staring at the

ground. Slumped shoulders. For the sake of art. Hannah had decided to
start a YouTube career. Maybe she'd turn out to be a born influencer. She
was always searching herself for some sort of talent. Her channel was called:
Life in the Cellar. Mostly she shot the others crawling around downtrodden
locations—a fashion show with clothes from the Salvation Army, interviews
with the homeless.

"How did you end up in this situation?"

"Well, I got sick."

"Okay, got it, thanks a lot. Have a nice life."

The earnest social reporting was not very successful. Not even a hundred
views. There were far more clicks when Hannah convinced boys to glue their
eyelids with superglue, get SpongeBob tattoos on their foreheads, or crash full
speed into a wall on a stolen bicycle.

On the day they were all supposed to make dead faces, she recorded a
makeup tutorial. Karen, Peter, and Don looked despondent, quasi hopeless,
the light of a crummy afternoon seeped into the factory. Hannah made up the
dead-looking children and filmed it.

Hannah looked like one those manga characters, the children who traipse
around with bodies like Barbie dolls. Her hair now platinum blonde and one
centimeter long, coupled with her odd, gangly body,

Just look at them,

Thought

KAREN

"A totally new world order is nearly upon us," said Hannah into the camera, and Karen found herself in a really bad mood. If cartoon figures were
going to explain the world now, she might as well just go home. "What do you
mean," asked Karen. "What new world order? You talking about the role of
the Vatican? It's said in the Book of Revelations that the Holy Roman Empire
will rise again during the end-times. An orchestrated apocalypse in which
the Catholics are left as the new world power, now that's an idea. Speaking of
which, did you guys know that there are now drones that are smaller than the
palm of your hand? They can drop a small amount of explosives right on the
forehead of the target and take them out."

"Oh man, that's just a fairytale,"

Said Don, and

"Um, no," whispered
MI5 PIET
Though probably
KAREN
Was

Just in a bad mood that afternoon. She was increasingly moody of late, was nervous and anxious and dispirited and enraged, and all of those things alternating within minutes, and Karen knew what that meant. It was starting. "I have to go," she said, because she couldn't stand the others or herself, and went home. Well, that is, she went to where she lived. To the tower blocks. With tiny balconies where because of the constant rain, of course, nobody ever sat or grilled—what would they grill anyway, their own legs?

So the small balconies filled with poor people's mattresses and cabinets, whatever sort of crap you needed as a loser. The entryways scrawled with graffiti, musty smelling from all the bad food cooked there, a high level of noise—people were always screaming at each other, some children were always crying, there was always something going on, the elevator was nearly always out of service, and when it wasn't it sounded as if it should have long since given up the ghost. The apartment was happily empty late in the afternoon, out the windows a good view from the twelfth floor, the sun hung behind shreds of clouds, a few cars wandered through the streets below, downstairs in front of the buildings some bored boys. For a moment Karen was happy, because her life wouldn't play out here. After her studies she would go to the US or Israel, but first she had to survive her adolescence. It was time to say goodbye to her old self and take a break from her intellectual development. The hormones created a constant hum in her ear, and she knew what that meant. Karen, still a model student and biology nerd, Karen, the future scholarship earner, knew that her body was now preparing itself for reproduction and her brain would soon be useless. She listened to Devlin while she packed up her biology textbooks and the microscope she'd borrowed from school, and then, together with her brain, stowed them under the bed, promising to return soon. She believed she detected her brain being replaced by a clump made of pure idiocy. After that was done Karen sampled her meager wardrobe, checked it for so-called sexiness, tried out makeup and new hairstyles. Welcome to the world of sexual imbecility were the last sensible words Karen heard herself utter. In the same year artificial intelligence took the first steps toward its own lumbering creativity, humanity lost another thinking member.

A little bit later

Karen began to experience the normal misery of young people. The transition from a child to a grown-up asshole was set in motion and expressed itself in bad moods, which is understandable once you understand what will soon become of charming children. Karen did what pubescent girls do: masturbate, watch porn, stalk boys on Facebook. She even carefully observed the two complete idiots who were her brothers. Well, one of them. She looked at boys at school and before school, she looked at them on the main street, where they hung around in front of the bet shops, she looked at them when they closed their eyes and when they slept. Karen didn't want to get interested in something that was intellectually inferior to her, and yet she was powerless against and obsessed with staring at bottoms, necks, and legs. Which didn't lead to any results, no interactions took place, because boys her age didn't consider Karen a sexually useful being. Karen was the geeky albino. The girl with glasses and red eyes.

Unlike during her time as a thinking being, Karen no longer went straight home after school to read; instead she showed great interest in the goods on display at charity shops in the pedestrian zone. That is, the area where groups of handsome young men milled about looking to transform their inner excitement into something productive—like fucking or beating someone up. There was never contact between Karen and these boys; even if one of them had been interested in her it would have impossible for him to enter a relationship with Karen without losing face. In the male hive mind Karen was only a step above copulating with a bulldog. She was finally chatted up one day when she wanted to go home—well, wanted to go home isn't strictly true; she had to go home, because her bed was there—a young, good-looking man who presumably had Pakistani roots.

THE PAKISTANIS

Were not necessarily the most beloved subpopulation in the United Kingdom. They had their own neighborhoods, their own gangs, their own rules, and there was hardly anything you'd have to do with them, unless you needed a truck or a taxi, drugs, prostitutes, or cheap vegetables.

The Pakistanis were too plentiful. Nobody is prepared for the realization

that the world must be shared with billions of others. It's too much information, it brings up questions like:

Am I possibly not unique?

What are they all doing on my planet?

As long as those billions kept a proper distance and lived quietly in their
own countries, everything was fine. You could watch impassively on television
as the people in faraway lands cut each other into pieces or otherwise died.
That was the moment when you went to grab a beer. But now they were there.
Here. Across the street. On location. They came with buses and boats and
airplanes, on their feet or swimming, and many people had the impression that
millions of dark-skinned people were holding on to the edge of the island all
at once, trying to hoist their bodies onto land. It was the time when lots of old
men started to warn about Islam and refugees, about foreign infiltration. They
wrote books which sold spectacularly, and articles, and founded movements,
and the people—people who had never before thought about why it always
rained—found an explanation and began to regard Pakis and others, that is,
simply put, Muslims, with mild reservations. Which

Didn't surprise

KAREN.

Humans were not capable of developing compassion for large groups of
strangers. Sympathy that extended beyond those you were related to or friends
with was best limited to individuals who were attractive or who looked sadly
into cameras.

"Hey, wait a second," said the Pakistani. He grabbed Karen's arm. Her
arm melted. The young man stood close to her, he was tall and slim, with
broad shoulders, a white shirt, beneath which a smooth chest was discernible;
his hair was medium length and almost blue-black, and he wore very tight
black jeans. Karen didn't say anything. What would she say? Mania flooded
her speech center when she noticed the young man's elegant hands. The young
man whose name Karen had already forgotten the moment he said it, said
something, but only a few odd words managed to reach Karen's brain. Often
seen you, never dared to approach you, where did she live, oh right, he had to
go that way as well, we can walk together, and then they walked together, and
as they arrived at Karen's after far too short a walk—the stupid short distances
in this absurdly small city—the young man, whose name Karen still didn't

know, reached for her hand and pulled her to his warm chest. Did I just think warm chest, thought Karen, and did I just think that somebody might jump out of the high-rise at exactly this moment and land on us? And then wrench him away in their death throes. Thought Karen and said not a word, because words were made of letters and she had just forgotten them all.

The young man looked into her eyes, and his face was a little too close to hers, she could smell some sort of product in his hair; he asked if she'd like to see him again. Karen nodded, she might have thrown up out of excitement, staggered into the stairway, ran up what felt like 678 flights, entered the apartment, where it stank, where the idiots were lying on the couch, and for the first time Karen thought: Fuck you guys.

Then

Followed weeks set to a soundtrack of violins. During which Karen thought about every inch of the young man. His ears, his hands, his skin, his pants, his voice, and then she started over again, and at night she hoped to dream of him. That didn't happen though, such dreams are never delivered on demand. Karen walked through the apartment she had nothing more to do with, it just didn't affect her anymore, this apartment, and she saw the place for the first time, with its torn shower curtain, the stove with burned-on stains, the ochre carpeting where various people had apparently bled out, and the view out over nothing nice at all. It didn't matter. She had. A boyfriend. A boyfriend. It was so unreal that Karen felt as if she'd suddenly lost her mind. As she went about all the daily activities life entailed, teeth brushing, getting dressed, being insulted by her brothers, Karen said Patuk's name to herself, and the adrenaline rush followed, causing her heart to skip a beat, and hormones flooded her body in such concentrations that she would be immobilized. Not even her big brother's announcement that he was converting to Islam so he could marry four women was enough to upset her, that's how absolutely she didn't care about what happened at home. As if seeing it out of the corner of her eye she noticed briefly that her brother seemed to have a problem that expressed itself in his constantly scratching his body parts.

KAREN'S BIG BROTHER

INTELLIGENCE: *it'll do*

TEMPERAMENT: *out of control*

CONSUMER INTERESTS: *porn, weapons, drugs*

HEALTH PROBLEMS: *toenail fungus*

Never thought: Man, my limited intellect is depressing. He was.

Bored from head to toe in his too powerful body.

Karen's big brother had pumped iron like all his friends. They'd done pull-ups at the playground until the loser passed out. They threw rocks and did sit-ups in such numbers that it meant they couldn't move the next day. Now, though, he had nothing he wanted to do with this perfectly defined body. To go to a club in Manchester on the weekend you needed money. Lots of money if you wanted to take girls with you. Where would you get that kind of money? You could deal drugs, but that didn't bring in much because practically every second person was a dealer. Stickups? What were you supposed to steal? The cash from a charity shop? A system was really finished if it couldn't even offer its criminals a future. Karen's brother was pissed off. He got no goddamned respect for his muscles and his physical presence. Everyone around him was a loser just like him. Children who sat bored on the metal fences whistling at

girls. Who exposed their Calvin Klein underwear with their low-slung jeans
and who greeted each other with complicated handshakes.

Karen's brother first became acquainted with adults when his friends got
into a scrap with a Muslim gang. At first they fought each other, then they bled
together, that was the homoerotic code among young men who could no longer even go off to war to get more physically intimate and cleanse themselves
of all things feminine. They got to talking to the Muslims and it turned out
that the Muslims were more powerful and more lucid. They didn't have so
many questions like Karen's brother and his peers. They were simply the coolest gangsters. Karen's brother grew a beard. And finally had a plan for his life.
Which

KAREN

Didn't care about at all. She barely slept, ate next to nothing. She stopped
reading. She didn't know who was at war with whom, which injustice was
taking place where; she wasn't informed about the Nazis' activities; she had
no idea of what the new, hot shit was that had just been invented and would
change everyone's life for the better. (It was neuromorphic chips, which in a
best-case scenario can be implanted and replace parts of the retina. But soon
enough they'd be used for biometric face recognition and so forth.)

Karen wasn't interested.

She was in love. At night Karen stared out the window and imagined
Patuk was standing behind her. During the day she sat in school and imagined he would be waiting for her in the bathroom; she'd glide quickly into the
stall like an eel and he'd do it there. It. The thing she knew nothing about.
How it felt. Despite her prodigious knowledge. Former knowledge, since her
hormones had shrunk her brain. When Karen had a date with Patuk, she sat
on her bed a full hour in advance and hoped not to pass out. Half an hour
beforehand she stood in the entry hall of her building and tried not to lick
the walls out of excitement. She stood in front of the building and tried to
wait with absolute disinterest so it was possible to pull herself away from the
door in the event Patuk didn't show up. Which she assumed would happen.
But. Patuk always showed up. In his car or his uncle's car, who fucking cared,
a car, and then they drove to Hollingworth Lake or to Manchester. If Karen
were a girl who squealed, she would have constantly squealed: "He is so cute.
OMG he is sooo cute." And then she would have fanned herself excitedly with

her hands. Karen did that on the inside. Inside she was flailing about with every appendage and had crossed eyes and was hyperventilating. Yep. She was, however, a little less delirious than at the start of her—attention: love. The drugs Patuk always carried with him—it was as if he'd stuffed the secret interior pockets of his sports jacket, which he never wore, full of all sorts of merchandise—disburdened Karen of her personhood. She happily accepted the proffered chemical helpers. Light drugs. Fun drugs. Pills. Coke. They were Karen's salvation. They let her forget her astonishment at the volume of the sexual claims Patuk made, as well as his lack of complexity. The drugs that liberated her from her inhibitions. Finally she no longer had to be aware of herself stammering—she *was* the stammer. When she was high she could sit on the grass kissing Patuk and welcome his hand as it wandered into her pants.

Karen didn't know what to talk about with her new boyfriend, but it wasn't uncomfortable that words failed her. Besides—Patuk always had things to talk about. Things from television or his analysis of global politics, which always ended in the collapse of the Western world. Or he just kissed her and said that he'd never seen anyone with such white skin before and such beautiful hair and lips. Karen didn't know what to make of that. Either everyone who had laughed at her was wrong or Patuk came from a country with ideals of beauty unknown in the Western world. Maybe in Pakistan they also thought earthworms were elegant. An elegant, speedy creature, the earthworm. Maybe in Patuk's country albinos and earthworms were divine. Definitely.

It was the first summer Karen experienced in its full summery-ness. With the smell, the birds in the morning, and, once in a while, sun that fell across the pavement.

Theoretically Karen knew that her first time would have to occur, and she suspected that it almost always involved moist lawns or the backseats of cars, dark rooms, fear of parents, mosquito bites on your backside, and bad music. But of course Karen thought it would be different for her. Mind-blowing and golden, without the smacking of tongues or the smell of bodily discharges. And when the moment arrived, Karen knew it. They were sitting in a restaurant, and Karen wasn't eating anything because she had to gaze at Patuk. He looked so unbelievably good. Karen felt uneasy in the too see-through blouse he had given her, and the high heels from the charity shop. She drank wine. Tasted like shit, but helped her not listen too closely to what Patuk said. Karen gazed at him and wanted to touch him and lick him from head to toe and eat him or just strike him dead so she could have him next to her forever, that is until he decomposed. Unfortunately once in a while Karen caught what Patuk was saying. "I'm going to be a tailor because I like to be around people." Pause. Something in his ear, hand goes to ear, finds something. Fingers roll something before it is stuck in mouth. Don't look, take another sip, concentrate on the nice feeling, don't want to lose it. There was something stuck on the side of Patuk's mouth, quickly licked the knife clean. "I like cars best when they're fast. Then it's like flying." Of course, thought Karen. Like flying. The only thing tougher than being in love is being in love and finding the object of that affection is a bit stupid. A dire conflict between hormones and brains. Karen didn't have a chance. She was delirious. And another sip. And a bottle later they were lying on a blanket by a lake; it was damp and a little too cold for the see-through blouse; one of the high heels had got stuck in the grass. Then kissing, groping, and underwear pulled aside, and then he was inside her; it was painful and not the slightest bit magnificent, not at all, and Patuk banged his lower body against hers, the noises too loud in the silence. Patuk groaned; Karen was worried she had hurt him. Patuk pulled out of her, wiped his penis on the blanket, didn't look at Karen, who straightened out her things, which were damp and crumpled.

On the way home not a word. They didn't kiss goodbye. Karen went to her room. And began to cry. She was sure something was wrong with her, that this wonderful love would be over because she was weird. Because it must have been just as awful for Patuk as it had been for her. Somehow dirty. "Ah, come on, have another sip." Said Patuk

A week or two later

An that's how it started. With Karen taking another sip. Like most people here, she yearned for something that belonged to her, something nice, warm, because it was drafty everywhere.

And it's just ghastly when a warm place is nowhere to be found. For Karen it had been her brain, it had become useless as a result of all the chemical processes. There was no place where Karen would be safe. Only her boyfriend, who smelled good, had a car, complimented her, and kept the alcohol flowing. Her boyfriend, whom she'd slept with—that's how you said it, even if it was just a quick fuck, which was followed by another quick fuck.

Again Karen had felt nothing to write home about. During this second time, a couple days and a couple meals and kissing on the lawn later, on an old mattress in a cellar, Karen thought: Is he done? And Patuk was done and gave her some pills and said, wait, things will get better in a second. Things got better. The pills were magnificent. Karen's body got warm and seemed to drift away, same with her brain; she grinned strangely, unable to stop grinning, and the room spun. From far away she heard words. "Just this one time. I have a real problem." What pimps always say.

Then an old man was standing in Karen's field of vision. He opened his pants; Karen was already naked. He squatted over her, and Karen felt him push into her. She was still wet with Patuk's sperm, which the man didn't like either. He cursed, then pulled his pants up and left the room. Karen didn't know exactly what had happened. She also didn't see the friend of Patuk's who had filmed the incident on his phone. When Karen's head began to clear, Patuk was lying next to her, stroking her. But it didn't get better. Her boyfriend drove her home later and asked whether it was bad, and told her she had really helped him out and that he loved her even more. What pimps always say. Karen was neither stupid nor a little girl, but she was in love. She lay rigid in her room and barely dared to breathe, because that would mean she was alive and would have to think. Later Karen stood at the kitchen window and looked down. It was a long way. Then, a glimmer of her previous intellect, she thought momentarily of her friends.

Of Peter and Hannah

And of

DON

In whose apartment the roof had collapsed. While they were all sleeping. The electricity was out and her brother cried. Don's mother brandished a flashlight. Everyone had survived. Hurray. When dawn broke they saw the sky above them. It was almost romantic. The sudden radiance illuminated the family members and the remnants of the furniture. Sitting on her dusty bed, Don watched her mother comfort her frightened brother. She felt no connection to these slightly overweight people whose skin, as a result of their lopsided diet, was gray and plastered over an overly soft structure. A slanted table, a chair with torn upholstery. This layout of organic and inorganic material wasn't going to win any prizes.

Until the damage was repaired, the family had to move, it was announced. Unfortunately there were no social housing vacancies in Rochdale at the moment. "Sorry," said the contact person at the agency.

"The children go to school here, this is their environment," screamed Don's mother into the phone.

"Yes, I understood you," said the bureaucrat. "But there aren't any flats in—"

"We live here. This is our home. We have roots here," said Don's mother, weeping a bit.

"Yes, I understood you, but we don't have any space for you," said the woman.

"Because of all the foreigners, who are more important than honest British citizens," screamed Don's mother into her phone, which was kind of funny, this latent racist statement from a person whose parents had emigrated from a so-called foreign country. But, people, you already know how it goes.

"I have no vacancy for you," screamed the woman back, "and if you continue to harass me, I won't help you find a space anywhere else, either."

The only flat that was immediately available was in Manchester. More precisely, Salford, and more precisely—it doesn't matter. It entailed a certain excitement. Moving to the big city. It was almost like relocating to London. The family no longer owned much they needed to pack, the collapse having already completely ruined the ugly furniture from Salvation Army. A few bags and boxes, mattresses and lamps were quickly gathered up, then an old Pakistani turned up with a moving van. The shabby, dirty belongings were loaded up. One last look at the fences, the people in wheelchairs—bye-bye, home.

Don didn't even have time to say goodbye to Hannah and Peter. Karen was busy dealing with her sexuality anyway. Hannah and Peter with their lives. But it wouldn't be for long.

At first glance the surroundings varied negligibly from Rochdale. Beige and mold-colored little buildings, flowerless yards, a few broken-down cars, a few attack dogs, groups of hostile-looking youths. Nearly all light-skinned. Lots of bicycles. Probably stolen. No trees. There wasn't a single goddamn tree. In Rochdale there'd at least been a few stunted, mostly bare-branched, wretched trees around the fenced parking lots and the football pitch. Here stood—nothing except—buildings. Front yards with scrap metal and streets with grim youths.

Anyone who lived in this area stayed here—most of the residents often went no farther than the end of their block because they lacked the money for any means of transport. However did they find their lust for life, these simple people, without well-cultivated distractions from the tedium that came with life, without cinema, theater, concerts, restaurants, dinner at friends' places, weekend trips, visits to the salon, to the zoo, to the café, to the spa, planning holidays, shopping expeditions.

So.

The little family had arrived in front of the new flat. A row house with a broken garden fence and rocks in the front yard. And now Don had to get out of the van, and this new life became reality. Suddenly she missed her friends so deeply that tears welled up in her eyes. Most of all she missed

HANNAH

Who'd gotten a mysterious message from Don that morning.

"Place destroyed. On the way to new place in Manchester-Salford. See you soon."

WTF.

Hannah would figure it out later. First to get up. Or to stay seated a little longer, staring out the window.

In the front yard stood burned-out car chassis, ironically. They were always found in poor areas. Bones thrown into the grave by the wealthy, which the losers could still gnaw on a bit.

Peter lay on his mattress with his eyes open and was perhaps deceased. He'd been living in Hannah's room for a few months already. And had said possibly ten sentences, all of which began: "Where is . . ." It would never stop. Hannah's loneliness would always be the same. It began upon waking up. "Good morning, Hannah!" it said to her. That there was nobody else who wanted to stick by her was obvious every morning.

Nobody who would lift her up. Nobody waiting for her. Out in the world—nobody was looking forward to her presence. It was unbearable. Sometimes Hannah's sense of isolation on the planet was so overwhelming that she could hardly breathe.

Hannah didn't know what she was supposed to do with another human being. Except with her friends. Who were perhaps not friends but rather just a last-resort arrangement of strange children. Outsiders in a world of normal misery. It started out brilliantly, that day on which Don fled to Manchester for some reason or other. The cold of the room uncomfortable on her feet. Various registers of coughing in the building. Outside it was raining, the drops so large they looked like snow.

And Peter, the idiot. Lying there growing. He grew ten centimeters every day it seemed. He did nothing but eat, sleep, and grow. A bit like a cancerous tumor. Hannah looked at the cancer in the corner of the room, which looked like every room in every squatted building everywhere on earth. A clothing stand, a pile of clothing on the floor, broken shades, broken floorboards, a chair, a bed on bricks. And, of course, cold. And, of course, a bit dirty in case an adult were to enter. None did. Children don't notice the dirtiness thanks to a dysfunction of the iris. "Are you listening, Peter?" said Hannah. "Don moved."

PETER

Opened his eyes and nodded.

"Thanks for the terrific conversation." He heard Hannah say as she ran out of the room. Peter didn't know how he was supposed to act now. He'd made progress in mimicking so-called normality. He pushed himself to look people in the eye, they had a thing about that. He even let himself go so far as to allow minor physical contact. He did everything to integrate this "having friends" thing into his life. He learned to listen and give answers. He functioned within the bounds of others' expectations and that way made a huge contribution to his resocialization. But at the moment he was overwhelmed. Don was gone. And Hannah upset. Peter had learned how to look when she was upset. Tight mouth, strangely baffled facial expression.

Peter lay there. His bodily functions were decelerated, his metabolism barely registering. He waited. Until there was a reason to move. Up to now that had only been when Hannah ordered him to leave the room to go hang around with the others. Or to be the lookout when the others went shoplifting. Food, potatoes, vegetables, that sort of thing.

Peter no longer went to school. For a long time now. He did better studying on the internet. Thanks to stolen electricity. Thanks to logging on to strangers' Wi-Fi. He learned interesting things. About the Tempora project, about people who wanted to put their brains on computer chips to live forever online. He traveled the world with Google and strolled on beaches; he learned to make small talk in Portuguese and French.

From the other rooms in the squatted building came noises. Children arguing and laughing, they clattered pots and pans. They lived. They were young and had never known the collective structures that used to give people a strangely uplifting feeling. They were amazed at how nice it could be to live in a pack.

There were no mail carriers. Mail was delivered by a private company that used harried slaves. There were no junctures to connect people with a sense of shared existence anymore. No bureaucrats, no shop assistants living next door. It was all migrant workers, temporary workers, wage slaves, or fucking machines. When people no longer know anyone around them, the lonely become increasingly venomous. Anonymity allows all civility to disappear. They just didn't exist anymore, moral authority, feigned cordiality, it was kill or be killed. Everyone was the enemy, anyone who walked too slowly on the street or blocked the checkout at the supermarket, or the empty seat, any fucker who was just fucking there diminished others' chances of survival. It was obvious the immigrants were at fault, the Muslims who wanted to fuck over and subjugate Europe. They were the least trusted. New immigrants came to the city daily. Hurray, new people. They moved into flats in social housing units, received social benefits, and if it had taken four hours to see a doctor at the hospital before, now you had to reckon on an eight-hour wait. Food handouts from churches and generous private do-gooders were inundated by foreigners. From countries where the language sounded abrasive; who could hold it against them that they pushed their way through the exhausted zombies of their new homeland who'd already been dead for two generations? The government, which at the moment consisted of loutish populist Nazis, fanned the flames of these unpleasant tendencies. A populace where everyone hated everyone else was a preoccupied populace. It was old hat.

It was the time before the perceived downfall.

Or at least—it seemed that way to the old people. To old people, every change seems to be the end of the world. That they knew. The years of people unbound. Of people before—Before something.

Who gives a shit.

Thought

DON

After a few weeks in Manchester-Salford. Far away, beyond the invisible border that divided this area from the world, another crisis was taking place once again. Self-learning algorithms had allowed themselves a bit of fun and had added extra zeros to the endless zeros of a few people's accounts.

EX 2279

```
> + + + + + + + + +
[> + + + + + + + + + + > + + + + + + + + + + + + + + > + + +
+ + + + + + + + > + + + + + + + + + + +
+ + + + + + + + + + + + + + < < < < < <-]
> + + >—-> > > + >
< < < < < <
> . > . > . > . > .
```

DON

's intellect was like a luminous sword, but she had never understood these zero numbers. Was there such a thing as hundreds of billions? Was it sitting around in some cellar? In any event: crisis. Banks went under, brokers jumped out the windows of office towers, lines at the bank machines, virtual currencies boomed, the whole fucking thing, all over the world again, it goes without saying. Portugal and a few other countries that Don would never visit went bankrupt. Don thought: So what? We're bankrupt, too. That's the advantage of being poor.

Don had other worries. She was in a new school and had to reestablish with a hoodie and sullen demeanor her position as a child everyone should be scared of. In their circles there was a clear hierarchy: thanks to the equitable poverty they all shared, there were only those who were afraid and the rest. Amazingly, Don didn't need to maximize her tools in the new school. There were no knife fights, no battered children, and barely any drug dealers. The school director believed in wonder and had hired good teachers, she made sure there was acceptable food for lunch, and after school there were workshops, courses, and in the evening a youth club which even hosted a weekly event for homosexuals. Most of the children preferred to be at school rather than at home; they didn't hang around bored on the streets or engage in minor break-ins just for something to do. The director would later be let go for cost-cutting reasons.

Don's idiotic brother stopped pissing his bed, their insane mother looked for a job and found nothing; she had pills and booze. Don never knew what condition she would find her mother in when she got home—lying on the floor blocking the door from the inside, or just cowering in the kitchen staring at an array of pills on the table.

After a few weeks in Manchester-Salford Don had nearly forgotten that she once lived somewhere else. She was sitting in front of the building and waiting for a miracle when a convoy of SUVs drove into the neighborhood. It was a film crew.

An hour later a nervous, severely underweight woman who, it seemed, was smoking three cigarettes simultaneously, stood at Don's door, and it was truly strange, because other than the absolutely lowest rungs of the underclass, nobody smoked anymore. Being seen with a cigarette was like appearing in public in puke-smeared underwear. An affectation of her peculiar job. The woman was a location scout and wanted to take pictures of Don's apartment because she was looking for authentic, original scenery. There was to be a social drama shot. England was known for its gripping social dramas. In case that hasn't been said yet. Television viewers whispered excitedly: "Wow, these social dramas."

They were always set in places like this. Poor flats, poor buildings, blah blah blah. Sometimes with a yard, sometimes with clotheslines, sometimes with Staffordshire terriers, American pit bulls. You could train the animals very effectively for dogfighting, you just had to smear a rope with meat, let the dog bite it, pull up on it, and then beat it with an iron rod. The four-legged friends wouldn't let go. Amazing!

There were some social dramas that showed the owners of such dogs— chronically unemployed, totally bored, pathetic, angry men. Some of them had had their faces chewed off by this or that dog during an alcohol-induced stupor. Most of the dramas, though, were about honest women who had their honest children taken away. Honest workers who had lost their honest jobs and then landed in a room where a bare lightbulb always hung from the ceiling, swinging from side to side.

It was out of the question, said the chain-smoking woman, and left the building where Don's family now lived and which wasn't shabby enough for the social drama even though it could have effortlessly won any Olympics competition for shabbiness. The place consisted of a kitchen which at the time the family moved in was full of moldy food, empty beer cans, and insects. A broken cabinet, a stove that used gas cylinders. A narrow hallway led to the master bedroom, with grates over the window. The ceiling of the children's room, upstairs, had water stains. In this room the previous tenants had lived out their propensity to hoard bizarre items like rags, pizza boxes, and streamers. There was one more room, for which you had to pay the so-called bed tax. It was one room too many for the number of family members, and the state assumed that the residents could rent it out. Which is why Don's mother had to sacrifice twenty of her weekly seventy pounds. Most residents in social housing units solved the problem by growing marijuana in the empty room. Every few days the police came through the area and conducted raids to remove the hemp operations, and some overburdened parent landed in jail and the children in a facility. So much for drug prevention.

The support Don's family received was enough to eat potatoes three times a day. To be able to eat potatoes three times a day Don's mother had to go the agency, wait for hours, but—there was always something that made disbursement of the payment impossible; for instance, you'd missed some course because somebody had been ill, or you had no bank account where money could be wired. Ten million people in the country had no bank account because the banks wouldn't accept them as customers. But the banks had problems, too, such as the aforementioned crisis. Don wouldn't have wanted herself as a customer, either.

"Okay, what else have we got?" the location scout asked her crew. There was a practice pitch in the area that had been financed by Manchester United. The young millionaires trained there, watched by lice-covered blond children. Who dreamed in turn of becoming football players, which of course wouldn't happen. For them, life had other surprises in store. Like a movie shoot, for instance. That was the hot thing in the neighborhood for the following few weeks. "Great, just like that," called the director, an old man, whenever he encountered a teenage mother in a bathrobe in front of her place. Soon all the girls in the area changed and stood by their doors with their siblings to get into the movie. The men walked around in undershirts with beers; people had quickly figured out how to make the film crew happy and perhaps snag some free beer.

The children dressed themselves extra wretchedly, they hustled around the neighborhood in dirty clothes, their eyes darkened with makeup, and coughed when they found themselves near the director. The director would buy them a Coke—and talk about the injustice done to the Palestinians by the Israelis. The children didn't care, but they took the cola and nodded at the old man who as thanks for their head nods let them walk through the background of a film scene. Not all of them. Don wasn't allowed. She would have undermined the concept with her pigmentation. It was about the left-behind white working class, who in their colorlessness came across as so pitiable. People whose skin tone looked as if they just came back from holiday tended to be the stars of social dramas about drug dealers.

The white children passed through the picture while in the foreground young child actors from the neighborhood played. Nobody here would be so idiotic as to run around in old track suits. Others wore underwear and slurred their speech. Presumably to properly depict the misery and show that the people here were honest and didn't even have clothes. In some families' apartments, the ones without marijuana growing in the spare room, they shot inside the place, for which they pulled down wallpaper to give an authentic image.

When the film crews left again, boys threw rocks at their cars as they drove off. They felt dirty without being able to say why. Then things in the neighborhood went back to the normal routine.

Don

No longer thought

After a few weeks

Of her friends in Rochdale every day. The WhatsApp messages became ever less frequent, since what had connected them were the trivial details, chitchat, shared places, shared enemies. Now without a daily life for them to share, there wasn't much left to say.

Don's life was here now. With new children who weren't friends, would never be, because among other things Don had a bad conscience about missing her group from Rochdale so little. The boys here were angry—they raced around the treeless streets on stolen bicycles and were so stupid that time after time they passed within the radius of a surveillance camera, and—yet another boy with a criminal charge. The girls watched in order to get a little affection. The meaning of which they didn't understand. And which the boys understood to mean sex. There were lots of girls who had babies at thirteen that they carried around like dolls.

Adults—the ones who weren't too depressed or strung out, it must be restrictively added—were all right. Nearly everyone in the neighborhood had been born the children of former workers. In their genetic code still floated homeopathically dosed memories of "the union," of "solidarity," of the power to be able to bring the entire country to a halt with a strike. The owner of a pub in the neighborhood made sure children could warm up if for whatever reason they couldn't go home. Don was content.

A strange feeling.

For Don, Manchester-Salford was that pub where children could hang around, the girls watching Beyoncé and grime videos on their phones, the boys who left their stolen bicycles and mopeds in a pile in front of the pub.

It was the place where her brother started committing robberies in order to be accepted by the white boys, it was the place where she learned to hate the police. And to fear cell phones, which were wondrously connected to the police. Who always showed up when the children had plans to meet, and conducted degrading inspections, which included the pulling down of pants.

Manchester-Salford was the last moment before the premature coming-of-age, when Don's world still represented an adventure playground and companionship.

At some point, after what felt like years and two centimeters of growth—only two? Yes, only two—a letter arrived from the Rochdale social welfare office. Their building—or what passed for one—was once again suitable for occupancy. The living quarters in Manchester-Salford had to be cleared out because new buildings were supposed to be built there for the disappearing middle class.

In order to enhance the value of the neighborhood, moderately appointed single-family homes would be built throughout the social housing estates and sold at so-called prevailing market prices. This made a great impression on the statistics, which would indicate that the residents were doing progressively better. Which allowed the city to look good, which for some reason or other was good, and pushed the people who truly had no money to move away. To an even more dismal area, farther north.

Don called the movers. This time the nephew of the Pakistani citizen, who had in the meantime become a British citizen, came, a greasy young guy with gold chains. Probably smart to have invested in gold. Thought Don randomly. She had packed, and now her fat brother and spaced-out mother loaded. They got into the moving van and Don would surely have cried if she were the type for it, but instead she just averted her eyes and stared at the brown neck of the Pakistani.

His name was

PATUK

DISABILITY: *left-handed*
HOBBIES: *betting, gold chains, nice trousers*
INTELLIGENCE: *average*
POTENTIAL FOR AGGRESSION: *high*
CREDITWORTHINESS: *not available*
USABILITY: *unclear*
ETHNICITY: *Asian*
TERRORIST DANGER LEVEL: *of course*

And he had landed in Rochdale as a youth. The moment to make a grand restart in England was a bit ineptly chosen. The big attacks in London hadn't yet been totally forgotten. Same with the one on the World Trade Center. And Paris. And so on. The imaginary memorials were still hung with notes, prayers, and teddy bears, all sorts of pop stars had sung stirring songs in front of the bears and notes and hearts, war against the axis of evil had been declared, and the first conspiracy theories about the gradual takeover of the West by Islam were circulating. The moderate distrust of Muslims by the non-Muslim Western world hadn't diminished. To put it mildly.

9/II, as the thing would later be called, was probably one of the triggers of it all. The retreating into populist sentiment on all sides, the mass surveillance, the new dictatorships, the conspicuous transformation of the Western world. Later there were adherents to the conspiracy theory that the first attacks and the refugee crisis had been engineered. Planned by a few American industrialists who wanted to profit from chaos in Europe and the probable wars. Or the Vatican, which wanted to prove its theory of the apocalypse. Or China, which wanted to tip the West into chaos, in order to . . . doesn't matter.

Anyway. The EU broke apart, people ran around like chickens. Of course there was no plan behind the fleeing refugees. It would have been great if there had been a plan. But there were as many ideas and interests as people on the planet, and none of them were really wise. It's gotten too crowded on earth. It made people nervous and caused scientists to make foolhardy prognoses. They all ended in catastrophe, having to do with a halving of the world population, with war, euthanasia.

The place Patuk's family had sought out, because of an already large community from the old homeland and a few distant relatives there, had just been voted the most depressing city in England for the first time. Abandoned factories, abandoned lives, but—Patuk didn't notice it as they drove down the faded streets on the bus that had brought them from London. A few ill-tempered locals stood on the street and looked at Patuk's family without any particular indication of welcome. What was he supposed to do with these unattractive people, was Patuk's first thought. Then first contact with the paved street. With no potholes. The rolling suitcases glided over it like weasels, inside the things that you take with you when you leave your homeland. Photo albums, table mats . . .

So this is England. A bit dark, the houses, but not leaning the way buildings did at home. It was cold. But the family had gotten used to that in transit, which, compared to the conditions refugees would face in coming years, had been relatively drafty, sure, but not dangerous. Family consolidation, forged documents, the whole routine. The closer they got to the home of their relatives, the more people they encountered on the street from their old home. Everything would be fine. The family had hopes.

How sweet.

Patuk was for the most part barely present during the initial period in their new home. Like most people he was a creature of habit, and when everything familiar disappeared, people can fall into a sense of paralyzing helplessness. Patuk saw himself from afar as he walked and talked and breathed. The large family with whom they were staying, all the children, the crowded rooms, sleeping in one bed with his parents. Strange shit. Touching his father's leg while asleep. Sharing the rest of the house with strangers, no place to sit undisturbed and think about the world, about girls—profoundly awkward. Patuk was young, his hormones made him crazy, though he didn't know that, he just thought he was going nuts. He thought about death, and then about girls again. About god, and his life, and above all about the people he was supposed to live with now, these pale, scowling people, until he died. The town, which you could walk entirely across in half an hour, was unusually clean compared to the place he'd spent the first part of his youth and about which he had never thought: Man, it is filthy here. Back home he had thought his family well-off. After all, his father was an engineer with a firm that broke down old ships. Now his former home suddenly seemed unbelievably shabby. The looks from the white people probably had something to do with the shabbiness that oozed out of all his pores and those of his relatives. The country's prime minister made it easy for immigrants to come. He wanted to set an example for an aging population, multiculturalism, openness, who the hell knows what he was thinking, but whatever it was, the prime minister hadn't thought very carefully about what exactly he wanted to enlist all this fresh immigrant blood to do. It would be sorted out and then self-regulate, the market regulated everything after all, it would all work out. As in all European countries, the people in England weren't reproducing satisfactorily because of feminism. With new, reproduction-friendly people, one hoped to ensure the funding of old age pension payments. That was before they eliminated old age pensions.

For Patuk's family, the initial situation was optimal. Free doctors, and you got a passport after three years. The fact that contact with the locals was dysfunctional—yes, you could talk of a hostile ignorance with which they confronted the new arrivals—allowed a defiance to form in Patuk. A pride in the lost homeland. A sense of superiority based on his intact family, his intact beliefs, his intact complexion. He would just sweep these white, tired people aside. Patuk put together a gang of sweepers. He wasn't afraid of the drunks who sat on their chain-link fences and yelled insults at him. He'd fuck them all. He was young. He was strong. And he was many.

Months later

At times when Patuk wasn't planning something with his buddies, who all came from a family context similar to his own, he walked around and tried to figure out the rules in this new world. Complicated. The girls had on short skirts. In this weather. With so many legs he didn't know where to hide his erection. The girls were easy to get. Their brothers and fathers were busy drinking, the mothers worked. Patuk had tried it once. Alcohol. It had proved a failure. There'd been vomiting. After his strolls past high-rise apartments out of which strange ill-tempered people stared, past boarded-up houses and factories where imaginary rats that had died of boredom lay in piles, he tried to understand what it was all about for the people here. Nobody was really happy. There were not many families, no open doors where you could see people eating in their kitchens. Instead the residents scurried around the wet streets, the fenced-off yards in their fenced-off housing blocks. Patuk tried to analyze this scurrying. It had to do with a downcast look, hurried movements, and the desire for unconsciousness and death. None of them wanted to be there. And couldn't even dream up an idea of where they'd rather be.

Patuk sat on swings in playgrounds that were too sad even for the rotten, pale children here; he inhaled deeply and tried to be optimistic. He rummaged charity shops, made bets on horse and dog races at the town's betting shops, and was harassed by the white residents. There was a somewhat heated atmosphere. The residents of the countries partitioned by drunken Englishmen and Frenchmen in the Near and Middle or whatever else East had through crazy leaders, parentheses male, discovered their hate for the Western world, which had to do with inferiority, aggrieved love, and waning self-confidence.

Europe had discovered the hate. America had discovered the hate. In particular for itself. For its make-believe version of democracy. For the transformation of the world into one where you could barely get ahead without a considerable fortune. For the others, those who laid claim to a share of what little anyone else was entitled to. For the downtrodden they ignored. For globalization, which hadn't proved its worth, but most of all for life, which turned out not to be so special.

Things went well for Patuk. His father had found a job in his cousin's workshop. They could rent a house. A little house on an access road to the motorway—and finally Patuk's mother could put out some things and mess around with the feather duster, and Patuk had more time for his new friends.

There were an astonishing number of young Pakistani men in this little town. They had shared interests, knew what a good family was, and were interested in girls. Not the girls they met in family circles or through acquaintances, since they were taboo, but the pretty, blonde, new-homeland girls who were very exotic and uninhibited. So to speak. Something had to be possible there.

Even later

Patuk had made money delivering various packets of drugs, and he had bought himself his first-ever Gucci shirt at Selfridges in Manchester. His lucky shirt. Because right afterwards he got a job with a relative. He would become a tailor. It wasn't necessarily what he had imagined for himself. What kind of young man, other than a weirdo, passionately wanted to sew clothes? But it was better than going to school forever, and it was possible with a tailoring business to be self-employed. That's what Patuk pictured. Something with autonomy, a car, and a house. And perhaps not here. London. Why not. No idea what London looked like, but since the whole world talked about how great London was, there must be something to it. Patuk had, like most of his friends, no clue about the kind of country he lived in, about the unwritten rules and the questionable traditions. He didn't know what colonies besides India had been exploited by the crown, he didn't know that the government of the country had for all eternity been made up of graduates of just two universities, he didn't understand oatmeal or twinsets. Winter, rain, hunting, all that crap, the quiet background music that in the past accompanied the people of any country from birth on and socialized them, had as a result of globalization and concomitant immigration become unimportant. For more and more people it was just about somehow scraping by. Surviving. The concept of homeland had been gutted. It was, if at all, artificially instilled, overstretched by empty statements that nobody inhaled anymore. Patuk was indifferent to all of that. He was young, he had a future, and he had met a girl.

Right, so

DON

Stared out the window and suspected that her life would now pick back up right where it had stopped in Rochdale. The stupid house, the stupid brother and—no idea. No idea. No idea. Her head hurt. When she thought about seeing Hannah, Karen, and Peter again, her head hurt even more. My god, this country. Even tied up and dangling from ropes Don could identify what

distinguished an English landscape from a non-English—that is, inferior—
landscape. Everything here seemed to have been washed too many times at
high temperature. Whites with colors. Where it was always just before or after
rain. Before or after a natural disaster that had irradiated everyone. The animals, too. Not a landscape that touched people in such a way as to make them
think: a little house here and a few sheep, I wouldn't need anything else to
be happy. Then, after half an hour, when the family was standing with their
boxes in front of the house in Rochdale and Don's mother tried to unlock
the door, it was suddenly thrown open from within. A man (undershirt, un-
shaven, belly—to flesh out the scene) shoved Don's mother away, whereupon
Don's mother kicked him in the shin. And so on. The fight, in which several
neighbors lustily took part—nothing much happened around here—ended
with the appearance of the police, who then figured out that the social services
office had apparently made a mistake. Until it could be cleared up the family
would be put up in a homeless shelter.

The homeless shelter

Represented the lowest point of self-inflicted failure even in Rochdale.
There weren't people who slept on the streets in Rochdale. Not yet. But. The
homeless shelter was overflowing. Every day new people arrived from bigger
cities. From all over, wherever elegant owner-occupied flats could be built in
place of social housing units, the hardship cases were resettled in unattractive
outlying districts. So they could die off there without any opportunities for
anything.

The little family arrived at the shelter, which looked just as fucked up as
all the buildings in the city, door made of steel and equipped with a camera
that recorded everything that happened in front of it. The alcohol and drug-
addled dregs who jiggled the door in winter because they wanted to sleep in a
dry place. Crazy idea.

In the entry were fluorescent lights, a carpeted floor, a water dispenser.
A sweet scent of disinfectant fought with the effluvium of poverty. Bad food,
secret smoking, and alcohol made milder contributions to the bouquet. More
difficult was the biting, sweet-sour smell of filthy people. Dirt under the nails,
greasy matted hair, folds of skin, genitals. Some of the residents stood in front
of their rooms. If they didn't live here as families, they shared rooms with six
beds in them. You looked forward to some quality time by yourself.

Wary people, open sores, many with tics, most of them, though, rendered calm with pills courageously distributed here. The pills made sure nobody was too clear on his or her situation, nobody felt hungry. These wonderful medications assured that most of the indigent didn't jump out of windows or grab for pitchforks and shout: "What are you doing with our tiny, short, worthless lives? Is there really no place for us anywhere?" Most of all, the pills: dulled everything. As if half asleep the undead shuffled through the halls in greasy bathrobes and smelly sweatpants. Speaking of which—*The Walking Dead* had just been named the most successful TV series of all time.

Don briefly panicked. What if she never got out of here? If this was it? Here, with her family in a single room. Her brother already installed on his mattress, busy playing a first-person shooter game, mouth open, drooling, the idiot. Mother swaying on her bed.

It was Sunday. Don lay on a daybed and listened to the sound of her family breathing. Nobody said a word. Each on a personal island of horror. Normal people, members of the disappearing middle class, those employed in insurance and travel companies, always thought this could never happen to me when they studiously looked away from those on the side of the road. Maybe so. Maybe not. Every day thousands of new entrants arrived at shelters, at emergency overnight accommodations, on ventilation grates above underground stations.

Don tried not to think. What was left was the so-called emotional life. Everything inside her yearned for normal young people things. For the chance to fall in love, kiss, have sex, for loud music and fast motorcycles. Don wanted to be anywhere where there were no homeless shelters, no Rochdale, and no family. The expectations of what was waiting for her outside positively pained her. An outsider from, say, Ukraine or Malawi or Bangladesh, from, how to put it, precarious conditions, could chuckle bemusedly at Don's self-pity. That person could say: "Please understand that we are considered to have no value. Our lives are only significant if we distinguish ourselves in some way. With wealth preferably, or a mind for startups. Some extraordinary gift, like piano playing or ball playing, some shit that somebody else can make a fortune off. If you don't contribute to the strengthening of the economy or divert people from their existence with your singing talent, it's a bit presumptuous to ask for a prize for the fact that your parents managed to fuck. You had dreams of something because you live in a halfway civilized country, meaning there is only a possibility that you'll be raped or shot, plus you can go vote. Hey, how cool is that? Anything above and beyond that is, however, not intended for you. This is it. A bunk bed in a putrid homeless shelter where the screams of other people, who understand that they've been abandoned here to die, keep you from sleeping. Eat it up."

Someone would say, someone observing Don from above.

But

There was nobody. There wasn't even a god for fuck's sake.

After a few days

Don felt better. She'd gotten used to it. Humans. If it's necessary they'll grow fins. And then

Something strange happened. One of those things that could only happen in a small town

Because all of a sudden

HANNAH AND PETER

Arrived at the homeless shelter. Hannah's squatted house was being razed, and a grim building thrown up for somebody. Whatever—

HANNAH

Had lost a bit of momentum of late. Her career had stagnated somewhat, her YouTube channel had been a bust, every day thousands of unimaginative young people started their own channels and provided the world with product recommendations, cat films, comedy clips, and tips for makeup and removal, sports, and burial. It was yet again nothing that distinguished her from others. She had no particular gift. There must be someplace in the world for her talents, if only she knew where that was. Hannah wanted so badly to pursue something with fire. But nothing set her aflame. She tried to write but stopped again for lack of excitement. She had been able to convince the boss at the bar in Manchester where she had until recently worked to let her do a dance performance. Okay. So, a dance performance. Hannah had no idea. She asked a percussionist if he would accompany her. And then developed an idea to perform a life from birth to death. She rolled around on the floor halfheartedly, beat on her chest, balled herself up. And realized that it was complete rubbish. Hannah quit the job in Manchester, questions about her age had come up anyway. Underage was not a favored age on the job market just then. She didn't look it, but she was still a damned child who should have been going to school and should have had foster parents or been in a juvenile facility. Luckily the country's bureaucracy was being dismantled. Mass redundancies, digitalization, and so forth. And Hannah didn't exist in the system. She didn't have a bank account, no credit cards, no address of record. She was granted a spot in the homeless shelter, which would normally require a voucher, only because the building was being razed. She had simply gone into hiding among the throng of youth. Contact with any sort of officialdom would have meant the end of invisibility. Subject to official grasp, security forces, procedures. Hannah didn't trust the state. Any good experiences she'd had with the state were negligible. There were doctors. There weren't people lying along the roadside starving, but there definitely were people lying along the roadside. They lay around like rubbish, these people, but any efforts to dispose of the rubbish in shelters fell apart. Let them be, these people, so as to scare others. The way mafiosos hung their enemies from bridges in order to spread fear, the government left these people to lie around. Off you go, run, get yourself together, man, otherwise you're next. Don't complain, work, don't create any costs, shut your mouth. Nobody starved yet. Maybe they got sick from malnutrition, maybe they got sick from stress, maybe they died at fifty, looking eighty, maybe they caught pneumonia that proved deadly. Maybe they died of an infection, maybe they hung themselves with less than a pound in their pocket because it was no kind of life. But no, nobody starved. "You see, nobody's starving here, the world is improving, and outside the water is rising." A reality TV star had become president in America. The Ku Klux Klan had an influx unlike anything since the 1960s, people gathered in Facebook groups and set fire to refugee shelters, and in Paris, tent encampments where thousands of homeless people and migrants lived—well, lived in a way—were cleared. Every second day there was a terrorist attack somewhere in Europe. Doesn't matter.

Because

PETER

Had hugged Don. Well. Somehow put his arms around her and then quickly removed them again. The new surroundings became somewhat more bearable once the familiar people were together again. Once Don was suddenly back. He felt safer in this shelter that seemed to him like a cheap horror film where the dead tramped around grabbing at the living with their bony hands.

Peter didn't want to be apart from Don and Hannah for the time being.

When he was on his own in the building he was touched, spat on. He didn't belong here. Like always. Along with the unease of the new surroundings, Peter missed above all having his own computer. He didn't want to use Hannah's device so often, because she looked at him so expectantly of late. What was she expecting? What did people expect in general?

Over there, the

OLD WOMAN

SEXUALITY: *unimportant*
USABILITY: *not available*
CONSUMER BEHAVIOR: *not available*
VISUAL ACUITY: *same*
HEALTH PROFILE: *sold one kidney, the second damaged*

From boozing. Naturally, it was obvious. That she was sick. Until recently

She'd been a punk and straight edge. Now she was broken down. And old. But she didn't know it, just as no person knows he or she is old. To others, because everyone stays a certain age inside. For most people it is mid-thirties. And only on bad days do they see the devastation left behind by the slowly deteriorating cells. But then people forget these horrible moments in the mirror, and they are lost within again, in their mid-thirties. But now the old woman was too broken down for such self-deception. Legs full of fluid, eyes cloudy, ears deaf. And always the coughs and bone pain, that's the worst, when all your bones hurt, when you want to rip them all out. The old woman was fifty or eighty and just didn't care anymore. She no longer hoped for a miracle, she was bored and sick of everything, and she just wanted to go to sleep, because she saw her future as nothing more than a hospital stay where various machines would barely keep her alive so they could make their contribution to medical advancement. Medically assisted suicide was illegal. It was more agreeable to the decision makers to let death result from illness and age in all its excruciating lack of speed. Hewing to a mildly sadistic proclivity. From the moment she awoke she clenched her jaw in rage, as there were no teeth left. A couple of idiots sat around parliament and decided how long she had to lie around a homeless shelter. They signed papers with Montblanc pens and then went off to brunch. And she lay here unable to pursue medically assisted suicide. Like in civilized countries, where friendly social democrats turned up with a bit of poison, observed with blubbering sympathy, and put out your light. The humiliation of being dependent dragged out to the last meter. At which point some fucking assholes forced an old woman to go up to a rooftop in her condition and jump and possibly hurt a few other people upon impact. The old woman had imagined all the possible ways to check out. None was tolerable. They all involved shitting your pants, a lot of effort, pain, or frightening other people. All because a few well-off fuckers had decided to make it so. The old woman would stop eating and drinking, which, after four days, ended in admission to a clinic where she would be force-fed so that she could be returned to her six-bed room at the homeless shelter where she would once again refuse to eat. And her rage would become hate and disgust related to her own humiliation. She left this earth with these feelings, and if you wanted to give any credence to religious nuts, these feelings would accompany her for all eternity in hell, where only people like her ended up.

The atmosphere at the shelter is uncomfortable.

There's no other word

PETER

Can think of. It was like being in a haunted house, where the unhappy souls of the dead staggered around. Except that here they were still alive. Barely.

Nobody knew what anyone else wanted, understood anyone else's feelings. They were unable to comfort each other. They were inconsolable, they were lonely. The poor people. Peter at least understood that he couldn't make connections to anybody here. The others believed they could connect with their small talk, their endless stream of meaningless words. Or show something of themselves, something brilliant, with all the lies they told. Every word that flowed through the filter of, and was monitored by, an adult mind in order to meet the expectations of others was a lie.

At the shelter Peter began to radicalize. He had always thought the freaks were his friends. The sick, addicts, the disappointed, he'd always believed them to be his friends, that they accepted him and liked him, just as he liked them, those with prison tattoos, with Rasta braids, the sad sacks, the lonely. But now once again he was just the stranger. The outsider who was stared at. People loved to look down on everything that seemed inferior. Here, too. There was no redemption. No peace. No quiet. The fluorescent lights crackled in the long hallways with gray flooring, where people stood in front of the yellow doors and fell silent when Peter approached. When Peter didn't understand something he began to hit his head against the wall. When he hit his head against the wall, he thought of his mother, who had been the only person able to make him stop. Then he hit his head against the wall even harder.

And

DON

Sat next to Peter. She didn't touch him, just sat there until he calmed down. The poor nutter. Who always fell asleep after these fits. And even then didn't look any more relaxed. Or happier. None of them knew this feeling, though they were all so desperate for it that they bought drugs to try to attain it. Didn't help. They just got fucked up. Tired. Passed out and got skinny legs. The people. I'd love to know what it's like to be happy, thought Don, lying in her bunk at night. Listening to her brother's grunts and her mother's heavy breathing. Outside, the clank of a bottle somebody was kicking along. Don suddenly realized that her relationship with her family would never change for the better.

Mother, she thought, Mother, these are our final days. Our inner farewell tour. One could talk about feelings. My feeling is that I'm going to take off. See you one last time, smell you, listen to your yammering, to make it easier to go. If I stay with you I'll become what surrounds me. All these children and youths pulled into the abyss by their parents. Flung to the ground from life or—shall we say—from a vegetative state, these parents. And there they lay. Drunk, depressed, ill, spent, mumbling unhappily, yammering, and the children place a pillow beneath their parents' head and leave with the feeling that the world owes them something because they have such pathetic parents, who are everything to them. Are. Their world. Which is collapsing. There is nothing more dangerous on earth than children without a foothold. And I don't want to end up there. I don't want to let my life be influenced by someone who despises me. Even if that word is a bit of an overstatement. Even if I know it's really just yourself that you don't like. Mother. Because you blame yourself for your misery. Because you think women bring unhappiness upon themselves. And even if I realize that the world, this wonderful world, where ever more people come into money, and yeah, yeah, infant mortality rates and all that, that this world has made losers of our parents. Because they didn't inherit anything. Because they were born into the wrong families. Because they just passed on what was inside them. Thought Don. She would like to have said these words, but didn't know what good it would do. Don had collected enough information about her situation to know that it couldn't be much worse. She had to get out of here. The bottle clanking in the empty street, the sounds of the small, damp city—just not cool. These are small-town sounds. The squeaking of pram wheels and sparrows. Aside from the sparrows no birds even strayed into this town.

On the way to school,

Which Don for reasons that are not clear is the only one from the group still attending, she hears a couple of cars and Pakistanis fighting with each other. She hears the sparrows and thinks for a moment what a real city must sound like, Chinese advertisements, cars honking in traffic, all sorts of languages, helicopters, sirens, and she becomes dizzy with the desire for excitement and grandeur.

People push their way out of a bus that stops in front of the shopping arcade and set off in search of either the dinosaur museum or squalor. They've read about the criminality in Rochdale, minors have been forced into prostitution by foreigners. Now they stand here in the pedestrian zone with the unsure look people get in unfamiliar surroundings. Removed from their environment, they suddenly feel it. They feel how vulnerable they are. It's quickly destroyed, that sense of one's own importance, in a knife attack or a spray of puke far from home. They realize they aren't in a foreign land, the people, and now they spot Don and put on forced smiles. There's a minority, you have to conjure up an open expression on your face.

The art enthusiasts, the lefties, the well-meaning people who still had occupations, could no longer keep themselves together when they encountered a
Black person or other sort of minority; they tripped over themselves, shat their
pants for fear of using the wrong terminology. What did you call Inuit and
Roma and Sinti these days, and which form is correct for someone apparently
transitioning genders, and are you still allowed to say missus? Refugee was still
acceptable. The collective joy in chattering as well as humor had given way to a
great uptightness, and people were once again busy regulating themselves and
making their lives hell. On the streets and online. From which Monty Python
had disappeared. In order to make room for a few billion hate posts, as if
something had been suppressed for years with all the supposedly democratic
governments and the privileges granted to even the most absurd minorities.
Unisex bathrooms and gender studies—and then

Finally the long-pent-up exploded, the suppressed burst out of individuals
who as a result finally labeled themselves with malice, contempt, and hatred.
These sentiments crawled out of the net and into the streets, became knife
attacks, brawls, acid attacks on women. The slaughter of dogs. Imported dogs.
All dogs except English dogs. Rochdale became unpleasant, too. Ever more
people armed themselves, there were fights daily. Gays didn't dare go out on the
street after dark, same for women. But this was only on the edges, on the outskirts of the world, which was lurching into a new phase of repulsiveness. Sure,
everyone was doing better. In Ethiopia babies were no longer eaten by locusts,
but the world had very few places left to dream about anymore. Places where
you could enjoy watching the sun set over the sea and feel an all-encompassing
love, they barely existed anymore. In this strange era. When everyone seemed
to have been left to sink or swim, everyone competed against everyone else to
try to somehow survive.

When

Don

Went home after school, it was

Stormy again. These strange weather events alternated so quickly. Wind
and rain, flooding and frost. People held paving stone–sized hailstones in their
hands and took selfies in canoes as they paddled on rivers that were actually
streets, they made V for victory signs and laughed.

Although—

There were

Days when the children couldn't even go out on the street, couldn't go out on the roof, and squatted haplessly in the entryway of the shelter. Lost in their own memories. Lost in hate for those memories and the people in them. Hate for their own weakness.

And

They began to worry about Karen. She didn't respond to any calls. She wasn't home. Nobody except Karen's stupid brothers there. Her big brother now wore a long nightgown and a beard, her little brother was attached to a portable ventilator. The children allayed their fears with the thought that Karen was having sex in old factories and driving to the lake on the weekend with her fantastic boyfriend, she was just so busy, the way it probably is when you fall in love for the first time, something the others had not yet experienced. And that is just

Brilliant,

Thought

KAREN

A hundred men later, a hundred pills and bumps of coke later. It's brilliant that I'm alert. Thought Karen, and was alert. Perhaps because her body had developed a tolerance to the drugs or because something in her wanted to survive. Karen had no clue as to how long it had been, as the time had merged together into a continuous film loop of fog, babble, kisses, Captagon, crystal meth, sperm, alcohol, and things Karen couldn't even name, in which she was able to see herself in moments of clarity. While walking on the street, lying on mattresses, bleeding from orifices, nightly. Mentally present only for short periods. Just as dementia patients snap to for a few seconds before they sink back into forgetfulness. Patuk was always there. He had other women, girls; Karen could have screamed, not because she was being abused but because he was together with other girls, but

No screams ever came, she was too dazed, too absent, and what she wanted to scream sat up in a tree somewhere and looked down at her. Since the beginning of her love—pause—seriously?

Patuk had monitored Karen, topped up the drugs when she threatened to come out of her haze, soothed her when she cried, threatened when she wanted to leave. He had really not been with her only during a few hours of sleep and during classes. At first. When Karen was still going to school. Before her duties had intensified.

Even with symptoms of poisoning and under the influence of drugs, even compulsively asleep during class, Karen's performance was better than all the other students. The teachers, who were used to all sorts of behavioral problems, didn't speak to Karen about her condition. Which was better. Because Karen didn't have a condition. She had no sense of anything, she was wasted. And moved like a machine through the daily routine she hadn't chosen. At night, or early in the morning, when Karen went to sleep, she perceived vaguely that her disabled brother had died. Mother was crying. But perhaps she had dreamed this. Her older brother seemed to pray nonstop. Later Karen stopped going home or to school. She had a room in a factory. Clients were serviced there and children like Karen were housed, and she no longer saw Patuk so much there.

A strange empty time elapsed, from which she suddenly awoke. Karen sobered up. She had a headache, pain in her arms, legs, in her stomach, in her ass. The light in the room was too bright, the noise too loud. There was nobody else around. Maybe clients' diminishing interest in Karen had made the minder careless.

Get up, then. Everything dull, and her legs, goodness, don't think of your legs, they hung pale and thin from a somewhat swollen abdomen. Karen let herself drop from the second-floor window, barely feeling the impact of her body because there had been greater trials in the last few months than an embarrassing jump from a window, and ran through the night to her former home. Nobody was there. The little brother dead and buried, the other probably off with Allah.

Karen washed herself for two hours, knowing she was fulfilling all the clichés about deranged girls, who were themselves somehow to blame for everything, primarily because there wasn't a penis attached to them. She threw her clothes out, took from her older brother's dresser a hoodie and army pants that he didn't need anymore with his new nightgown look, sat down in the kitchen and waited for the rest of her family to turn up.

Hours later,

KAREN'S MOTHER

Came home and was so tired that she wanted to fall to the floor as soon as she entered the apartment. The apartment would fall in around her and bury her, and life would stop tormenting her with letters and phone calls, with bureaucrats, handymen, robots that parked her in telephone waiting lines. And never to need to look for a job again and fail to find one—cost cutting, you know how it goes—and never to need to come home and run into the idiots her older son always hung around with now. The dumbfucks who can only speak in half sentences. And see the empty bed of her youngest child and feel somehow happy that he was dead and hate herself for it. And what was up with Karen lately? She seems to have grown up and lost twenty kilos. Probably smoking hash. And hates her life. Great, that made two of them. On the table alongside ten bills covering all aspects of personhood was mail from the building management agency.

KAREN

Saw how her mother didn't look at her. With a flurry of motion, her fingers, which looked oddly arthritic, fumbled around with the envelopes while Karen told her about everything. About the drugs, the men, the pimps, the other girls, some of whom had gotten pregnant. Two had killed themselves because they didn't dare go home, but most of them were on drugs and still half alive. "I'm going to call the police, okay?"

"What did you say," said her mother and looked vacantly at Karen. Karen reached a

POLICEWOMAN

HEALTH CONDITION: *obese*
HOBBIES: *addicted to sugar, ordering clothes online and returning them*
POLITICAL CLASSIFICATION: *left liberal*
SEXUAL BEHAVIOR: *Tinder profile has for quite some time had no matches*

"Yes, I've got it. Sounds like quite an adventure, from what you're describing. But yes, thanks, we'll follow up on these leads. It's possible that we'll need to speak to you again. Good night."

The police officer acted as if she were writing down Karen's address. Then she deleted the record of the telephone call. Nobody here at the station house wanted to be opened up to charges of racial profiling. There'd already been about twenty reports. Girls had been questioned, transcripts made. And then destroyed. Computers had killed ten jobs in the department in the last year. Archives, clerical, emergency call center, accounting, all of them displaced by machines. Who wanted to risk their job for a couple of girls, who in any case were pregnant at fifteen and would get social welfare benefits? The policewoman sucked on a sugar cube. And

KAREN

Hung up the phone

After a few minutes of silence—

Karen thought her mother was shocked or concerned or outraged—her mother looked up and asked: "Did you call?" She let the eviction notice.

Fall to the floor and

Breathed shallowly, her eyes wide open, unblinking. Karen had in the meantime read the letter, looked at the bills. In lieu of a sky, both stared into nothingness.

One week

Later

Karen and her mother were also sitting in the homeless shelter, and that is the coincidence that isn't one, but rather the normal progression of the changes in the world on a small scale. The changes were the result of the increase in poverty, which often meant the loss of an apartment, and the reality that in Rochdale there was only one homeless shelter, where Karen and her mother now landed. A bunk bed. A tiny window. Who came up with the idea of painting the window frame green so that looking out at the crossroads felt like staring at a television from the previous century? The room was tight for two people, but Karen didn't care as long as she had her peace and quiet. Withdrawal hadn't been dramatic. A bit of nausea, trembling, shivering, an emptiness, an emptiness that was better than the memories which followed, that she now suppressed with viruses. Hurray for viruses. Karen busied herself with adeno-associated virus serotypes. These beasts were truly devil spawn. All the things you could do with them. Like making testosterone harmless, for instance. She read through a theory the basic idea of which was that eliminating testosterone would solve 90 percent of the world's problems. She felt there was a great idea there that she couldn't grasp, not yet. She would finish her schooling at the end of the school year and at that point would have skipped four years ahead. Not bad for a fucking gifted student, thought Karen, wondering which of the four microbiology scholarship offers, from Aberdeen, Nottingham, Reading, and London, she should accept. The university in London was only fourth place in the rankings, but hey—London. Karen pushed off the decision because at the moment it was impossible to leave her mother, who was in a really bad state. As if her night shifts and the usual way home had been the only thing keeping her alive and she now had found a chance to think about her life for the first time. Terrible idea. Karen's mother trembled, because the sudden cutoff of thyroid hormones didn't agree with her. Health insurance no longer paid for such luxury products. Aside from tranquilizers, insurance barely paid for anything anymore. Karen's mother had tried to find work. There was no longer any demand for night nurses, same for day nurses, and what else was there— prostitution, pole dancing, bar girl—the things that hadn't been displaced by machines weren't exactly suitable for an overweight older woman, parentheses forty, with thyroid issues. It wouldn't go well for a tired woman in a world where 40 million people looked for work every year. Where thousands arrived daily thanks to development. Automation. The robots. Hurray, we now have robots for every fucking aspect of life. They perform, do you get that, you idiots? Perform. We've tried for a decade now to mold you to our needs. Wiry, overtrained, overly conforming. All that shit. And what happens? You got burned out. So now, bye-bye.

Speaking of which . . .

Karen's remaining brother had married the first of what with Allah's help would be followed by a few more women, and had moved into her family's apartment in London. Just until Karen's brother was able to meet his obligations as head of a family. Until Karen's brother realized that four wives meant providing for four women and the children they bore him. And satisfying them sexually. The women, that is. Karen's mother went to the capital once a week to see the stupid fucker.

When Karen's mother was in London, Peter, Karen, Don, and Hannah lay on the bed and looked at the internet. Everyone in a household on social benefits was entitled to a device. It was important for the future. What future? Doesn't matter.

Outside in the hall

A couple of men had gotten deep into their cups and were drunkenly ranting. Water whooshed. People shouted at each other, and a woman had taken issue with it all. She'd gone crazy. Job gone, husband gone, apartment gone, moved onto the street, in winter. Dumb idea. Then a wound on her leg, inflicted by a rat, infected, collapsed at some point, taken to hospital, leg amputated. After the amputation they'd taken her to the homeless shelter, where she had a bed, with her one leg, and a social worker who brought her marmalade once a week. The woman, she sat on her bed and whimpered in a tone that didn't sound human. Perhaps there's a fuse in humans that blows when the level of humiliation crosses a certain line. Perhaps they keep a lot at bay, the adaptable people—loss of families, of flats, security, limbs, and sleeping on park benches—but at some point the limits of tolerability are exceeded and they start to rock back and forth and to cry out in grief. The children, who were barely children anymore, lay together like little hamsters. They peered through their devices at the world and were sure that something big was waiting for them out there. Now came the news. London

The city where

KAREN'S MOTHER

Was heading up to the thirteenth floor of a high-rise. The building where her son lived, which looked like a vertical city for service workers. Nannies, paperhangers, Uber drivers, people with by-the-hour contracts. Karen's mother looked with alarm at the plastic ceiling of the elevator, which was slow and wheezed like a chain-smoker. Stacked-up slums, with partially exposed electric wires, gas stoves, moldy window frames. Along with her son and his veiled wife, another ten people lived in the three-room flat. Karen's mother sat uneasily among them on a sofa wrapped in plastic film. The people spoke Arabic. Just not with her. She sat, bored, and wondered why she had bothered to come. Then she noticed that it smelled funny. Then she heard screams from outside. Karen's mother looked out the window and got

Smoke in her face. There seemed to be a fire on the lower floors—the third and fourth floors were in flames, it crackled, windows shattered, the smoke grew thicker, pressed under the door of the flat. The coughing began, eyes burned. In the hall, nothing like THIS WAY OUT. In the hall, crying children, screaming women, people in underwear, carrying bundles, not carrying bundles, with dogs, all tripping over each other, kicking each other, shoving their way to the staircases and elevators—seriously? Ceiling boards fell on people, smashed their heads as they stumbled over people fallen to the floor. Karen's mother was pushed into the staircase. Nothing to see but smoke. Nothing to hear but screams. It was dark and overcrowded. She shoved her way back into the apartment. Surely the fire brigade would be there momentarily and save them. That's what you learn: the fire brigade saves you. Sticking your head out the window didn't work; the flames had reached as far as two floors below them. People were jumping out of their windows. You could hear them thud below. The fire brigade instructed those still in the building to lie on the floor and seal their doors.

Right.

THE CHILDREN

Were lying on the bed like—children. They put their feet in each other's faces, tickled each other, and had just watched *Black Mirror* after watching *Utopia*. Then the news came on, the news barely anyone could stomach anymore, could grasp: ISIS was tearing across the desert beheading people, some icebergs had fallen into the sea, the sea was rising, the Russians looked forward to new sea passages, a researcher warned of centuries-old viruses that had survived in ice that was now thawing, in India a couple of women had been killed, some fascists had taken power somewhere, all over Europe now large groups of unbelievably ignorant, loutish people appeared, who screamed their hatred of everything into the cameras, in London a building was on fire. Be quiet. Just be—

Quiet. Said

KAREN

She had quietly looked at the burning building. Had thought. There are so many social housing blocks in London. And waited for her mother. But. When the following day no message came from her mother,

When the next day no information was available from any hospital.

When the next day it didn't rain but there was no sun, Karen realized that she no longer had any family. "You have us." Said Hannah when they held their daily meeting on the roof.

"We have each other," said Don to herself.

"Let's just take off." She said out loud. Nobody answered her. They all sat there lost in the thoughts this suggestion provoked. Taking off was something to think about at night. Something tinged with glamour. It was a completely different story to break away from the everyday, pack a bag, and run off with other children to an unfamiliar place.

"Let's double-check the list first," said Hannah. It was a delay tactic that put an end to the moment of daydreaming. "The list of people who tormented us or hurt us or whatever."

The others looked a bit vacant. They'd long since forgotten about the whole thing in this era when news was already old after an hour. Hannah pulled a little notebook from a jacket pocket.

"Right, so far we have the following people to punish:

Walter, Don's mother's ex-boyfriend.

Dr. Brown, the doctor who caused my mother's death.

Thome, the programmer who drove my father to suicide.

Patuk, Karen's—um . . ."

Brief pause. They'd never talked about what exactly had happened to Karen. It didn't feel appropriate just now, either, or perhaps it never would. And yet everyone knew that this Patuk rightfully belonged on the list, that there was no doubt about it, that there was good reason for it.

"Karen's ex-boyfriend," said Hannah, continuing on quickly.

"Peter's mother, the Russian,

Sergej, the man who, um . . .

hurt Peter."

A strange shyness took hold when it came to all subjects related to the body. It was an area that made all of them insecure at the moment, a strange and dangerous and perhaps forbidden place. They were still children. Their bodies in an in-between state, their feelings not yet grown-up. They were children sitting on the roof of an ugly building, looking out at the familiar, endlessly boring city, scared about leaving. Leaving everything here. Which wasn't nice but was familiar. It was the same fear you feel right before you jump off a precipice attached to a bungee cord. The brain panics at the last second, trying to come up with a way out.

There wasn't one.

BEFORE THE INTERMISSION

If you were the idiot director of idiotic dystopian movies, you could lower your gaze and say: "A new era has begun. The machines are becoming intelligent and humans are modifying themselves." DNA optimization was the hot new thing. For those with money. Which barely anyone had, but if they did, they saw to the perfection of the future branches of their family tree. There were hardly any children born the so-called natural way anymore anyway. In vitro, of course, technology, no need for rigid organs or agile sperm.

None of the horror scenarios dreamed up by dystopian thinkers came to pass. No giant concentration camps, no brutal dictatorship. The development of the world is elegant. Quiet.

Inconspicuous.

It wasn't good.

For the human brain. The wonderful digitalization. How does the brain change in offline mode when existence is increasingly virtual, music is on the cloud and streaming services, movies, books, friends, shops, social life exist as a user interface that perhaps isn't real. What happens then in the 1.0 world, with wetware you have to drag around in the winter at human speeds that are so slow? While life online functions at such a furious pace. Some idiot comments on what some star, who also only exists online, says or does. Some doctored deepfake video of something goes viral. And—and the media picks it up. On TV, which everyone watches online, Twitter and Facebook posts and film clips by random dumbfucks or bots are cited by online newspapers. Someone or other posted something or other. Hey, fantastic. Totally understandable that people find politics boring and vote for washed-up reality stars or bad comedians. If they vote at all. Because in countries where voting takes place online it might be bots voting, or malware from China. In the end it was impossible to tell from the bits and bytes whether it really was a person who had pushed the button on the screen of a device or not. Doesn't matter. Nothing at all matters because less and less is real, less and less produces any feeling other than irritation. Humans seem to have developed a hate for their existence beyond the net. Demonstrating, for instance, or joining a party, vigil, or opposition—all that crap is unappealing, exhausting, the only exceptions are actions that include violence and hate so that they trigger a feeling approaching what you get online. Otherwise it's better to stay online. Where you can operate so brilliantly politically. Become part of a troll factory, or doctor video or audio recordings. What happens to humanity when on the one hand they only believe what's online but on the other they are deeply distrustful of everything online? And have no clue.

Speaking of which.

Ever since people started commenting in some form or other, became part of the public, were given Likes, found friends, who might be bots, the certainty of one's individual importance has risen to pathological levels. People all believe that the world revolves around each of them. Their opinion is important, their rating can ruin a restaurant, their comments chasten politicians, their disease is unique, they looked it up, humans, they can do anything, humans. They'd seen tutorials. Climate change: got it. CERN: yep. Gastric surgery: can do it themselves. Come here, Gertrud. Gertrud's dead now. But she still lives online. *Second Life* was the dress rehearsal. Billions live in a new world whose basic functions are less transparent to them than the so-called real— You know, that thing out there. Billions have no idea how a computer works, to say nothing of algorithms. How they can be manipulated, what is being manipulated, they just stare at the pixels and trust. Which is actually touching. It makes you so angry, so angry that online you feel as if everything hinges on your own deranged opinion. And outside, when you walk around in slow motion in your freezing body, you don't get any respect for the importance of your existence. What happens to people when nothing is tangible anymore, when everything might be fake. Nothing real. Will human beings themselves become fakes who can only be transported back to reality by inserting chips into their cortexes? The ability to think is atrophying because it's too demanding. Empathy is withering because stimulation online occurs in fractions of a second. Frustration is growing because life offline is so slow and boring. The fucking internet has become the Leni Riefenstahl of the world. A place of dumbing down, inciting, of manipulation and frustration.

So everything's going just great. Time for the next level.

INTERMISSION

While the story of Hannah, Don, Peter, and Karen takes on a new dynamic that consists of packing their bags, the silent departure from their childhood, and a failed trip to London (the bus to Manchester was delayed, there was no connection, the children stayed overnight in Manchester-Salford and continued their escape the next day).

An opportune time to talk about acceleration, something taking place abstractly in the world and which had a paradoxical effect on many people. They felt their lives were stagnating. Or going backwards. Or just stuck in a loop. Or simply couldn't catch up with the speed around them. You wanted to install a voice-operated computer in your home or a robot hoover to crawl around your ten square meters—but it wasn't any faster, because the mind's limits are already set. That nothing in their existence was gliding toward a glittering, luxurious future; instead everything more difficult, more unpleasant, and more hopeless. Was. Only the upper echelon of the populace was entitled to services; the rest toiled with online reservations, used self-check for airplanes on which they squatted in their compression stockings, waited on hold on their devices just to get information from a fucking robot, no longer knew who governed them or why, who ruled the world, didn't understand Alphabet and the delivery drones, the electronic cars that had increasing numbers of strange accidents, the headaches that disappeared when one took one's pills, and worried about their jobs, for good reason. The number of people who died of overwork was rising, the number of unemployed was rising, poverty was rising; they became more radical, less human; it was the time of acute housing shortages in big cities around the world, the time when tent camps sprang up in industrial wastelands, the time of total surveillance, of surveying the brain, the watching, recording, evaluating of people, classifying them as valuable and worthless, the flowering of neo-Fascism, because perplexed people wanted clarity, please, clarity. They didn't understand the developments anymore. Artificial intelligence, that nobody had ever seen but that dictated everyone's daily life, collected their data, made them transparent. Arrests, being fitted with electronic ankle bracelets, elimination, increased due to errors made by artificial intelligence; cash was phased out, same for animals and insects; floods became more frequent, the climate was irrevocably out of balance; the raw materials needed to manufacture all the wonderful servers and computers and batteries dwindled, no problem. Whatever. As always, it didn't matter to people. The important thing was what affected them—in their daily lives, their narrow surroundings. The oddly slow-motion way things became ever more unpleasant and harsh while the transformation of the world, in case it hasn't been said, began to pick up pace.

So, the increase in speed

"The aforementioned concept, discussed by Stanislaw Ulam and John von Neumann in the 1950s, that the exponentially accelerating progress of technology will converge in a finite amount of time in a technological 'singularity.' In 2014, I discovered a beautiful, incredibly precise historic exponential acceleration pattern that wasn't about technological progress alone but rather reached back all the way to the Big Bang: the history of what are perhaps the most important events from a human perspective seem to suggest that

The part of history dominated by humans

Will 'converge' in approximately the year Omega = 2050. (I prefer to call the convergence point Omega, because that's what Teilhard de Chardin called it a hundred years ago, and because 'Omega' sounds better than 'singularity'—it sounds a bit like 'Oh my god.') The error bars on most dates below seem, according to current knowledge, to be less than ten percent. Why the time intervals between decisive historical events are always so perfectly distributed, I do not know."

$\Omega = $ ca. 2050

$\Omega-$ 13.8 billion years: Big Bang

$\Omega-$ 1/4 of this time: $\Omega-$ 3.5 billion years: first life on earth

$\Omega-$ 1/4 of this time: $\Omega-$ 0.9 billion years: first animal-like life

$\Omega-$ 1/4 of this time: $\Omega-$ 220 million years: first mammals

$\Omega-$ 1/4 of this time: $\Omega-$ 55 million years: first primates (our ancestors)

$\Omega-$ 1/4 of this time: $\Omega-$ 13 million years: first hominids (our ancestors)

$\Omega-$ 1/4 of this time: $\Omega-$ 3.5 million years: first stone tools ("technological dawn")

$\Omega-$ 1/4 of this time: $\Omega-$ 800,000 years: first controlled fire (next great technological breakthrough)

$\Omega-$ 1/4 of this time: $\Omega-$ 210,000: first anatomically modern humans (our ancestors)

$\Omega-$ 1/4 of this time: $\Omega-$ 50,000 years: first behaviorally modern humans colonize the earth

$\Omega-$ 1/4 of this time: $\Omega-$ 13,000 years: Neolithic revolution, farming and animal husbandry

$\Omega-$ 1/4 of this time: $\Omega-$ 3,300 years: beginning of the first population explosion in the Iron Age

$\Omega-$ 1/4 of this time: $\Omega-$ 800 years: fire and iron combined; first firearms and rockets (in China)

$\Omega-$ 1/4 of this time: $\Omega-$ 200 years: start of second population explosion during the Industrial Revolution

$\Omega-$ 1/4 of this time: $\Omega-$ 50 years: Information Revolution, digital nervous system spans the globe, WWW, mobile phones for all

$\Omega-$ 1/4 of this time: $\Omega-$ 12 years: cheap computers more powerful than human brain; artificial intelligence at human level?

$\Omega-$ 1/4 of this time: $\Omega-$ 3 years: ??

$\Omega-$ 1/4 of this time: $\Omega-$ 9 months: ????

$\Omega-$ 1/4 of this time: $\Omega-$ 2 months: ????????

$\Omega-$ 1/4 of this time: $\Omega-$ 2 weeks: ????????????????

(a simplified treatise based on Prof. J. Schmidhuber, computer scientist, AI developer)

It's going well

For

HUMANITY

They keep getting older.

People. And why not, since life is getting more enjoyable even in underdeveloped countries, as the Western world calls them. Ever since Western firms started selling clean water there and with the aid of China created blossoming landscapes in Pakistan, Uganda, Somalia, and wherever the hell else. Mechanized agriculture operations as big as countries, battery companies, solar farms brought work, prosperity, development and devices for the natives.

And technology. OMG.

Technology cures cancer, makes disabled people walk, deaf people hear, it provides old people with robot seals to cuddle and nursing staff to love. Ever more exhausting, sickness-inducing occupations disappear into the open arms of artificial intelligence. All the world's knowledge is available online to everyone, computers have become a foodstuff that's increasingly available to the entire population. There are so many positive, exhilarating aspects of development that it doesn't seem improbable that our daily life could soon be like a shining utopia, with laughing people who, well-educated and equipped with wonderful opportunities for self-actualization, stand around green spaces hailing flying taxis.

Abolishment of the monarchy happened as quickly as the opening of the Berlin Wall that had divided East and West Germany. Or the fascist power grab in Europe. The outbreak of encephalitis in Africa that mushroomed into an epidemic in Europe. These moments that fundamentally change some people's lives, that seem unimaginable but that are completely wiped from the hive mind hardware a day later. Because they don't affect most of the other eight billion.

The new king appeared in front of the cameras. He announced his resignation, he was the most modern member of the royal family and therefore the least liked. Then. Nothing. Happened. Amazingly. It had always been whispered that the monarchy was a fundamental part of social cohesion. A rock of stability in a burning sea, a foothold amid hopelessness. It had been thought that just the presence of a few anointed ones, in order to bring god into the lives of the subjects, was important in preventing revolution. And there followed—no street battles between royalists and monarchy-haters. Everyone shrugged their shoulders. The royal family packed their bags. The queen had gone to fashion shows before her death. She'd tried desperately to make the monarchy hip again. Which unfortunately didn't work. Marriages to two commoners were the low point, the marriage to a Black woman the last straw. You know the story. The deep-seated hatred of anything nonpink among the segments of society that supported the royal family could no longer be placated. You could even say a nonpink person sealed the fate of the monarchy. The palace was transformed into a museum of the British Empire. Elements of MI5 were given space there, too. The former royal family moved to Scotland, still in possession of their billions, of course.

Another jittery blink of the eye and the whole thing was forgotten . . .

The mind of the world population. You know how it is. The people who came of age without the influence of mobile devices

Are dead.

Every child in the Western world spends more than five hours per day on a device. They check their social media accounts, messages, and chat forums in intervals of ten minutes, and that's a conservative estimate. The addictiveness of an entire generation has gone up by 300 percent, the ratio of gamma-aminobutyric acid to glutamate in the anterior cingulate cortex has risen sharply, if you take the dead as a baseline value. The third generation of addicts, fear-stricken, and depressives are no longer able to concentrate on a topic for more than two minutes.

Or to develop

Creativity

Or

Empathy. They operate with reduced motor skills and exhibit significantly reduced brain power.

What are you going to do?

Later. Which is to say, now.

Everything is quiet. A different kind of quiet from Rochdale.

Thinks

DON

Excitingly quiet, she thinks.

It's nighttime in the big city, where it doesn't get dark, there are no stars visible in the sky, a place where you don't feel alone, where you suspect there are people all around who could become a friend. Or lover. Behind some window or other could be the person who would change your life. Something Don had never thought before. She knew virtually everyone behind every window of her hometown, and didn't want to be expected by any of them. The air smells like old oil. Of petrol. Of tar, and there are frogs somewhere.

During the night watch Don feels she's in the right place. At the perfect time. Grown-up and—excited. Their security is up to her. Being responsible for others has a positive effect on the brain's reward center. A reason people still have children. If they're even able to, which is ever less frequently the case. Humanity's sperm seem to know that something's up.

Quiet. A shimmering quiet is what Don might have thought if she were a fuckwit. If she'd been a person who always walked around barefoot in order to absorb the electrons from the earth, she would say: "I welcome the night because I sense a deep connection with nature only in the absence of light."

Nature.

Right.

In the—let's just call it—environs where the children's—let's just call it—dwelling is, there isn't much nature left. A true Anthropocene landscape deep in East London, dotted with enchanted lakes whose surfaces are covered with green sludge through which little gas bubbles pop. Something is happening in there, deep in those lakes that stink of sulfur; they sit among the industrial complexes like pools of blood oozing from dead robots. Nobody comes to this area who doesn't have to. Except for a few undead and unemployed night watchmen who because of old habits still occasionally check on the empty buildings, a total absence of people prevails in the area. A few years prior this area would have been overrun by the excavators that were digging foundations in even the most unlikely corners of the city for luxury condo towers being built as investments by idiots who wore diapers because they'd lost control of their sphincters as a result of stress. But construction had tapered off. Too many high-rises sitting empty for years on end. Though now it's so pleasantly quiet. Controlled. Here. What a time it was, when the country was being sold off to dictators, fundamentalists, oligarchs, and whoever the fuck else. What a time, when everyone thought it would go on like that forever. Taller, faster, prettier, more golden. Affluence and exoskeletons for all.

It's so quiet. A stream gurgles in the distance. A motorway junction where elegant electric cars stand in traffic. A beautiful spot to set up camp. Everything's good now.

After the first three somewhat problematic weeks.

Don had imagined it more euphorically, this

New start

They'd arrived at the bus station she remembered well, with two drunken parents.

She'd thought this time would be different. They would romp through the streets and things would be offered up to them, she'd thought.

Maybe they would meet interesting kids who had a—let's say—villa where they could put up the four of them. It wasn't clear what the others had pictured, what they had dreamed of for that first day in the metropolis. Nobody talked about so-called feelings; that sort of thing wasn't sufficiently concrete. What were they supposed to talk about? Their troubled childhoods? Their distrust of the world? The horrors of the night? When the ground seemed to open up and they vanished into the abyss. Blaming their childhoods for their fucked-up lives had been a pointless quirk of the disappearing bourgeoisie. The over-fifty set, teachers working on behavior therapy based on trauma inflicted by their mothers, constructing a new family tree with amusing, colorful pictures they'd drawn of their pain. WTF. If there was an upside to the end of the world then it was the collapse of the psych industry. Nobody had money anymore for family constellations and Kleenex boxes. There wasn't any money for nonfunctional members of society.

Men like

THOME'S FATHER

Had seen to that. Thome's father looks around. He's alone in the library. His so-called wife is hanging around with some Russians in Dorchester, which belongs to some Arabs. And Thome's father scratches his testicles. Well, "scratches." He checks on the basis of his masculinity. Everything's present and accounted for. Still alive. He shoves a cigar into his mouth. Things are rolling. Withdrawal from the EU has been forgotten. But not by Thome's father; he likes to remember it. It was the first step of the reconfiguration, and it still makes him smirk, yes, he thinks "smirk" when he vaguely curls his lips, thinking about the fact that bots took the blame for that. Back then he had no clue about technology, only about psychology. A divided populace is a controllable populace. One that wants an enemy and a leader. Voilà, thought Thome's father. Here I am. Thome's father was a rabid supporter of Murray Rothbard's libertarian manifesto.

Exactly.

Here

SIR ERNEST (EARL)

HEALTH PROFILE: *gout, incontinence, pronounced anxiety when he thinks of his own
demise*
HOBBIES: *hunting*
FINANCIAL STATUS: *unclear, more than a billion*

Comes into play.

"Sir, if you were to offer a concise version of your ideas?"

"Yes, very happy to. So. You see. I would regard the privatization of the military and police as a breakthrough. Absurd to think that a fickle state apparatus holds a monopoly on violence in its hands. It belongs under the control of a sovereign, nonpartisan board of people for whom it's important to maintain order and stability in the country. I'm conservative in a good way."

Says the earl.

He understands this to mean that he longs for a Great Britain that exists exclusively in BBC series.

"During my childhood," says the earl, "the contours were relatively clear. There were the Highlands, Cornwall, et cetera—places you went on holiday to your manor and it smelled of hay. The stallion grazed on grass moistened with dew. The English stallion. Life in the cities was orderly and the structures tried-and-true. A calm, friendly atmosphere reigned. Those whom tradition and the labor of their own hands had brought prosperity didn't mix with the simple, industrious fellow citizens. Typical Englishmen strolled in Hyde Park, kept themselves tidy, and respected government authority. Woman and man knew their places in the bedrock of the body politic. Woman: internal. Man: external. Both important. Both according to their worth. Bearing children, looking after them. Hunting, conquering. Soft and hard. No ambiguities. No misunderstandings. An agreeable sense of organization existed in the country, which precipitated ever-increasing dividends and allowed Great Britain to become one of the most powerful empires ever."

Sir Ernest longs for a time when words like *morality*, *trust*, and *pride* were used. He wishes for an orderly manageability and tidiness that he no longer sees. When he looks around he gazes into an abyss of filth, he sees rubbish in the streets, decay in the faces, people on the side of the road, women who are aggressive and unladylike, men wearing laughable women's clothing. He doesn't see a cohesive unity of Britons loyal to the crown, but rather splintered groups of immigrants, feminists, Blacks, and white Nazis. Nobody can tell him that anyone could be happy amid this disorientating mess. "When the acquisition of goods," the earl continues, "is the only gauge of a person's success in life, then the system falls apart through nonconsumption. The human being. Here I'll pause for a moment. And I believe, the person entrusted to us, the person calling out for leadership and rules, for a controlling hand to keep things in check, needs a handrail to grab hold of along the frightening path of his short life." Said the earl.

"Look at China. A nation of rules, strong laws, and yes, the death penalty is not an unknown term there. The death penalty for child abuse, for acts of terrorism, and for treason. That's right. Give me strength, for I am working on making my country into one for the native-born descendants of greater England once again. I'm angry. This is my country. Listen up, you idiots disrespectfully urinating on the very foundations of our history! That you flood with false ideas and filthy fantasies. Without any regard for the accomplishments of our people.

"Time for a new start!"

Which is also what

PETER

Thought,

When the children had arrived three weeks before,

After an unsettling voyage during which there'd been many fires to look at. Tent camps on the wastelands of abandoned industrial sites, on dead acreage.

Did I really think "new start," Peter had thought, this stupid esoteric nothing phrase that people use in order to pretend they have things in hand? As if they're not just sheep who are only superior to their four-legged comrades because of their gripping tools.

Once in London, it didn't look any better. What was going on? A war, and nobody had said anything about it in Rochdale? Traffic stood still, people pushed their way through the gaps between the cars, it looked like a demonstration in the street in front of the station. But. It was just rush hour traffic. The pace was dizzying by comparison to the speed of people back home, who seemed to barely inch forward at a crawl. Here people ran to show that they could keep up. Jaws set, eyes, too, they were always ablaze. To show that they had ridiculous powers of consumption at their disposal. "I'll buy the shit. Just tell me what. I'll buy all of it." After work—or various work, as you have to say to properly describe the system of multiple jobs—the wage earners and employees of London did their shopping in automated shops—"We also accept bitcoin!" The products all packed conveniently for single people, in cardboard containers. For the sake of the environment. The stove in the smart home, which meant eight square meters in some back court, turned on in advance with an app; ditto the oven. Lights switched on, the Underground ticket taken care of. A great hurrah of digitalization, which saved people time so they could take on a fourth job. In order to buy another device which would then save them more time. So. After they'd bought some shite or other in a plastic box, feeling modern—"I'm part of the fucking industrial revolution 4.0 thanks to shitty precooked pasta packed in plastic!"—they ran to the buses that would take them to their back courts. The news beamed at them from giant screens on every corner. There were fewer accidents now that people didn't have to stare nonstop at their devices in order to overstimulate their synapses. Moments with nothing to do, moments without information, were damned as wasted time by the brain and punished by short episodes of depression. Moments without information to keep up the stimulation curve, since stimulation was mistaken for liveliness. People stared for a moment. Then kept running. Stopped again, came back. Double take. The reports on the flat-screens on an endless loop.

Something big was happening. As if to fittingly celebrate the arrival of Peter, Don, Hannah, and Karen, as if to mark the date of their "new start" in the collective consciousness.

One of those motherly, concrete-blonde television presenters, the only kind of women who seemed to have a right to exist on the island, announced the decision made the previous evening—"Yes, just last night"—by the government.

Effective immediately

Every citizen of the country

With a valid British passport

Would

Receive

A basic income,

Which was not tied to any conditions whatsoever.

Passersby stood frozen before the screens. You could see how the words went into their ears and then painstakingly burrowed into their brains, arriving at the Wernicke area at the back, the upper part of the left temporal lobe. This takes time. But then. The realization erupted in the form of a collective shout from hundreds of

People.

They fell, within the framework of their typical British contact aversion, into each other's arms. Money. Free money! It would be said many times that Great Britain was as a result the first country in the world to rise to the challenges of the future, and so on. With a basic income, welfare, retirement benefits, sick pay, and disability pay would be dispensed with.

The collective mouth was agape. This policy, it was further said, would necessitate a laborious registration of all residents; citizens should sign their claims in the next few days by appearing at registration offices. And don't forget proper ID. And kiss my ass, thought

DON

It's nothing to do with us. We're not citizens, we're runaway children. Meanwhile

What had upon their arrival seemed like a demonstration had become a riot. As if the money the state was giving the citizens would be shared only with the quickest, everyone seemed to go mad with greed. Taxis were stopped.

People ran, fell, stumbled over those who had fallen, and everywhere single shoes lay dubiously in the streets. Peter got scared. It seemed advisable to leave this scene of insanity. The children took their bags and pressed through the tumult. It took a quarter of an hour to shove their way into a rich neighborhood a hundred meters from Victoria station. The contrast between the wretches in the street, the riotous common people, the homeless, and these elegant living arrangements was amazing. The general public apparently stuck to the division between the classes. Residences as big as ships, with golden light shining from within, overlooked a handsome park that seemed perfect for their first night, a night on which for once it wasn't drizzling. The four children had barely sat down before two security guards with a dog, which was probably mechanical, turned up. They told them that this was no public park. Because there were no public parks. That is, there were parks that the public could use under certain conditions. Every green patch and open space, every square in the city, belonged to somebody. Russians, Arabs, mobsters, and it was up to the owners to determine the rules.

So

The new life

Started with a delayed euphoria.

Over the course of the first few weeks, the nearly still—children of parents of undefined ethnicity slept on the street in front of a Bentley dealership, in a youth hostel, in a squatted building, and in office buildings they managed to get themselves locked into. Office buildings were the best overnight locations, as they were heated. During those nights in office towers the children had longed for a regimented life. They came up with plans during those nights in the towers. "Before we put down roots we should get to know the city first." Said Don during this time. The others agreed.

So the children got

To know the city.

The central districts seemed inhabited exclusively by Chinese, Russians, and Arabs. Whom one glimpsed only through the windows of golden cars with five gold-plated exhaust pipes. These inhabitants of the central districts insisted on their petrol motorcars, and law enforcement forces turned a blind eye. They knew who owned most of the city. The rich sat in traffic in their golden vessels, same as the electric cars and the little self-driving vehicles. Nobody wanted their right to individual transportation taken away. A car was freedom where there was otherwise little freedom left. With a car one could drive around, at least in theory.

The children began their confidence-building explorations in the City of London. Barely three square kilometers, just eight thousand residents. With its own laws since 886 AD. Only reptiloids hung about Temple Church.

There wasn't much else going on. White men in suits who looked so similar that you might think it more practical to condense them into one man. What he would then be good for was, however, unclear.

Aside from the rich idiots in golden motorcars, the central areas of the city seemed made exclusively for tourists. Chinese tourists who wanted to buy marmalade worth its weight in gold in authentic shops. Aging models who'd married Russian men and now shopped with wicker baskets for superfoods in organic groceries, still a bit unstable on their feet because of surgical belly button revisions and vagina rejuvenations. Standard operating procedure. You know how it is.

In the entire city center, from Nottingham and Chelsea to Mayfair and Kensington, there were no children. They'd probably been sent off to boarding schools, or were dead. The looks that followed Hannah, Peter, Don, and Karen could be interpreted without difficulty as greedy. "Maybe they eat children around here," said Hannah. "We should get out of here."

Like everywhere in Europe, the streets started to look squalid as soon as you left the city center. No trees, no limousines, no gold. No good honest red brick, organic cafés, fitness studios. For a hedonistic world metropolis, these, shall we say, "locales" looked depressing. Garages and sheds had been turned into flats, signs had been put up in warped window frames. Solicitations for flatmates or offers of sofas to crash on were posted everywhere. And the rates,

You can guess.

In the districts

Beyond the manicured white villas, the expensive shops, the charming private parks, the government's announcement reverberated. Long lines had formed at the registration offices. Those in line emanated confidence, hope, and fear. Perhaps this incredible basic income would be gone by the time they made it to the front of the line? Inside the offices, people were attended to at long tables that had been set up temporarily. The customer looked into a camera. The facial image was transmitted to a database, in fractions of a second a chip was loaded with all the data of the person in question. Device IDs, biometric passport details, bank accounts, addresses, medical files, police record, sexual predilections, friends, family, social peculiarities, legal troubles. At info stands, trained staff explained the typical applications of the sensational new technology. They spoke less about the personal information which could now be ascertained even when a target wasn't within the catchment area of a biometric facial recognition system and went around without a mobile phone or ID. The personnel praised above all the simplification of the cashless transactions and the ease of use of public transportation. "And see, you don't need a credit card or proof of insurance; you have all your passwords in one place and can manage your smart home with this chip."

"What smart home," one or two asked. "More on that later," a staffer would respond. The registered citizens left the office feeling buoyant. Finally! They seemed to be thinking. Finally it was coming to fruition. The dream of progress and future. Finally things would be looking up,

Felt

The young

COMMUNICATIONS CONSULTANT

HEALTH STATUS: *two abortions*
DEFORMITIES: *foot fungus*
SEXUAL ORIENTATION: *Tinder*
POLITICAL CATEGORIZATION: *on the left side of the spectrum, critical of consumerism*

Well, theoretically a communications consultant. At the moment nothing was being communicated. And certainly not by her.

She'd had no idea what she wanted to be, like most of her classmates. Studied something that sounded nice. Something that involved people. Speaking to people sounded nice. The communications consultant didn't want to put herself out. She didn't want to be hated, get caught up in any shitstorms, didn't want to reinvent the wheel, be unloved. Wow, how exciting.

Her studies didn't provide her with anything substantive. Linguistics, story framing, modern media, to name just three meaningless subjects. Then she'd gotten an internship at a startup that was launching a new messaging service. Something like WhatsApp. Snapchat, Instagram. Before them though. Just not as user-friendly. Together with an external thought-reading device that could put sentences from your head directly into a message. Or was supposed to. Didn't work. Nothing but gibberish came out. The communications consultant covered the cost of her shared flat and her spaghetti by working at a bar in Soho and worked ten hours a day for herself, for the optimization of her portfolio, meaning she wasn't paid by the startup. Which went bankrupt after half a year. The communications consultant then found other internships at ten new up-and-coming IT firms that were developing some shit or other and dreamed of making it big. Two of them even paid. Well. Sort of paid. The communications consultant was gender-fluid and polyamorous. Whatever—it had always been clear to her that she was unique. She believed in equality for all. Respected religions, sexual preferences, gender self-identification. It wasn't that she didn't care how others lived. She just pretended she didn't care. The communications consultant had been opposed to Brexit, her arms were covered in tattoos to such an extent that they looked like black prosthetics. Her stated enemy was neoliberalism. About which, just between us, she didn't know too much about what it meant beyond rising rents and a generally more fraught societal situation. Take Amazon. Oh, man. Amazon. When the communications consultant still had money she had ordered books from Amazon, of course, even if she had held her nose. Who had the time, blah blah blah. And when Adidas brought out a new Capsule Collection from a grime star, she had camped out in front of the shop. She was a totally normal, self-important windbag whose cluelessness was touching. Since birth she'd been preached to about the sacred value of individuality, for the sake of selling Capsule trainers to her, and now none of the promises were coming to fruition. No prize for gender-fluidity, no certificate for juggling seventy-eight different social media accounts featuring seventy-eight possible genders. But

From the cute, tousled experimental stage of youth she had reached an age when her lifestyle began to stink, and suddenly a number of uncomfortable happenstances began to pile up. Shocking moments as the communications consultant felt the downturn in her life in a nearly physical way. It began on the day she got her chip. The government bureaucrat had scanned her head with some kind of machine.

MI5 PIET
"That was the IQ test, sweetie.
And it wasn't so exhilarating in your case."
And the
COMMUNICATIONS CONSULTANT
Lost her last job a few weeks ago. She was a social media specialist at a big

real estate firm. Had been. A company primarily concerned with privatizing public housing. With her look, i.e., the gender-fluid one, the communications consultant didn't necessarily find favor among the overwhelmingly conservative male workforce. After a week a film clip that, thanks to new software looked deceptively real, went around the internal office mail system. The face and voice of the communications consultant had been placed in a bestiality porno. Keyword: *stallion*. Though viewers knew better, the fake news, images, videos that made social media a battlefield always left a lingering doubt. One knew better, but could there be something to it? And hadn't the communications consultant paged through a horse calendar at a rather slow gallop? Didn't she look at the office pooch with an unmistakable desire?

So she was let go. And subsequently, thanks to the fraught economic situation, didn't find a new job. Not at an established firm or a startup. Not even one of the one-pound jobs was available, and the communications consultant bounced from one shared flat to the next, always having to leave after a short time because someone always came along who could pay more. It was as if the weeks and months ran together into one day that always consisted of the communications consultant standing in some apartment, being greeted indifferently by the occupant, and then lying down in a dark room. And she was always afraid to go onto the street. Because outside, with her ambiguous look, the communications consultant got beaten up once a week. And someone always recorded it. Humiliation was a powerful and always effective weapon. She huddled in her room. Looked into the courtyard. A shadow in the window on the opposite side. Tomorrow she'd register and then she'd have a basic income. Then everything would be okay.

And it wasn't raining.

"They've gone mad."

Said

DON

Looking with amazement at the excitement of the natives. People with ragged clothes, bad teeth, bloated faces, gazes muddled by alcohol, danced downright boisterously. They had faith in their government again. Pride in their country again, pride in being British. Pride in being part of a global empire. This wonderful country that gifted them an income. "Fuck off." Thought Don. Loudly. The atmosphere was perhaps best compared to the

feeling laboratory apes feel when first released into the wild. A completely exaggerated cheerfulness reigned in the streets. There was silver confetti coming
from somewhere, which now covered the streets. On the oversize screens on
every corner came images of spontaneous basic income parties and interviews
with happy citizens. Various politicians appreciatively praised the decision to
take this important step for social justice in the country. "We're surrounded
by complete idiots," said Don. "I don't know what exactly is going on here, but
they should leave us out of it." Hannah nodded. None of the four was really
what you would call an IT nerd. They just knew it was advisable for them to
go underground if they didn't want to end up in some sort of child welfare
institution. They knew that as children they had no human rights. Knew that
adults didn't have any human rights, either, and that the idea to let themselves
be implanted with a chip like a pet was weird. The four stood with their
mouths agape, looking at the crazy big-city people as dark fell.

On their further explorations of parts of London where a delighted Chinese tourist would never end up and where there wasn't a single aesthetically
pleasing millimeter on which the eye might happily light, rubbish containers stood before buildings where people lived behind boarded-up windows.
"Check it out, a gathering of the undead." Methadone clinic, suggested

KAREN

When she saw the long line of unsteady figures. But it was a blood bank.
Twenty pound payment. The place was hopping. Donate blood, people's last
idea before hanging themselves. Junkies, alcoholics with cirrhosis and covered
with rashes, who urgently wanted to support the Swiss blood plasma industry
and who were too fucked up to have picked up on the whole basic income
thing, stood in line unsteadily waiting to have their daily liters of blood drawn.

In the first three weeks,

During which the four tried to get a sense of London and find their place
in the city, they all had to deal with their disappointment on their own. Nobody said: "I'm so disappointed." Each of them thought he or she was the only
one feeling that way. They all tried to make jokes and to seem adventurous in
a manner suitable for children. What good would it have done to say:

"This city seems strangely cold. I can't explain it any better than that,
except that I'm always freezing here. Everywhere we stop the windows don't
seem to close properly, and the rain is sharp, as if it's frozen. And always this

cutting wind, I'm sure you know what I mean. The cold also has something to do with the standoffishness of the buildings. They're like ships. There's always bright light in the buildings so you can see the people sitting in their libraries. But they're just decals of book spines, because real books smell too musty. The cold has to do with the peoples' faces, the way they look through you. The way they all seem to know what they're doing."

The

PROGRAMMER

Knows what he's doing, right? "Yes, exactly. Right now I'm studying a fascinating report, unbelievably good. So. Have a look! What do you see? LED bulbs, right? But did you know that information can be transmitted by—I'll put it in the crudest terms—waves? The frequency plays an important role in it. The frequency of light is—well, unbelievable. Do you know how much information you can fire through space and time? LED bulbs could be used as communications devices. An LED reaches transmission rates of eight gigs per second:

"That's about one hundred and sixty times more than the fifty megabytes per second a private individual gets over Wi-Fi for the TV. One of the CERN superconducting wires can move one hundred gigs a second, which is gigantic, but only twelve times as much.

"This LED shit is enough, right, you could multiply the entire surveillance capacity of China many times over, and across the entire planet. By combining a few thousand LEDs you can attain much higher transmission rates, with no cables at all! Just imagine—you take in all the data from the chips, from the internet of things, with its networked minisensors, plus smartphones, and let's bear in mind, the amount of data doubles every twelve months, and in the future every twelve hours. And all that data has to be moved. Have you seen the 5G towers? Massive, right? In many countries they struck down limits on radiation just for them. It randomly occurs to me.

"The next thing that comes into play are artificial LED suns—a new form of satellite called sun simulators because of the glaring light they emit, though they aren't about light but about communications that are hidden in the light waves . . . and they operate from space. Somewhat more lax regulations on privacy up there, if you know what I mean. From space it goes to quantum computers, with which AI runs a superintelligent globe-spanning surveillance and control system.

"The German automobile industry is investing in quantum computers. Germans, eh?"

Just as an aside.

The programmer had never given any thought to Nazis. Except in video games. There he mows them down. But otherwise—they meant nothing to him. Maybe he understood their urge for a cleansed world . . .

It's all quite sensational.

Only

MA WEI

No data

Finds the whole LED thing rather lame.

He isn't so quick to get excited, because he

Is so old that he lived through the Three Years of Difficulty. It was later whispered that about 40 million people starved to death back then, which was probably propaganda. Ma Wei was ten at the time, and he had heard the stories about other difficult times. They scared children with those. People said to kids: "If you aren't disciplined, you'll starve." Nothing worried people more than another period of difficulty. And when it arrived, young people thought it was just a temporary situation. Virtually nobody had supplies on hand, there was a drought, and the emerging nation found itself being restructured. Which meant that the farmers who had previously owned land were suddenly part of a large family with no land. Ma Wei remembered the hunger. Whenever he thought of the hunger, it pierced him deep inside his body in a way familiar to people who have suffered trauma. An amputation without anesthesia. Or rectal penetration during which their intestines are ripped out of them from the inside. The rest of the memory ended at the point when he ate excrement. When the dead were consumed. It ended in shame. Eternal shame and the feeling of being able to accomplish anything because he had survived. The only member of his family. Ma Wei didn't find most people from Western countries unpleasant. But rather, just—laughable.

But

THE PROGRAMMER

Knows what he's doing.

"What I'm doing,"

The programmer often tells himself, "is important for humanity."

EX 2279

```
>++++++++++
{>+++++++++++++>+++++++++++++>+++++++++++++>
+++++++++++++>+++++++++++++++>+++++++++++++>++++
++++++++>+++++++++++++>+++++++++++++>+++++++++++
+>+++++++++++++>+++++++++++++>+++++++++++++++>++
+++++++++>++++++++++++++>><<<<<<<<<<<<<<<<<<<<-]
>———>—>—>+>——->++++>+>->++++>———>—>>++
++>+>>
>>>>>>>>>>>>>>>>
>.>.>.>.>.>.>.>.>.>.>.>.>.
```

And

Welcome to Holyroodhouse.

"Just look how nice it is here." Says

DON

To herself. At night, when she's on watch, she likes to talk to herself. At night, when she stands guard over an imaginary fire. If a social worker were to show up, one of those single women about forty years old, with good intentions and bad hair, she would say: "It's delightful here." Like at a children's overnight camp. "You know, I used to be in one, too. Oh, good old Bath— how I loved it there." And then she'd look at Don as if she, a member of the white former middle class, and Don, a descendant of the various waves of guest workers, were somehow comrades because of her memories of youth, which were guaranteed to be about bad sex. As if she knew what was going on here. As if she'd suddenly developed pigmentation that would release her from her pink existence and bestow upon her an agreeable physique. "I have lots of friends who are foreigners," she'd say, because she wouldn't be sure which shade of nonwhite to classify Don as. And the social worker would hang about, as if she were expecting an award for it, as if she wanted to show that in a pinch she, too, would eat vomit. Then she'd enter the factory building expectantly. Images in her head. If you said to someone, "Listen, we live in a commune of neglected children in an old factory building," it conjures up images from American movies. Large windows, plank floors, wood stove, cashmere blankets, and dogs. Not something that looks like an art installation put up as a critique by some student from St. Andrews looking to grapple with social ills. Aha, the social worker would mumble helplessly while using all her might to conceal her disgust. Despite the efforts of the children to make the place into a home, to adult outsiders it still seemed a bit. Jarring. It was damp and smelled of unwashed children, there were things lying and hanging all over the place, old clothes, jam jars, pots stuck with spaghetti, broken windows, drugs. Okay, not drugs. Next, in the dusky light, the social worker would take the mattresses on the floor for beds and the candles for a romantic quirk rather than the result of the fact that the children could steal electricity only sparingly. And the solar panels—yeah, well. It rained a lot. And it was hot. And very cold. And these extremes alternated maddeningly. Strange weather, thanks to the failing gulf stream. But—

"Don't the kiddies look cute? The way they cling to their pillows," she'd say while patting one of the children, who would then bite her hand. "Oops," she would say. Looking at the bones laid bare in her hand. "Like a sailboat, don't you think, the bones," Don would say, smiling at the bones.

The children lounged about, relaxed, calmed by the trickle of the stream outside, the branches scratching at the windows, at least the windows that still had glass in them and Don hadn't had to cover with plywood. "A bit nippy," the social worker would say, and Don would explain it was healthy to sleep in damp conditions in freezing temperatures with no heat.

"And . . . those aren't real weapons, right?"

"No, no," Don would answer, winking at the machine guns, "we made them. You know how it is; doing crafts is calming. We all have our psychological security zones, which make those affected feel they have some kind of illness they can blame for their inability to function in a socially idiotic context."

"And what do you do when you need a doctor, are you just out of luck if you're not registered?" the valiant fortysomething woman with energetic calves and red cheeks and, one suspects, a sip of liquor in the evening would ask while wondering whether she was breathing tuberculosis-infected air.

"Yep, that's right, you only have access to doctors if you have a chip. But there are tutorials for everything online. We don't need the state," Don would say. "That's why we're here, that's why we have weapons, that's why we've planted potatoes out there and other stuff that will taste like potatoes when it ripens. And as for a bit of tuberculosis—everybody gets that."

But

There were no more social workers. The last one had been rushing around Rochdale before, as if she were constantly walking headlong into a storm. She looked lost. Somehow picked apart and depressed because she couldn't live out her calling to save the world. There wasn't even money for boxing clubs for the area boys anymore. A service that had been very popular. After all, who wouldn't rather be a well-trained criminal? The social worker had sat helplessly at Don's kitchen table looking at the mold infestation and the mother, who had emerged from bed in a dirty nightshirt for the occasion. Through the open bedroom door, the metal bucket where Don's mother relieved herself could be seen and smelled. Don't ask. The social worker had broken out in blotches and said: "So, I wish you . . ."—she had stood up—"all the best, right. I must be on my way." She had hopped up and stumbled over her bulky bag, which was filled with applications for food aid, and was gone. Suddenly,

Three weeks after their arrival

DON

Thinks

Of her family.

Who are probably still hunkered down on bunk beds in the homeless shelter. Mummified. And the social worker has surely transferred into the civil service. The place where middle-aged women who've been sufficiently disappointed by their leftist ideals always found a home.

Up in the sky a drone approaches with the typical lawn clipper sound. Don tries to blend in with the floor. Private drones had been banned by then. If you spot one of the little comrades on the horizon these days, it can be assumed that it's a government surveillance overflight. Drones. Right. Don sits up and thinks she'd like to smoke a cigar. Just because it would make a cool image. And to poke around in a campfire with a stick. Don likes the night. She likes to be alone at night, nothing to do, as if she has things figured out. She likes the night and the idea that millions of people are lying down in the city, dreaming of solutions.

Like

CARL

HEALTH STATUS: *high blood pressure risk group*
POLITICAL ATTITUDE: *conservative*
POTENTIAL FOR MANIPULATION: *easily susceptible to right-wing propaganda*
SEXUAL ORIENTATION: *porn*

Who had worked as a foreman on the building. Until he'd been replaced by a Polack. Which is why he's against Islam. And against all that shit. For which Carl has a theory. In his opinion, the imbalance, the lack of respect, the poverty, change as a background noise, all of it was the result of women in the workplace. It stood to reason, after all, that a new generation of mothers had been raised who preferred to go to work rather than bother with bringing up growing—go ahead, say it—children. Carl didn't have a wife. He was ill. He had some fucking disease, the name of which he could never remember and which, given the current state of science, could be cured with a one-week course of tablets. Could be. Which didn't happen, because it was more lucrative to support Carl's lifelong decline with medication. So no more work because of the illness and the Polacks. And now. No idea. Cunts. The latest thing was that they wanted men to have themselves sterilized because the birth control pill had side effects. For example, women on the pill had no sexual desire and got cancer—"Divine retribution," mumbled Carl, thinking that was just the sort of madness that would lead to the end of the world. Women who fucked their way around and men who weren't supposed to come anymore. Carl had lost three molars to his nightly grinding, and he hadn't recovered them in his stool.

Carl

Had for a year now liked to drink milk. He'd seen a report on it, how baby cows are separated from their mothers after two days. Both parties scream. Even cry. Most of the baby cows are slaughtered for meat. Which the mother cows once again greet with tears and screams. Since then Carl drank milk with a grin on his face. He often sat up nights in his kitchen with a glass of milk in front of him, sensing it wouldn't be his kitchen for much longer. Even in the southernmost part of the city, where Carl lived, the soy milk–flat white cafés had arrived, always a sign of transformation. Transformation, right. The streets would be repaved and Zara shops would replace Sudanese greengrocers. And then: See you later! Carl sat in his kitchen and looked into the yard, where he could see a light. In the apartment across the way lived young, urbane people of indeterminate gender with dyed blue hair. Assholes. And Carl sat in his kitchen because he didn't want to sleep, he didn't have enough teeth left, and it was cold, creeping up from his feet, and it was nauseating or at least it smelled that way, and there was nothing but mayonnaise in the fridge, and nothing grew from the walls, nothing grew into something he could disappear into, where he could stand in a glade in the forest and breathe deeply, and then everything began again from the beginning, counting down, and at night Carl counted, there were ten more years, then he'd be retirement age, and then another ten and he'd be dead. His breasts sagged and so did his balls, and he wasn't going to find a wife now. They'd gather him up somewhere along the imaginary walls of the city. What was that goddamn mongoloid poof doing over there in the light? A light that made him restless. A person that made him restless. That woman in homo rags.

Or the other way around. The fact that she was unable to keep things straight. That the restlessness and disorder in her sexual statements had to be dragged out into the world. "Listen up. That thing sits at the kitchen table with blood in the face. I'll show you what blood is." Says Carl. And heads out. He'll give the communications consultant a piece of his mind.

It

Had been worth it.

For the

CHILDREN

The long search. Wandering around various parts of the city, because otherwise they'd never have found this useless district. Just when they thought they would never find a spot that wasn't already occupied by a vacant condo building, they had taken the last tube on their list to the end of the line. They'd passed old rail tracks and ponds in an area that seemed ready-made for ironic dystopian photo shoots. Dystopia had been the big thing in recent years. Everyone was filled with an overwhelming end-of-times fear. Fear-based laws were passed in a matter of days. Laws against: covering your face, gathering, disguising yourself, hate speech. Internet-blocking laws, asset-freezing laws. But all the loving attempts by the government to calm the people, to protect them, hadn't helped. Like ants being hunted out of their colony, or hive, or hill, or whatever the hell you call what ants live in, people ran around scared to death, shitting their pants with fear. Scared of multiresistant microbes, Sharia law, feminization, the abandoning of traditions, poverty, and, well—they were still alive. Fear still lingered in the Western populace's DNA, but it was already half forgotten. Now there was—a basic income. Everything would be all right. Oceans were still rising, the ice caps were still melting, resources were getting more scarce, but everyone had returned to their religion as if nothing had ever happened. The religion of shopping.

In any event, there was

Nothing in the area where the children did their final round of scouting the city. Other than the aforementioned poisonous ponds, a few old warehouses, junk heaps, and motorway on-ramps. The group had checked out a few derelict buildings, old factories with collapsed floors, with rats' nests in the corners or with drafty, horrible karma.

And then they'd found this space.

"Holyroodhouse," whispered

KAREN

Impressed. Indeed a light fog hung over the wasteland, the contours of the factory hall became one with the sky and the world, and the building looked like a watercolor painting of the Highlands. Don opened the door, which didn't even creak. "Please take note of the light in this architectural gem. We've spared no expense on the wood flooring, which is sourced from organic, sustainable forests. Significant, too, is the small but charming brook in front of the property, a feature sure to stand out in any portfolio," said Don in the old warehouse, which upon first sight they knew was the reason they'd come here. A flat-roofed building with nearly intact windows, solid walls, and a wonderful view of—nothing. That was the day the four of them found their new home. A beautiful property. Beyond the gentrification ring. Meaning: a right shitty area. The financial resources of the investor class had run dry about five kilometers from Holyroodhouse.

And now

The sun is coming up. Within the limitations imposed by the fact that this is Britain in winter. Let's just say the sun forces itself to insufficiently illuminate the area.

It becomes light gray instead of dark gray.

The others are still sleeping. It's cold in the hall. Music's on. The advantage of life without legal guardians: listening to music. All day. Listening to grime, recognizing the stars' voices without seeing the videos—Kozzie always sounds like a tin can being kicked across a field by angry children, Ruff Sqwad like heroes, Stefflon Don sounds like she's not afraid of anything, Abra Cadabra sings like he's seven feet tall, with that deep booming voice that lifts you up. That voice that's ruined the larynxes of millions of white men who tried to pitch their voices down until they sounded like talking Ken dolls. Whatever. Thousands of acts, thousands of teens, squatting in masks on top of garages and who wanted so badly to be threats to the world. Who were bored. Who wanted to change the world. But the world has its own plan. It watches the humans, who became too important as a result of the stupid accidental discovery of fire, and who can't handle their position at the top because they're simply too stupid. Maybe the earth is the god everyone yearns for and she will bring peace to humankind and a break from all the self-improvement and growth, and from fucking up every possible thing. She will just raise ocean levels by twenty centimeters, puff out a few clouds, and free herself from all the idiots with a wet ice age.

Right.

Don goes to make herself a cup of coffee in the kitchen—they have a kitchen, well, a stove and a table. None of the children like coffee, but it goes with adulthood. Adulthood. Which had felt better in its imagined form. They had assumed they would all suddenly know exactly what to do. Which is absurd, since most adults are just big children who think that if they wrap themselves awkwardly in clothing and toast with crystal glasses and swirl wine around in their mouths they will be imbued with adult wisdom.

They're not adults. Just little criminals.

"Would you like to tell

HANNAH

How you get money?"

"Happy to. It goes like this.

You find yourself a solitary, average-looking, middle-aged, well-to-do man. You approach him and say: 'Hi, I'm new in the city and I'm trying to find a good swingers club. Not that you look like the sort of person

Who would frequent a place like that, but—

The men are always interested. Always. Blame it on nostalgia for their past virility. Morons.

Sometimes if they look just too buttoned-down, I ask about a good bar that's open late. After a bit of chitchat they always accompany me into some dodgy spot, they start to grope me, they get careless—and Don films it."

DON

Continues. "Exactly, I film it, then I step in, we show the nutter the footage and ask him politely for his credit card and PIN. Usually there're a few hours during which we can relieve their accounts of cash and go shopping in a select few shops.

There's just been a nationwide conversion to cashless payment systems. If our current strategy ceases to work at some stage, we'll come up with something else."

They always come up with something else.

That's the upside of a childhood without parents putting on Mozart at dinner, without a father admonishingly saying: "Sit up straight, Benedict." The advantage of growing up without the limitations of a so-called education, without the active imposition of moral definitions and without any inculcation of a sense of right and wrong.

Children driven in opulent electric SUVs to school and afterwards to go horseback riding or to ballet class, who were read bedtime stories from the collected works of Ovid, and for whom the biggest conceivable catastrophe seems to be the possible separation of their parents, grow up with the idea that the world is a threat and they can protect themselves only with the help of the police. Children like that would stand helplessly in front of the cold heater in the case of an EMP bomb and they'd be the first ones eaten by the rest in a nuclear bunker.

One can say this for an absolutely solitary childhood: a fearlessness surrounds the four children, who had learned that it could always get worse, and thus they fear nothing. No panic during a power outage or a flood, no tears when there's nothing around to eat, the four don't believe in the system. They don't believe in the fucking system and trust only themselves. People who survive a childhood without love, in poverty, surrounded by brutality, do not expect any gifts.

They just get by.

And

Don

Is satisfied.

The hall looks almost

Well—

If sunlight were to stream through the leaded glass windows it would almost be romantic. The children have pushed their mattresses surprisingly close together. They could easily have a huge amount of privacy in this nearly four-hundred-square-meter space, but they lie close together around a TV, with green plants scattered around. A homemade table of brick and boards, stools.

Once they'd declared the hall their hall, the children, who are no longer children but adults, who drink coffee, had taken great joy in furnishing their life. The ark is now very well equipped. One of the first donations from a friendly mid-forties man had financed the solar panels on the roof,

Eventually, in a clumsily constructed garden, potatoes, cabbage, carrots—and all the other shit nobody wants to eat—would grow. Nitrogen fertilizer—you know, the magical stuff that multiplied the world population a thousandfold. For a few weeks they were busy getting money, shopping, transporting things by tube and bus, moving things around, covering the furniture with doilies, and now inside the hall and in the area in front of the hall it looks like the home of mentally ill, nudist survivalists.

Once their existence

Is sufficiently furnished that they're able to comfortably hang about, they start the search for the people on their now expanded death list, in order to give their days structure. All of the idiots have posted photos of their surroundings and their acquaintances on some stupid social media site or other. All the idiots have websites with the appropriate registration info and IP addresses. All except Thome. His registration is listed as a boarding school and signed by his father—politician. Cheers. Sorting out all the results takes a few hours. A few hours' farewell, during which they order weapons, listen to music, frantically watch the latest tracks,

And then

They close their laptops, and, after a tender caress, the children put their smartphones and devices in a trash bag. Smart watches, GPS, tablets, all that stuff.

Following instinct rather than any well-informed wisdom, the children had decided to bury their devices. Beneath an old shed. A good distance away. They stand around the grave transfixed for a moment, then silently make their way back inside. Each feels as if a body part has been buried. And it doesn't even rain that day. Endless emptiness lies before the children. No mail, no Google Street View, no Tor browser, no Instagram, Twitter, Snapchat, no online shopping, no way to stalk anyone—especially that: no way to stalk anyone. No movies, no music, no contact with the world. After just ten minutes the first signs of withdrawal appear. Hannah's fingers start to tremble, Peter sweats heavily.

I represent for the jobless, that have been made redundant
That have got four kids and don't know how to fund 'em
Ever since the wife and her husband
Both lost their jobs at the office in London
Now they feel financially trapped
Now they're locked with rats in a dingy old dungeon

Devlin on the turntable. In an endless loop the next day. Cold turkey—no news upon waking up, no looking at photos on social media to kill time, no weather report, no searching the name of some idiot, and no music. No. New music. It's as if the days are suddenly too long. Don starts to hug trees outside. But there are no trees. The withdrawal drives Hannah to reflexively look at her hand as if it were holding a phone, and then to bite her hand. Karen stares with wide eyes at the ceiling and scratches herself now and then, and Peter rocks back and forth. The devices were home, brain, confidence, and a life purpose. Had been. Now there's nothing. Don distributes small doses of heroin (Victoria station) during the first few days in order to keep the group calm.

After a week

HANNAH

Tries

To find peace by taking walks. She's grown recently and now constantly stumbles over her limbs, the length of which she hasn't gotten used to yet.

Taking walks is completely useless if it isn't connected to looking at shopwindows. If it isn't connected to the acquisition of products. Such an obsolete activity is unimaginable. Long gone are the times when families had Sundays off and traipsed through various forests with the goal of reaching some gastronomic establishment to consume drinks or pieces of cake with other families or individuals, happy that something has happened other than being with oneself and the trees. For modern families there were no Sundays anymore that would allow time for such useless undertakings. You always had to work. Either in the service branch or in preparation for a fulfilling Monday of work. The only people with time for taking walks are the unemployed.

The unemployed.

The unemployed are the rejects of the ant colonies—ants again, isn't there any other metaphor? No, what would ants do with ants who sat around the house and smoked and scratched their balls all the livelong day. Unemployment isn't really intended in human life, unless you're part of the upper class, and then you have to represent. Represent the upper class. The value and tradition. Be a role model for working people of how stupid you can look while idle. Which inevitably leads to golf or alcoholism.

Speaking of which, thinks Hannah, the history of humankind is a succession of contempt, degradation, and cruelty. The easiest to hate are animals. Animals, say humans, have no feelings and are dumb, they're things. Animals will be eaten.

Children are not people. If they can't work, you can scald them, lock them in the cellar, chain them to radiators or abandon them. Or kill them before killing oneself. Women can be raped, splattered with acid, burned; you can shove broomsticks into them, you can buy them and fuck them and piss on them, you can lock them up, you can dictate what they should wear, when and how they bear children, you can stone them to death. Other people, whose skin is different from your own, are not people, they are objects that you may despise, they're dumb (see: animals). And if they resemble each other, people, as far as status and gender and skin color and income, then they hate each other because they are neighbors, because they think everyone else is stupider, deem them less dignified. So, do something, do something with these people whose expiration date is set from birth.

Who would want to walk around in the company of such beings?

The others, real people with employment contracts, who don't sit stuck to a sofa somewhere waiting to die, go crazy while taking a so-called stroll. The body, accustomed to speed, produces stress hormones. Nobody can take it with their overtaxed muscles, with worn-out synapses trained only to digest short info captions in seconds.

Thinks

Hannah.

The things your brain will speculate about when your fingertips are burning with desire for the touch of a keyboard. My goodness—just look at this place. Hannah has been walking for fifteen minutes, and the area looks. The way she pictures the surface of the moon.

The user interface is defective: you see here the detritus of long-ago progress. That's the absurdity of the earth, that because of gravity, everything you put on it just stays: the skeletons of old factories, rusted fences, plastic waste, unidentifiable metal junk, liquids that turn ponds green. An old pharma plant or a brewery? Or a trout farm? Hannah had never walked so far. Behind the former trout farm was another factory. And inside glowed

A light.

THE FRIENDS (BEN, KEMAL, PAVEL, MAGGY, RACHEL)

MENTAL LIMITATIONS: *various obsessive-compulsive disorders*
CLINICAL PICTURE: *psoriasis, actinic dermatitis*
HOBBIES: *bad food, gaming, uh—nothing else*
TECHNICAL ABILITIES: *satisfactory*
AVERSIONS: *Marvel movies, fascists, the ruling class*

Had gotten lucky. When their old clubhouse sank into the ground, they were asleep. All of them. At home at their various parents' places.

The old clubhouse had been in the cellar of a building in Tower Hamlets. The building is gone now. The whole thing went down like this: Chinese investors had bought the extraction rights for some Scottish oil and natural gas. In order to transport these resources, a subterranean pipeline was to be built. The Chinese had slightly modified the plans of Elon Musk's hyperloop. How. Only they knew. Gas, oil, and passengers were to be carried in seconds from the north to a newly built port at Canvey Island. That was the concept, until that Thursday at about quarter past noon when substantial parts of the tunnel imploded. Twenty-three people lost their lives—approximately. Two hundred buildings were sucked into the abyss. Which entailed only moderate financial losses because the pipeline route ran for the most part under social housing projects. So much for the disappeared hacker space of the young people who, because of a lack of acquaintances in 1.0 life, call themselves "the Friends." The Friends have established rules for membership and talked a lot while looking at the ground to live up to their designation as Asperger-afflicted nerds. They exchanged notes about programming languages, their devices, servers, racks, cryptography, and soldering irons, and they were so excited, indeed still are, that there were other people like them. Outsiders who, because their sense of outsiderdom was so strong, felt a calling to fight for all outsiders. They'd found a mission that was bigger than themselves. Young people who stutter, who are incapable of looking others in the eyes, who have no connection to other sorts of people because none of them have a clue what other sorts of people talk about. Concerning the 20 million IP addresses that had been blocked by the government in the last few months. "WTF is an IP address," they would ask, the normal people, with blank looks.

The Friends. Who now sit around an old factory celebrating the collapse of the financial system, because if not for the country's market restructuring, this area here would long since have been developed into condos and organic cafés and yoga studios. They'd found it in the course of a targeted search. Very much like the climate mission GRACE, which supposedly measures the earth's gravitational fields, primarily looking for disappearing water resources so that Western military forces can be deployed to places in the global south in order to keep people from fleeing drought-prone areas. Similarly, the Friends had looked for interesting data on the cloud from the most popular fitness tracing app. And found this pearl on the edge of the city. Not a soul jogged here. No heat cluster, no network. Meaning: there were no surveillance cameras here. Meaning: there was nothing here. No animals, no drones. No drones linked to robot dogs. Nice neighborhood.

MI5 PIET
Chokes on a sip of pinot noir.

THE FRIENDS
Have been busy for two days setting up their infrastructure again. Stealing electricity, server, network, cables, and so forth, all the shit you need to have the virtual world up and running. Now stand up and introduce yourselves!

That's Ben; he's already eighteen and supplies the group with money. He tests corporate IT for vulnerabilities. And in his free time he's trying to develop a decentralized network. Which he'll probably manage to do in fifty years. Well, maybe. Or maybe not, because he doesn't have millions at his disposal to hire a swarm of top programmers to set on the task. He doesn't have millions at his disposal because nobody who has millions at their disposal is interested in a new internet. The old one is working just great.

That's Maggy, who's very young and has problems with people. Well, actually, people have problems with her, as Maggy is too heavy and too manly to fit the social conventions that determine how a young girl should look. Rachel, over there in the corner in the plush coverall with bears' ears, is just fourteen and doesn't like to talk. Talking bores her. She's also not too good at it. She constantly has cold fingers and chews on them while staring at the internet—it's warm there. Over there are Kemal and Pavel. The children of some immigrants or other, groups that have started to be hated of late, and for good reason of course, because they're to blame for global warming. And privatization. And tax evasion in the Cayman Islands.

These are: the Friends.

Who are angry at society but don't know who they mean by that. Who talk about anarchy but don't know what it is. Who pine for action but mean things online. They're the good guys. Whatever that means. There're also the others, the bad guys.

Everyone has logical-sounding explanations for the state of the world. The Vatican, intelligence agencies, the Koch brothers, if they're still alive, and if not, the people who represent the Koch brothers, a coalition of free marketeers and old Nazis—someone is to blame. Someone wants to usurp global power. Their minds won't tolerate chaotic situations and rule out coincidences. The Friends here are looking for a hold in a parallel world, because the real world is unbearable when you have a bit too much intellect and also too little to just blow out the candle. Save the world. Meaning, actually, themselves.

Ben has a theory that all the agitation—the terror attacks, the mutual antagonism among the citizenry, the Nazis, the hatred of foreigners, the unrest—was just a diversion from, well, something. Whenever he's almost able to grasp the answer to the big question of Why, he's distracted. By some bridge he needs to solder, or some new information from some hacker about the fact that you can now infiltrate a computer via electric circuits or an aquarium thermometer. It seems they are hammering against concrete here. So to speak. With a bit of encryption against almost all governments of the world, all intelligence services.

"Cute." Says Hannah when she sees all the flashing devices and the little rough-and-ready soldered robots. She had followed the light, entered the factory, a visit to the neighbors, so to speak. The Friends' distrust of Hannah lasts only a few seconds. Until they notice that Hannah doesn't exhibit the intellectual capacity for an espionage job. That she's a user. And with that the group's interest is extinguished, the attention span stretched excessively. It's back to staring at computers.

The Friends had once believed they'd win. That their numbers would continue to increase. The cool new youth movement. Though they hadn't considered the fact that nerds don't wear erotic clothing or that the masses had no clue about technology or politics. You can't dance to technology or politics. The Friends grew less numerous rather than more. Their people disappeared more and more often. Into prisons or mental health facilities. Too much information isn't good for the human brain. They know that the so-called internet isn't just a place where people watch cat porn and search for travel deals. They know that everything is online. Electrical infrastructure, traffic controls, stock markets, world trade, trains, life. And that all life ends when systems are attacked. Or when raw materials for the manufacture of computers are no longer available. They know that there are wars over these raw materials. That they are called wars against terror. They know that people are manipulated online, that people are monitored. At all times. That their voices and bodies and mails are faked, that lawsuits are brought and that malcontents are eliminated. It is serious. It always had been, but in the past it hadn't been life-threatening. When they fought against intelligence services. They'd done incredible things and celebrated online. Leaked secret service data banks, hacked the fingerprint scanner of a smartphone manufacturer, proved that every five minutes access was granted or an arrest was made based on glitches in algorithms. Right, and so forth. They had believed they were the next revolution. And now.

They sit here. In this shitty factory. And don't know what to do next.

Virtually nobody had been interested in their revolution. What people don't understand, they don't care about. They care about terror. Which is why attacks by random fundamentalists take place regularly. After such attacks, people are all too happy to let themselves be x-rayed, stripped, and filmed before boarding an airplane. Nobody has anything to hide. The Friends. Hadn't managed to mobilize the masses.

Hadn't deployed an army of bots in the battle for votes over Brexit, hadn't manipulated, hadn't distributed false reports, hadn't set up any fake social media accounts, or done any microtargeting, because they believed in what was right, or what they believed to be right. And now they're sitting among the rubble, a ruin, and don't know whether to stay still or fight, and if so, how. Most of the people they know had surrendered, conformed, watching the nationalist revolution taking place in the Western world. Nearly every little country had voted in a right-wing conservative government with more or less cravenly fascist agendas. In nearly all Western countries it was the men who had carried this revolution to victory.

"Right," said Ben, "the servers are working again."

The Friends are one of two underground movements still in existence at this particular moment in history. Until a few years before there had still been anarchist youths who demonstrated or squatted buildings, who set out to hunt down fascists, who covered their faces and believed they could turn England into another Freetown Christiana, an area beyond the law where carefree young hippies sat around eating vegan mash. The militarization of the police and outfitting them with machine guns had meant the end of that. Squatters had in some cases been chased from their accommodations with grenades, a few children lost limbs. A demonstration was shut down with armored vehicles and live ammunition. It was quiet after that. Since then there are only a few young people who haven't submitted to the system. Only a few who don't believe they live at the greatest moment of all time. The few malcontents who still rap or hack will soon find their place in society, too. And it's good for them. The only way to partake in the successes of a society is to conform.

Whatever.

Most of those who live here in this space are unpopular. Were. Because they don't meet today's standards of human normalization. Because they're too loud, too quiet, too tall, too small, too fat, too thin. They move too quickly or too slowly, they're too gay or asexual, too uncoordinated or too nervous. All were lonely. Still are when they leave the sheltered workshops and with poor eyesight look at the surroundings beyond the net. Most of them want to save the world. A few just want to show off. And all suspect that they won't achieve anything. The superiority of strength has grown too much, or, let's just say, they are gradually realizing who they are fighting against—

Against intelligence agencies, countries, multinational corporations, radical right-wingers, crackpots, conspiracy theorists, and murderers. Where to start? They've barely finished off a Nazi network before thousands of bots mushroom up again. Knock off a few surveillance cameras and through some miracle new streetlamps with biometric recognition systems have already sprung up to grace the motorways with their presence. The group turns to Hannah, trying within the limitations of their abilities to show hospitality.

They make tea, sit down together, and Hannah tells them about the others and the buried devices. The little group, in a room with a gaping hole in the middle of the floor, is happy not to be alone in a strange world. Where at the moment the news is being shown on one of the computers.

There's

THOME'S FATHER

Speaking to the people:

"The reintroduction of the death penalty for capital offenses and civil disorder is an effective measure for the protection and strengthening of democracy. We've noticed that even bringing the full weight of the law in some cases, such as terrorism, fails to create a deterrent effect. In the battle against terrorism we must as a result be able to impose drastic punishments alongside the ubiquitous surveillance of potential terrorists. Terrorists are increasingly moving away from suicide attacks. Perpetrators are surviving attacks with cars, knives, poison gas, which in turn emboldens other terrorists. For that reason we have decided to send an unambiguous message through bold and resolute action."

Jubilation

Applause

Elation

New day. New location.

Back to

HANNAH, KAREN, DON, AND PETER

The markings on whose faces, to undermine the facial recognition capabilities of surveillance cameras, sometimes done with duct tape, look like war paint. They go off to war in their military outfits, overalls, boots, marching aggressively. They love the fact that passersby jump out of their way, they jostle people, they kick, they scare, this is music, this is power. They listen to Little Simz. On a portable CD player. Magnificently retro. Don grabs the mobile out of the hand of an egg carton–colored man and drops it elegantly to the ground, a joy, this feeling of being part of a formidable army.

And so forth.

Arriving at the observation site, the four of them sit down on some steps. They look like the cast of a music video, embodying various parts of the country's unbelievably interesting and multicultural youth. None of the children believes in the mission. None has an overarching sense of vengeance. The past is so far removed that it seems like a yellowed old photo. When there were still photos. When there was still a sense of vengefulness. Vague is the memory of excitement—back on the roof of the homeless shelter, the oath and the motivation. They'd imagined that they'd need a mission in their new life but now they realize this new life is itself mission enough. That it's interesting enough to recognize the transformation of the world and of one's own body. But. The children are human, and humans don't talk about important things. The conversation could be short and everything that followed would move in another direction. "Hey, cops-and-robbers is a totally shite game," one of them could say, to which the others could nod, then they would go home or build a bunker or entertain the idea of constructing an ark. Or emigrating to Iceland so as not to have to attend Europe's downfall live in person. But they don't talk. They sit at the observation site.

Two nights earlier

Hannah, visiting the hackers, the Friends, the new acquaintances, had received more information about their victims, which she had jotted down on the list.

Walter, Don's mother's ex-boyfriend and sadistic failure,
Lives in one of the smart homes on the outskirts of town.

Idiotic. A little hack in the thermostat controls and you already had access to their network and private documents. They learned from the hackers,

Walter is married, a sex addict, and had taken a remote course to become a religious instructor. Address below.

Dr. Brown, the doctor responsible for the death of Hannah's mother, heads up a private practice in a basement office, address below, where he conducts abortions and outlandish cosmetic surgery. Lives in a sublet room (address below) and sexually assaults unconscious patients from time to time. Athlete's foot.

Thome, developer of Dream Island,

Frequent visitor to gay porn sites. 99 percent homosexual. Hasn't come out. Father plans to take over prime minister's office. Just as an aside. Lives in a villa on Holland Park, address below. Works in Silicon Roundabout, failure.

Patuk, Karen's—um,

Owns a nearly bankrupt tailor shop in Savile Row (address below)

Lives in Luton (address below)

Profoundly frustrated. No sexuality, impotent, strikingly frequent visits to Islamist/Daesh/torture/nuclear terrorism sites

Financial problems, single, frustrated,

Peter's mother

The Russian

Villa on Regent's Park (address below), operate child prostitution ring

She visits a fitness club (address below)

Whole Foods delivery day, smart apartment without password, ha ha ha.

Sergej, leader of a paramilitary organization, right-wing radical.

Mini sublet east, on Campell Rd (address below)

Conducts survival training in various parks without surveillance cameras.

PETER

Checks the address. This is the right spot. This is where his mother, according to her log-ins, comes to the gym four days a week. Today is one of those four. But his mother is nowhere to be seen.

Chants can be heard in the distance. A demonstration? What about? They have everything, the people. The weather is, well, yeah, weather. They are getting money, don't have any serious diseases, don't die shortly after birth, their land isn't decimated by locusts, since there are no locusts. Scientists have modified a bacteria to eat plastic. So the world's oceans might be saved. Okay, so they'll be polluted with bacteria. But does that make sense? To demonstrate against bacteria? Speaking of which—where is your goddamn mother, and how are you supposed to react to her? Peter starts to rock back and forth.

Whenever Peter works himself into a state, it's up to Don to calm him down. "We're sitting here planning and thinking about our lives, because we think it's totally important, because every human thinks he, specifically, will enrich the world or even allow it to survive at all. And then comes a meteorite and the world is gone in a flash. Or a volcano that darkens the sky and lowers the earth's temperature to minus ten, and so on. I'm just saying," says Don. And Peter calms down. "We don't have the power," says Don.

"Amen," says Hannah. The four of them stare at the entrance to the Bulgari Hotel. An exceedingly boring street full of Victorian red brick buildings and rich women who obviously work out. That type of women, who seem to live only to fulfill men's expectations, are unknown to the children from Rochdale. It's as if they've been produced by a 3-D printer. Without anything objectionable. Without pores or fat, without cellulite or brains. They'd probably have been influencers or models. They'd thought they could take a shortcut. Have their hair removed and sculpt themselves, and just like that, a sumptuous life would be there for the taking as a reward. But it isn't there; their sumptuous life consists of service and fear. Fear of losing out to the new sex robots can be seen in their eyes with the surgically tightened upper and lower lids. Presumably it's helpful to have deterioration as the only thing to fear in one's life. It makes you so damn stupid. Speaking of which, it smells almost like spring. The holly bushes rustle quietly in cast-iron pots in front of the entrances to buildings where exclusively millionaires live, millionaires who are somewhere else. Sparrows express themselves as well. The sound of sparrows in the big city always produces a vague sense of longing in people. Perhaps for blossoming landscapes and serious songbirds. Karen is reading a book about viruses, Hannah and Don have their eyes closed, their heads leaning together. Peter stares at the entrance. "They're really doing it, the bodycams," says Peter. He points to a large man with a little camera clipped to his cap.

BODYCAM MAN

ETHNICITY: *white*
POLITICAL ORIENTATION: *malcontent*
SEXUAL ORIENTATION: *asexual*
FRIENDS: *not really*

Had picked up his equipment the day before at the newly opened bureau of citizen points.

THOME'S FATHER

Had spoken to the people a few days before:

"Now we come to a brilliant added feature of the chips in your wrists. Last week we launched a new program: 'Social points for a good life.' From now on you can boost your basic income through environmentally friendly, socially conscious conduct. You can lower energy costs by using less heat and showering less frequently, lower insurance premiums with sensible eating and sufficient exercise. You can earn a number of attractive benefits on the public transport system or on holidays if you're willing to engage collectively. Of course, this new offering is strictly voluntary."

Then Thome's father turns away from the camera. He feels an outburst of laughter welling up inside.

And the

BODYCAM MAN

Also smirks. Just now. The point system has been in place for a week now.
And has already persuaded, so to speak, nearly half the population of the
island. Just picking up the equipment (pulse transmitter and bodycam) racks
up three points. Use of the bodycam gets you five points a month. So.

The bodycam looks like a pair of glasses. Google Glass, the great flop of
Intel Glass, and Amazon Glass. Body Glass allows uninterrupted access to
the social behavior of the wearer. No fistfights, no crossing the street on red,
friendly greetings, goodwill in the neighborhood.

Hang on

THE PROGRAMMER

Adds: "And first and foremost access into the areas not covered by con-
ventional surveillance tools. Like alcohol consumption, an unusually high use
of vulgar language, racist statements, the persistent scratching of body parts,
lies, antisocial behavior in cellar spaces."

And

BODYCAM MAN

Is excited about the new possibilities to turn his behavior into cash. His
behavior, which was always impeccable and still is to this day. He had allowed
himself one mistake, luckily before the introduction of the point system. A
mistake that to this day he can't recognize as one.

The bodycam man is a forensic architect. Was. With the help of 3-D models and VR animation he investigated the causes of construction failures and
fire damage. In recent years there had been increasing numbers of fires in social
housing. Brutalist blocks with 267 units, high-rises with 400 units, burned
down just like that.

The bodycam man figured out that all the evidence pointed toward arson.
Since in the wake of the fires the buildings were invariably razed and condo
buildings were then built in their place, it was logical to examine the relationship of the owners more closely.

In the course of his research the bodycam man found for instance a real estate firm that had acquired 357 social housing facilities around the country. Of
them, forty-three had been condemned because of fire and another twenty-one
because of collapsed roofs or load-bearing walls. It must be, well, a coincidence,
thought the bodycam man, but it emerged that the owners had realized a few

cost savings in the run-up to the events. The bodycam man wrote to the housing authority, to the buildings department, to the House of Lords, the prime
minister, the mayor—and subsequently lost his job.

Today, in his new life, he runs every morning, confronted with vacant
luxury buildings standing around as if bored.

Speaking of which. A new business idea hit him upon beholding his new
living situation. It's important to know that he lives in a pipe. Tube housing
was a concept to combat the housing crisis that he had also worked on during
his studies. Nine-square-meter apartments inside concrete water pipes, fitted
with everything a person needed to live: mini kitchen, shower, bed. Plexiglas
on the sides. At first the tubes were installed only beneath motorway bridges
and on the edges of industrial areas. Later they were stacked—up to twenty
meters high—on other financially uninteresting expanses. The bodycam man's
tube lay next to a wastewater treatment plant. At night his home looked like a
beehive. With one in each honeycomb.

One person, that is, of course.

One evening as he looked from outside at all the solitary people in their
tubes, a new business idea hit him, and he became a toucher.

It's like this:

Most people no longer have physical contact. People just don't interact with
other people anymore, and whatever this circumstance offers individuals as far
as peace, the flip side is that it takes a negative toll on the body. They book online, people, check in online, shop at stores with automated self-checkout, talk
to service bots, have food delivered by drones, mail by postal robots. All good
fun. But it causes sadness and loneliness in one's body. The bodycam man understands the body. He's extraordinarily physical. He looks like a two-meter-
tall red-haired bee. He smells like vanilla. And his business is working. He's
just come from a large office where he works once a week. The staff, low-level
IT personnel, have pooled money to pay him. Each of them gets five minutes
of bodily contact. For many, the only contact they experience each week.

The bodycam man hugs, presses, pats. The art is to do all of it without
any sexual undertones whatsoever. For a moment, these tense English people
soften in his arms. Many cry. And afterwards they function phenomenally.
So. Door open, here's his studio. A little cuddling package is available for just
ten pounds, a deluxe session costs fifty. He works nonstop. Weeping oligarch's

wives convulse beneath his hands on the mattress, bankers who have because of stress ground their molars to blackened stubs curl up in his arms, sobbing. When it comes to collecting plus points, the bodycam man's business is perfectly suited. Nearly every customer gives him a good rating. Immediately, with their mobiles. In the points app. Kiss my ass. You can access the public point standing of any citizen online. If someone has accumulated a certain number of points, it indicates a cash value that will be added to the basic income. If someone has no points or even a negative point total, you can reckon with a shitstorm, though a more civilized one than prior to the era of points. Nobody says things like "You should be gassed" anymore; women are no longer called "cunts" and "sluts" and "whores who should have their brains fucked right out of their bodies," because you get points subtracted for verbal abuse. Quiet, disdainful censure by others is almost more painful than the previous vulgar attacks people had been accustomed to. Apart from praise or criticism from the hive mind, the point system is also interesting for landlords, banks, insurance companies, and potential sexual partners. Or not. Every week a Loser of the Week is announced, someone at the very highest rung of the negative rankings. The losers, who appear on the karma points home page, see their status follow them online in the following weeks: with a drop in social contact (people shun losers), with the loss of their flats, their jobs, their heat, their water. Societal satisfaction reaches its apex when such a subhuman ends up on the street after all the public attention. At which stage the point system losers get beaten up. Beating up a point system loser does not entail a points penalty.

Once a week the bodycam man turns off his camera. On Friday. After his final client. And he writes additional reports. Requests. Letters of complaint. In order to bring attention to the connection between arson, unlawful gains, and fraud and murder of the real estate firms. He won't give up.

Good that we persevered—

"There she is," says Peter, pointing at

His, which is to say

PETER'S MOTHER

Who is standing with a group of women in front of the hotel. Maybe they're exchanging dates for some designer sample sale or news of a successful new beauty procedure, and they look eerily similar to each other. They're all thin and have nearly identical facial features. Straight noses, high cheekbones with a natural shine and full but not-unnatural-looking lips. Difficult job for five-factor biometric facial recognition. The faces were constructed by a plastic surgeon using knowledge of the optimal "calculable beauty," an algorithm that has to do with how the various facial features relate to each other and their symmetrical arrangement. And these faces are what come out of it. The women's legs are thin, their breasts firm. Fuck puppets. They think they can control men. That they can fleece them for a bit of sex and feigned love. What they don't know is that men don't care at all what women think. They value the feeling of having bought women, seeing them dependent, they like being conscious of their financial subjugation, their greed. That way they leave the man in peace and don't demand any emotions, which the cruel oligarch displays, if at all, only to people sprung from his loins.

The locations where these types of women mingle always have to do with chrome and liveried doormen. They always have to do with the ostentatious display of money, which should damn well produce a sense of euphoria. It doesn't. But whatever. The means by which the rich shape the contours of their lives is just as depressing as those of the poor. It would seem that people with assets of—let's just say—ten million have to live in a gated community where they learn a standard way of dressing and how their apartments are to look.

The flats. Ostensibly mimicking the royal family, not knowing that the king in exile spends his days with drafty windows and, thanks to the dogs, ratty carpets.

There're always heavy curtains, hanging uselessly in the room, with those tassels. The fucking tassels that you compulsively want to stuff into bodily orifices. The orifices of your parents. Even if they're dead. Also indispensable: an interior designer who buys up old engravings to be resold at a steep markup and sticks them in equally steeply marked-up antique (according to the seller) frames. Hanging things salon style gives the space a sort of eyebrow-raising flair. Interior design is a recession-proof job. Design apps will never be able to miss the tasteful mark to the absurd extent a real person can. Even in a decade of decline, there still needs to be gilt work in a flat. Gold, the immortal burial gift on the voyage to the next life. If it would just come already. The constant stress is no good for the nerves. Peter's mother is constantly afraid. Of having her cover blown. Of being traded in. Of having to go back. But where?

Peter's mother's story of being an oligarch's girlfriend features tedious triv-
iality and humiliating dependence. It consists of blowjobs that Peter's mother
gives the Russian upon waking up. She looks for a moment into his slightly
bulging eyes, then slides down his well-defined, shaved body, takes a deep
breath, and sticks his genitals into the space within her mouth, which has
taken on an unpleasant taste overnight. She read somewhere that according to
Jerry Hall, the secret to a long marriage is to constantly blow your husband.
They love it. Peter's mother does her job. Sucks the appendage. Laughs effer-
vescently. Throws her head back coltishly. Her sex life involves shit-and-piss
games. With piercings and diapers which the Russian wears. But their home
is top-notch.

It's a beautiful villa. Peter's mother works out, keeps herself fit, squeals
delightedly at the Versace dresses the Russian buys her. And the quiet contempt with which he regards her. She wears size 2 or 4. That's, well, that's not
a size 0. The old idiot's forgotten that you simply can't get silicon D cups into
a fucking size 0. Peter's mother. Squeals with delight at the Russian's jokes.
Which mostly have to do with humiliating the staff or making derogatory
remarks about Poles. She thinks: I'll get you. She doesn't think. Of her son.

Unless she forces herself to. Mostly she forces herself to think of her child
while sitting in front of the three-way mirror in her dressing room. The view
of her beautiful, pain-drawn face sometimes puts her in a self-pitying mood.
She cries then. The few times she'd felt something for her—go ahead, say
it—child had been long ago. Sometime before Peter's third birthday, before
he started to become weird, and before she realized there was something worse
than living in a shithole in Poland. That was living in a shithole in Poland
with a fucked-up child. Peter's mother had been so poor that she now deems
it her right to be rich. If that means sucking on a sausage for a few minutes a
day, then please. She's the perfect lover. Good-humored, open to experiment-
ing with drugs. Charming to her Russian's colleagues, a perfect hostess. She
had, as mentioned, had her breasts. And lips enhanced. Every centimeter of
her body is taut and groomed. The Russian's taste has for decades been un-
waveringly old-fashioned. Triple-A women had to look like 2017 influencer-
hookers. In Europe this look was a bit embarrassingly antiquated and betrayed
one's origins in the developing world. Or what the English took for the developing world.

"Show me *Shit Happens*," says Peter's mother to her fucking Amazon Echo device. The latest episode of the beloved BBC show appears on her flat-screen. Ever since the BBC had been privatized, the programs, unlike the unbelievably dreary old garden shows, are supposed to elicit huge interest among the viewing public. *Shit Happens* is one of these shows. People are crazy for it. The show's about the greatest possible humiliation you can inflict on a person. Friends and family members nominate candidates to the BBC, algorithms take care of the rest. Search the net, create a profile, and hit the candidates where it hurts them the most. They take mothers hostage and isolate them from their newborns. Show wives recordings made in a brothel. Show butt plugs in teachers' backsides. People in front of their computers wanking to cat videos. Speaking of which. Peter's mother is beyond humiliation.

She's someone who had stoked the fire with furniture in order to stay warm. Someone whose neighbor had cut a hole in his floor and taken shits into the space above her ceiling, someone who during one hard winter set traps in the woods and consumed highly questionable game. Someone who'd been beaten up by alcoholic Nazis. What on earth could a little Russian, shaved head to toe, add to that? She lets him shove her off his lap in restaurants, smiles when he introduces her to acquaintances as "my whore." Thinks of Poland, which she escaped, while he absentmindedly fucks her, and thinks of the absurdity of humankind. Beneath all the expensive bespoke suits, beneath the table manners, the ritualized small talk, beneath all their supposed importance and irreplaceability, they carry their genitalia. It doesn't matter if a new era has begun for some out there, what remains are humans with their testicles, ass cracks, holes—draped in silk underwear, sat on toilet seats, taken in their hands, cradled, always ready, always on the lookout for a chance to get it on. When Peter's mother is downhearted, when in rare moments she has the feeling that everything she is now living, the perpetual stress over looking good and fucking good, is all for naught, because she takes no joy in her home, her clothes, the view of the park, because she has nobody to share these things with, then she imagines all the people she encounters in the expensive boutiques and clubs as big, smelly genitals.

Then things are fine.

Meanwhile

THE CHILDREN

Have followed Peter's mother, and the home address corresponds to the info provided by the hackers. The first target can be watched.

In order to attack at the right moment

Speaking of which

After

CARL

Had beaten his dim-witted neighbor to death. Well, what does that really mean, beaten to death? He rang at her door, a teary woman opened up. Actually a totally normal young dim-witted woman, as he had noticed to his surprise. Okay, so there was no fucking tranny or whatever standing there, but there was no going back. He punched her. Kicked her backwards into her room, then bit out her larynx and jumped on her corpse. Yep, the woman was dead at that point, and a few minutes later a division of the private police turned up to arrest Carl. One of the surveillance cameras had captured the whole spectacle from outside. And once again the populace was supposed to owe its gratitude as a result. The days when young women were shoved down stairs, old women robbed, respectable citizens beaten up by roving gangs of foreigners, are over thanks to the tireless expansion of security systems. The current absence of aggression in the public sphere speaks volumes. Which volumes? Doesn't matter.

Now Carl sits here, and outside, in front of his cell, preparations are being made for the event. He'll be the first client to have the pleasure of the new disciplinary measures the people wanted so strongly. The referendum had been unambiguous. Eighty percent wanted the death penalty, and all of them had their own image of the bad guy. Kiddie diddlers, woman killers, or perhaps just people who were somehow different.

Carl doesn't understand it all yet. Not the evening of the murder, and not the fact that he is about to die. He understands only his fear. Which floods his body with stress hormones, an ice-cold sensation. He wants to live, and to forget the depressing evenings in his apartment. He thinks of spring, birds, food, all of which will be gone forever, never to take another walk, never—

And

Now the door opens. Two elegantly uniformed women lead him outside. Carl can no longer feel his legs.

In a well-lit room fitted with a range of cameras sit various representatives of societal authorities. There would be enough space for family representatives, but. A judge is there, a doctor, a Plexiglas box, sealed airtight. That's where Carl is taken. Now he loses control of his bladder. Now he sits on the floor whimpering. The cameras broadcast it.

To every screen in the country, on the BBC.

Peter's mother sees the execution only vaguely, as she is kissing

THE RUSSIAN

The Russian shoves her aside like a leftover scrap of food. He's watching TV. The glass box is filled with gas. Maybe sarin gas, who knows. The death throes come quickly and entail convulsions and foaming at the mouth. A camera pans along the corpse, lying curled up on the floor. The first execution is over. People will notice. So.

The Russian goes back to working out. When he's working out, he can forget his rage. He is an angry man. He says of himself: "I'm an aggressive man." He's not tall. And a short man has drawn evolution's short straw. A small man must become rich, become powerful, he must always have at his command the option to have someone killed in the case of disrespect. Thanks to a fatal mix of inferiority and delusions of grandeur, the Russian had felt untouchable. Like so many rich men, he was sure he was the only one able to catch on to things. What things? Doesn't matter. All things. Then a recorded voice message turned up online where he called for overthrowing the government. He was sure it was a Lyrebird fake. His voice had been mimicked by a very intelligent program. That was the latest technology back then, dreamed up by some twat. He also knew that it must be possible to disprove the fabrication, but not if you were sitting in pretrial detention.

So now he lives in this foggy place in a pompous flat and is

Within the ranks of the wealthy, part of the underclass here. The Russian had invested what was left of the fortune he had parked in the Cayman Islands and Patagonia into this piece of real estate in Regent's Park as well as a sex business. Done.

The Russian heads into the private gym and joins Peter's mother, who is working out on a rowing machine. The Russian stands next to her. Peter's mother looks at his face, with its narrow lips and bulging eyes. "What an ugly frog," she thinks.

"You need to pay attention to your figure," says the Russian. "Have you stopped wearing your fitness tracker?"

The Russian sees himself as a nerd. As clever. As a modern man. His apartment is a smart home. He's got the smartest fucking apartment in all of London. Not open source–slash–Raspberry Pi smart, but rather, simply user smart. Even before the sheep allowed themselves to be implanted with chips, the Russian had one. It's how he opens his car, his safe. It's what he opens the lock on his Polack's cunt with, which he secures when he's not around. Little joke there. The Russian is disgusted by his feelings for Peter's mother. He hopes the hormones that turn him into a complete idiot whenever the woman is around him will calm down. When she's not around, he misses her. An unfamiliar feeling. Goddamn hormones. To spite his hormones, the Russian treats Peter's mother worse than his staff. People and their feelings. Utter chaos.

The Russian owns a refrigerator that restocks itself with the help of a Whole Foods app that delivers goods in the blink of an eye. All the home technology runs on a voice command system—the blinds, the climate controls, the music, the lights, the washing machine. The Russian had the first Tesla in the city and now he has the first self-driving car. The Russian loves technology, he loves the feeling of controlling something. The Russian is planning with some experts to transfer his brain onto a chip. The Russian has never grasped that he will die. But he shares this quirk with many others.

Dying,

THE PROGRAMMER

Knows,

Is for losers. Mate.

This is so cool.

The programmer stares at the wondrous monitor, divided into hundreds of little screens. He has set the AI, which he programmed, for interesting optical key stimuli. Keyword: *weapons*, keyword: *sex*, keyword: *violent crimes*.

His little band of thieves, his codes, the extension of his ego, now trawling the world like tentacles.

And still not yet functioning perfectly. A huge amount of boring shite is also transmitted from the delinquents' bodycam glasses. A man who looks like a giant bee—running him against the database, it says he's a former fire investigator who aside from his tendency for troublemaking hasn't distinguished himself—has a woman in his arms. One of those plasticky oligarch's birds, who is resting in the arms of the bee, weeping. Man, oh, man, people. Windbags.

The oligarch's bird

Sobs

Because

For

PETER'S MOTHER

Her longing to be hugged is unpleasant. The man who looks like a bee has barely put his arms around her before she starts to cry. She cries for twenty minutes and can't say why. Or what about. She doesn't know a better version of herself that she could miss.

The beginning. Which consisted of excitement. The four-hundred-square-meter building on Park Square East with a view over Regent's Park, service staff who cleaned the boxwoods at the entrances to the buildings with feather dusters, and Peter's mother thought: kudos, boxwood leaf miners have no chance here. Peter's mother gave the Russian blowjobs euphorically, he fucked her in every room, on every piece of furniture, he fucked her the way she was accustomed to men fucking her. Like a hamster. They drove around in his Tesla convertible. They went shopping, they went out to eat. To the plastic surgeon. It was an exciting time.

In the meantime she has become—lonely. She's grown accustomed to the staff, to the flat, to the delightful private park with its guards. She's grown accustomed to the days at Harrods and Selfridges, to the comfort behind silk curtains, to appointments at the salon, to pedicures and manicures, she's grown accustomed to being stared at, and to the children on the first floor of the building.

Whom she hasn't seen for a week now.

Because of the risk of infection.

One must pay attention.

And

DON

watches the news coverage on a screen while sitting near the Palace of Westminster. The reporter is wearing a mask. First she's in front of an entrance to a hospital. Her voice is high: "Ladies and gentlemen, I'm here at the entrance to St. Mary's Hospital. Behind me you see—

Ambulances, arriving virtually"—say it already—"every few seconds. This is in all seriousness also a moment to be happy about our functioning, right, yes,

Now we enter the building . . ." (The reporter with the too-high voice enters the building.) "My god, it looks like the third world, when it still existed." When the third world was somewhere in the southern hemisphere. When the third world wasn't part of the Chinese colonies. And as a symbolic image you see here the European, white—well, yellow. Dying on the floor. There are patients lying all over the floor, the corridors are overflowing, the staff are outfitted in space suits, and so forth. The reporter has to gather herself, she is visibly shaken. "Children are dying," she nearly screams. And bends over a dying child. She holds herself—unsteady, but stabilized by the task at hand. "Doctor, a moment." The reporter pounces on a bleary-eyed assistant doctor in a protective suit. "People are dying, children are dying. What are you doing, what is the government doing?" The doctor answers, sounding strained behind her mask: "Nothing. We're doing nothing. We're just providing palliative care to give people some relief. We amputate rotten limbs. But. Multiresistant means multiresistant."

Appearances of the multiresistant microbes had skyrocketed, so to speak. Public water supplies are badly contaminated, which could be the result of wastewater from hospitals being channeled directly into the Thames and other public water supplies. Or the cause could be something else. Animals pumped full of antibiotics, antibiotics in milk, in groundwater. And now. Measles, pneumonia, abscesses, norovirus, the flu, infected wounds. All are deadly. Particularly for the aged, the poor, the weak, and children; children are dying. Though principally it is the poor dying. Passersby hurry along the streets with masks on; most people wear gloves. The story of deadly microbes will have disappeared from the media again in two days, the poor and aged and children, children will continue to die in larger numbers, but nobody will be interested; attention spans, you know how it is.

And another ambulance with lights flashing

Blocks

Don's view. She's been watching the activity at Westminster for four hours.

The House of Lords. Or, to aficionados: the Right Honourable the Lords Spiritual and Temporal of the United Kingdom of Great Britain and Northern Ireland. A third of the mummies who vote on the future of the nation are over seventy. Half of the honorable politicians live in London. No point. Unlikely that the infirm gentlemen roam around abandoned industrial wastelands in Leeds or Birmingham holding out a basket in order to cultivate relationships with good-hearted degenerates. The ignoble lord moves between Westminster and his club in Mayfair and his apartment in Hampstead or Kensington. On the weekend he heads to the Highlands in order to shoot a few poor beasts with his trembling hands.

Don is bored. Westminster is one of the saddest parts of London. Open-roofed tourist buses every minute; photographs are taken, for what reason nobody knows, you just do. And not to forget the bridge. Quite creepy. The bridge where earlier cars had constantly driven into tourist groups, catapulting people's bodies into the water, leaving them lying around crushed. Or some-body with a machete or knife went crazy—which stopped happening some time ago. No more terrorist attacks here anymore. Tourists see the world as subject material for photos to be taken on their phones. That is, they don't. Hurray, it's still going brilliantly for me! I can fly from Prague to London for ten pounds on easyJet, push my way across this fucking bridge. Take a few shots on my mobile, then sleep in a youth hostel, get bed bugs, and then tomorrow fly back to my wonderful European city, where I'm doing as well as the people here, who get out of London on easyJet, too, and take a time-out, so to speak, from their many jobs. That's the situation.

Don waits for Thome's father. Observing Thome's environment is for the purpose of figuring out a sufficiently humiliating penalty. That's what they're doing with all the victims. Figure out the weak spots. And use them. To give the idiots an unforgettable moment. He has to come past at some point to get home, since he's an old man. Don can't imagine being so old. In her world it's all over at forty. Forty is the oldest Don can imagine. It must be awful. It must be like being dead. Like standing here and staring.

There's nothing happening. The private police stand at the entrance to Westminster. They look as bored as Don on their side of the street. The two of them have to go work out after their shift. Don knows about steroids. She's seen everything online. The two men are a good two meters tall and must weigh 180 kilos. Each. They probably feel indestructible. Poor idiots. A well-placed shot and they're a heap of dead muscle tissue lying in the street. The tourists would be thrilled.

Don stares at Westminster Palace. She can think of thirty-six other places she'd rather be. The first place would be with Hannah. At home on the mattress. Various places in warm locations, though imagining it quickly becomes boring because Don has no idea what it feels like in such a place. What it smells like and what you do there. Don can't know that hardly any of those so-called holidaymakers, who had in earlier times let the world become an overcrowded place, that none of them know what to do on vacation, either. Since there's always an awkwardness about being in unfamiliar surroundings. How long can you lie on a crowded beach and shimmy through markets; how many T-shirts can you buy?

Which brings us back to the morons standing in front of Westminster, hoping Lady Di will come out of the building. Some of them look at Don and take pictures of her in their desperate search for things to photograph. Don, we remember: war paint, oversize overalls, over which she has on a US Air Force B-3 bomber jacket. Don loves the mildly paramilitary statement of the outfit. She likes that the clothing doesn't offer any clue as to her gender. Don still has the feeling that she's a man, which sometimes makes her ask herself what this feeling is tied to. Most of the time Don feels like—nothing. Nondescript, too small, not particularly intelligent and not overly strong. Sometimes she sees herself from above and wonders whether everyone feels the same way. Whether they, too, feel ashamed about what kind of statement their every movement makes. Don had borrowed a giant book of anatomy. Fascinated and disgusted, she'd studied human remains. The corpses of drowning victims, autoerotic mishaps with deadly consequences, decomposed corpses, bloated corpses. Now she can't look at passersby without imagining them decomposing. That's what is left. Of all the important people who now run through the streets with masks on and are afraid it'll get them. As if on cue, Thome's father enters the scene. The old fool stands on the sidewalk, stretches toward the not-shining sun. His eyelashes are stuck together oddly, like in photos of corpses. Looking at which always made Don wonder: "Why the fuck do your eyelashes stick together when you die, and why is there always a shoe in the picture?" And what about this unusually nice weather . . .

THOME'S FATHER

Takes a deep breath. Beautiful day. Weather fit for a king. He thinks. The spry, nearly two-meter-tall man with a gloriously full head of hair that has turned a sort of piss color, with a rosy, nearly crease-free face and a very small penis, briefly smooths the vest of his bespoke three-piece suit. He has a good day behind him.

Thome's father had been able to convince the House of Lords about a new strategy. Roughly speaking, it has to do with the point system, which he has dubbed karma points, and right of access of some segments of society to basic foodstuffs and medical supplies. The prospect of his vision for a just world being realized during his own lifetime has him in a mood to strut. Thome's father opts to take the hour-long stroll through Hyde Park to his villa. His Hyde Park. His villa. His triumph. Thome's father likes to cite Randolph Hencken: "Democracy is a dated technology. It has brought prosperity, health, and happiness to millions of people in the whole world. But now we want to try something new."

Thome's father is a great admirer of Richard Thaler. The two hoary heads share a disdain for the irrational, utterly moronic masses. Thaler is a cofounder of Nudging, a brainwashing method that uses framing and reformulation as an intelligent, manipulative way of lying. He was awarded a Nobel Prize for it by a bunch of old men who later were to attract attention for sex scandals and corruption. Suddenly the masses are constantly manipulated by their heads of state. Take the weather. Everything cold has for years been negatively portrayed as an anomalous emergency. The permanent spring and summer heat as normal. This reduces people's fear of climate change. This system of dumbing down now just has a name and a Nobel Prize. Thaler was the godfather of the breakup of the EU. Thome's father really didn't believe in the EU. At its core, the EU was, even for him as a neoliberal, too much. Too blunt, the idea of control behind it. It was all too clear that the goal was to allow Germany, this still occupied nation, to become a superpower again. Thaler, incidentally, had inspired in Thome's father the idea of karma points. The word *inspired* made Thome's father purse his lips. Inducements, controls, getting rid of cash, dividing society, total surveillance, militarizing private police. Thome's father wants more. Wanting more gives him a feeling of limitlessness. The foundation of this desire for more is vulgar greed and the urge to hoard, an affliction most wealthy people have.

Thome's father has a plan. That he had come up with at his club, along with a few colleagues. Boy, had they been drunk. The Earl of Caugingham pissed into the umbrella stand. Which he had mistaken for one of the wait-staff. "One must govern the country," Thome's father had said. "We already do," answered the Earl of, wherever. "Govern correctly," said Thome's father. The earl shoved his phallus into his trousers, which he did not close. "One must make Great Britain a place of tradition again, liberated from filth," said Thome's father, looking at his colleague's open trousers and the white sausage that seemed to beckon from the dark.

On that night years ago, a plan was hatched that still stood the next morning. One must again marshal people's fear. Thinks Thome's father. Hire once again Harris Media, a toxin-spewing PR firm from the USA, in order to give fear a face, buy a few newspapers, hire a couple online manipulators, and call his friends. Friends in business, in government, in media. The content of the campaign is simply brilliant, and nothing more than a somewhat optimized rerun of the Brexit number; basic principle: fear. Alongside the desire for sex, the fear of death is the biggest trigger for people, as idiots would put it. There is nothing that can't be sold by the clever activation of fear. Thome's father just needs to come up with an idea as to whom he can use beyond the Muslims to raise the level of fear. Because they aren't so stupid, the people, so as not to notice that while withdrawal from the EU succeeded, the foreigners are still here. They have British passports. The idea that at least 80 percent of the citizenry is as dumb as rhubarb seems drastic. Though it is accurate, the earl knows. And he knows how to win them over, this silent majority, and how to unleash them. A raucous leftist minority had for decades compelled the majority toward civilization. Introduced the curse of political correctness, of embracing others as you would yourself, and so forth. Though people's empathy doesn't extend beyond themselves, and most can't even manage that. And then, owing to the new openness, people were supposed to celebrate gay marriage, let women abort babies, sort their own garbage, save water by flushing their excrement just once a week, and in exchange for all this effort people got: nothing. Or more precisely: less for their money, less money, and in the end the total assurance that work alone is insufficient to finance a life if that work isn't to do with programming, biotech, research, the defense industry, or big pharma rather than with some antiquated 1.0 bullshit.

The people.

Thome's father is turning seventy-one. A fact that with the help of his new wife he does not forget. The birch in the forest of his inner sense of death. He doesn't think to look at his body next to hers and ask himself what excites her about nuzzling his liver spot–covered skin. He is a man who doesn't question why a woman would fancy him. He assumes his manhood is sufficient reason, and nevertheless asks himself in the company of the Russian what actually connects them, him and this woman who could be his granddaughter.

Thome's father clears his throat in disgust, there's a vagrant sleeping on a bench. The city is full of them, almost as objectionable as the Muslims. Thome's father freezes. He has an idea. He's speechless, his heart beats double time. He practically runs home. Ducks into the entrance of the private road where his family seat is. When he sits down at his desk, he excitedly sketches out a campaign that has just occurred to him. He hears the door open downstairs. His son.

The only disappointment in his life.

That was nothing.

Says

DON

By the fire in front of

Holyroodhouse.

Hannah puts on music. That, too. That, too, is a human trait, to cover everything up, drown out any quiet in a room or in a mind with noise. There is a difference, after all, between you shuffling across a concrete floor to go to the moderately clean toilet and then grabbing some sour milk out of the refrigerator and hearing all the ridiculous human noises you create, which make clear that a human is nothing more than an organism that needs to be fed. And using music to turn your life into a track.

And while we're on the subject.

The children have tried to make music themselves. To become grime stars, a collective, Ruff Sqwad 3.0. As in

Hoods over their faces, the intro to a Lady Leshurr track in the background,

Bobbing their heads to the beat. Don began to read the lyrics that she used to have on her phone but now, now she's standing there with a piece of paper in her hand and her handwriting, which she can barely read because nobody writes by hand anymore and

If you want hate,
You can have it,
I'm staring at you but you won't look.
If you think that we should die,
Then I guess you just don't get it.
This is the downfall of the people,
that's already gone on too long,
This is the world of the living dead.

At that moment Don ended her attempt—that is, her career, so to speak. She had suddenly seen and heard herself, to an extent, and it was incredibly embarrassing. The others stopped awkwardly bobbing their heads. "It's not going to work out, eh?" Hannah had said.

"Somehow I don't want to comment," said Karen.

"Maybe we just need to practice a bit more?" Don said to herself but knew: no. Hannah and Peter had already gone to the kitchen, they silently began to peel dinner. The kind of stuff you peel. Instead of scary gangster rappers they stood in a moldy jerry-rigged kitchen peeling proletarian vegetables. Don was disappointed in herself. Disappointed in the day about which she had dreamed of giving interviews in the future. Interviews about the moment. When something magical happened. But. There was no fire waiting to burst out of her.

"Too bad," says Don, now back by the fire in front of the building. "I guess we'll just have to keep being criminals." The others nod. No career after all. Just staring at the fire, staring at the sky, and trying to come to grips with the fact that they're nothing. A few dots on a little planet hurtling through infinity.

MARS

Which you can't see. But it's up there, up to the left. And soon people will arrive there. Yay, people.

Good luck. And

BEN

We may remember him as one of the Friends,
One of the nerds, who is sitting at his computer in the new hacker space,

looking at what's happening on Mars. Living environments are going in. A covered oasis is being built. Which brings up questions. The questions are: Can the will to survive defeat the gratification of shopping? There are, after all, no Dior boutiques on Mars, no electric limos, no gold cigarette lighters. Instead there are palm trees, lakes, pelicans. Why pelicans? Anyway it certainly looks more compelling than the little egg carton modules that had been planned for a bunch of idiots. The idea of staging a reality TV show with poor bastards running a dress rehearsal for the billionaires fell through. They couldn't even line up some white trash willing to stagger around the craters in permafrost with no return ticket. So now it'll have to be done without a test run, now there'll have to be a way to get back, now it'll have to be the luxury version. So people who were instrumental in the destruction of the earth can ruin a new planet. An exclusively male club. Based on what you hear, the first inhabitants should arrive soon, in the next few weeks. Musk will be there. Musk is always there. His leg begins to twitch. Ben can't concentrate anymore. Of course, he never could for long unless he took Ritalin, but now he's barely able to stay on one topic for more than ten minutes. They can't fucking concentrate on anything anymore. Three years ago they had begun to rebuild the entire net. As a computer-to-computer network with no centralization. Peer-to-peer. A genuine alternative to Tor, which from the start hadn't been prepared to fend off powerful intelligence services with global capabilities. So then, build a new internet with a few activists who are still nearly minors. Do it even though the other side includes highly funded secret services, the FBI, Homeland Security, Mossad, and whatever all their brethren are called, who are kitted out with the most expensive programs in the world. With budgets in the billions. Some days it seems hopeless, this idea of saving the internet. And barely anyone is even interested in it; people don't understand how a mobile phone works, much less the internet. You push something and you can post a picture online. Cool.

Ben's legs begin to twitch. As always, whenever it occurs to him that everything they're doing here is just to avoid surrendering. Forgot that. Which is easy to do online. So that you melt away, you idiots, so that you get hooked, without creating any medical costs. Without lying about on the street covered in abscessed needle wounds. The not-so-intelligent disappear, along with everything they represent, even if that isn't much, online, rendered unable, or perhaps they were always unable, to read long texts, understand complex information.

They live as headlines, churning at the speed of instant news updates. The more clever go insane as a result of the amount of accessible information. Ben and his friends are inclined toward going insane. They're inclined to lose themselves, to become computers. The constant stream of information through implants and metadata stored in synthetic DNA, and the deficiencies of AI and multiresistant diseases and conspiracy theories and bitcoins and quantum computers running through their brains without leaving any traces behind. They don't know where it's all leading, though they have a feeling that it won't end well, this endeavor to digitalize all spheres, and the effect of this is that your limbs twitch. Ben stands up. Since he's been able to think he's wanted to save people, protect his friends, everything, he just didn't want to be a man. Ben had a deep, physical aversion to taking on the designated role as a lackluster member of society. He didn't want to booze or fiddle around with his penis, to speak derisively about things he didn't understand, and most of all he didn't want to become some fucking scatterbrained idiot. Until recently the men he knew distinguished themselves by the fact that they wanted power and that they pushed people onto train tracks. Every week approximately seven people were pushed in front of oncoming trains. Just because it was possible. Every week paramedics were beaten up, police, nurses. That's over now. People have calmed down. They get points. Assholes. Speaking of which, a nice hacker space has taken shape here—as always, with a sofa where pizza grease can be wiped off, servers, a refrigerator full of energy drinks to help stay awake, and some heat lamps. The others are lost in their screens, and Ben says: "I'm going to stretch my legs." He stretches and walks toward the full moon, little ponds create noises that are almost romantic, the gurgling of putrid gas bubbles replacing what once would have been the sound of frogs. Whenever Ben is without his devices, when he is alone with himself, he descends into such deep despair that he can barely move. What is the fucking point of wandering through the landscape with this body, sitting with one's thoughts, staring at walls, and

How long can you live like this?

It is all

KAREN

Can think about. How long is this all supposed to last? Strange thought for a fifteen-year-old, a member of the merciful age group that assumes every-thing is eternal, right?

Karen cowers within sight of the factory and is too much for herself. Her thin arms wrapped around her thin legs, white hair shooting up to the sky. Karen looks as if she has just landed. From somewhere else, fallen from Musk's car, which is careening around as space junk. Her face glows, it's a child's face on a stretched-out alien body. Karen rocks back and forth and looks over at the fire. There the others sit, they're hopelessly far away, on an island of nor-mality. She hears their laughs, their low voices, they're trying to rap. It won't amount to anything. Karen tries to breathe but it's difficult. At least once a day she falls into a certain state. She's developed such intense fear of this state that she tries to take shallow breaths and move slowly because she doesn't know what sets it off. It always starts with shooting pain in her abdomen. Like she's survived an operation where they removed all her innards and her body is remembering it. After that comes despair and rage. Karen is furious. Rage is her second name. She stares into the half-darkness that reigns over the city. Shite area. Even by British standards the immediate environs here are breathtakingly ugly. Old barrels, old corrugated metal and chain-link fencing, rubble, scrap metal, factory runoff ponds, the empty streets—what the fuck is wrong with the world? Is there nowhere beautiful? Or warm? Is there nowhere with people in normal relationships? Where people pass pastries and run their hands over each other's heads? Karen knows about the power of endorphins. She has experienced it. So much hate now surges through Karen that she has to stand up, because she's afraid she'll explode otherwise. Karen knows that the cause of her fucked-up life is to be found within her. She doesn't want to grant anyone else the power to have caused her pain. She is to blame. She was weak the day she let her brothers beat and humiliate her. The day she fell in love. She doesn't remember individual people, individual situations, she remembers her rage at being female.

A hand is placed on Karen's shoulder.

She screams. Screams and cannot stop screaming.

You maggots.

Yells

HANNAH

As she stares at the noodles. Noodles. Every day noodles. Young people, practically still children, love noodles. But not every day. Noodles every day until that horrid green stuff outside is ready to be picked. Until they come into some money again, which is increasingly difficult because cash is accepted in barely any shops anymore and cards are disappearing as well. Replaced by the ever-so-practical chips implanted in hands. More and more shops function exclusively with facial recognition. But—

There is a problem.

With, how to put it exactly,

Blacks. White programmers still haven't developed a properly functioning biometric marker for Black faces. They're just too—dark.

But first the noodles.

Ten more minutes. Another ten minutes of staring into the pot of water. "Come on, you maggots, come on in," calls Hannah, and the others tiredly come to the so-called kitchen table. "Imagine we're in a romance film and this is the second date, and here comes the scene in the movie where the man, in an effort to create intimacy, tells a story about his childhood, like: 'Back then I was always with my grandfather at the seaside, and he showed me how to skip stones.' And the woman takes his hand because she is touched by his manly vulnerability.

"I have no idea whether I have any grandparents," says Hannah. Taking another scoop of noodles because she's never full. Nobody here is full, they eat and eat, but the hunger remains, their bodies grow by the hour. The mind and feelings stay hungry. That's it now. Thinks Hannah. Nobody is going to come and make her life into something extraordinary. And the realization that she must do it all herself is so unpleasant that Hannah has to brace herself on the stove. She looks at her hands bracing. The fingers like spider's legs. The truth that Hannah is incompetent and untalented and that she must live with this uninteresting person for an eternity does nothing to improve her mood. They've been here in the city for several months now and none of the grand visions have come to fruition. They've constructed lodgings for themselves as if they were putting up a tree house in the garden, though none of the children ever had a tree house. None of them thinks of apple trees, grandmothers, there are no childhood memories that involve the smell of cake. A place that is safe, where you don't have worry about anything because there's always someone there to protect you.

It goes on.

Thinks

PETER

As he stares utterly emotionless at the private road, until all he can see blurs together into an indistinct slurry of white and green. He wonders if it's possible to privatize the air. Earlier in life, Peter—it is rather sweet when such a very young person thinks "earlier in life"—anyway, earlier he'd not had anything against people. They just didn't matter to him. They could live, who cared. In the meantime, however, animosity had developed in Peter toward most. They're just so unbelievably stupid.

Who needs them? As if they had a sense of their own uselessness, they stand around pubs at night and beg for oblivion. Just a little smoke and alcohol and a feeling of intimacy, Peter had thought, waiting for Thome in just such a pub, which was patronized primarily by men. Hannah had with the hackers' help found all sorts of information about Thome. Education, address, favorite pub, and his fondness for young men, at least if you were willing to attach any significance to his search history.

When Thome entered the stuffy room one evening, everything went swimmingly. Peter just looked at him until he came over to him. They always come. They come like moths, they don't even know what they want from him, perhaps to be touched, perhaps just to be near him, the way it is with beauty, it makes people crazy.

THOME

Has been unable to sleep since that night when he first spoke to Peter. And when he can't sleep, he plays the entire conversation back in his head, every word he said to Peter. Every word was stupid. And he had been sweating. And, when he'd gone to the bathroom, had realized leftover bits of kale chips had been stuck in the corner of his mouth all day.

And now

PETER

Is standing at the entrance to the private road on Holland Park. Security has been stepped up. New addition: the thousand-volt fence. Now in stock: the constantly circling quadcopter drones. The guards are equipped with the latest machine guns and the full authority to use them. The situation is coming to a head, you could say. Online, more and more stories are popping up about the threat posed by the homeless. The homeless and other unregistered total failures as vectors for multiresistant microbes. Or something.

And yet.

Everything seems so peaceful. The charmingly nostalgic double-decker tourist buses make brief stops and idiots take photos of what they take to be English normality.

The scum—that is, the people—can access the city center only after extensive security controls and mostly do jobs that even a robot won't stoop to. Mop under beds, peel potatoes, clean up vomit, disburden S&M dungeons of feces, deliver drugs or prostitutes. The villas on Thome's private road are owned exclusively by senile patricians, one is proud of one's degeneration here, and home ownership is often the last thing that remains. The crisis, you know the story, some crisis or other, the unbelievably bad investments, you can imagine what happens when men who consider themselves the top of the food chain take action. Peter leans against a tree, as if he's doing a photo shoot. Though he has no idea the effect he has. It's not going to be easy for him with his appearance, which evokes something in everyone who encounters him. Desire, hatred, envy, denial, longing—all sorts of things, but inconspicuousness is one thing he will never be granted. The guards look Peter up and down with the utter disdain of those who think they are better off. Are they wondering what minority he belongs to? Blond, yeah, sure, but he's not one of us.

They're stately white men, the guards. But soon they'll be replaced by weaponized drones and robocops. Then it'll be: "Welcome to the gutter, you morons!"

Little golf carts scurry around the private road, driven by drunken patricians who are recognizable by their pale skin, worn cashmere sweaters, and bleary alcoholic gazes. They hate rich Arabs and Russians, they hate Black, brown, and yellow people, but above all they hate the poor. They had believed that if they offshored the jobs of the underclass, sourced their crap from the third world, sold off the rest of the country to foreigners, it would all take care of itself. Then the poor, together with the empty factories, the lousy rotting social housing, the outbreaks, football and foul odors, would simply disappear. This did not come to pass. They're still alive. Like cockroaches. And they're increasing in number. By the hour. Coming in boats, paddling across the sea, reproducing. Somebody has to.

The guards are still staring at Peter, but before anything can burst out of them, something best described as hate, Thome turns up in his golf cart. His ears seem to waft behind him like those of a basset hound.

Nervous, sweating heavily, he drives with Peter past white villas. Each worth at least 30 million. If through a kidnapping or airplane crash a family were wiped out and one of the villas were to go up for sale, the owners' council, parentheses male, because women don't own anything, would advise about suitable buyers, parentheses male. Acceptable are exclusively Britons who can trace their family lineage back at least fifteen generations.

"So, welcome," says Thome. He suppresses his nasal Eton/Oxford/bullshit accent in order to adapt to Peter's level. He squints. Hey, we understand each other. I also squint at animals. Thome hops around his quarters—there are two rooms with an en suite bathroom, probably five hundred square meters—as if he's well and truly nuts. Men in love tend toward excessive oversharing. Family photos, diplomas, sports equipment. Check it out, look at this, what quality things I've accumulated. Thome nearly fell over in excitement. Barely avoiding the Regency furniture, whoops, the round library table. Why do all rich people furnish their places the same way, why do they all dress alike, why do they all look so unbelievably pasty? Thome's limbs are awkwardly attached to his trunk, they wobble with every breath. His face has something horse-like about it. Not a beautiful person. But clearly a member of the upper class. Whose sexual gratification consists of looking at little boys. And now, now he's sweating, and his eyelids twitch nervously. He stares at Peter and wants something, but it isn't clear to him what that could be. Thome, who isn't homosexual. He just doesn't like women. He doesn't want to sexually possess Peter. He wants, well, simply to be near him, isn't that right? Peter is silent. "You can talk, too," says Thome, trying to sit calmly next to Peter. He can barely look at the boy without trembling. Peter has a discomforting beauty that turns people around him into complete idiots. "Shall I give you money?" Thome asks. A surprise turn of events. Peter shrugs his shoulders. He has no idea what the man wants from him. His mission is to find out a lot about him, so he stays, he listens, he finds things out. Peter flows onto the sofa. His limbs sprawl out like a greyhound's, his shirt is crumpled, letting part of his smooth stomach show. Thome is out of his head. He would like to suck this beauty out with a straw. Peter finally says: "Why not." Thome jumps up and retrieves his briefcase. "Would five hundred be about right?" he asks.

"For what?" says Peter, looking directly at Thome.

"Watching, filming, that sort of thing," Thome stutters, pulling more bills from his wallet. "This is the last of my cash," says Thome. "From next week on, all systems will be cashless."

"Thanks," says Peter, very slowly slipping the money into his tight pants. He has no idea where he's seen all this shit, in some movie or report, he smiles.

So this is the wealthy. This is how they live, cloistered away with their ugly faces and their stultified furniture. Peter doesn't envy this existence; his own life is more exciting, more intense, he has friends, he doesn't have to pay for boys to lie on a sofa so he can stare at them. Well, okay—friends. That's something he's seen in movies, too. What Peter has is three other children who are always around.

Thome aims the camera at Peter, he assumes a speaking pose, face in profile, makes a better impression. No chin. Okay. Have to do without. He tries out a speech—he's always trying out speeches that he wants to post online or give to tech journalists. Or to new employees. Or to nobody. He probably just likes to hear himself talk. The sun is shining outside. A rare occurrence to see sun like that in the city. It doesn't make the place any more beautiful. But it is affecting. People immediately feel more hopeful. Hey, you see, the sun is shining after all those weeks that felt like years, there is a sun. Winter will pass, and then things will grow from the earth, and perhaps things will be better for us . . . That's what they think as they frolic on the yellowed lawns of the adjacent Holland Park. Climate change is not having a positive effect on the island's inhabitants. For a long time there's been maybe a month of sun per year, and that's an optimistic estimate. It seems to have gotten colder, probably because for some time geoengineering has been going full blast, as the conspiracy theorists in Thome's circles well know. Sunbeams being reflected back into space, aerosols in the atmosphere. The weather is mild. Bearable. Except in Africa. Asia. South America. Australia. But hardly anyone knows people there. Speaking of which—

"Can you open your shirt a little bit more?" asks Thome, fidgeting oddly.

From invisible speakers comes Schubert's *Winterreise*, which Thome likes to listen to ironically. This German whining. The forest. The griffin. Idiots. Should have vanquished them for good—

Thinks

THOME

In passing

Before his mind clouds again. And he stares at Peter. And is at a complete loss.

But it's good not to be alone anymore, they're visiting the

FRIENDS

Hannah, Don, and Karen are, they're maintaining a neighborly relationship and at the moment are crafting latex masks that biometric cameras can't. Well, you know. They look pretty stupid. The Friends hunch over their devices, looking for a way to get around the power of the chips, because soon it will be impossible to get by without them if you want to participate in society in any way other than sitting in a field grilling rat meat. The Tor browser has been blocked, various activists' pages have been blocked, next some AI will break the encryption of their email. Before it gets to that point, a definitive blow to the system must take place. The cards are stacked against that, you want to say, as more people had taken part in demonstrations around the world in the space of ten years than had in the previous fifty. Millions had demonstrated against their elected governments, against the dismantling of everything, against rent prices which practically doubled every week, against the privatization of the last public resources. They demonstrated against everything, they'd yearned for new leadership, voted for Nazis who had promised. Well, actually nothing and that's what happened. Now it's quiet.

The cooling fans buzz quietly. The keyboards click, lazy conversations about the revolution. "I'm for armed resistance," says Hannah, imagining something under that term having to do with uniforms and weapons.

"And who do you want to shoot?" asks Pavel, who comes from some country where the inhabitants wiped each other out in a civil war. The children think about following up the attack on Westminster by wiping out the City of London, the Silicon Roundabout, banks, insurance companies, stock exchanges, commodity traders, all the typical things that occur to a young anarchist. Armed resistance is set aside as unrealistic. There isn't enough manpower for a cyber war. Founding a political party takes too long. "There's nothing we can do." Hannah looks around the room. The lights flicker, and perhaps these are the last people she will ever see, she thinks. If outside there's a tidal wave coming, the polar ice caps and all that, then she'll die here with these children. Which wouldn't be the worst fate.

"Maybe a revolution," says Ben.

"Exactly, a biological reboot."

It is on this afternoon, which could also be morning, that Karen's idea will be born.

The others are listening to music,

And

HANNAH

Is thinking about her earlier life. Back when there had been responsible adults. Neighbors or teachers who had given hours-long lectures about mediocre music. Hannah had never understood why men couldn't just listen to music and keep their mouths shut, why, if they had to think about it, it wasn't obvious to them that music was a legitimate medium for inhibited people to express their feelings. No, they had to waffle on about it. Every little twitch of suddenly perceived vitality has to be exaggerated. So the Beatles, right, Liverpool, our white geniuses who reinvented music for white, young people. Sting. Fucking hell. Sting. These bands as the most polymorphic, controversial, and magnificent pop musical documents of contemporary society and so on, and then eventually they always, always land on Bob Dylan. The greatest white male poet of all times, who shook the world of poetry with

Lines like

All the tired horses in the sun
How'm I s'posed to get any ridin' done?
(Hmm . . .)

The tired horses, aren't they a metaphor for an old white man? Who at the end of his life is taking stock of his so-called life's work. And what does he see? Nothing. Life fucked them. The old Beatles fans. They're probably driving Ubers, at least until self-driving cars take away that tenuous purpose in life, too; they drive through Paki and Arab neighborhoods and spit in front of every mosque, as if they haven't yet realized that hating Muslims is out. They've given their all: they were in the Nazi Party and deposited pig heads in Arab areas. They were furious, and for good reason, because an old man like that, over forty, can sense that nothing more is going to happen for him.

"Do you have a few chips you could spare?" asks Hannah, snapping out of her thoughts, back to the room, where nothing has changed. The lights aren't flickering, the music isn't playing anymore, the hackers are talking about a plan that has to do with tunnels.

And

MAGGY

SEXUALITY: *ambiguous*

HEALTH QUALITY: *suspended development*

SOCIAL MEDIA: *nonuser*

COMMUNICATION: *encrypted. We're working on it*

The girl, who looks like a boy, gives her three chips. Wherever they're from, they represent shopping. Riding the tube. Going to the library. And to the movies. If you're into that.

Maggy sits next to Hannah on the dirty sofa. She figured out the trick with the chips, or, let's say, the location and surveillance implants, at a funeral. More precisely her grandmother's funeral. More precisely, when her grandmother, who was only fifty, was beaten up by Nazis, and it went like this. Maggy was on the way to a food pantry with her grandmother. That should make it apparent that the pair's financial prospects were negligible. Maggy's mother had taken off for India a few years before. "Don't be so egotistical," Maggy's mother had said to her weeping daughter. "I have to take this path for myself; it'll be useful for you, too, to be able to learn from my experiences later." With that she left, and Maggy moved in with her grandmother in a one-and-a-half-room flat in the south of the city. Her mother now lived in a commune on the beach. Pumped full of hallucinogenic drugs all day, which makes the colors look amazing, and the ocean, man. The ocean. Such a cool setup, and best of all reality just disappears.

The reality

Is that the commune is on the edge of an emergent Indian IT city, the residents of which despise the filthy tourists who take drugs, fuck, and piss in the bushes. Maggy's mother is extremely malnourished, tanned to leather by the sun, and she laughs a lot. Including at the five locals who surround her and toss her around like a doll until she collapses, then kill her with a rock. They didn't even want to fuck the filthy woman.

But back to the grandmother and the food pantry. You could almost call it a family curse, because when Maggy and her grandmother were on their way to the food pantry, they were surrounded by some Nazis, who shoved her grandmother to the ground and then stomped her with their boots. The result was severe brain damage and her demise after a few weeks in a coma. And it's strange—that on the one hand the death penalty had been reintroduced and negative points were given out for fistfights, quarreling with the neighbors, and even giving the middle finger, but on the other, violence against the poor entailed no consequences whatsoever for the attackers. But back to the point. At the funeral, Maggy noticed that chips weren't removed from the deceased. They also weren't voided or erased. Nothing happened, which might have something to do with the excessive demands on IT personnel. Which meant there's nothing more to do than remove chips from the deceased, which is relatively easy, as the dead are of no consequence for capital growth, which is evident in the custody of the dead, in the laughable locks on morgues, in the fact that morgues are not even equipped with surveillance cameras.

The only thing you need to get hold of chips are a blade, bodies, and patience.

Which is something

THOME

Does not have.

For him, this is the greatest moment of his lifetime, in fact the greatest moment since the invention of the steam engine. Everything is possible right now. Every goddamn area of life is being reinvented. By people like Thome.

Another way to put it:

The era of uninteresting men has begun.

The decade or—hey—the millennium, when brain power is more important than banal fame as a rock star or actor. Models consort with unsightly men like Ayers and Spiegel. Applebaum can have anyone, girls masturbate to digital 3-D fanzine puzzles of developers. What a gift, that the world is currently in the midst of a thoroughgoing renewal. Thoroughgoing—Thome loves to intersperse his thoughts with quirky terms. It makes him feel nifty, which by the way is another unfairly forgotten word. Today. The most exciting moment since the invention of the steam engine. And Thome's on the team, meaning: men; meaning: he is one of the men making the transformation happen. The men planning the establishment of city-states on the high seas, the colonization of Mars, and various cyborg ideas of immortality, all of which, of course, always include leaving earth as quickly as possible after restructuring it. "On Mars. It'll work on Mars," calls

Thome. He's talked himself into a strange condition of weightless euphoria. Without really even thinking about it, he has pulled his member out of his trousers and had a wank to his fading thoughts. Peter stands up, takes the mobile phone from the hand of the trembling man. Sends the video to his own device, which is resting beneath a shack almost beyond the city limits.

It's quiet in the room

The silence

Is as heavy as a sack of coal, which

MR. M.

FINANCIAL STATUS: *leader*

HEALTH: *tip-top*

MENTAL CONDITION: *manic depressive*

POLITICAL INCLINATION: *indifferent*

Feels on his chest. It's time once again to get up. Mr. M.'s current life, which is to say for months now, consists of a montage of waking-up moments. "I'm happy to go through my life without saying anything to anyone." This saying, which Mr. M. had nicked from a wise man, white, dead, and which served as his motto, seems embarrassing. Beside his bed—no weapons. Weapons are banned here; the danger of ruining the glass dome is too great. If the glass dome were destroyed as a result of—let's say—a weapon, the residents would have very little time to reach the shelter. Because outside is. Well.

Mr. M. is, as mentioned, a clever fellow, who, on top of it all, had a hand in the fact that people in America are increasingly shooting at each other again, that a vulgar man with an IQ of 98 is president, and that the Nazis are once again proudly staggering through the streets of Europe, singing. He had a hand in making it possible to hate Jews again and to despise the poor, he had a hand in largely dismantling government. Hurray. More impressive than his model railroad, which he reconstructed 1:1 here. Not yet seventy and untethered from the world. Quasi immortal. For those down below. Up here that doesn't matter. There he's nothing, there he notices his perishability. He recognizes it by his crinkly knees, by his scrotum, when he kneels over a woman and his balls hang down nearly to the mattress. The real reason for his presence lies in his overabundance of knowledge. Increasing blackouts are to be expected, and the raw materials for circuit boards and semiconductor plates are nearly depleted. Just to mention a few arguments against the earth. Not to mention increasing climate catastrophes, civil wars, mass migration. Yep. So now he's here. Cheers. On Mars. Beneath a dome. With a giant reactor artificially polluting the atmosphere. Right. He had thought it through carefully beforehand. His wife, who remained on the estate below. For example. Had told him there was no water. No problem, Mr. M. had explained to her. It's possible to divert ice comets from their paths, necessitating a mere circa 3 million tons of fuel in order to change the velocity of a comet by circa one hundred meters per second. You would need only divert circa 33 million comets per week. Well then. In the meantime, water will come from earth. And to make up for the lack of a magnetic field there's the wonderful dome—and the atmosphere. Mars has in essence no greenhouse effect and an average planetary temperature of −63 degrees Celsius. The shit factory under the dome is tasked with discharging greenhouse gases. Though one doesn't yet know exactly what effect the gases will have. Chlorinated hydrocarbons build up ozone, but even if an ozone layer develops, Mars isn't attractive for microorganisms because of the lack of UV protection. There'll also be a problem with the tilt of the planetary axis and orbital wobbles. And the force exerted by Jupiter causes variations in the axial rotation and orbit for periods of 51,000 to 2 million years. Mr. M. continuously ponders these problems. Also as a way to divert his attention from the new reality of his life. Which consists of a group of older men, at the moment there are fifty, with a couple of hookers, hunkered down beneath a glass dome, bored to death. Sure, there are amazing chefs up here, vegetables and livestock are cultivated in greenhouses and barns, nobody has to forgo the devouring of intelligent life forms.

Mr. M. wakes every morning—well, actually, he wakes up at some point in artificial warm light. He washes up, he talks to his virtual assistant, it plays Frank Sinatra for him. Frank Sinatra. He could eat him up, he loves him so. The feeling, the elegance this great musician embodied, combined with white, superior manliness that oozes out of all of his songs. Mr. M. has a light breakfast and heads out to golf. Ricochets don't threaten the glass dome. He runs into a few interesting men while golfing. Unfortunately Ray Kurzweil died last week. To the end he hadn't managed to digitalize consciousness. He had so hoped to live on in the form of a chip. He departed bitterly. Now he's gone, they had him buried outside the dome. There are a lot of machines here. Funny Boston Dynamics dogs, which can also kill, in case aliens, ah, what nonsense. Nobody here believes in aliens. Mr. M. plays golf, then it's off to the club, then to the pool, evenings at a restaurant for a little chitchat with the scientists who are trying to help the men produce offspring by means of cloning. Live on at least a little. Mr. M. cannot imagine that all the IQ points assembled here will simply disappear upon their demise. Hastily buried on a planet where meteorites constantly rain down. It sounds like hail. It sounds like home. Down on earth. This shit is no fun. What is the point of being better than others if the others aren't present? When his mood bottoms out, he calls the hooker. The women live in a space at the far end of the golf course. A woman comes over in a golf cart. When Mr. M. sees her, he becomes nauseous. He's finished with all the women here. They no longer excite him. They're not worth slurping down a Viagra and imperiling his health. Though obviously they have a first-class medical facility here with the best Indian specialists. Why Indian? Doesn't matter. None of it matters. Mr. M. is so hopelessly bored that he begins to scratch himself bloody. Before he steps out of the dome onto the surface of Mars without a protective suit.

You can't see Mars
From below. From the outskirts of the city,
There where wolves once lived,

DON

Is preparing
Dinner.

"Potatoes?" asks Karen, who is sitting with the others on the terrace, which is to say, a muddy bit of garden they've covered with a tarp from a freight truck. Of course potatoes, potatoes are always passed around the fire. In the half-darkness, the building lit up yellow from within, whatever did they use this space for in earlier times? Back when there was still an economy that wasn't online. Perhaps this was a warehouse for spare auto parts, or maybe they manufactured rope here, who knew. And who needs rope or wire or watering cans or jam jars anymore? Nobody needs real products when there's no real life anymore, just a nervous waiting on the state of things. The potatoes roast over the fire. The young people stare at them. Like a group of English teachers at Stonehenge.

> *Down, down*
> *Yellow and brown*
> *The leaves are falling*
> *Over the town.*

Silence. The fire crackles sporadically as potato peels pop. Planting food is such a *The Day After Tomorrow* thing. Youth in paramilitary outfits, dirty and armed, gathered around a fire in the middle of nowhere like in an old cyberpunk comic. Back when young people still had time for so-called youth culture. "Anyone want another potato?" asks Don, breaking the tinnitus-like din of the distant city that is otherwise broken only by helicopter rotors.

They're coming again, thinks

ROGER

HEALTH CONDITIONS: *high blood pressure, aquaphobia*
CONSUMER BEHAVIOR: *irrelevant*
SEXUALITY: *none*
POLITICAL SUGGESTIBILITY: *very receptive*

Who is sitting by the river. It's dangerous by the river, but at least this way he can keep an eye on it. Under control. He can react. That way the fear is bearable. The fear he's had since the flood. Although—fear doesn't adequately describe his fundamental feeling of discomfort. Roger has lost his inherent human confidence. The self-conception of existence that protects one in daily life. Roger reckons with the very worst at every moment. Since that night, when he still had a little house on the sea, up north. The night when he was watching television and suddenly had wet feet, the night when the water slowly rose and all the neighbors stood on the street until their ankles, knees, thighs were submerged, it'll recede. It didn't. Then came the helicopters. Since then he starts to scream whenever he hears the whoosh of rotors, since then he can't get the vision out of his head of the life that sank in the flood. For years the residents of his cute little town on the sea had resisted. Had trekked to London with cardboard signs, protested against carbon emission trading, warned of global warming; they had no idea what exactly it all meant, or whether it really was the cause of the changes in their world, but somebody had to bear the blame. All these boring, abstract things that mostly sex-starved old ladies demonstrated about, things that gave them a purpose in life before they were composted, all of it had burrowed into Roger's cells. That and the knowledge that people had destroyed him and his home, his life, just because they could, was comparable to what people experience during a war. The loss of faith in oneself. And the world. So Roger sat by the river. He knows that he is nothing. Insignificant. With no rights. With no purpose. From afar, noises—

HANNAH

Puts on music.

Cheers to retro turntables. As always, there're new rappers daily, somebody somewhere, in some social housing block, is always trying their luck at becoming a grime star. This movement turned business. That's had its rage sapped and replaced with Gucci. Never have so many people tried to make art as now, with the basic income making everything possible. That's what had been predicted, that people finally freed from the drudgery of work in the digital era could pursue their creative urges. Now they're all sitting around, building ships out of matchsticks or shooting pornos. Speaking of which, there are no more birds. Either they've all died of boredom. Or they've all left the island because they wanted to have a look at other places. "What would you guys think of me contaminating the groundwater with a virus?" asks Karen. The children try to play dead. They're worried about getting a lecture from Karen. It's no use. Karen starts to speak. Only a few disconnected sentences make their way into the brains of those present. ". . . obviously you have to do it again, if pregnant mothers drank uninfected water during their pregnancy, you have to redo it," Karen is saying now. The effect is irreversible because the virus stays in the brain cells and they cannot reproduce.

Don pretends to doze off and accidentally

touches

Hannah's

Leg.

Hannah carefully pulls her leg away, because she doesn't want to be touched by Don's extremities. That became clear to her last night.

When they made a young-persons' outing into the city. A grime party in Wimbledon. Too flimsily dressed so that the youthful flesh looks good, too well lit, bad music from the sound system, paper cups on the floor, disappointment and too many freezing youths waiting so hopefully for a miracle. The same since all eternity. Young people with hormones that cloud their thinking, who today nervously show pictures to other young people in dating apps even though the other young people are ten meters away. The great hope that the answer to all questions would emerge and they could escape their awkward bodies to heaven, where something wonderful would await them. "Fuck, she's too close," Hannah had thought when Don stood too close to her, and it was suddenly clear what that meant. What all the looks and touches from Don meant. Then it got dark and loud, and finally the moment arrived, the moment of that "we're young and love life in a perfect fusion of body, youth, and lust" feeling. People kissed in the hallways, they groped each other in the crowd, the music was the way they themselves wished to be. Fearsome. Quick and dangerous. And there stood Peter. He stood there like a lighthouse. Sex. Popped into Hannah's mind for no apparent reason. An embarrassing word, because sex was

The only great freedom that remained to most people. The freedom to buy cheap shit and to fuck. There was so much sexual intercourse in spite of declining sperm quality, more than ever before. Hobbies thought long since dead, like S&M, gained mass appeal. Everybody was sitting around tearing at their genitalia, visiting swinger clubs and dark rooms, giant sex parties in every corner of the city.

And nothing had changed in the communal life of the wonderful digitalized modern people. There were no points deducted for an exuberant sex life. Agile sexual curiosity was more or less rewarded. You could in essence fuck your way to your next bonus holiday.

Before the basic income there had been an ever-growing number of frustrated men who gathered online in incel forums. Involuntary celibates, in short: men who were unfuckable. And who do nothing other than create a worldview based on the annihilation of women. Now and then the hate posts became deeds. One of the unfuckables went out with a knife and stabbed passersby, went on a killing spree at school, or strangled a prostitute. But that was over now.

The hate suppressed using plus points that allowed you to fly to a European city. The hate that had reigned for an entire decade disappeared.

Even in the club, where, of course, surveillance cameras hung in every corner, things went down peacefully.

Like always. The brilliant night, when a miracle could have happened, ended with Hannah sitting on a toilet seat cover, music and bass from outside, feeling alone, as always.

Hannah's scalp shows through her hair; she cuts it so short that sometimes she wounds herself with the scissors. Hannah would love to look like a Ken doll. Cast without gender attributes. She'd like to be made of plastic and invulnerable. She'd like not to be touched by Don. Hannah opens her eyes. The sky is yellow. That'll be the new day.

On which

KAREN

Sits at a café in the city center and waits for the start of her lecture. It is an early morning in the city, with all the sights and smells that can thrill a contented person with the deep satisfaction of living at the right time, in a well-functioning system. Electric transporters bring deliveries for shops and restaurants. The sun is nearly visible, it smells of freshly washed sidewalks. People who still have jobs head enthusiastically into shops and offices. Every one of their steps is a cheer: I am needed. So much has changed so quickly that most people's brains just hadn't realized and continue to slowly operate in another space-time plane. The only thing connecting people is that there are no more dreams. There's no "If I work really hard I'll be able to buy a house, or go on holiday, or find a love that transports me away from reality." People reside in the here and now. That's fucking *ZEN*. They get by. Their eyelids twitch. Perhaps most of them will die off from being overwhelmed, and a new race, the strong, the dull, the loud, will keep going on a planet that will then need to feed only two billion people. Perhaps the world is at the beginning of its decline. Possibly there were plans to wipe out a large part of the populace. One would get used to it. The viciousness of humanity as the status quo is always something one can get used to. The chaos before an old order collapses has subsided.

"You're doing great, right?"

THE AVERAGE ENGLISHMAN

All data under LM62810228
Somewhat sluggish midsection, mild form of alcoholism, nationalistic, minor sexual
perversion, loves Britpop, football, gardens

"Yes, exactly, nice of you to ask, right,

One comes to understand the new order very quickly. I have, that's right—I had drunk very many beers, cleaned up garbage off the street, at night, and bathed drunk before dawn. I've parked illegally, given people the finger, not visited my mother in the nursing home. So. No big deal. Then suddenly the water bill tripled. Same with insurance. These two bills alone ate up my basic income. Meaning no food for a month, except the leftovers from mum's nursing home cafeteria. No tube, no bus, walking and hungry. Believe me, you learn quickly. Look at me today. I follow the rules. It's not so difficult, and it pays."

And

KAREN

Looks at the people in front of the window of the café. Only rarely does she manage to find anything joyous in the faces of adults. Their heads look like those of lizards. Speaking of which,

Today is one of the key lectures at university,

That's how people say it. Key lecture, key speech, nothing works without keys anymore. The key lecture about adenoviruses. By this point Karen sits in on lectures at University College London nearly daily, among hundreds of young people who don't have anything even approaching her mental abilities. But Karen can't attend university. Not officially. Not with a scholarship. A degree, a PhD at twenty. Her own research team—not going to happen. For that she'd have to register. And for that she'd have to have a chip implanted.

Karen sits alone on the bench. The others shun her, the others watch her. They stare at her. If a famine were to break out, she'd be the first one to be eaten.

The professor explains the effects of the fascinating virus. "If you infect pregnant women with the virus, the fetus will also enjoy the virus's effects. The virus will thereby be able to overcome the hematoencephalic barrier. The placenta is another story, but the Zika virus demonstrates that this, too, seems possible, even if no one as yet has been able to figure out the mechanism. However. Today's problems, having to do with violence, depression, drug addiction, criminality, would disappear from the world after one generation."

The professor takes a deep breath. Almost dreamily she looks out the window at the sky. The students don't understand a word. Except Karen. Karen is excited. What she's learning matches a prediction. It's the confirmation of her theory.

"Alongside reduced aggression and sexual listlessness, those affected should be able lead a happy life, even if not a sexually active one."

"If you are ready,

I am, too," Karen greets the lab director later. A wispy crane-like fellow with a giant Adam's apple. Over forty. That is, from Karen's perspective not just old but long dead. After she had the idea about the virus, Karen befriended the man, though that's overstating it since the friendly contact is one-sided and verbal only. Karen is allowed to use the lab when it's empty, and she can order some shit using the lab director's account. It's of no interest

To

THE LAB DIRECTOR

INTERESTS: *A collection of miniature living rooms in matchboxes. Trading pornographic images of underage females*

CRIMINAL ACTIVITIES: *stealing used underwear for sexual stimulation*

CONSUMER INTERESTS: *see 1.2*

"So, where exactly am I supposed to speak into?" asks the lab director at the interview to determine whether his contract would be extended.

By now, in almost every sector, Precire-based software makes the decisions about. Everything. Personnel, actuarial science, court verdicts, death penalties, the granting of loans, acceptance to universities, schools, kindergartens. Sure, incorrupt and finally gender neutral. The AI system breaks down the voices of lawbreakers based on thousands of vocal frequencies of people whose personalities had been investigated for months. It inexorably determines the character, weaknesses, strengths, and it errs only 0.03 percent of the time. That's only three hundred people out of a million who. Well. "Right, I guess I'll start talking," says the lab director. Then he waits for an answer that doesn't come. Just him and an empty room. And overly bright light. That was never eliminated, overly bright light, even though the opportunity to do so existed.

"I'm very good at my job. A terrific lab director. A still youthful, ahem. I don't look over forty, because. Nobody ages on the inside, it would be unbearable if one were to notice how time was slipping away, and realized that it was all a big joke, this Life, in which everyone believes a big yellow bird will come and reveal the meaning. Nothing comes. No bird. The only enjoyable thing is the fact that you barely notice the way time passes, because most people are just filler, tiny cogs, meaningless, not even affixed to the earth's surface. Just organisms. Goddamned organisms. Over forty. The time when most people, unless they're complete idiots, know whether their way of life, whether chosen or stumbled into by accident, works. Most people I know and with whom I don't intensely interact are nose-diving. They're getting out of shape, losing their hair, they're quickly trying to have a child, getting divorced, being broken up with, they stand around morosely at gay parties and worry that all the dreams they had for their lives have turned out to be nothing more than a pile of laundry, left wet in the dryer. Nobody pulled it off. Nobody except a few assholes with companies that develop Mars rockets or eavesdropping equipment with cute women's names. Nobody from the so-called middle class managed it. The insurance agents and craftsmen have been swapped out for a new type of person who studied, works in IT or nanotechnology, is mid-thirties, and now partakes of gluten-free food in various downtowns. People like us have clearly not made it. We're the new underclass. And sink deeper by the day into the morass, knowing that we still have half of our lives ahead of us. How is it supposed to go, if somebody like me grows more unsightly by the day, and gets sick, and it's too late to start over, too early to die, one can't just stay in bed, particularly when that bed is in jeopardy, the bed no longer stands in its ancestral location, not since the harassment. Excrement was shoved through the mail slot at my flat, the windows smashed in, dead rats left in the corridor, grime came from the empty flat next door. Twenty-four hours a day. When the water and electricity were shut off, I gave up. Nearly all of my, shall we say, acquaintances, that is people I know from shops and the university, have been kicked out of their flats. Half the city has been evicted, you never know. Perhaps there are a few fucking Russians who'd be interested in the shitholes if you smeared some antique pink on the walls and put up tasseled curtains. And then the usual thing happens. Showings every day. In the end I found something in Luton.

Mate. Luton.

Nothing against Muslims, but. Fuck. So many of them?

It's a nothing part of town. There's not even a Selfridges. Or a normal, go ahead and say it, chemist's. No Amazon or Google shops, and they still use cash. Where the hell do they get cash? What kind of rags are those they sell there, crumpled up old kaftans? Anyway,

That's where I found myself. In Luton, amid large families wearing night-gowns and sacks. The name Mohamed was more common than William, just a random aside. Should I keep talking?"

Silence in the room. White walls. Fluorescent lights no longer hum; today they're energy-saving bulbs that don't hum. "Fine. I'll keep talking," says the lab director.

"During the first few weeks in my one-room flat in Luton, fucking Luton, with a view of the interior courtyard, kitted out with a hot plate, the bathroom had a shower at least, I tried in the good, enlightened way of a social democrat to get to know the new neighborhood. But—

The new neighborhood ignores me. The young men spit on the ground, the women are veiled. Why do they all shuffle about so? Where are they shuf-fling to? Nothing but Arabic script, ugly people, garbage in the streets, they slaughter animals in their flats, flats they've taken away from British people, animals that are probably smarter than they are themselves. No cafés, prayer beads. Demonstrations for Allah. And always acting insulted. Pulling in a basic income, driving a swank car and still whining. More, more, more. And blowing themselves up and driving lorries into people."

Speaking of

Cafés,

They wanted to meet up in the city, Karen and

DON

Who is sitting on a chair in front of one, without drinking anything, why should you always be pouring things into your body, it's really not that exciting after all, filling yourself with liquids, unless it's alcohol, which fucks up your vision and makes you embarrassing. But take heed. Alcohol consumption by the citizenry is assessed favorably, but any peculiar behavior in public spaces, that is, spaces that are for public use but which are actually private, what the hell are you supposed to call those spaces, carries with it penalties that can vary from having one's hot water shut off to a reduction in food allotments. So drink at home. Which leads to the risk of waiting, as a rummy, twenty-four hours at the hospital instead of nine.

Don sits with her legs spread far apart, her arms resting on them, looking at her muscles. Her hair is standing up, Don looks like a warrior. In a children's movie. A glorious baby warrior. Inside the café, which is owned by a chain, because these days everything belongs to a chain which belongs in turn to a multinational firm, and which as a result looks like all its brother and sister cafés, the white-skinned slaves are gathered together and discussing what to do about the Black youngster sitting on a chair outside. Not consuming anything. Who poses a threat, just as most Blacks pose a threat. A thousand years from now, the chance of people not connecting their hate for each other to differences seems low. The city is waking up, the pregnant are waking up, they can't sleep any longer, their bladders, you know how it is. Don has never seen so many pregnant people. As if every woman has been forcibly inseminated, they shimmy off with their round bellies to some remaining service industry job. They shimmy off to cut the hair of IT nerds, to massage them or prepare their food. Abortion carries a risk of up to ten years in prison. Contraceptives are no longer available. That's good; it is greeted with approval by

HONEST MAN

FAMILY STATUS: *single*

HEALTH SITUATION: *problems with impotence*

POLITICAL TENDENCIES: *conservative, well: vulgarly anxious to achieve a status he*
never had

"If I impregnate a woman, so that a life starts, so that something is growing there, put in her by me, in the woman's belly, then I expect her to fulfill her duty. Feed the child, let it ripen, my mini me, that's what I expect. And if, not facing an emergency, she decides to murder my child, and do it legally at that, then there's something wrong with the system." The honest man looks at his legs: they're cracked and red. He scratches them constantly. He dreams of an amputation. Then he could fuck the tarts out of their minds with his stump.

"Right, thanks, we've heard enough."

Says

MI5 PIET

"And it reminds me—

I haven't talked about myself. Which is normal for people in my position. You see, the thing is as follows: When one deals full time with the surveillance of failed life plans, one very quickly comes to the conclusion that there's nothing more ridiculous than opinions or life plans or—doesn't matter—people.

With their so-called aspirations and their priorities. Their conversations and actions, which, after all, primarily consist of the fact that people shit someplace. I can't take anyone seriously. It's a job-related affliction. No psychological shock over the liquidation of a few subjects, no mourning, just—ridiculousness. I observe myself in every act, in every word, in existence. And can barely stand it. Professionally I know that anything of seeming importance can be terminated in seconds by, for instance, imprisonment. A trial or none, a hearing or then again none, a cell, a little torture, an open pit in the dirt, and that's all that's left of us. A helpless pile of biomass. Everyone wants only: sensations they can't fabricate. And they try so hard. Be it through sex or intellectual work, through murder, brutality, auto racing. They try to relocate the excitement that humans lost when they started settling in place. When they started carrying out duties every day. This much is certain, the sensations they wish to reach will never be attained. If they only knew that I don't even bother observing them after a while. That is the true penalty, not even being interesting enough to be surveilled. So

I'll get back to"

DON

Is now surrounded by men from the mobile strike force. Who are asking her why she's sitting there. Don, who tends to be short-tempered, answers them with "Fuck you." The men of the strike force, there're five of them, and they look like killer dolls, order Don to get up if she's not going to consume anything. Don is furious and scared, and together it renders her unable to move. The men once again order Don to get up, this time kicking the chair out from under her. A small crowd of pink-colored citizens has gathered around the incident, awed to be present at this humiliation. People love to watch others in dire situations. The illogical thinking goes, a catastrophe won't hit the same spot twice, so they feel safe if they see another person die. Or get arrested. Or in some other way land in the shit. Almost every day now there are harsh reprimands of Black people to be watched when they sit unauthorized in a private space, that is in cafés or restaurants or in parks or shopping malls. Ever since social points superseded political correctness, the orderly pink-colored populace no longer needs to hold back. They can give free rein to their skepticism of nonpink people or gays or invalids. To the extent that they don't act in accordance with the rules, one can also report them. "Get that rubbish out of here," yells an overly fit man whose suit reveals its shabbiness only on the second glance.

Don lies on the ground; she's not afraid, not angry, she's just humiliated. The men point their machine guns at her. Slowly she stands up.

Raises her hands.

One of the strike force members kicks her in the buttocks.

Everyone's alone. With oneself and one's misery.

A few hundred meters

Away, the

LAB DIRECTOR

Is talking about his life. He's waiting for the end of his interview, he's unsure, glances down at himself, his belly has gotten soft. "I was at the Tate Modern yesterday."

Silence. "Okay," the lab director clears his throat. "I always go to museums before I have to go home. There's no modern art in museums anymore. And if there is, it's only British. And even then, only images of nature. The study of art is like all scholarly avenues closed to most young people. Since the complete privatization. Only super wealthy oligarchs or the old upper class can afford to let a child study art. That's how it goes.

I've had terrible headaches ever since the encephalitis jab," says the lab director, who no longer has any idea what the AI expects from him. And at that moment, the door opens. An energetic woman enters the room. She is the manager of the Human Resources department. "Thanks very much," she says. "We'd forgotten you here. Apologies.

You've spent the last hour talking to yourself. But the good news is we were already able to process your evaluation in the meantime. That is, our program evaluated it, to be more precise. Without considering your gender or your"—a quick glance—"outward appearance, it has reached the conclusion that it would be best for both parties . . ."

A whooshing sound fills the lab director's head.

There are two moments of fundamental debasement in the life of a human being. The moment when one truly grasps one's finite nature. With all the embarrassments that come with it. With all the: What am I doing here if it's all going to end anyway and I'm going to be eaten by worms when I'm gone and everyone else is going to go on as if it is perfectly reasonable to do so without me? The second moment of debasement is when a person recognizes one's mediocrity. Many people are not gifted with the intelligence to be able to really savor this moment, they're just suddenly grumpy, and it never ends, and their hair thins, and they look for scapegoats. That is the instant when people go into offices with knives. The gig is up for the lab director. In a week he'll be out of work.

But until then.

KAREN

Sucks

The lab director's genitals. She has to push up his stomach so it's not constantly in the way. The lab director grunts. In a second he'll put his hand on Karen's head. An extra rush of power.

The fatuous think it excites women to have a flesh sausage rammed into their uvula. Or perhaps they don't even think that much. It's enough to take out their penis. Seeking a feeling of transcendence. They completely lose their minds as soon as there's an orifice in their vicinity. "It was good for you, right?"

Asks the lab director, tucking in his genitals.

"Yeah, it was super, let's do it again tomorrow." Karen extends her sperm-smeared hand, the lab director grasps it. Karen leaves. She notices that she's strange. Has become strange. She's beside herself. And doesn't know how to find her way back to some kind of inner peace. Suspects that it isn't the injustice of the world that's so enraged her, but something about herself. About her humiliation. About her first love. Rage, because she had briefly believed herself to be a normal girl living a normal love story. Only for everything she had planned to suddenly be called into question as a result of a guy with too-tight pants and a gold chain. Karen suppresses the thoughts about the fact that, as with most people, it's not going to be about saving the world but about saving herself.

Karen had

Ordered nutrient solution with fetal bovine serum to culture adenovirus. She'd also ordered via the lab 293T cells for reproduction of the little bastards. With a pipe fermenter, 37 degrees, and a little blast of CO_2, Karen sets up a starter stock of the beasts which she will soon need to transfer into a new home. For today there's nothing more to do. Karen looks out the window— there's an incomprehensible light outside.

Waiting outside is

DON

In that light, which occurs only in areas near the ocean, creamy, pale blue—pink.

After the outbreak of violence which, unfortunately, she'd been at the center of, Don is in shock, as if she'd survived an accident and is now standing on the street, in front of her the wreckage of her convertible. Nice cue, thinks god. A few Russians glide past in an electric sports car with the top down. Nobody at the wheel. Probably for the best because they're drunk. Bad Eurotrash music coming out of the giant speakers. The Russians laugh, pass a bottle around, and hold their arms up in the air, a move they probably picked up in the primitive music videos that people like them enjoy. They're all wearing designer combat clothes. Camo with golden trim. It's the thing of the moment. Uniforms. Fatigues, gas masks. But ironic. With gold. People love it. They want to survive. Want to look as if they've been to battle. But nobody knows what they should fight against. Everything's calm, after all. The Great Replacement—whereby whites were to have been displaced by Arabs—hadn't happened. If anything Europe had witnessed an increase in Chinese people buying up properties in so-called prime locations. The Russians, too, are barely noticeable on the street anymore. Karen's eyes follow the people living out their own promo film clips. The others are still not happy.

The city is full of tense people for whom the basic income hasn't provided genuine peace. It just isn't enough. The money just isn't sufficient, even though the official numbers are so brilliant. Thanks to the basic income there's no more unemployment, for instance. Thanks to minijobbers and job-hoppers and minicontracts and temp work and

JOB NOMADS

HOBBIES: *gaming, making videos of themselves, being free*
HEALTH CONDITIONS: *bad teeth, sleep deprivation, trouble concentrating*
POLITICAL TENDENCIES: *none.*

Who live a truly free life. Well, kind of. And who are constantly being visited by BBC camera teams. Used to be. Before. When there were. Bye-bye.

In the Philippines, for instance. There sat young, urbane digital natives in front of rental houses, always in flip-flops, always with tattoos and beards, well, like, building websites for consultants and motivational coaches. That is, for the unemployed. And they would say: "I work hard, I'm available for my clients 24–7, but just look at this setting." The camera pans to simple, good-hearted natives, who've just robbed a bank. Are there even banks in the Philippines? Perhaps they were just members of a terrorist organization. But these days the digital nomads aren't even sitting around with terrorists in Guatemala or Malaysia but in warehouses in Leeds, gathered around a campfire, and the only things in working order are the charging stations and the server and internet. Anyone who can use a computer is doing some shit or other online. Mostly content managing or building bots that are supposed to get people to do something, when in doubt getting them to shove a poker up their own asses. It works.

"Come on," says

DON

She pulls Karen along behind her, whose face is paler than usual, and usually she is very, very pale. Karen looks as if she's asleep. And dreaming. Dreams are a neglected arena for the children. Other than imagining themselves as grime stars (Jet, Rolly, Brilli, Bling), hardly any pleasurable experiences occur to them that they might lose themselves thinking about. What are they supposed to dream about? World peace, ecologically sustainable housing, functional sewers, or saving the earth's climate? Nobody knows what the matter is with the climate, which had earlier been constantly used as a threat in various scenarios. Nobody had been interested. Warmer is better. Now it's even warmer, and it rains more often, and the water can't soak into the ground because it's too parched, soon millions of people in distant parts of the world will disappear. Or want to. To go to nicer areas. So far, so good.

In the park, the first few homeless people are setting up to sleep for the night, or at least until anxious citizens chase them off. Don and Karen walk through the masses of people who are moving along the streets in order to enjoy their lives. Yay, hurrah, enjoying life. Going out to eat in the city, a little celebration of daily life. Come on, let's indulge ourselves. Come on, we'll run into other people like us, people in our social strata, who are in a position to partake in a tasty pad thai with organic bean sprouts for £6.70, who can afford to have people, in this case a cook and waiter, work for them. The slight excitement at being able to decide between rewarding and penalizing. About rating the waiter, which follows after payment occurs. "Would you be so kind as to rate me?" How good that sounds, that submissive tone and the fear in his voice, something they the guests recognize in themselves, as they, too, are all rated at their jobs.

Don and Karen haven't talked to each other. Don hasn't said that it is more and more unpleasant to stay in the city with nonpink skin. Karen hasn't said that she plans to sterilize all men. They don't talk, they walk. Slowly. Because running or other hectic motions lead to alarm and the dispatching of drones. Or strike forces. Deep breaths, movements. Hoods pulled down over their faces, they stumble over one of those moronic delivery robots,

Which, instead of the

COURIER

HEALTH CONDITIONS: *varicella zoster virus, spleen problems,* HIV
SEXUALITY: *heterosexual*
QUIRKS: *crying fits when looking at wet dogs*
FAMILY STATUS: *very much alone*
HOBBIES: *lying about*

Distribute Alibaba's wonderful wares these days. The tons of shoddy rubbish made in Bangladesh and the Eastern Bloc, you know how it is, the stuff people would virtually go insane without.

XIANG MAI

The products that people in the Western world buy are, surprisingly enough, made in Western countries by Western workers. Twenty years ago, the first Chinese workers arrived in England on tourist visas. We say simply England, but they also arrived in Spain, Germany, and America. In every country that used to be considered rich. They went to run-down areas. They went as cheap laborers. Slept on the floors of warehouses, worked twenty hours a day, didn't bother anyone. The next step was for them to open their own companies. Where they worked twenty-two hours a day. The companies grew, brought recovery to regions long since thought dead. A mafia developed, a Chinese middle and upper class developed in Europe. The Chinese take care of the fixed assets, distribution, expansion, structure. The Europeans work. That's how it goes.

THE COURIER

Was a courier for ten years. Had been. He'd started during his university days (literature and education—WTF?). "I like to be around people," the courier said. "I get to exercise my legs and be out in the fresh air." He said, unprompted. To other couriers. Because soon he broke off his studies because in order to afford his studies he had to ride his bike so much that he had no time left to study. Yes, well. There were no jobs for literature graduates anyway. Nobody read anymore, either. "I'd love to read a book," people said, unprompted and a little sheepishly, "but—time." Of course, time was spread thin. There were online chats to be had and houses in Costa Rica to look at, hate comments beneath articles nobody read, and after that TV series, TV series. Series that prepared people for actual conditions. Everyone remembered—like the cherry blossoms in grandpa's garden, which they never had, that is, no garden and no grandpa—the wonderful effect of a good book.

In the meantime the courier was over forty and in excellent physical condition, as long as you look past the bronchial infections he contracted during the era when the cityscape was still dominated by combustion engines. And if you ignore his HIV. Which had been totally ignorable. The medicine is infernal stuff, but

Then the health system was revolutionized.

Something that

THOME'S FATHER

Emphasizes in one of his talks in the House of Lords: "Too much inequity marked our previous health system. The costs to treat the so-called uncooperative members of society, who wantonly endanger their own health, fell on the shoulders of the common man. The system is deeply unfair. With the new system, each person pays what they should. You're hardworking, keep yourself in good shape, don't take drugs, don't drink? Then you are like ninety percent of the population, who up to now had to pay for the ten percent of spongers. For people who engaged in overly prodigious sexual activities, who put parties and drugs above the willpower it takes to lead a healthy, responsible life. Now that the free primary health care has been eliminated as a result of abuse by parasitic foreigners, the fair system of health insurance . . ."

And so on.

THE COURIER

has not received his medicine for a month now. He is no longer able to pay the premiums for the new, wonderfully fair insurance. He already had pneumonia, but he's getting by at the moment. If you look past the Kaposi's sarcoma lesions on his face.

Right. Suddenly he was unemployed, the carts and drones, you already know all about it, and as an unemployed courier in his mid-forties, his chances in the labor market—mustn't grumble. The courier had been one of the first in line to sign up for the new basic income, he was one of the first to have a gorgeous sum of money land in his account every month. That's something. The place where he sleeps, on a sofa in the southern part of the city in the three-room flat of a single mother with two children, costs three hundred pounds a month. Insurance comes out of what's left. There's 150 pounds left over for him. It's possible to get through the winter on that as long as you cut back. As long as you don't get another bout of pneumonia.

People are becoming ever more sickly. You see them without prostheses, sitting in little pushcarts on the sidewalk, with sores on their faces, missing teeth, everywhere, and they're back again, the measles, shingles, and polio. Shit happens. The courier's doing fine so far. He rents the sofa at the single mother's flat from eight at night to seven in the morning. The ex-courier leaves the flat at seven in the morning before the single mother gets the children ready for school. When the ex-courier steps out onto the streets of the city's south side after seven in the morning, he's never alone, regardless of the weather conditions. There are other ex-couriers and a striking number of old women hanging about the streets. The usual faces. Raised three sons on their own. And not one of them became a grime star. The grizzled old women, who are forty, kicked out of a council flat by one of the sons, these women, who huddle apathetically, extinguished, not a spark of rage in their gaze, which is okay, nobody would see it anyway, the people who are still able to walk go past them quickly, don't look back, don't want to get infected, everyone is so scared. That the promises that were made to them of wonderfully partaking in the exciting dream have not been fulfilled is clear to everyone at this point. Before health care reform, broken-down homeless people were patched up in the emergency room and put back out onto the street. How inefficient. Now they just die. Losers.

From all the entryways, ex-couriers slip out with looks of helplessness on their faces. How long can you sit around a playground without attracting attention, how long can you loiter in a shopping center? How long can you wander a train station, sit in a park, look at shopwindows? How often can you go to Hampstead Heath on the bus? You can go to a VR space once a week.

Virtual reality rooms are the amusement arcades of the new era. Nobody goes to put on embarrassing goggles and play shooter games anymore. A lot of people go on holiday. They lie on the sand and travel to Thailand or South Africa. With breezes, aromas, the whole deal. Finally multisensory. To touch, feel the breeze, the warmth of the sand. The ex-courier likes above all else to go the rain forest. He loves the rain forest. Once in a while someone turns up nude.

So. Seven p.m. Another day spent bumming around. Watching time slip away. Is this how it's going to be now? It really will be like this until the ex-courier dies—without any role or function, together with all the others with no role or function, who jam the streets with too little money to travel the world, to shop, or do whatever else you've learned to do to avoid thinking. This thinking. What's the point of it in the end?

The courier stops. A placard. How 1.0 is that? A prepper group advertising its next meeting. To be prepared. Next weekend in Colne Valley Regional Park. The courier has never been there. The class is cheap. The instructor is named Sergej. I'm going to do this, thinks the courier. In his excitement, he nearly trips over a delivery robot.

Nobody complains about the delivery robots anymore. At the start, all the obvious symbols of the digital revolution had a hard time of it.

They were kicked, thrown into the Thames, and then suddenly you had points subtracted for that sort of thing. So now people just stumble over the white robots darting about, equipped with cameras.

DON

Also

Stumbles over a delivery robot.

They've reached Savile Row, the lovely museum of a street from the old days, back when the latent homosexual upper class had peacock-like clothing made here. In one of the little, semi-elegant shops for bespoke survival uniforms, a light is still on.

Overtime is being worked.

For

PATUK

Lives in Luton.

He hasn't landed in a town house in Mayfair. He lives in Luton, because friends of the family live there, too. He lives in a little flat above a butcher shop. He likes the smell of dead animals. He likes death. He doesn't like much else in his life. As mentioned, it has gone poorly. Patuk has his own business. At an address that any tailor would kill for. He likes death. The Mount Olympus of gentlemen's tailors, a *Michelin Guide* five-star rating in street form as far as bespoke tailoring. Patuk owns the smallest business on Savile Row, the best address for dapper men's suit since 1740. It's on Patuk's business card.

At the end of his apprenticeship, Patuk had taken over the shop with the money he'd earned honestly in Rochdale. He had believed it would be a short hop from embossed business card to membership in an elite club. Which would in turn lead to a house in Belgravia, where a useless British upper-class spouse would be permitted to spend her days on the sofa with migraines. But. Unfortunately. Even his employer during his apprenticeship didn't have it easy. He came from a country created by the British—they had given birth to the Pakistani tailor, so to speak—which conferred on him the status of a farm animal. For thirty years, the owners of other tailor shops greeted the Pakistani with a tip of the cap and a contemptuous downturn of the corners of their mouths while simultaneously smiling. No people on earth could ruin a smile like the English. No people represented so starkly the concept of a class system. And have yet to overcome it to this day. Just as in the bombers there were only two ejector seats for the two upper-class pilots while the third man, the engineer, a commoner, had to reach the ground without a parachute. That's how Patuk felt. He's the one without a parachute. And now—

The businesses are slumping on top of it all. The wealthy are investing in personal security, weapons, and houses in other countries so that if the situation, whichever situation, comes to a head, they can relocate. The old middle class, which could indulge in a bit of bespoke clothing as a status statement, no longer exists. The tourists are hordes of losers from all over Europe. The rich Chinese have stopped vacationing on the island. They own it. Beyond real estate, corporations, automobiles, and whores, the Arabs who still live in London have no interest in the culture of the natives; British fashion is not ostentatious enough for the Russians; and the IT billionaires dress in athletic gear rather than like daft poofs.

At the start of his apprenticeship as a tailor, Patuk had been surprised by the colorful fabrics worn by British upper-class males, whose female counterparts came across as particularly dowdy and shapeless. Since then he's come to better understand the deeply rooted nanny-cult system of the upper class. Women here have to resemble governesses to attract any attention from their sexist spouses, in whose minds the only women who exist are prostitutes and strict governesses, who are also somehow prostitutes.

The men don't come anymore, and Patuk will never find his way into the city's elite, into the company of men's clothiers who keep company at their own private club, White's Club, or some other club, any other club for god's sake, because even in a three-piece, herringbone tweed suit and a bespoke cotton shirt he doesn't look like a gay man of the upper class but rather a gay maître d'. On his computer, Patuk looks at his surveillance video appearances of the last few days. A service that was enthusiastically welcomed by the people. You scan your chip and immediately see in orderly sequence any surveillance clips where you played a role. Alongside that is your current point tally.

Patuk was at the shop yesterday, which is documented. He had two customers. Who ordered shirts from the bargain fabrics. Then he went home. Patuk looks at himself on the screen. He's gotten ugly. From a young man handsome enough to have starred in any Bollywood film if he'd been Indian, he had with absurd speed turned into something that could be stuck to a rubbish bin. His scalp shines through the sprayed-on hair. Sweat gathers in the glistening bald patches, then runs down his face and neck, across his chest, and down to his stomach. There the rivulets stop. His stomach isn't large but it's hairy. A belly button people make fun of, one in which you could hide servers or fruitcake—

"Look how his bell end shines,"

KAREN

Had

Said yesterday.

They'd been at the hackers' place next door. They'd watched videos from the old thumb drive.

Patuk having a wank next to the mattress where Karen lies unconscious. About ten men stand in line ready to shove their penises into Karen. Karen, who is obviously underage in the video.

When the video ends, uncertainty fills in the room. It's not every day one sees a friend lying on the ground while various sets of genitalia pass in and out of her.

And now

PATUK

Notices

As he's watching his videos that he had several points deducted yesterday.

His antisocial gasoline-fueled motorcar is to blame. Every vehicle owner transmits data to the insurance company upon entering the vehicle. And to MI5. There are no bonus points for that. It's mandatory. Not being surveilled by insurance (and MI5) means no insurance. But—Patuk is a careful driver. And for that he gets a point. A small accolade amid daily life, how good it feels. But—a gas-guzzler!

So Patuk

Had accumulated minus points, and with the feeling that today would once again not be his day, he had driven into the city center. Braking genially, nodding pedestrians across the zebra crossing. The new system had contributed to people being very careful when interacting with others.

Everything will be fine

Thinks

HANNAH

She looks at men.

Well. Men. Things. Boys. She's back at a club with Peter and Don in order to have youthful experiences. When if not now, and why are they in London, the metropolis, the heart of the country, if not to waste away their youths in silly ways, to get excited and at the same time to be endlessly disappointed at how boring it is, because nothing matches the impact of one's own feelings. In that regard, nothing had ever changed about these venues that are always too loud for everyone in order to drown out the embarrassment that accompanies the search for mating partners. Loud, so you don't smell the cold sweat. Loud, so you don't think about what you're doing here. Dance, yeah, well. Of course. Lust for life. But how it all looks, for god's sake. That awkward self-conscious movement, the self-conscious feeling of being observed. Everyone is afraid of embarrassing smartphone videos landing online, afraid not to be rated well if videos from the club are watched by others. Hannah despises the smartphone morons. No revolutionaries, no solidarity. Just an idiotic mass of supposedly individual young people who all look the same and who hassle anyone who deviates from the current norm. Hardly ever has a minor deviation in hair color or BMI led to such bitter contempt as during this wonderful era when everyone has the feeling of receiving too little. Too little space and recognition, too little money and love. A new narrow-minded generation has developed.

Assholes.

Inside this club it's like every other club ever. The young people feel superior to old people, they're immortal, and, of course, they believe they're the first ones to experience everything. No living being had ever felt the way they feel. Nobody had ever been so wild, had engaged so intensely with oneself and one's fears of adulthood—that time when everything will be gray and over. Here in the club, everyone has just grown out of childhood. Grown out of total denial, no longer cute but also not yet full of greed and duplicity, not yet calculating, something that will also affect their willingness to couple up. The perception that well-being is dependent on others choosing you. Is not helpful.

Grime is playing. It's made it into the mainstream. Yet another revolution that's been sold out.

Many of those present are wearing their bodycam glasses so they can post cool videos of their antics. Hannah is uneasy and young and longs for something but doesn't know what. She looks at men. Well, okay. Men.

Boys in uniforms with army caps. With bulletproof vests, helmets. There's an oddly controlled atmosphere in the club. Everyone is standing up straight, nobody pukes behind the bar, no pogoing, no fistfighting. Civilized young people with the expectation of an event. Orderly young people. Even grime suddenly seems sweet-natured. Gentle. No longer angry. Nobody's angry anymore. Nobody dares to chat anyone else up, it could be unwanted. It could be intrusive. After a brief phase of civil revolt against political correctness, which was catalyzed by right-wing nationalist bots, after a brief pause in the British collective agreement that openly stated hate and racism are lower-class matters, after a brief time of offensive hate and contempt, now

A new era of progress has been reached. Well-trained people having fun.

The music is loud, the young people stand around shyly and wait for another shy person who is less shy to save them from their own shyness. Hannah has spotted a boy she can imagine engaging in a sex act with. The sex act she can imagine has its origins in a thousand pornos that served for her like everyone else as her only sexual education. The boy looks at Hannah, and Hannah looks at the boy, then she brushes past him toward the washrooms. She probably saw this move in a TV series. Or a porno. The boy follows her. Right. And now, now Hannah stands in a bright, unisex washroom. The boy enters the room, and at this point Hannah's fantasy ends. She stands opposite a stranger in a too-bright washroom kitted out with too many mirrors. What good are all these technological advances when people are still people?

"Hello," says Hannah. The young man nods and unzips the fly of his army overalls. His penis sticks out like a baby's arm in the bright washroom. He turns so the camera catches his penis at the right angle. Cameras in loos, offices, bars, brothels, wherever. "What now?" says the young man. Hannah's hands tremble. Hannah doesn't want to do anything. She doesn't want to deal with the baby's arm, she suddenly wants to go to bed. Without him, that is. And anyway, she doesn't have a bed. She has a mattress and friends, and she wants to go to them. Hannah sees her life elapse in the course of a few seconds. That is, the life that will not happen. She will definitely not find out what sex is today.

The boy slowly zips up his pants again and leaves the washroom. Hannah looks straight into the camera, and wonders for a second whether the bars on her face really make her unrecognizable

MI5 PIET

"Um, no."

HANNAH

Imagines that tomorrow half of London will give laughing smiley emojis to her fail on some website. "Now get out of here, you stupid cow. Fuck off and don't take yourself so seriously,"

Mumbles the

BOXER

Who had retreated to the washroom to snort a mixture of fenethylline and other strong narcotics. Which he does. And then makes his way toward the cellar of the club. The boxer has a strange feeling today. At least it's a feeling. Which is a change from the norm. The norm is being dead. The boxer is actually a chemistry lab technician. He came to England a year before. He came by tractor from Chad, Syria, or one of these—go ahead, say it—places that won't be around much longer. Because there's no more water or the ocean is full of plastic or oil or because there's a civil war that nobody gives a shit about because there aren't any natural resources there that can be used to make car batteries or computers. So. The boxer took leave of his previous life in some shithole or other. He didn't consider what it meant to leave the smells, the air, and above all the natural way you navigate your own homeland. That occurred to him only when he landed in London. Together with five other illegals. In one of those toolsheds that's touted as a "charming carriage house." He had cold feet and homesickness and didn't understand a word spoken by any of the others, all of whom were from different shitholes that had also been rendered unlivable for human beings. For a few days he had just lay on the floor; his roommates shared their bread with him and were considerate, which manifested itself in their beating each other up outside the room. After a week came the pimp. One of those handlers who finds illegals all sorts of shite jobs, from prostitution to burglary, money collecting, intimidation, and drug dealing. The boxer was hungry and wondered whether it might have been better to have remained at home, back in the place that might have been in the Bikini Atoll. The boxer's first job had to do with people. "OMG, I love being around people." Nearly every day he was taken in a lorry or bus along with others like himself to London or some other location in the country, where there was a demonstration taking place. The illegals' task was then to form an aggressive counterprotest, with the additional duty of beating up demonstrators. The boxer beat people up every day. Until the introduction of the chips, which eliminated the problem. Since then there are no more demonstrations, as a result of the point system.

For a few days now the boxer has had a new occupation. It takes place in the cellar beneath the club. For a fee well within the bounds of the current basic income, people can practice on him. Mostly older men of the former middle class turn up to courageously beat on a naked man, that is, the boxer, or somebody like him. The great thing about it is that the victim doesn't defend himself. That's the deal. The victim is naked and doesn't defend himself. Being naked makes the wounds easily visible and gives the whole thing sexual connotations. It's reminiscent of homoerotic-tinged time at boarding school, in the army, back then. The victims get punched, have their balls yanked, get kicked with boots, have their faces stomped and kidneys kicked while lying on the ground. Ribs and noses broken. It's a tough job. But better than sitting around silently.

With the

sadness.

In

DON

Who is sitting on the footpath in front of the bar, looking wonderingly at her hand. She imagines she's cut off her hand and attached an embryo in its place. The skin irritation has become an oozing rash. Don stares at her hand and the skin, and thinks of the surface of a planet.

Where does it come from,

This sadness, like a persistent cough, that takes all the color out of everything? It often seems to Don as if she sees the world the way it really is. Nothing sacred. And nothing changed. Actually. And yet everyone suddenly—so peaceful.

And—

It's become so quiet in the city. It's shocking. Unimaginable that something like an uprising could take place here. A civil war. Against what? There's food. The cars drive without any noise; same for mopeds, delivery drones. The malaise of recent years, the chaos before the new beginning, has yielded to a calm.

There are no more terrorist attacks. No drugged-up dudes mowing people down with semiautomatic weapons at concerts. They're gone. As if they had achieved a higher purpose, all the massacres had disappeared, or nobody believes they happen anymore, or you just never think to consider that the explosions caused by smart toasters or the self-driving cars that ram into crowds could be terrorist attacks. That was just technology, nothing but misunderstandings between man and machine, all in the name of progress.

EX 2279

```
> ++++++++++
[>+++++++++++++>++++++++++++>++++++++++++>+
+++++++++++>
+++++++++++>++++++++++++>++++++++++++>+++++
++++++>><<<<<<<<<<<<<-]
>——>++++>——>—->++++>—>++>++>=>>——>
<<<<<<<<<<<<
>.>.>.>.>.>.>.>.>.>.>.
```

DON

Doesn't know about AI efforts to preserve the planet. She looks at people.

They look tired. As if their synapses have been partying too hard and now it's—quiet time. They're all busy self-monitoring. It has to be done right. The facial expression, the words, the interest in their counterpart, the smile. Is real. They have hope again. That there is a chance again. To go shopping. For underfloor heating. For an intelligible world for god's sake.

"You're rubbish." Don screams.

A few people, who look alike, cringe. Loud outbursts are no longer welcomed. "You're going to go extinct, you idiots," screams Don and then sits down again, quiet and empty.

In the greatest of all eras. The education. The opportunities. The infant mortality rate. Hurray, look how we propagate in this, the greatest of all worlds. How do we propagate? Doesn't matter. And we eat meat. No generation has ever eaten so much meat. We eat meat morning, noon, and night, meat in sausages, meat in soup, meat in aspic. We eat anything that can't talk. We're people; we eat meat that is grown in animal form in giant factories, and then you cut them open, still alive, it makes the sausages taste better, and we like to see them kick their legs, we like to see things kick that we're going to eat, perhaps while it's still trembling, or better yet we spoon brains out of an open skull, that's the latest trend, to grip animals' heads in a vise and lick them clean.

Speaking of. Licking.

MA WEI

Interjects briefly. "Yes, I'd like to briefly interject here. Because—I'm also a bit proud. Because what the entire world consumes comes from our facilities in Africa. There's space there, indeed, space is something Africa has. Tens of thousands of beef lots. The livestock stand in self-cleaning stalls with a tube in their bottoms, which sucks out the excrement, and another tube in their mouths, to pump in food concentrate. And antibiotics. Who gives a fuck. In China nobody would even think of eating the stuff."

That's great, thinks

KAREN.

With a bit of blood on her face.

She's squatting on the footpath next to Don. It's still cold. It's still London. Soho, the streets full of quietly cheery people. "Is he still alive?" asks Don. Meaning Patuk, the tailor. Karen pulls a wad of bills from her jacket. And a blood-smeared chip. The moment when Patuk will realize he made a huge mistake. Is nearly here. The moment of definitive revenge.

While

The

ATTACKERS

INTELLECTUAL CAPABILITIES: *added together the two have 110 IQ points*
THREAT LEVEL: *10*
HEALTH CONDITIONS: *hormone problems, skin problems, problems with everything*

Are inconceivably bored with themselves, the contradiction between the hormones racing inside their bodies and the lifeless drabness outside cripples them. One of them came from Rochdale and moved in with a friend here in the city just a short time ago. They share a fondness for

Nothing. The two young men are not humiliated, just vacuous. They might possibly have parasites in their brains. *Toxocara* roundworms, carried by animals that are common in poor areas, lay their larva in sand and grass, where they are picked up and from there make their way to the brain and cause significant cognitive damage. Bye-bye. One of the two is studying electrical engineering. The other isn't studying anything. The two dumbasses live with the mother of one of the morons. A single mom, textile refiner. What? Doesn't matter. The two youths spend most of their time lying on the sofa watching terrorist videos. Or pornos. The effect is the same. A stiffy. Good Western citizens are constantly faced with the mystery of terrorists. What made them like that, so hard, so inhuman? What drove them to it? It must have been real hardship. Meaning, the attackers must have been humiliated, lived through a tough childhood with an unloving, aggressive father from the Arab world. While searching for a father figure, they'd tumbled into the open arms of a preacher of hate, become radicalized, stopped listening to their mothers, because contempt for women goes without saying. They'd been discriminated against, unemployed, and angry. Also because sex isn't an option for an unmarried Muslim and so on. As if any woman would get in bed with these dolts. Nobody seems to recognize the possibility that there are just complete fucking idiots, people who inflate frogs, slit open cats, because they're bored to the point of insanity. Well now. The two loll on the sofa and satisfy themselves orally with chips. "We should attack the electrical system," says one. The other looks up from his porn film. "Cool. Or—we could blow up Victoria station." "Cool," says the first, looking online for explosives. "It sounds complicated. Or wait—maybe a lorry would do the trick. Can you drive a lorry?" "No, I don't know how to drive a lorry." Right, neither of them can drive a lorry. They look for automatic weapons at an illegal online market. "Hey," says one of the buddies. "How does Bitcoin work?" Another hour passes while the two of them try to set up a Bitcoin account. "Maybe something with a machete?" suggests one of them, wandering into the kitchen to butter some toast with margarine. The other has already pulled up machetespecialists.com and ordered two of the things. They spend the evening watching snuff videos. "We can go to Soho. And slaughter a few poofs." "Cool, and then we'll kill ourselves." "Right, but how?" "We'll count to five and then chop each other's heads off." "Formidable."

Google Clips is always on. The tiny camera which decides on its own when to record things. For absolutely authentic shots.

MI5 PIET

"Yes, that's correct. It's always on. Of these two utter morons I can only say: Who cares?"

THE ATTACKERS

Are over the moon. The machetes have been delivered. Good, solid, sharp machetes. The idiots pump themselves full of Captagon. They giggle away their fear. Finally, some action. They get dressed. With masks and all in black. Then they tramp to Soho, take deep breaths and begin to dismember passersby. The first slash is difficult, after that it's like it moves itself. Like dancing in a trance. Body parts flop to the ground, a head is almost completely severed from the trunk. What is supposed to happen? They catch ten passersby. Whether any of them is actually gay doesn't matter. They catch ten passersby, and the quick-response rescue units can't get through because other passersby are filming the incident and blocking the way. That will mean minus points. The two idiots are shot only after half an hour by a member of a private militia.

DON

Hears the shots of the fully automatic weapons. They don't sound as impressive as the results-oriented effect they have. They sound. Dull. Like little New Year's crackers. Don

Has no idea that her unbelievably stupid brother is dying just a few meters away.

And suddenly the door opens. It is three o'clock.

In the morning and

KAREN

Stares at the ceiling. The little TV is on, the others are sleeping, they sleep well when the TV is on, like the voice of a family member reading a good-night story, right now it's

the news.

An account of the day's violent crimes in the far reaches of the city. In other words: troubled districts. Or: the poor. Again. It's about the poor again. Like every day for the last two weeks.

Images of the tide of refugees, which in the past had put the masses into a panic three times a day and set the stage for panic and fear-based voting, are now being replaced by coverage of spongers. It begins with reports about crime. Always perpetrated by the poor. A wide array of crimes are highlighted in dramatic tones. Bank robberies, insurance fraud, false claims to supplemental social benefits by organized scammers, verminous children with weapons, drug-dealing housewives. Undocumented foreigners, wasters who've supposedly managed to secure multiple basic incomes, culminating in various multifaceted commentaries alleging that the poor are just as harmful as immigrants had been in the past. Nearly every day there are interesting reports about incest in social housing blocks. There where single parents with five kids live on one basic income. There where the father pisses away the basic income on booze on the first day. Toothless people speaking on camera while high. Women are beaten up, babies play with the unconscious bodies of beaten mothers.

TV off. The silence of the hall interrupted by the grunts of the sleeping children, by the rain outside, so quiet and nebulous that it could just as well be fog that is fraying. Inside it's damp and cold. It smells of dirty laundry and noodles.

Karen rarely thinks about the weather. It's just there. Like her. She doesn't waste any mental energy on this circumstance. What good does it do anyone to act self-important? To spend quality time with yourself, to analyze yourself, to meditate, to be mindful and to pretend to be the center of the universe, except for being constantly aggressive because the world doesn't show you any respect.

Karen gets up and goes outside. In the dampness she mutters the names of the Big Sixteen.

"Bill Gates, Warren Buffet, Jeff Bezos, Mark Zuckerberg, Larry Ellison, Charles Koch, David Koch, Michael Bloomberg, Bernard Arnault, Larry Page, Sheldon Adelson, Li Ka-shing, Wang Jianlin, Sergey Brin, Carlos Slim Helú, Amancio Ortega."

Women are the new China, Karen had read. Not in her mind. She's the new Hiroshima.

Warren Buffet, Jeff Bezos, Mark Zuckerberg, Larry Ellison.

Karen can't sleep. She needs to move, like a sleepwalker, a somnambulist, and she thinks about the richest people in the world. No women. No Blacks. No albinos. Not even a fucking albino. No point. Karen has declared men the root of all evil in the world. Not a particularly original thought. Karen has gone mad.

She stumbles across the wasteland and ends up standing in an old brewery she recently discovered. The viruses she cultured in the lab are swimming in the old vats. "Multiply," she'd whispered. And behold—

100 trillion per milliliter of drinking water. All will be well. Karen stands in front of the vats, she looks at the sky. There are even stars tonight after the rain.

It's cold.

In the freezer

Where

DON'S BROTHER

Is lying, thinking about his life. He thinks of his mother. He thinks about what it was like to be able to sit around.

It wasn't bad. This sitting.

In the shelter there'd been a window you could open and close and look out; that is

No longer possible.

Back then, when there were still windows and air and sparrows—for fuck's sake why did he ever leave? He weighed 120 kilos. He ate everything he could get his hands on. What he could get his hands on were crisps. He ate crisps and played video games. He was at home among the undead, night elves, worgen, and orcs. He fulfilled his quests by successfully killing opponents and his mouth always hung slightly open. Used to. Now he was light. At 120 kilos, Don's brother had developed sores on several spots on his body. The sores wept. And so mother determined that a doctor needed to address the problem. One gray morning the two of them waddled through the idyllic little town, which became more wretched every year, because as a result of automation the last sources of income in the form of betting shops and trucking companies had ceased to exist. At that point the people sat quietly and waited for the giant bird that would carry them away.

No bird.

No relief.

After a day waiting in the hospital because of the open wounds, he was sent home. Unfortunately there could be no treatment

Because

After importing data from the chip, it became clear that the condition was the fault of personal misconduct. Keywords: *gaming, snacking, failure to exercise.* The nurse, who had yet to be replaced by a robot, urged Don's mother and brother to put in some effort and then they could try again. Don's brother and his mother waddled back through the town to their lodgings. That had been just recently. And now he was lying here, that is, his corpse was. Next to which he sits. Thinking. I want to go back. I want to go back and do everything differently. Not sit in a room and eat, but learn a foreign language instead. Dutch, for instance. And then take a ship across to Holland and run a farm there. And smell the sea and the freshly cut grass. No idea where he came up with freshly cut grass, but he imagines it smells good. Don's brother lies there and freezes, and he can think but not move, and he starts to cry, which also happens only inside. So they're all still here, the dead, thinks the brother, hoping this is a temporary condition. Then he imagines his burial and the dirt on top of him and the eternal boredom and cold and darkness.

If only he wanted to wake up

Thinks

THOME

And wakes up.

The dream had been horrid. In the dream, he was a total loser. And ugly. Suddenly it's over. Now he's only ugly. He hears gagging through the walls. Probably his Russian stepmother throwing up in the bathroom. She's pregnant. Hurray. Thome will have a new sibling. He can eat it up in the cellar. Whose child is it, anyway? His father is seventy. He hears his desperate attempts to reach ejaculation every night. Nothing doing. Thome has taken over the camera in his father's computer and watches him arranging his free time. His stepmother's sexual exertions nearly elicited respect from him. That is, if his stepmother weren't a Russian hooker. The stepmother wears latex and uses a whip. She has sex with a male sex robot with a forty-centimeter penis. She has sex with underage prostitutes of approximately eight years old.

THE EIGHT-YEAR-OLD PROSTITUTE

INTELLIGENCE QUOTIENT: *under 100*
HEALTH STATUS: *multiple badly healed broken bones*
Injuries in genital region
Syphilis—stage 2
DREAMS: *none*
HOBBIES: *sleeping next to the heater and pretending it is a bear*

Is ferried to Thome's father's house on Holland Park by a, let's call him a minder. After an hour she is picked up again. And taken to her lodgings, which are on Regent's Park. The owner of the eight-year-old prostitute is a Russian. Actually, you don't say that anymore. Not politically correct. His wife is also from the Eastern Bloc. You don't say that anymore, either. They are guests of the Empire. They are people.

(Shouted: *"They are people!"*)

As if that means anything, being a person. As if any person would care that other people are also living. They can't even imagine the pain of someone who's having a fingernail pulled out.

So

Now the usual story. As if there are only two types of CVs left in the kingdom—that of the upper class—

Which has to do with oily hair and wealth.

And the CV of the people.

Arrived here from somewhere or other, the result of some factor or other, and then a life whose only aim is survival.

The eight-year-old prostitute ran away from home because she was constantly beaten by her father after her mother died from jumping out a window. After the precipitous demise of her mother, which had to do with the fact that she could no longer stand her life, the eight-year-old prostitute kept looking for new places to hide in the little flat in order to protect herself from her father. The father of the eight-year-old prostitute was a cultural loser as far as modernity, who had no idea how his computer worked. A restless user. And angry. And with a hurt sense of manhood. He could momentarily regain his manhood when he ferreted out his daughter in her silly hiding places and beat her. It was—

As if pressure was released from his chest and his head when he showed this small witness to his failure who the boss of the house was. With the palm of his hand to her face. With fists to her face, with kicks when she stopped moving. With a hot plate that he pressed to her hands. When he began to break things over her, the eight-year-old prostitute took off. She moved into the cellar of a nearby building. Stole marmalade from nearby storage sheds until locks were installed all around the area. After that she slept in staircases and in those bays where rubbish bins are kept and which have no formal name. The eight-year-old prostitute wasn't unhappy. She was a long way from being able to categorize her emotional world with stereotypical terminology. She didn't think anything. She didn't miss anything. She didn't feel anything. She marveled at the world. She wandered around department stores. Rummaged in dumpsters behind restaurants. She then landed, through a series of connections that had to do with a Bentley, in the villa on Regent's Park. And from there to the parlors of various old men. The villa on Regent's Park was agreeable. Though she knew only the apartment within it that she shared with ten other children from families broken in various ways. Children don't know what's good or bad. You can turn them into murderers, thieves, or prostitutes, they don't know what's good or bad, they have feelings, they feel when something is disgusting. Old men are disgusting. But nothing you can't get used to. Such a nice, warm flat where they now live, pressed against each other, thumbs in mouths, watching the lights of motorcars on the ceiling; in this warmth you can tolerate something disgusting now and then.

Who cares?

Jesus, mate! Watch it, thinks

THOME

Looking at his father, whose face is deep red. Thome's father looks the way one pictures someone about to have a heart attack looking. Has the old guy already changed his will to benefit the little half-Russian in the fake blonde's belly?

But

To Thome's great disappointment, his father reappears in the camera's picture. He's crawling across the carpet on a dog leash. Thome could watch this pathetic spectacle for hours. People never come up with anything original. Rubbing your bell end with chili pepper or hanging from a chandelier by your cock. Though surely those things are already being done somewhere. Anything that people in their excessive simplicity can get themselves into exists—somewhere. Thome had discovered a dating app where heterosexual men in total ignorance of the parameters of female arousal upload only photos of their foreskins. That's reducing things to the basics. Who needs faces, bodies, thoughts anymore? Who needs people? And especially so many of them, who stuff themselves, shit, drive motorcars, and above all they: want something. Want more. The populace is divided into those who try to consume and fuck their way out of despair and the new people.

Whenever Thome thinks about his theory of the new people, a group he counts himself among, he gets sexual. Used to. His lust has disappeared of late. Is that how you say it? Do you say "lust"? You say "making love" when you mean intercourse, and "lust" when it's just about a discharge. Thome stands in front of the mirror, a Colani mirror. Piece of shit. Thanks to his new mother's tastes, the house looks like a chill-out lounge at an insurance company.

Thome pictures himself spiking a sterling silver candlestick into his skull, sees the hole in his head, splinters of bone, there's the brain, as suspected, nothing special. Thome still doesn't know whether it would have been worse to have spent the last years of his youth at home instead of at boarding school.

The years at boarding school—

As a result of his mildly masochist proclivities, he thinks of them often, they sort of blend together like one continuous humiliation.

That consisted of pulled-down pants, groups of boys who went silent when he drew near. And super glue, with which his foreskin had been sealed shut, soap in his mouth, feces in his mouth, and shame. Because he's homosexual. Or probably asexual.

Back to the present day.

Thome blames professional overload for his lack of sexual interest. The excitement of forming the world anew in digital form is greater than anything his sexual organs can generate. It's a glorious time. Right now. For boys.

All areas that had necessitated women are being taken over by devices created by men. Sex, services, birthing—WTF. Engineers and programmers watch the lumbering steps of their children rapturously. The bodies and brains built by themselves. Just look how funny they are, and how curious. In a few years a computer will surpass the collective intelligence of all mankind. Almost every one of the 98 percent—male IT buffoons worldwide—the startuppers, linguists, programmers, coders, hackers, engineers, whatever the fuck else—is god. It's like being gay without being gay. We build electronic monster-dogs, have you seen the dogs? LS4, 2.50 withers at the shoulders, up to a hundred kilometers per hour, equipped with baby rockets, automatic weapons. They learn autonomously and independently recognize—for example—Arabs? We have sex robots, robot insects, we have outsourced every area to algorithms. Our drones can now also autonomously kill, and the people who, well, those who are left, can devote themselves to their hobbies. Play chess against robots. Here, at the creation of the world 4.0, we keep it between us. We create the brains that will establish the new world order. We determine what is right and wrong, what is beautiful and ugly. Beautiful is white skin, Thome thinks as he looks at his foot. Man, oh man, this foot could tell some tales. It could star in a blockbuster, people would follow spellbound the delicate play of the toes, which, white, absurdly crooked, like tiny grapplers crowned with a few cheeky long hairs, seem oddly worldly.

So the new people—can finally look the way they want, because they decide that it's beautiful not to wear deodorant, to have a potbelly and no muscles.

We decide that women like to gather up our socks and that nose hair is au courant. Right. And? Finally just be, off to Silicon Roundabout with a ruck-sack and orthopedic shoes or sneakers. Aside from a few lesbians and a few customer service reps: be among ourselves, make jokes about lightsabers, do guy stuff. Thome laughs today about his old classmates from boarding school. About the great athletes, the lads who were assured a government position after graduating university, or an even cushier job in the diplomatic corps. They're sitting in a smelly office in Nairobi now, sweating it up in the House of Commons, they are the disappearing representatives of the old world. They're married. Thome imagines the English spouses of his former classmates. En-glish roses, who had passed their prime at the age of fourteen.

The new people,

In this wonderful world.

Just look at:

KAREN

Stares

Into the vats. Normal. The way one normally stares into vats. The con-crete floor beneath her bare feet is cold; Karen sweats. She is the wood from which revolutionaries are carved. She is the resistance. The Rosa Luxemburg of biohacking. She is the avenger of all women and children, and now she looks completely crazy, she jumps around the brewery, today her work is complete. She's done it. Here swims her work—harmless-seeming little cells, inside of which the virus has gestated. Zombie babies. Aliens. Now the cells must have disintegrated and she can siphon off the virus. Siphoning off virus— something everyone should do once, siphon off virus. Feel their life. One liter will yield about 2.5 trillion of them, which she can easily transport in small containers. Maybe it won't be enough to effectively contaminate the drinking water. It's a first attempt, and after a week there should be discernible results. Once absorbed through the oral mucous membrane, the infernal stuff will show its effect, blasting through the hematoencephalic barrier and deactivating the effect of testosterone. Right, and then. Listen up.

No sexual excitability, no aggression, no desire in men to impress sexual partners, to eliminate competitors, to bugger up the world. The effect is irre-versible. Ir-re-versible. If it works. Here goes. Out. Into the world, where it is still drizzling, where it no longer smells. It no longer smells of anything, isn't that strange? No longer like earth and flowers and petrol, tar, or food, it smells flat. Concrete and plastic. That is, nothing. This lack of olfactory sensations increases people's feelings of alienation. They live without any participation in the actions of existence. The people.

Karen lugs the first container full of her little friends, excitedly awaiting their mission, toward the Thames. The artery of the city, Karen would think, if she were daft. The strong current, which for some time has no longer carried corpses—the hope, you know, there's hope again, which holds many people back from jumping to their death. She sits down on the bank, which is primarily formed of old plastic waste. Karen looks at the dark, brackish-smelling water, she sees the distant lights of the city, she imagines how calm it will soon be. And wonders how she can expand her project to the entire country. Karen supposes she can see the curvature of the earth over there, where the sea must be,

Ha ha.

KEVIN

FAMILY STATUS: *single*
PROFESSION: *aeronautical engineering, so to speak*
HEALTH STATUS: *insane*

Curvature, ha ha. So, you know, when someone is told a lie at a fundamental point, then a basic sense of trust is lost. Then everything is false. Kevin knows that he lives in a construct, manipulated for the goal of the Great Replacement. The white man is supposed to disappear. That is explained with the round earth and the inevitable barbarian invasion. If people knew that the earth was flat, they would also know that having too many people in the northern half would change the axis.

Kevin had stumbled upon the teachings of Samuel Rowbotham at some stage. He had read *Zetetic Astronomy: Earth Not a Globe*. The truth had hit Kevin like a blow to the head and—

Destroyed his trust in everything. He had read the book several times. Reenacted the important experiments in it. Like Rowbotham he'd waded into a canal. You know the story. Rowbotham used a telescope at water level to watch a toy boat float from one bridge to the next. The top of the mast should have disappeared from view once it was ten kilometers away if the earth, as is claimed, is a ball with a circumference of forty thousand kilometers. But—

the boat remained visible. A follower named John Hampden later made a bet with Alfred Russel Wallace, one of the developers of evolutionary theory, to replicate the experiment with other visual cues, having to do with a black scarf. This was the Bedford Level experiment. It involved, well, boring.

The experiment worked. The earth was flat. Kevin didn't need to know anything more. Now when he lies in bed he's afraid the earth could tip because of all the emigration and he and his bed could slip off into space. Kevin always tries to wear clean underwear to bed because his body might spend all eternity floating in space. Without decomposing.

The North Pole in the middle, a wall of ice all around the edge that people take for Antarctica in the false ball image of the earth. Sun, moon, and stars are just a few hundred kilometers above the earth and far smaller than claimed; gravity is a fictitious force derived from upward movement of the disk. The anger at established science accompanies Kevin from the moment he awakes each day. He trusts nobody, not even people from the Flat Earth Society. He goes to work. He still has a job. He works in a small firm that repairs drones. In a small firm that has yet to convert to robot labor. He has a tracker on his apron. He has a two-minute bathroom break. Twenty minutes for lunch. He is filled with anger.

Again and again.

About twenty times.

KAREN

Goes between the vats and the river, carrying a bucket, back and forth, the virus slipping into the water like wet lynxes and swimming toward the city, which in the morning light seems to glow in the distance. A place of promise in the dreams of millions. The objective of their lives. That they've reached in wagons and boats, by ship and swimming, only to find themselves in the heart of a machine that is fueled by people. Money comes out the bottom and is channeled directly into the cellars of a small number of idiots. But most people don't care. They identify with the winners. Because nobody counts themselves among the losers. Because everyone is oriented upward. Because nobody assesses their worth realistically, because everybody wants to feel superior to some other group. Because the masses share social media with the rich. They're practically neighbors or colleagues of Stormzy. Kendrick Lamar. Drake. Fucking rap stars, with annual incomes equivalent to the cost of an intercontinental missile. So. Enough.

The world is ready to die out.

It is done says

THOME

Every day after his morning defecation. People like him are—first of all, chronically tired, since he had read that geniuses can get by on four hours of sleep. For several years now Thome has had his virtual assistant

(which additionally transcribes his conversations, forwards them to Tempora, where they are scoured for interesting keywords with XKeyscore, the search engine of the intelligence services, and then sent on to cave age in a Swiss bunker, all of which Thome must know, though perhaps his father is right in his assertion that he's not the brightest)

wake him after four hours, after which he spends half an hour absorbed staring at his feet. He'd had electronic skin grafted on his feet. A no longer popping-fresh invention from the university in Boulder. He likes to remove his socks in good company and garner admiration for his feet. It was a painful procedure to have such an extensive patch of skin removed, but worth every millimeter. "And what can this artificial skin do?" the meddlesome will ask. "It can sense warmth and contact," Thome says in such cases. That is, the same thing his skin was able to do before, only in modern form. His feet with the artificial skin stand for the realms in which Thome works. Digitalization, which can do anything people can, only without people.

Now Thome stands up and looks at himself in the full-length mirror. So, right. Well. If he hadn't have been born rich, he could jokingly picture himself as one of those sweaty gamers who constantly eat pizza and are trapped in *Second Life*. Is that still around? *Second Life*, for all the amazing virtual stuff people could think up who had already been shut out of Life 1.0?

Time to get going. Out. The world awaits. Before the sun rises Thome is engrossed in VR, always in the same scenario, thanks to his imaginary Asperger's, which craves repetition. He is sitting on the beach. Then—sunrise over the bay of Khao Lak. He always gets goose bumps as a light breeze blows in with the sun. And always when the goose bumps set in, an unbelievably handsome boy turns up, whose genitals are barely hidden by a sarong. Just the bell end peaks cautiously out. Thome starts to nuzzle the boy. What an absurd word— earlier it was exactly at this point, at this word, that a wonderful stiffening took place. No longer. Perhaps he needs to take his fantasies further, Thome thinks, but the alteration of habits causes just the sort of panic that he'd read about concerning his clinical picture. Following the failed erection Thome leaves the virtual world in order to take his hot-and-cold contrast shower.

Soon he'll look for a new flat. Far from his parental villa and so forth. But—

At the moment there are things to do.

Silicon Roundabout buzzes with viral lust for life. Thome strides happily from the subterranean garage on New Oxford Street, runs into a colleague who looks like Thome. Somehow.

"The world consists of mathematics,"

Says Thome.

"And violence," answers the young, lithe man, who works at one of the metadata analysis firms, which officially go bankrupt nearly every month only to reopen under a different name. The two men give each other friendly punches to their sides. Too hard. They knock the wind out of each other, then they trot off, full of strength and grace like untamed wild horses. Snorting, they enter the café, which everyone just calls "the café." Every morning, the under-forty, white, male future of the nation meets up here. Many with initial signs of hair loss, many with rucksacks and sneakers. Unathletic young men.

Like

THOME

Who sucks in his gut in the morning. He gets a smoothie at the bar and in so doing deftly slips past two women. Blockchain bitches. Unimportant. *Bam,* you'll just have to wait, you little butch dykes. The women don't protest; the constant company of men has left them listless and tired, as if the testosterone has crept into them and benumbed something in their brains. All the men in the room move in a similar way: arms held away from their bodies as if huge muscles are preventing them getting closer. Chins held high. All have attention deficit syndrome. Another way of saying: we stare at various screens until four in the morning, program, chat on the side, and watch the stock price indexes. It makes us agitated.

Long strides, somewhat uncoordinated. These are people at the top. Who, thanks to cybernetics, have managed to offer the people a better life online than they would ever have offline. Who have contrived to replace the old globe-spanning 1.0 monster corporations with new globe-spanning empires. The ones who had rethought every field. Mobility, the finance sector, telecommunications, entertainment, trade, agriculture—come up with something. Come up with a sector that hasn't been turned on its heads by these lads here.

Why?

Because they can.

Cheers.

A moment of silence.

On screens out in the street, adverts for a weekend in Ireland. Smiling people in front of herds of sheep, cliffs, blue skies.

It's been ages since I've seen any animals, thinks Thome. Where are they, actually?

Smoothies are being tipped back. At the moment, Tasmanian pepper with spinach is the in thing. The blockchain bitches have withdrawn to a corner. From afar they seem as if they are already dead. They had at some point worked on a digital currency that was supposed to make the banking system superfluous. Cryptocurrencies had been the revolutionary tool a few years prior. Ethereum, Bitcoin, Ripple, Litecoin, kiss my ass—Thome had already forgotten all of their names, just as their democratizing concept had been forgotten. These days so-called alternative currency was just the currency and under the control of financial institutions. Lucky them.

As mentioned. Everything new, but somehow also

Well, you know.

Lolling about the café's only seating area—

De Sede, naturally—

Are the AI aces. A couple of professors and their coder boys. The rest of the men stand at a distance from the gods of IT. AI is the thing of world domination. Whoever understands AI

EX 2279

```
>++++++++++
[>++++++++++>++++++++++>++++++++><<<<-]
>—>++++>>
<<<<
>.>.>.
)
```

Has found the Holy Grail. Business analysts calculate that even in the most conservative scenario AI will account for 14 percent of global economic activity. Ignoring exponential growth, that means: $15.7 quintillion. Jesus, mate. Respect. Create brains that develop further on their own. It's better than sex. When it's not possible to further improve the human brain, why not a new start by non-fleshly means?

In the back there, by the toilets—the women's bathroom was removed last year for lack of women; the lesbians can piss in the urinals—sits a man who as a sign of his defeat had SpongeBob tattooed on his face a few years back. Embarrassing story. His startup was one of the first to have worked with brain implants. They promised to push IQs to dizzying heights. But then there were deaths. The cortex is a delicate flower. No hard feelings.

The firm has in the meantime overcome this loss of confidence–inducing faux pas and is a leader in interpreting brain signals. Reading thoughts is the hot new shit. In his last TED Talk, one of the firm's founders showed how a deaf-mute, the politically correct name for which is probably something else, converted a touching speech in his head into words. Many of the viewers wept.

Another AI freak, neural networks and so forth, drinks his coffee standing up and then disappears. The gazes of the others follow him. He is the deadbeat who doesn't have his devices under control. They've developed their own language, the little bastards. Incomprehensible to humans. All this loser could do was remove the robots from the network.

EX 2279

```
>++++++++++
[>++++++++++++>+++++++++++>+++++++++++>
++++++++++++++>++++>++++++++++++++>+++++++
+++>++++++++++++++>++++++++++++++>++++++++
++>++++++++++++++>++++++++++++++>+++++++++-
++>++++++++++++++><<<<<<<<<<<<<<-]
>—>+>++++>+>+>++++>—>+>++++>+>++>—>>>+>
<<<<<<<<<<<<<<<
>.>.>.>.>.>.>.>.>.>.>.>.>.
```

THOME

Had bought shares in the company that converted thoughts into text. He was sure that the shares, which he'd bought for £32, would triple in value once the interest of the intelligence services had been piqued. Currently they're up to £789, Thome just couldn't keep track of all the new cryptocurrency mergers.

He remembered the day the beta version was launched. One of the programmers had conducted a thought–sound experiment just as the founder of the firm entered the airy workspace. With a creaky but clearly audible voice, the programmer's device thought aloud:

"Here comes the little pervert. I saw his cock in the bathroom. I'm sure there's an implant in there that he cradles in his hand while two dwarves fuck in front of him and he smears them with shit."

Though the creaky words were stated in breathtakingly bad grammar, astonishing for a beta version, the test did not go well. The development of the speech transfer tool was tabled as a result of the all too predictable fisticuffs, and efforts were instead devoted to the transfer of thoughts in written form.

There's a strong odor in the café.

The gang has talked itself into an adrenaline rush. They all try to one-up each other with over-the-top jargon. Except the AI aces. They're relaxed. They don't smell. They're already there where the rest wish to be.

The AI aces speak only to other AI aces. Nobody else understands what they're all about. Unfortunately they barely understand each other, either. Artificial brains. The interplay between 86 billion nerve cells, 100 trillion possible connections, 7.6 billion variations, what the hell.

The freaks from National Security are also standing at the bar knocking back smoothies. They wear expensive jackets now, they have healthy color in their faces. They have balls. Most of them, who had been involved in hacker culture, the only cool youth movement that had still existed back then—they wanted to save the world, fight against surveillance, expose flaws in so-called democracy using funny hacks, disable Nazi networks, leak secret documents, and so on—

Nearly all landed at National Security. Because that's where the money is, the super servers, the research, the power. Fuck tinkering on homemade servers. Fuck pizza.

The National Security people have come up with the most brilliant inventions. Keyloggers, which transmit every keystroke from a keyboard. The Dumbo project, voting manipulations about which they're still proud.

Yeah, great.

And, hey, who do we have here? Pressed against the wall in genuinely cheap clothing rather than expensive clothing made to look cheap?

The virtual reality nutters, who are building a world where you can engage people whose jobs have been outsourced. It's something nobody can afford or wishes to, these millions who are busy keeping busy. Just so they can go home in the evening and slide into their slippers with the trite feeling of having accomplished something. Conservative estimates put the number at 20 million nationally who are kept from committing suicide with absolute nonsense. Even now they stream to firms where they sit at computers and move around numbers that mean nothing at all. Insurance risk assessments, just to offer one of the stupidest examples. Consultants, bank administrators, all these schemes to placate people, the first of the cutback measures were the one-pound jobs. Work on demand. The attempt was aborted. Waiting for a job was not something people wanted to do. They wanted to be important, to justify the frivolous accident of their existence with an even more idiotic job. Virtually nobody is equipped to just be. Aside from millionaires, nobody is made that way, among the dull masses they want to earn an honest living, among the stupid masses they want to be able to offer a proud answer to the question of what they do.

"The smell, the smell is still missing."—"Yes, but if you atomize the scent."—"No, that's not the same." Exactly. VR nutters among themselves. Nobody takes the *Matrix* shit seriously. Keyboards that hover in the air, for meetings and virtual operations, the ability to hang out in the same room as holograms, that's the kind of stuff that made money. Giving people a sense of purpose without being able to skim a lot of money off them? Hard to see the point.

And there at the window stands a cloud architect. The cloud, or in other words, the Upload-your-data-here-you-idiot-so-we-can-access-all-of-it-at-once. Next to him, standing around with utter arrogance, are the half-wits who run the system of karma points, citizen points, or, if you will, idiot points. All paid by people like Thome's father. Cheers, lads. Great job.

The currency is being converted to 100 percent cryptocurrency. The crypto freaks, many from Holland, are new to the island, and not entirely of their own volition. Instead it's thanks to the flooding in their own country. Since their country is 70 percent underwater. And that, dear friends, shows how serious the situation must be, for somebody to voluntarily move to England. Thome glances at the social media boys. Technologically uninteresting, but they are responsible for 50 percent of the new world order. Memes have the impact of atomic bombs. Bots can fell governments, send shares tumbling, put companies out of business—therefore: respect, lads.

Hello all you clever developer twats who've come up with all the clever shite that functions only with

Hallelujah—an app, and now soon the hand-implanted chip will, you can already guess, optimize performance. All the devices, the TVs, radios, virtual assistants, tracking watches, automobiles that report and record driving behavior, texts, conversations, banking activity, printers that read and save all images, passenger information. Fingerprints, blood types (Hey, test your blood online!), urine (Hey, your toilet checks your alkaline balance!), the smart vibrators and artificial vaginas. Political disposition, health status, life expectancy, risk potential, creditworthiness, the chances of a tendency toward violent outbursts. Consumer behavior, sleep habits, alcohol and drug consumption, religiosity, criminal energy, social conduct. Because of terror. Terror, terror. Terror. Terror. There could be a plan behind it. Or maybe not. Thome spreads his legs wider and plants his feet more firmly on the ground. He is part of the elite. Performance, dominance, merit, virility.

And outside in front of the window the fanboys stand around with their paper cups of cheap coffee in their hands. Script kiddies who have no idea about anything, who wear hooded jackets, have no skills beyond a few tech catchphrases, the idiots, and they stare at the masters with open mouths. The little failures, who have completely buggered up their synapses with nonstop chatting, listening to hacker radio, trying to program, to blog, watching Netflix, reading, talking on the phone, taking photos, and then comes another message in a completely encrypted chat, where little poseurs talk among themselves about hacker radio shows and Netflix series. They'll never belong, to anything. Losers. Thome belongs to the winners. It's like being a rock star, in the past, when there were still real rock stars. It's like belonging to the illuminati. Here—right fucking here—is where the power is.

Well—or a few meters away.

In the office of a friend of

THOME'S FATHER

A few old men are sitting around feeling pleased. Red velvet curtains, thick carpets, porcelain dogs, bookshelves, fireplace, all the shit that signals tradition and power.

A man who is sweating profusely had just given a PowerPoint presentation about various steps in the campaign.

"PowerPoint? Really?" Thome's father had asked, leaving the young man briefly unnerved.

"So," he said.

The young man.

So—this stupid word that people use to introduce something to which they wish to give extra heft,

So.

"As you know, a new crisis must be engineered, potential unrest, indeed, that is before the surveillance tools can be fully utilized and linked to private security operations, before all citizens can be documented and the point system establishes itself . . ."

"Would you be so kind as to tell us something we don't yet know?"

Thome's father interrupts the

SWEATING MAN

ANXIETY DISORDER: *worm phobia*
SEXUALITY: *obsessed*
FINANCIAL STATUS: *not creditworthy b/c of compulsive gambling*

Who is in his early forties, and who has a breathtaking career as spin doctor, internet strategist, and campaign advisor

behind him

And is now a crisis manager. He features, promotes, and markets crises, and though they're the constant state of the world, one isn't permitted to sell them as the normal state of things; they must rather be used, focused on, highlighted in order to—feature their core brand value.

Though there had never been an even-keeled, calm, wonderful life. The calm, peaceful life is an invention of the advertising industry to fuel the economy, to sell diapers and all that shit in order to keep the people quiet, whose natural instinct is to run through the streets plundering and savagely killing game. Or other people. Or just breaking shit. This instinct needs to be channeled into profitable avenues. "It's no bed of roses," says the sweating man whenever he is asked about his profession.

Having spent recent years working abroad—the sweating man never refers to his clients by name—during which he had rebranded Islamic terror, in part

by curating attacks himself and coordinating the entire press relations operation in order to fuel the deterioration of the European economic zone, in order
to boost Brexit and the defense industry—yes, it was just as dull as you can
imagine when you're sitting on the toilet—there is now a new domestic project
lined up. The sweating man has no reason to feel bad or guilty, because people
need a bogeyman, it intensifies their lust for life. Awareness of the peril of the
evolutionary fight for survival fine-tunes the intensity of their lives. Treat every
second like it is the last. But

His penis. The sweating man, as befits a highly eloquent man of action,
has a lot of sex. He has on overly tight pants, which stretch across his overly
voluminous posterior; he's wearing light brown welted semibrogue shoes, a
must for assholes; his sports jacket, Savile Row, opens over his bottom like
little wings. His hair, once pale red, has yielded to a very high forehead and
these days he dyes it a striking rust tone. He can't get an erection anymore,
or rather, for a week now he has had no desire for anything. That is, neither
for his work nor for women. He looks at the naked bodies lying before him
and thinks: So, what now? What good does it do me to ejaculate into this
orifice? He looks at the white bodies before him—humans really aren't overly
aesthetically pleasing. The red spots caused by epilation in the pubic area; the
wetness, probably created artificially in the bathroom, that makes the slit glis-
ten; the makeup, the ears, my god. Puzzling, this absence of desire. But even
more astonishing is that he has occasional misgivings about his occupation.
"Yes, I get it," he says to himself. "Humans are a herd of absolutely moronic
animals. I can't even think of another animal that is so moronic that you can
make them do anything—well, no, we can go further, to the stirring event in
New York, which must be seen as the beginning of new era. As the accelerant
for the reconfiguration of the structure. After the event the entire world spoke
of Islam, which up to then nobody had given a shit about, to put it charitably.
What successful linguistic fireworks were sparked there. *Islam, Islamist, fundamentalist*, doesn't matter, all the same, the enemy. But it's so boring, so simple."
The sweating man is no longer excited by his occupation. The parameters are
always the same—specify an enemy, disparage, ridicule, generate fear, have bots
programmed. Dull.

The sweating man has for some time been downright crazy about wormies,
as he playfully calls them. He loves videos of people showing any sort of worm

infestation in their bodies. Worms in their feces, tapeworms that have been removed, worms in infected wounds.

But even fear and disgust no longer reach the sweating man's arousal center. Nothing gives him a feeling of being alive anymore.

Who cares.

Thinks

THOME

He has nodded off on the toilet of the café. From outside he hears the excited breathing of one of the workers behind the bar. Is it possible to complete a visit to the bathroom including proper hand washing in under a minute? Fast excretion raises one's point count. Was as little water used as possible? The use of less water is achieved by a solid consistency of stool. That can be achieved with a good, fiber-rich diet.

Thome takes a glance at the new app that he created. Well, it was built by a programmer who is a bit more on the ball, but what counts is the idea.

Your Fear

Is the name of the app. Wherein you can share your deepest fears with the community. One could of course also find out people's phobias in their harvested metadata, but it is much more fun with the app. Once in a while Thome indulges in a bit of fun by fulfilling this or that fear of app users I.0.

What's this then?

Respect, lads—sunlight?

The unfamiliar sight

Leaves

DON

Squinting.

Wow.

This light in Shoreditch, how beautiful the present is. Never before had a present been so beautiful. The formerly poor district of the city. Social housing, seven children, three stillbirths, boozers, fighters, leukemia patients, TB bacteria shuffled down the damp, narrow alleys shared with rats. And just look what's become of it all: an open-air museum of a successful lifestyle. Organic bakeries, oat milk lattes, muesli, smart clothing boutiques. And the people. So international, so colorful, with such incomprehensibly interesting lifestyles.

Don watches the breakfast café in one of the former industrial buildings.

A few hundred men crunching disgustedly on kale chips. They built the new world order. The reinvention of the world by—men. It's simply up to them. One fucked-up system swapped out for the next fucked-up system. Always done within the limits of their comprehension. The women were busy. With their children, their makeup, the question of how to find a fascinating, world-altering man. And because they don't understand, the bitches, why a hoover needs to talk to a soldering iron. Or why dildos need to talk to a pizza delivery service.

Everyone talks too much already.

There's no more escaping the sound of talking now that the giant screens have been installed all over the city. Don looks at the screen next to the nerd café.

"Have you never had the need to work for a living?" asks a blonde reporter with a microphone. A man, whose teeth are all missing, starts to laugh. He inadvertently spits in doing so. In the background, bedraggled children play with a dead cat. Ah, it's about suicide in social housing blocks. "I'm in therapy now," says a train driver accusingly. A woman had thrown herself onto the tracks. You see various body parts and hear the sympathetic voice of the reporter, who commiserates with the train driver. A boat pilot on the Thames complains about recurring nightmares after an old man splattered on the roof of his boat. The mother of two private school children grumbles about coming upon a corpse hanging from a tree while driving through Hyde Park in her SUV.

Next to Don a man stops, sweating heavily. He leans against a wall and tries to get control of his bodily secretions.

He's applied that particular hair dye, the one that is supposed to get men's natural hair color back but is in every case: rust-colored.

"These losers can't even manage a proper death," says the man with the rust-colored hair, sweating. Don looks at him; he looks wretched.

"You have on pimp shoes," says Don.

"Yes, of course I have on pimp shoes," says rusty.

On the giant screen now is an old man at a rubbish heap, in the background the body of a rat is turning on a stick over a fire.

"Loneliness is only tolerable with money," says the sweating man. "If you have money, you can buy things, and parcels will arrive. Someone will want something. At least someone will take an interest in you, even if it is just an algorithm. Without money, all that's left is the kitchen, the clock, and the yellow paint on the walls, a park that belongs to somebody, the parking lot in front of the supermarket where you can stand until the security detail shows up. Most people's lives consist of waiting. For something to happen, which will jolt them out of their waiting, which will make them take stock and realize that they'll regret not having enjoyed life. But how? How do you enjoy life if nothing is burning inside you? And how much TV can you watch? Especially if the electricity has been cut off. Especially if your bottom hurts from sitting and from being reamed out by all the bullshit you stuff yourself with, and that's what we mean by freedom. The freedom of self-actualization and possibility that was bestowed upon us all by the free market in reality gives most people nothing more than the possibility to watch the rich being free. The poor are theoretically entitled to freedom, but they just have too little money to live it out, freedom."

"You put that well," says Don, who had stopped listening after barely a second.

The sweating man nods quickly and disappears into the unbelievably multicultural neighborhood. Don watches him go. She scratches her hand, scratches off the scab that had formed over the red splotches that look like disgusting little islands.

The first few dynamic, nonchalant young men are coming out of the café across the street. With the crumbs of chips in the corners of their mouths, they flow into the street, which had been filled with tourists enjoying the last great amusement. Take a flight for ten pounds from someplace or other, day ticket, and then wander the streets, hit McDonald's at lunch. There you can get cheap meat in a kale wrap—back in the evening, or, if it is to be a really wild outing, to one of the box hotels for £19, where people sleep in something like lockers, stacked up in sheds next to motorway on-ramps.

They stand in the streets. The tourists. In front of buildings where every flat cost at least £30 million, with ten subterranean levels where the Chinese store their Ferraris or stash their whores. Time and again a street somewhere in the city center collapses, bringing down a building with it. Structural integrity, you know how it goes.

Speaking of which—

Don has never traveled. But she has Google Street View. Had. Google had explored every last corner of the earth, mapped it, that's the kind of thing you do only if you want to own it. You have to have an overview of the inventory.

Don could always imagine exactly what it would be like elsewhere. And what she would do there. On those unspeakably ugly beaches in Spain, what are you supposed to do there, in the sun, with a view of high-rises, surrounded by burned pink-colored people with swollen feet? You'd sit on the beach and wonder: if this is the high point of my life, there's no reason to be present for the rest. This principle of going on holiday as a reward for a shitty life. These so-called destinations around the world whose very names used to sound out of reach. And now—thanks, Google!—you can spare yourself any effort at all. With Street View you can walk down the street in the middle of any dream destination. There are no trees, just the same buildings everywhere; they look like they're from another millennium. In the south they're moldy. People in little boxes. People everywhere and far too many for them to possibly be able to be happy still. But. Nobody promised that, the whole happiness thing.

A new breaking report on the screen. A drunken couple have killed their two children, the shot lingers on the corpses. Baby children. Very small.

Then back to the father. Unpleasant face,

Right

BERTA AND HENRY'S

SOCIAL CONDUCT: *don't separate recycling. no exercise. eat poorly*
FEAR: *losing each other*
HEALTH STATUS: *not available*
No karma points, you fuckers

fate is perfectly suited to a social drama, the kind that would certainly win a prize at a film festival. People would emerge from screenings full of concern. A couple women would have tears in their eyes.

Berta and Henry had a flat in Birmingham, where they led a bog-standard lower-middle-class life. The two children were talented, both could already read and write at four years old, when

Berta was diagnosed with cancer. That was at exactly the moment when some areas of health care that had previously been free were privatized. For some time now, the costs of unusually expensive care must be borne by the insured, unless they had bought supplemental insurance, which nobody did, because—not important. Right. So they tried to cover the costs with crowdfunding. Henry sat next to his wife on the sofa, the children in clean clothing beside them.

He spoke into the camera: "This is my wife, Berta. She has lung cancer and it has metastasized, and the insurance company won't pay for her treatment anymore, now that the departments of oncology and cardiology, orthopedics and oral surgery have been sold to a Chinese holding company. You out there! Any of you could be hit the same way tomorrow. Today it's us. These are our children. This is my wife, this is me. I used to be an architectural draftsman, but there are no more architectural draftsmen. I worked as a street cleaner before the automated sweepers came in, worked in construction, in industrial kitchens, and what I earn is enough for—nothing. Please help me save the life of our family."

Odd sentence. Perhaps a slip of the tongue. At the same time Henry's crowdfunding went live a startup began seeking funding to bring personalized trainers onto the market.

Within four weeks they had raked in £1.2 million. Henry £112. No joke.

Berta could now either die or take part in a study of a new experimental cancer drug. No sooner said than done. The cancer disappeared. But unfortunately Berta's brain was also affected, which led to her racing into a bridge piling in the family Ford. Which in turn led to her being paralyzed from the neck down. Henry picked her up from the hospital two days after the accident because the costs there would have exceeded his nonexistent budget. His two daughters walked next to their father, who carried his wrecked wife over his shoulder like a rolled-up carpet. At home he laid his wife in bed and became an expert at patient care in the period that followed. Washing, feeding, exercise, speech therapy. Henry lost his job as a night watchman. Because he kept falling asleep. He was exhausted, he had to cook, shop, wait at the social services department, clean the flat, pack (household and children and broken-down wife) in order to relocate to the outskirts of town. The children had obviously suffered a bit under the circumstances; they wet the bed, stopped reading, stopped playing, they sat next to the broken-down mother's bed and were afraid. At some point, after his wife slipped from his arms in the shower and lay on the floor like a heavy slice of sausage, Henry began to cry and could no longer stop. The children grew more afraid. Henry told his wife every night that he wanted to kill her, the children, and himself, and his wife said nothing, but her eyes filled with tears and she smiled. The euphoria surrounding knowing a way out didn't last long. There was a fear of the end, and how could you get rid of the hope that things would be nice again, that there would be another spring or autumn, you'd see the children grow up, everything that is implanted in humans, implanted even in a man, this hope for a so-called fulfilled life, which ended at some stage with the singing of a hymn. And then his wife vomited, and shat in bed and moaned, and the air was stuffy, and at the social services department Henry screamed because he hadn't received his basic income because he hadn't been in touch because he showed up an hour late because his wife had shat the bed again and now he had to wait until Monday, and he went home and placed a pillow over his wife's head. Then on to the two children. He suffocated the first but the second refused, she tried to hide, she screamed, defended herself, then Henry hit the child on the head with a frying pan until it was finally quiet, and then he sat next to the corpse in the kitchen and couldn't move, couldn't breathe, couldn't cry, nothing.

On the screen

Is a local politician in front of the family home, the bodies are being removed, the man carried out, ditto the wife, and the politician—camera pans to the residents of the housing estate; they look like zombies, impassively aiming their mobile phone cameras at the goings-on, a few stones fly, probably from the civil task force that is positioned between the residents—the politician is appalled, at least he looks appalled, and he says: "The welfare state means that the laws of the market supersede mob rule." They've all gone crazy.

In the city. And on the outskirts, there where it's calm. Out at

THE FRIENDS

Excitement is in the air, there's an atmosphere like a crappy old American TV series, where everyone talks hysterically to project a crazy performance. The young people jump around inside the factory hall, they're incredibly excited. They're doing some hacker shit. "We should do it with spoofing." "Bullshit. I'm for row hammer," says Ben toward the sofa where Hannah, Don, and Peter are lying half asleep. "Yeah, sure," says Don to nobody. The hackers don't even listen to themselves; they talk like they're on drugs, so fast, the same way code is generated on computers, always new synapses that, in their brains, connect the same theories, all having to do with the online world, as if the real world no longer existed. Where it has become strangely empty. Everyone somewhere else, nobody here. Nobody is in touch with themselves anymore, or with anyone else, everyone alone with their feelings, which involve sex. And insecurity.

The lightheartedness of the group is gone. Same goes for the fun. They feel awkward confronted with their own helplessness. As if children who up to now have always bathed together naked suddenly hop in the tub in bikinis. All unsettled by their own bodies, which are getting stranger by the day.

Now they sit around here and listen to the others breathing in an oversize room. They drink yerba mate and

BEN

Gives one of his long explanatory lectures in the dark. Nobody listens to him.

"Some nuclear power plants had to be removed from the net." He says. "The reason had to do with obsolete technology. The new technology exists somewhere, but mostly in academic papers. The computer animation of smart cities, where there are solar farms, where self-driving buses stream through car-free green zones, people sort their garbage, children don't put their little tits and penises online like zombies, like and dislike things, and off themselves as a result of online bullying—this new world, born of science, doesn't exist. It's not worth it. What's worth doing is making smart devices. And computers, computers, computers. Meaning: every year, in order to build these cool devices, there is a need for four hundred thousand tons of aluminum, three hundred thousand tons of copper, and one hundred ten thousand tons of cobalt. And every year more than fifty million tons of electronic rubbish is left behind.

The electricity use for computer users, cloud services, search engines, terabytes eaten up by cryptocurrencies, networked window shades, drones, the eight million surveillance cameras that take over three hundred clips per week of every single citizen, the speech-activated hubs, bar coding, big data analyses of algorithm-based trading. The communication day and night, insomniacs' online shopping, streaming, the hardworking robots, blockchain—that's not neoliberalism out there anymore, that's hurtling at light speed toward an iceberg. Which is cold. And dark. And it needs electricity, god damn it. Electricity, electricity, electricity; without it nothing runs; without it all the data centers go down, AI is nothing but junk, for god's sake, do you guys get it?"

Silence.

The empty, dark space. The beginning and the ending and everything in between filled with products and fear. With little moments of intoxication.

Here at

THE FRIENDS

Who have removed themselves from real life and transferred their existences into machines. Which would be washed away if there were no more electricity, if the water were to rise. But at the moment everything is okay. Some of them have become a bit paranoid. Adults would say: "Oh boy, that sounds like paranoia right there!" Which could be true, but isn't necessarily, some of them just know too much, they know about all the invisible things that happen, that go on in the world beneath the world, where people play no role.

"What the fuck are you up to anyway?" asks Hannah at some point.

She shouldn't have asked. Because now Rachel, the youngest hacker, starts to explain.

Ha ha, funny,

Thinks

MI5 PIET

At the window. He looks down at the Kensington Palace Gardens. Nothing has changed here except for the owners. Abramovich had to sell. Some sheiks had to sell. It's mostly Chinese living here now. And him. Well, "living." The London Cage, earlier a well-disguised interrogation prison or, to put it more elegantly, an interviewing facility, has for some time been back in business.

Piet, who looks like most other men his age—vaguely approaching retirement, vaguely thinning hair, no mouth, eyes too close together and a creased neck. Piet, who looks as if he smells bad because there's tallow in the creases of his neck, doesn't move his mouth. He laughs inwardly. It was always the case that he had a good sense of humor, but, well, a distinctive type of humor. Piet feels superior to everyone. Like everyone else. He goes back to his work space, Eames chair and all that. He'd always had style. Born with it. The flat he decorated with his husband attests to his extraordinarily good taste. A flat in Chelsea. Thanks to the pay. Which has been somewhat in jeopardy ever since he had to start passing off his husband as his brother-in-law. Since the campaign against homosexuality and the reform of the marriage laws. Compliance with which he oversees. Bizarre, right?

Homosexuality isn't punishable by law. Not yet. But it's only a question of time, now that the country has started to recall its Christian roots. But back to the little hackers, thinks Piet. As head of command, he sees only what doesn't bore him personally. The algorithms deliver him surveillance highlights. Live links to gay clubs, to opposition movements and shoe stores with a conspiratorial footnote. Piet is into feet.

The baby hackers have been under surveillance for a good long while already. They didn't register themselves. Not clever, as the registration serves exclusively to detect portions of the population that aren't registered. Nobody needs people with chips. In an era of biometric total surveillance. The firm where MI5 Piet works is private. It has a long, complicated name which even the people who work there can't remember. So they just say MI5. Despite the outsourcing into private hands, Piet and his colleagues are paid from the government budget—put another way: the citizenry pay for his service, which is completely sensible, since he serves the people. Somehow. The secret service is a close partner. Which also has been privatized. Which, together with the privatized army and the privatized police force fight together toward the goal of privatizing everything.

Mastering the internet. Whereas ten years earlier MI5 Piet could access 40 billion data retrievals per day, today the scale of retrieved data must be in the trillions and contains—everything. From bowel movements to vaginal dryness, conversations with grandmother about debt, attitude toward the military, high school diplomas, streaming services. AI gets it right with some irregularity. Rarely does something go wrong. Sometimes, however, it does appear as if the program has developed a humor of its own. So-called malfunctions.

EX 2279

```
>++++++++++
[>++++++++++++>++++++++++++>++++++++++++
+>++++++++++++>++++++++++++>++++++++++++>+
++++++++++>++++++++++++>++++++++++++>+++
++++++++++>++++++++++++>++++++++++++>++++++-
++++>><<<<<<<<<<<<<<<-]
>+>+>—>++++—>—>+>>+>——>>+>—>
<<<<<<<<<<<<<
>.>.>.>.>.>.>.>.>.>.>.>.
```

Don't exist.

MI5 PIET

Believes in the system. A good system. A violent, absurd misconception has developed out there related to individuals' own skill sets. Every pupil, every unemployed person, every complete idiot believes they are owed justice and the same life as a tech genius or a superstar. In the past people contented themselves with what they were able to earn given their abilities. A farmer was a farmer, the lord of the manor was the lord of the manor, and god watched over everyone. Amen, man. And listen, we need to give people rules and a god again. Nothing makes the majority of earth dwellers more nervous than a good, punitive hand.

Check.

The country, his country, is nearly back to an ideal condition. With a satisfying sense of order. Forget the unease, the imbalance, the absurd pressure to make his life into a shopping event and to go mad when through some mistake you can't buy cheap plastic shit from Africa. Go mad because people of a particular religion or skin color resent others their shopping fun. In the short time of the experiment astonishing successes have already been logged. They keep themselves and the streets clean, respect the rules and schedules. The need to be more than one is, seems to have dissipated in no time. People are busy just bettering themselves. Most of them are excited about the challenge of earning positive points. It stimulates their reward system. They want to accumulate points and be better than their neighbors. The basis of capitalism. Narrowed to unthreatening parameters like parking in an orderly manner, cleaning one's flat, the assistance one provides to fellow citizens, how loud one turns up the music at home, the environmentally friendly handling of resources. There are bonus points for lowering the heat in your flat. For showering responsibly. Owning an electric motorcar or doing without a car altogether, and meat; for doing without:

Cleaning powder, fabric softener, owning a pet, having children. Right, and so on, the catalog of rules is long and incomprehensible. Piet leans back. That's what he would say if someone were to ask him, which doesn't happen. Nobody asks him what he does for a living. That's considered impolite. Impoliteness is reprimanded with a point reduction. After the Me Inc. brand was built up for years, egotism, antisocial momentum driven by the demands of the market, after mutual solidarity was trashed, ditto unions, this development has now entered the well-ordered escalation phase. The battle of man versus man—why men, actually?—has started. Piet turns toward the screen. The image quality produced by the tiny drones is astonishing. Same goes for the sound captured by systems that have been taken over.

Piet watches the little idiots with something bordering on touching interest.

RACHEL

IQ: *156*
HOBBIES: *Linux, Python, and all that hipster nerd nonsense*
POLITICAL TENDENCIES: *oppositional*
SEXUAL ORIENTATION: *none yet*
FEARS: *MI5*

Is just fourteen. Her father is an engineer, her mother a mathematician. Under other circumstances, it's quite possible that Rachel would have become a fashion blogger, but then again perhaps not, considering that intelligence is hereditary. The sobering reality of biology.

Had Rachel been born twenty or thirty years earlier, she would have listened to Hawaiian punk music, collected comics; she might have conducted experiments with a chemistry set or tried to observe dark matter. Today, though, it's the internet. Nice that the net exists. With a computer that she'd disassembled. With codes, Linux, GNUnet, and accelerated developments that demand intelligence, a resource Rachel has not yet exhausted. It is the most uplifting feeling a human can be granted: not to hit a limit. Right, and so forth and so on. Rachel is happy here with the others whom she regards as totally normal. In school she always stood alone in the corner because she wasn't an engaging child and also wasn't necessarily good-looking in that childish way. Her ears are too big, same for her nose, and the rest of her doesn't conform to the norm that currently holds sway for good-looking girls, either. Today is by far the best day of her life. Her body is so flooded with adrenaline that she feels as if she could fly. Her pupils are dilated, her body trembles so much it's as though she were frozen. Today Rachel feels at one with the universe, like she's on an epic heroin high.

Rachel has told the others what she intends to do. To expose people out there to the giant joke, show them that they're nothing more than lab rats, show them how they're being deceived. "In a few days the time will have come, and the revolution will kick off," says Rachel, and . . . "Where is the other one anyway?"

By the other one she means

KAREN

Who has begun to train. She runs. She listens to grime. She listens to vintage music. Lady Leshurr and Scrufizzer and she's so angry, so angry, what a bunch of shit, that she can't rap and instead must run, past the sheds that pass as accommodations, where people celebrate the death of their hope. Running is rapping for losers. While

Dusk

is falling and

KEVIN

contemplates the darkness, which closes like curtains. The part of his brain responsible for survival sounds the alarm. Fear spreads through his body, ice-cold. In the night. Asleep. The disk of the earth could tip and dispatch him into space. Kevin overdoses on sleeping pills like every day at the arrival of darkness. The only joy in Kevin's life, which is largely poisoned by the feelings that come with believing in theories ignored by the general public, are the pills, which cost only pennies. For his mood, to sleep, to combat fear and worries. But. He hates the neighborhood where he is forced to live; a machine had on the basis of all his data selected the area as the one where he'd feel most comfortable.

And

THE PROGRAMMER

Knows,

People feel most comfortable among those similar to them. It makes them calm when they're surrounded by others who resemble them. "Just imagine a person with an income of a thousand pounds a month lives, however it's supposed to work financially, in an area where the average income is a hundred thousand a month. That would obviously create discontent. The calculation of the optimal residential area for each individual takes into account factors such as ethnicity, sexual orientation, hobbies, financial and health background, and character traits. We utilize the same system in the realm of the labor market and partnership matching. It's proved brilliant. Things have gotten calm."

Satisfied

Is something

KEVIN

has never been. And he awakes because his bed is tilted and is being jolted by violent blows. An unprecedented terror envelops him. It's happened. It's pitch black. It's ice-cold. He's going to float off into space.

Kevin suffers a heart attack around 3:30 in the morning, and dies at home a few hours later as a result,

Because

THOME

Disappears again immediately after his successful prank, not without having filmed the effort. Just for himself. For a laugh. He indulges in such a prank every month. Every month he chooses a victim from his Your Fear app upon whom to bestow the gift of staring their greatest fear in the face. Thome ignores mundane fears like the loss of a loved one or the loss of a home and instead embraces an unusual anxiety. Like the fear of a loss of an appendage, for example. That was something he had managed for a woman to wake up to last month. Morning, light, birds singing, and you wake up and want to get out of bed. You wake up and want to get up and pull the covers off and look down and see two bandaged stumps. That really gives your brain something to think about. Kevin and his slipping-off-the-earth-into-space phobia was easy to satisfy by comparison. His bed was propped up on a slanted machine that had been used to get dirt off potatoes. Between the slant and the shaking action the terror was perfect. It's helpful that all of these people totally voluntarily knock themselves out with propofol-containing drugs. Fun must be had.

Thinks

KAREN

As she runs past the losers. The immigrants, the alcoholics, the homeless, the number of whom seems to swell by the day. The homeless shelters were recently bought by a holding company and prices were raised. Karen follows the interesting research that began with the decoding of Neanderthal DNA in Germany. Years back, they had already grown mini Neanderthal brains, though only to the maturity stage of an embryo. But now scientists had succeeded in growing human brains with Neanderthal DNA inserted in them. It worked well. The next step was to abstract the feelings from brains. Goal! In the meantime they've produced fully functional brains. Brains without feelings, workers and soldiers without troublesome characteristics. And perfect, intelligent, troublesome-free brains for people who can afford to do well by their offspring. Karen knows she belongs to the second-to-last flawed generation.

Rubbish, thinks

THOME'S FATHER

Miserable do-gooders,

He mumbles. He's just presented his plan to eliminate child benefits without a replacement, and to put what's left of the health care system into private hands. He looks into the bright red, indignant, self-righteous face of a Labour woman. Unfuckable thing. She asks for the floor.

She is recognized and asks:

"The monstrousness our colleague once again recited here can only be understood as exhorting the needy to suicide. I have one question for him: When you create millions of homeless, ill and with no access to health care; when as a result of your actions millions of uneducated children are produced; when purchasing power is thereby reduced by the millions and subsistence crime grows by leaps and bounds; when these people completely disappear as consumers, where then is the economic advantage?"

Thome's father smirks. "If I might be permitted to answer.

"Esteemed colleague. That is extremely simple—it will take care of itself by natural means."

If you vanquish all things human.

Thinks

KAREN

Then feelings will also be under excellent control. Karen has become a machine. No fat. Only muscles. Bones. Sinews. She's grown strong. She injects herself with testosterone that she gets from the lab director. She runs, does a thousand push-ups and pull-ups.

As if her brain had likewise been battered by the hormone, Karen simply has no fear anymore. Afraid of nothing. Even now, in Hyde Park as darkness gathers. It will all start in the dark. The first homeless will be lit on fire. Hurray, light in the dark—

Karen walks past a bench around which a few young men stand, looking at a homeless person.

Students from Trinity College. Karen recognizes them by their ugly blue jackets and gray trousers, despite their ridiculous clown masks.

The unbelievably overwhelming demands on the collective consciousness, that now manifests itself in the form of flaccid groups of idle men roaming the inner city to hunt down beggars. He doesn't look up. The tramp.

"Hey, would you kindly get up," say the

YOUNG MEN

CITIZEN POINTS: *as a result of stable family relationships, no reductions despite multiple traffic violations, various accusations of sexual harassment*
FUTURE PROSPECTS: *pillars of society*
SEXUAL ORIENTATION: *perversion*

The homeless man doesn't get up. "So, you're resisting," says a tall student, nodding to the others, and they begin to punch the vagrant, almost half-heartedly. At first with their hands, which are covered in gloves, you certainly wouldn't want to actually touch him. And hands don't leave any marks, at least until you break the nose at some point, the snap is good, the blood is good, it gives you a rush. One of the three young men gets up on the bench and orders the tramp to the ground with a few kicks. Right, that's better, now you can really step into it, at first in the side, the body, then in the face, something breaks. Then the three of them jump one after the other on the tramp's head. Someone else can clean it up. For instance

KAREN

Who tries to find a pulse among the remains, but the vagrant is no longer alive.

Karen breathes to stop her urge to beat the shit out of the three Trinity College wackos. Fucking testosterone. So that's how it is at the top of the food chain, shot to the top with the injection of a few doses. These female babies that begin shortly after birth, still half blind, to stare into faces and start to think how they can push the very people who are looking at them around in a wheelchair. All these woman-thoughts—how will I find a man, how will I get everyone to like me, what will I wear at my funeral, am I too loud, too demanding, am I shaved enough, nice enough, pretty enough—WTF, it could be cured. One injection per week and world history would be rewritten. Karen sweats. She sweats more now and usually has a strong rushing sound in her head that exits through her ears, as if water has flooded her brain and is washing away her thoughts. Think about it. What would happen if I were to smash my fist through a window? She doesn't ask herself that anymore, the little delay that balances every act with a possible effect has disappeared. She has too much energy, which is why she started all this running, something she had previously regarded with contempt. It's always the most inconspicuous creatures who beg for a longer life with every step. Karen runs. She feels good. It seems to her that after setting the virus adrift in the Thames and with the pressure inside her gone, she might for the first time in ages be taking some joy in life again. She looks at buildings and trees and it isn't so bad to be alive. As long as there is something to do that challenges you and excites you, as long as that, it's not so bad. Karen has forgotten the homeless. She forgets everything of late. Including the reason she is running around here. In the park, past benches.

On one of which sits

DR. BROWN

He likes to sit on a bench of an evening. He runs his hand along his flat stomach, fit from working out. It had been a good decision to open a beauty-to-go practice in London. Members of the disappearing middle class love it. The startup slaves with their multiple degrees and foreign languages, Dr. this and Dr. that in all sorts of disciplines, hiring themselves out in Open Spaces without proper employment contracts in order to share in the great, prosperous dream of the developer family. For the most part they earn barely five hundred pounds a month, but on the other hand there's a refrigerator in Open Spaces with energy drinks and energy bars, a foosball table in the lounge, and you can speak informally to the bosses. The bosses are all men. Startup firms that take money off people who barely have any money left, by delivering diapers to them daily, dispatching cleaning slaves, dispatching old ladies who cook simple, good-hearted dishes, desperate pensioners who are living beneath the poverty line and can be had for any old shit, delivering socks or gluten-free food daily. That's the stuff they develop. Ridiculous platforms for a ridiculous life.

The startup slaves have cool job titles that always include the word *manager*, and in the evening they play ball with their coworkers, always good to be seen doing that. Nine out of ten startups go bankrupt after a year. In which case the job is gone. The rest succeed. And are sold to China. Job gone. But as long as you have the job, you want to look good. They come in during lunch and leave the practice with cheap muscle or breast implants from India, Botox from Russia, and whatever other cheap shit Dr. Brown can procure from around the world. Dr. Brown has also started giving abortions since they've been made illegal, and since you now have to pay for the pill yourself and reproductive decisions are in the hands of the state. Women disappear out the back door afterwards. Some of them take their aborted fetuses with them. Others have a little something done after the abortion. "This is just for me, so I feel good." They leave the practice with the hope of looking like everyone else. And thereby to be invisible. Please, please, if they just were part of the huge mass of identical-looking assholes, perhaps they'd be spared the downfall. They can pay in installments. They can pad their asses, have fat sucked out, have fake six-pack muscles put under the skin of their stomachs, they can be let straight back out onto the street afterwards where with their artificial stomach muscles they can duke it out with the little metal boxes that take away their jobs. Will. Dr. Brown knew the world pre-internet. It was unfair, it was dark and boring, but more comfortable. People sat in front of their buildings and—in the absence of other excitement or Netflix—watched cars go by. They spoke to each other. And when you killed someone, because back then the right existed to kill someone, it was a personal, almost loving act. Today that, too, is taken care of by machines. Killing.

"Pardon me, you're Dr. Brown?"

Dr. Brown looks up; in front of him is a peculiar person. Giant, scrawny, with high cheekbones, slanted eyes that glow red in the dark, white hair, and a giant mouth.

"What can I do for you?" answers Dr. Brown angrily, because the injections in his penis are doing their job. Dr. Brown clears his throat.

"Nothing," says the white ghost, not in a friendly way, and walks with long strides toward the darkness of the park.

Dr. Brown thinks he hears snickers. He watches the thing go and wonders what is off about the person. Some body part isn't right. As if the head were attached between the legs. Brown looks at the time. He heads for his practice.

And

KAREN

Follows him into the courtyard of a circular social housing block situated on a street of affluent houses. It'll soon be on fire.

The medical practice is on the ground floor. A bathroom window is tilted open, and Karen climbs in through it.

She passes a kitchen where sad yellow light illuminates medical equipment, a toilet, and—the examination room. Karen sees the open crotch of a woman and the back of Dr. Brown's head, hair is growing out of his ears. Karen leans against the wall. A flashback. Bodily details of all the male bodies of the previous few years pass before her eyes. Hair creeping into the light from ears and noses, yellow teeth, breath that smells like old rubbish, dried spittle in the corners of mouths, strings of saliva between upper and lower lips. Small, white, tapered bottoms with black hairs, between thighs testicles dangling down toward the knees. All kinds of little, crooked cocks, smegma on the cocks, drooping arms, hairy backs, eyes close together, inflamed. Stomachs in all shapes and colors with smelly belly buttons. Makes sense that people have such an unbelievable propensity for violence inside, people who look like that are evil.

Dr. Brown pulls down his pants. They gather around his ankles. His underwear stretches between his knees. Looks ridiculous, but

DR. BROWN'S

Penis still stands out from his body like an imposing architectural structure. As if it weren't part of his body, as if it had been retroactively attached. Dr. Brown is going to stockpile a fuck. A chance like this doesn't come round every day. Such a good-looking unconscious person. Conscious sexual partners cause hassles, since they talk, breathe, they make false moves, they lie, they feign excitement, excitement about his penis and his technique. The difficulties of a woman's bodily openings aren't unknown to him. The dumbfucks can't come unless he manually fiddles with their clits for ages. But what man wants to do that? So he likes them best when they're calm, silent, open. Just a few more thrusts and . . . Dr. Brown doesn't feel the blow. He doesn't feel anything. He is out like a light.

With a heavy metal ashtray

ARTHUR

HEALTH RISKS: *highly excitable*
POLITICAL ORIENTATION: *prior antifa activities*
HOBBIES: *drug abuse*
OTHER HOBBIES: *becoming a father*
Well, even though

Stands in front of the doctor's body. Well mashed. He thinks and breaks out in a fit of laughter that despite the term's misogynist connotations is best described as "hysterical." Now, it's not every day you strike somebody on the head so hard that part of his brain is laid bare. Arthur's wife is anesthetized. He looks with bewilderment into her open vagina. He's in shock. He's going to be a father. His wife won't abort the child. He's going to be a father, and everything will be sorted again. He starts to sing. His wife will not leave him. She wanted to leave him. That is, a few days before she had said she could no longer stand him. But you should know.

That Arthur can't stand himself, either. Ever since Scriptbox technology started to choose screenplays, that is for two years now, he hasn't been able to sell a single play or screenplay. At first he had still thought: Well, guess I missed the mark. You should know that Arthur is in his mid-forties and for twenty years had been able to more or less live off his screenplays and theater pieces. The plays ran successfully in off–West End venues. The screenplays were a bit more fraught. Up to thirty-two rewrites for independent films. But he was satisfied. He was an artist. Now he receives a basic income. The Script-box algorithm has saved every theater piece and film screenplay that's ever been produced, all of which are analyzed for profitability and risk, and the algo-rithm then gauges the prospects for success of new works. That is, based on what sentences and other elements appear in successful works. If little or none of that appears in a new work, the piece doesn't have mass appeal. Bye-bye.

Arthur sits in the one-room flat he shares with his wife and tries to think in terms of mass appeal. That is, to think up plots with mass appeal. Something about love. And problems. And twists. And a happy ending. The old Hugh Grant type of films. Or something about spies. Countless beginnings, legs twitching, increasingly agitated. Every day the same. Start. Something with sun, autumn foliage, a wild but at the same time sweet girl strolling through Soho. Then. Arthur begins to poke around on social media. From current events to newspaper reports to the filter bubble of idiocy—the Nazi accounts—he gets excited, then tired, then he has a nap. No success. He has no success at any-thing; every new attempt to produce something with mass appeal is met with a proverbial shake of the head from the machine. Arthur writes a script about a machine gone awry that makes decisions about all things, subject only to its own absolute discretion. Decisions about life and death in hospitals, couples' suitability for marriage, court verdicts. When it's finished, the Scriptbox speech generator asks: "Where is the gag?" That night Arthur rapes his wife. Well, really, come on, rape? He just didn't listen too closely when she said: "Nah, not tonight." His wife, who is planning her departure. Getting away from the grouchy dope smoker who sits home at night awaiting her return after her shift at a restaurant to the little flat they were recently allotted. Before them, a fitness trainer with cancer lived in this dark hole. There were still photos on the walls. His wife later got pregnant, and that, ladies and gentlemen, is a miracle if you consider that the sperm count in the gonads of the Western world have already dropped 60 percent and that by the year 2030 men will be infertile, which explains why they'd all become so angry even back then.

In any case, his wife was not so enthused about this fluky biological bull's-eye. She'd said: "I don't want this." And Arthur had thought: What do you mean you don't want this? He had already seen his life with the baby flash before his eyes. A life where he didn't sit at his desk all day and try to write a Hugh Grant film, god rest his soul, and in so doing despair about his lack of talent and so on, and instead he'd have a purpose. A meaning, in an I-can-raise-this-baby-and-do-baby-appropriate-things-with-him sense. He had figured out that his wife wanted to get rid of the fruit of her womb. Which is so incomprehensible. That a woman can decide what is to happen to a seed he planted. That a stupid cunt can kill his creation.

Which is why he follows her as soon as she leaves home. Why he hooked up with the group called the Others, who hunt doctors who perform abortions, which is to say commit murders. Or women who want abortions. Who are then—how shall we put it—pressured by the group. Their addresses are posted on a website. Easy.

And now he tosses away the ashtray and runs into the night. Perhaps he can still beat up a homeless person so as to explain the blood on his collar.

It smells of food

When

KAREN

Enters the factory. It's after midnight, and the others are lying on their mattresses, tomato sauce smeared on their faces. Leftover noodles still in the kitchen. "Dr. Brown died with an erection," she says. "From or with?" asks Don. "Eat something first," says Peter. The children who are no longer children— what do you call people who are still growing, for fuck's sake?—sit at the kitchen table with Karen and watch Karen shovel herself full of lukewarm noodles. She's not hungry, but sitting here, with the others, like a real family, is a ritual they've established, sitting together and talking, as if they could be each other's family. They sit at the table, because grown-ups always sit at a table and make serious faces. They make serious faces and discuss adult things. The price of water has risen in the city again. It's shut off every day for a few hours. People no longer bathe, barely shower, and there's powder to fight the odor created by an unwashed body. Showering. What a thing. The children sometimes wash themselves in the little stream outside, sometimes in the kitchen sink. Often, though, not at all.

Despite its loft-style loftiness, the factory hall still looks like something. That animals live in. The mattresses on the floor, the laundry they wash in a trough in the kitchen hangs from lines all over the place, pizza boxes in the

corner. Cardboard on the windows so as not to reveal at night to any poten-
tially passing drones that it's occupied.

The children leave the kitchen in its state, a state that looks as though
a set designer had set up a bombed-out kiddie kitchen, and they lie on their
mattresses to enjoy the best moment of the day. When the lights are out and
the TV is on, all of them doing something by their nightstand lamps, reading
or thinking or just not sleeping. I don't want to go to sleep yet. The moment
when it's like being in a cave, when we all breathe as one, should never end.
The moment before they're all alone as the heroes of their nightmares, before
you wake up in the morning in a light that illuminates the aimlessness and
loneliness of the group too brightly. And

DON

Lies on her mattress, her legs twitch, she tries to read but can't concentrate
because her legs are twitching. And her brain isn't trained for the grasping of
long blocks of text.

"Is there a lot of dialogue?"

Asks Hannah.

"What do you mean, dialogue?" asks Don. "It's a book about algorithms."

Hannah lies down next to Don, whose skin immediately becomes sensitive.
Nearly painful in the areas where Hannah's body touches hers. From outside
the wind blows through the drafty windows, a candle flickers in the kitchen;
another nod to adulthood, they always light candles, adults, and then they
drink wine. The children have also drunk wine today; it makes you bleary.

"My favorite part of books is the dialogue," says Hannah. She stares at
Don's book. "Do you mean comics," asks Don, shifting to the side a bit so she
can breathe. "No," says Hannah. "Dialogue, I can hear people talking, and
they talk the way we talk, it draws me closer to the story."

Don is silent. Her heart races, her head buzzes. She is. Simply out of her
mind. Don hates books with dialogue and is convinced that it's a lazy trick
used by writers, this whole writing of dialogue thing. It fills pages so nicely.
With the empty sentences that most people exchange, with all the incredibly
meaningless words they use to demonstrate their self-importance or to talk
about their relationships or just their fear of being nothing more than an aggregation of desires. "Do you want to kiss me?" Don doesn't ask, staring into
her fucking book. It's about the benefits of an algorithm-defined society. And

it has no fucking dialogue. But it is fucking horrible. Bots pushed it to the
top of the best seller list. Bots push all kinds of shit, but people have gotten
accustomed to it, or perhaps nobody cares whether they see real news or fake,
whether they're chatting with a bot or a human. The point is that someone is
listening to them. Back when they were still around, many media experts had
urged citizens to become critical, um, users. The truth of every news item, every
article, every video could be checked through time-consuming research. Well.
Okay. A kind of truth. Nobody did it. Truth is a feeling. A gut feeling, people
say, people who should be smacked for the use of the phrase. But everyone just
continues to believe what they want to believe—like an apocalypse brought
on by jet airplane chemtrails, the victory of anarchists, or that vaccines are
deadly. The more confusing the world gets, the more desperate individuals are
to create an inner catalog of the comprehensible.

Hannah has returned to her mattress, has turned off her bedside lamp;
now just the TV is on so the voices can calm the children, talk them to sleep,
sleep that doesn't want to come when it is too quiet.

It's going well, thinks

THOME'S FATHER

He is lying in bed, watching TV. He needs a few minutes before he realizes that what he's watching isn't the eighty-ninth episode of *The Walking Dead*,
that series financed by neoliberals, but rather a live report from the north of
the country. The sweating man has really done top-shelf work.

Thome's father needs to call him straightaway. But

THE SWEATING MAN

Doesn't really hear the phone ring clearly. The call reaches him just as he is

Tying a scarf to the radiator, putting his neck into the loop, and forcing
his body to defy its will to survive. Yes, and it's true that during the fight, flush
with hormones, he sees his life flash before his eyes, a life that had been made
up of nothing. Hanging oneself on an object near ground level, like a door-
knob or pipe valve, demands a strong will. At the very least. My goodness was
it torture, this living, when you wanted nothing more than the respect of alpha
males, who had never accepted you, how bleak is it when you can't love? And
when he, the sweating man, had ever fallen in love, it had always been short-
lived and ended with him sitting helplessly at a table with a woman, drinking
tea, and at some point she would always say, "Take your jacket with you when

you go." At least he has a strong will, the sweating man, who hears the phone ring in the midst of his death throes and in his fading consciousness pictures the ringing of the bells of heaven.

Nice images

Viewed by

THOME'S FATHER

In a BBC special called *The Poor: How Much Do They Threaten Our Prosperity?*

He straightens his blanket. Turns down the sound so his Russian hooker doesn't wake up, and follows the special broadcast delightedly.

In a talk show format the problems caused by the poor are outlined. They hinder growth of a recovery, they lead crime statistics (which never include white-collar crime). The basic income could be 50 percent higher for "normal citizens" if payments to degenerates were stopped.

The next program up is on child gangs.

The enlightenment of the people is bearing fruit. A homeless shelter in Blackpool is burned down. Fifty-seven people die. There's an expression of so-called official regret, not, however, without a relativizing comment by the prime minister that of course one must be aware of what one triggers among other, working people with one's lifestyle—

And now

DON

Has completely lost her way in her book.

Don's hand hurts so badly that she moans quietly. And doesn't notice that she's moaning, and only when Hannah turns on her bedside lamp and bends over her does she become alert, snapping to from half-sleep. "You can see the bones," says Hannah, holding Don's hand. From the bathroom she retrieves bandages, disinfectant, and antibiotics that the Friends bought via Tor. She disinfects the hand and bandages it and gets very close to Don while doing it. Don would only have to move a few millimeters and she'd be able to give Hannah a kiss. But she doesn't. She watches as Hannah puts out the light, feels the throbbing spreading out from her hand through her entire body, corresponding to the beat of her heart, and she can't sleep, of course not. Because it's cold.

Despite the stove.

They got the wood stove from a

STUDENT

HOBBIES: *masturbates (according to transmitted vibrator data) twice daily for ca. 1 minute*

HEALTH CONDITIONS: *passive-aggressive*

POLITICAL ORIENTATION: *inconspicuous*

INTELLIGENCE: *average*

CONSUMER INTERESTS: *TV series, magazines, cosmetic products, vegan, otherwise no interests*

The stove. Well. The young woman studies. Something. Authentic. That is—shall we say—she had studied, before student fees and so forth. Now she's more of an inner student or, as she likes to say: "I'm a student of life." She studies life at three different jobs. One consists of her showing her breasts. The student has an entirely representative average early-twenties urban white middle-class life plan. The student is from a middle-class family of teachers in Norfolk. Two mothers. That was still okay then. Now it is. Illegal. The student hates her body. She doesn't smoke—well, okay, who smokes anymore?—doesn't do drugs, takes Pilates classes, and walks ten thousand steps every day, it gets you bonus points in the social points system.

MI5 PIET

"Ten thousand steps. I knew it, you sloppy cow. If it is any at all then it's maybe one thousand steps a day. One thousand totally pointless steps."

THE STUDENT

Likes to earn points. She likes to walk ten thousand steps a day and would double that number if not for her breasts. Which disrupt the lithe, streamlined shape of her body. The student is saving up for a breast reduction and has lived for four years in London. Subletting. And so on. Online the student opposes: circumcision, *shechita*, factory farming, climate change, the financial system, low income taxes for billionaires, fracking and nuclear power, atomic weapons, and surveillance. She has as her social media profile picture the symbol of the anti—coal, fracking, and nuclear power movement.

MI5 PIET

Spits his breakfast onto his keyboard, laughing.

"They make their own profiles. Do they know what a profile is? In the old days they existed for use in police records departments to classify criminals and the mentally ill. An accomplishment, so to speak. Today billions of people willingly and meticulously compile their own profiles. Hobbies, sexual and political preferences, networks, friends, family relations, consumption patterns, they even send in their DNA so they can tell people what ethnicities are in their genes, they send us their data twenty-four hours a day. The really clever ones blast all their info into the cloud. I could practically sing an ode to the cloud. Sweet."

Is

THE STUDENT

A feminist, blonde, young woman who on dates insists on paying for her own organic falafel. Who gets very angry if anyone touches her without asking or comments on her body. The nude photos she considers art. The student regularly has her teeth cleaned, eats vegan, and yes, she makes a big deal about it. Some new superfood or other is always making it into her meal plan, usually the hype conforms to a blueprint created by the economic system of foodstuffs that are overproduced or underpriced. Stuff that just has to be gotten rid of. Oats, quinoa, avocados, coconut oil, spelt, kale, fork it over. The feeling of living in a body whose guts are forming good, healthy excrement from healthy, nutritionally valuable, environmentally friendly products is indescribable. These days the money no longer suffices for that sort of fun.

These days the student subsists on the same thing as everyone else she knows: good, cheap meat. The student is political. Like nearly everyone she knows, she is obsessed with freedom fighting. That is, theoretical freedom fighting for the oppressed. The Palestinians, for instance. She knows a few personally. She feels for them. She's opposed to Jews, well, not on the whole, she doesn't know any Jews except those at Goldman Sachs, who now control the cryptocurrencies, and those who have spread through the city of London. The student demonstrates in front of supermarkets against the purchase of Israeli chervil. It gives her a really good feeling. The student stage manages plays in fringe theaters with refugees who have experienced hardship. She had thought for a time about a theater piece with kids from troubled neighborhoods, but then it seemed too unattractive to her. It doesn't make sense to her, because the poor in this country aren't poor in the same sense as refugees. They speak English. They have themselves to blame for their situation.

To a certain extent.

The student overestimates her worth to society and leads a normal average young person's life. Meaning the student is going mad like everyone else. She can't keep up anymore, doesn't understand the immediate drop in value of newly purchased technical devices and the simultaneous pressure to always want the latest devices, doesn't understand what these devices that are falling in value want. They are constantly asking her to update her software, the refrigerator wants to newly configure its app, the hoover needs to fix a security breach. You could say that the student spends six hours a day with the devices, she waits, installs uploads, reconfigures, watches tutorials, fails at something and then is badgered by some other device. Her devices perpetually make noise, with which they demand respect.

And outside.

Something is hacked every day: banks, email accounts, airlines, chemical factories, governments. Personal devices are already bugged by the government before they're sold. Whatever. Who gives a shit. The student is nervous. Everyone is nervous and phlegmatic at the same time, thanks to the new order, passive-aggressive.

"The unrest in the world can always be felt before major upheavals," says

ROB

HOBBIES: *talking*
HEALTH STATUS: *optimal*
STATE OF MIND: *young man*
SEXUAL ORIENTATION: *interested in sex. But not with the student*
FEAR: *of being insignificant*

Who has for a while been the man the student is in love with. Theoretically, that is. In practice, this love hasn't led to an exchange of anything at all. Rob sits on her bed in her shared flat and talks. Something he can do well. "The world is developing the same way humans age. In stages. Before each newly manifesting stage humans experience crises. They sense something but don't know what it is. When they then arrive in their next age phase, this nervous situation dissipates again."

"Aha," says the student while thinking: Take your clothes off!

"Yeah, we are at the dawn of a new era. The revolution 4.0 during simultaneous overpopulation."

"Right, of course," says the student, opening her blouse. She suspects that Rob is a fucking know-it-all, but she's not the brightest, either, and her blouse is open. And she's frantically rubbing Rob's arm and brightly laughing and throwing her head back like a young foal. No reaction. Reactions from men have been missing for some time. The student is sure it's a result of her lack of sexiness. No whistles on the street anymore, no unsolicited penises flashed at her, no random brushing up against her body parts on the tube, and most of all no sex. The student confuses sex with affection and has felt cold for some time, she feels invisible when the gropes and shouts fail to materialize, she misses the feeling of superiority during the sex act, when she could observe men unaffected by the proceedings in her body. Jesus, the way they lose themselves. You really feel very little at all with such a small penis inside you. But—

Suddenly there's nothing there anymore. Rob has finished talking. He looks at his watch, which is connected to the chip implanted in his hand, and says: "I have to be going." And then he leaves. Not even a goodbye hug. The young men have no urge anymore. They're busy. On the computer. And with music. And games. And movies, and hanging around. And having no clue.

When the student lies down in bed, freezing because the heater doesn't work, the voice-activated virtual assistant consoles her. "You're sad because Rob left."

"How do you know it was Rob," asks the student, slightly shocked by the little tin can's attentiveness.

The little tin can answers: "Rob Walter, twenty-four, theater student, moderately gifted, poor marks, numerous missed classes, bank account currently overdrawn: three hundred forty-five pounds. Suffers from chlamydia, white middle-class family from Birmingham, parents divorced, previous girlfriend had an abortion, moderate threat potential."

WTF, thinks the student. That's cold. She's in arrears in karma points. When she went to buy beer yesterday the price had risen by a factor of six because she'd stayed out partying at the pub too long on two previous nights. Last night she was so drunk that she tried to cut off her breast with a razor blade. But it hurt, and on top of that she hadn't covered the camera on her phone and today two hundred penalty points had been subtracted. Which is why she gave up the heat. Children. Hopefully she would get positive points for that.

The next day

PETER

Is with Don in a so-called public space, which is accessible to the people but doesn't belong to them. How nicely the so-called populace conducts itself while populating when they're suddenly no longer anonymous. Aware of being recorded and evaluated every second. A totally abstract but somehow revalued existence, that transcends the meaningless performance of shopping, which has long since become hollow. Had. Over. Peace. They've been phenomenally well trained to be seen. Ten years of social media has left behind vast mental devastation. Speaking of damage—

Most webcams transfer their material to the internet, where it lives forever. That way everyone can archive all evidence of one's existence on the planet. Can profile and exhibit oneself, reread the comments about oneself in a bar yesterday evening. Hey, you in the red dress, you're hot, want to meet up? Super performance, thanks. The comments are almost all positive. It appears as if all the hate of recent years is being siphoned off to some gully, as if there's no more reason to be angry at the world now that one is taken notice of, now that there's money just for showing up, now that the island is swimming alone in the sea and everyone has for various reasons really shown the elite a thing or two. Now there's nothing left to hate, Brussels is gone, the elite defeated, the foreigners stuck in Calais, the poofs are afraid to show themselves on the street ever since a referendum repealed marriage rights for such obviously deranged people. And the public display of affection between those of the same sex is also punished as indecent behavior. People are no longer distracted by abnormality during social gatherings and can dedicate themselves to themselves. So to speak. Through the removal of paper from the street, driving in an orderly manner, showering in an environmentally conscious way, by the approved consumption of approved foods, by keeping physically fit, by refraining from visiting the doctor, and by picking up dog droppings. Even from other people's dogs. All dogs. Humanity picks up a giant pile of dog shit in order to grab bonus points in order to augment the basic income. Some earn as much as a hundred pounds, and their photos are pinned at the top of the karma points website. How pleasing. The new life.

A WOMAN

UTILITY: *utterly insignificant, appears only to illustrate the scene*

Walks into one of the concrete street barriers that had been erected all over the city to protect against Muslim-oriented individuals who, by order of some operator or other, had flattened people with a motorcar.

She had.

Seen.

PETER

like the cover image of one of those cheap tearjerker romances that had existed back when people still read books. The longish blond hair, the broad shoulders, the narrow waist, muscles and spermatic cords distributed along 190 centimeters, and something in his appearance causes erratic behavior in passersby who encounter him. Memories, perhaps. Sexuality has almost completely disappeared in the city or is limited only to tourists, men who stare and whistle and scratch their crotches. The local men have changed, though most wouldn't be able to say exactly what had changed. Peter feels uncomfortably tense from the stress of standing out, for whatever reason, whether it is a result of skin color, body type, intelligence. To be different from average people is to be in a constant state of crisis. Most people want to get rid of anything that's different from them, anything that doesn't look like them they want to see dead. Most people are comfortable being subject to this general view. Inconspicuous, out of harm's way. What an extraordinarily lovely boy.

Practically Michelangelesque.

Thinks the

PHILOSOPHER

SEXUAL PREFERENCES: *homosexual. Presumably*
CLINICAL PICTURE: *no abnormalities*
HOBBIES: *collects wooden toys*

Who rolls past Peter in a blue, self-driving tourist bus. He contemplates London. Such a pretty city, and yet also culturally cradlesque. The philosopher likes to make up words. He loves words and this city here is really something different. Different from the countryside where he lives, like very few live anymore, with a fireplace, with a library, and the investigation of the complete works of James Joyce. The philosopher had spent the last ten years retranslating an unpublished German translation of *Ulysses*, for which he first translated the German translation into English only to translate it back into German. Now, when his work was supposed to be published—parentheses: he was one of the few Joyce experts who as a native English speaker could also translate into German, a rare talent—now the widow of the German translator refuses to allow a new translation of her dead husband's translation. The call came yesterday. Today the philosopher, as he likes to jokingly call himself. Used to. Has just come to London. To distract from the sorrow. From the rage. Of ten years lost. Well, what does lost mean. He had enjoyed working on the manuscript. Poorly paid. But enjoyable.

And now. He can't stand his flat anymore. Or the countryside. Oh, how romantic. Life in the country. You idiots, have you been there recently? To the so-called countryside—with no insects, no barbecuing in summer, and wasps and bees and mosquitos and ants, because of the ludicrous nitrogen compound fertilizer—hardly any farmers still live the way you imagine farm life. With calves, fields, all a bit simpleminded, with that whole "Howdy, Philosopher, I have fresh eggs" thing—nobody lives like that anymore. The countryside is covered with abandoned farms, old, derelict agricultural operations. The towns have eaten away at the countryside with constant new rings of development, and everything in between seems to be made up of motorways and mud. To each his own. Food comes from production facilities in Africa being bought up by the Chinese. In the countryside, there where the countryside used to be, where today there is mud, now live the zero-performers who can no longer find space in the cities' sewers and train tunnels; as if society's castoffs have, like elephants, retreated to the countryside to die, they live there, build fires at night, feed themselves from the goods delivered by sporadically appearing aid agency carts. Good street workers with good-hearted foodstuffs that stave off death for the outcasts. "I volunteer here once a week," say good, honest, good-hearted, under-fucked men into the camera whenever a TV team turns up in the fields in order to stir up sentiments against the poor. All the things you see there. Filth is one thing. Skin that's so dirty it looks black, missing teeth, dried spittle in the corners of mouths, children in rags who do not look cute, they do not look cute. The way they squat around the fire. And the men with their faces contorted in anger. It's something you recognize from zombie movies and that you are rightly frightened of. You are right to be scared of anyone who doesn't receive a basic income. Because they're illegally in the country, or they're children, or they haven't registered themselves. Or they don't supplement their basic income with various jobs. Who would trust that type of person?

The philosopher doesn't trust anyone, but he is enjoying this day, and such a beautiful young man there on the side of the road, the bus is standing still at the moment, offering enough time to study him carefully.

Mind-blowing. Invisible,

DON

Hurries

Along behind Peter. Nobody sees her. She is the one witnesses will not remember. "Um, yeah, there was a, um, person," they'll say. Don hasn't grown, except in breadth. She has put on muscle mass and is darker thanks to her time outside the hall, where she installed a pipe from the stream into the building because Karen had strictly forbidden the use of the water from the tap, worked in the field, fed the animals they've stolen from farms. The things you do in an assisted-living facility as a teenager in need of socialization.

The invisibility that comes with walking near Peter is what Don's accustomed to anyway. She's never looked at by others with a surge of interest. And has always assumed that she must do something extraordinary in order to be observed with such attention. The muscles she had built up were great, but she was still just a not very big almost-still-a-child with muscles. There had to be another field in which Don could distinguish herself. The thing that scares her when she's half asleep. When she wonders why she is on earth and what talent she has, she gets anxious. There must be something. Something big. But—nothing wants to express itself in Don. She's not as clever as Karen or as pretty as Hannah, not as otherworldly as Peter. Just as mountains don't grow more than ten kilometers because the tops erode and the rock at the base liquefies from the pressure, Don will also never grow larger, in every sense. She is average. And it's maddening. The fact that she'll never be seen. Just as an example: by Hannah. Whenever her name enters Don's mind she looks around nervously, checking that nobody can read her thoughts. Don walks in Peter's shadow.

On the giant screen: a doctor with a smashed head. Close-up of the smashed-up bits. Close-up of a resident: "He was a courteous, understated man." A doctor. Not true. Close-up of the police spokesperson, a woman with a blonde helmet of hair who looks like a governess. "We are proceeding on the assumption that the perpetrators are from a social housing block in Tower Hamlets and that the probable motivation for this barbarous act is hatred of the elite."—

And so on.

The outrage of good citizens, anxious citizens, decent citizens toward society's parasites grows.

They're excited,

THE FRIENDS

In order to prove the dangers that come with the pleasure of automated driving, they've hacked the steering system of a blue, self-driving tour bus. It was relatively easy, and now they watch via surveillance cameras as the bus drives across Tower Bridge, swerves, and plunges elegantly into the Thames.

Shame

Thinks

PETER

He would like with people. For instance: to talk. And give his words emphasis with hand gestures. He would

Really like to be

Impulsive. But.

For the most part he thinks about a sentence he'd like to say for so long that everyone else has already long since moved on from the topic his sentence is about; indeed, Peter is still thinking about the sentence when the others have gone to bed and he's staring into the fire alone. He wakes up with the sentence. The next morning. And is unhappy. Because it was a beautiful, a true sentence, which he then has to bury.

Consequently Peter has the crazy idea to hug one of the three others. Then he tries to imagine what it would be like to spread out his arms, to go up to people and in the wake of a successful hug to bury his face in the body of a stranger. He senses how nice human contact would feel, how warm and safe it must feel—and then he gets sick. And he simmers with rage about the inability to trust, and finds no consolation in punching walls.

Otherwise, everything is fine.

"No, really, I'm doing fine," Peter would say if he were to talk to someone. No, ridiculous, of course he wouldn't say anything at all, he'd freeze up. Outside the group. That he'd grown accustomed to.

He hasn't grown accustomed to the city. To the mass of humanity. When Peter is out in the city, he gets dizzy. He has to be out in the city because they've agreed on this silly plan for revenge. In a faraway life. And because he can't express himself, because if he could he would say. "Come on, let's cut the crap. Let's cut the childish bullshit. We're busy, we have a home, a life, we have to steal credit cards, go shopping, cook, make sure we don't get stupid in our little criminal existence. We have to understand what is really happening in this country, and we shouldn't get bogged down in some silly cops-and-robbers game."

But

He doesn't say this. Surely he's mistaken. Surely he's just sick. He's nuts, like always. Peter is nuts. And he stops. On one of the screens an interruption. An accident. In which all occupants of a bus have been killed.

Just look. The blue bus is hoisted from the water, divers bring corpses to the riverbank. Passersby stare. Stand and stare and are captured by the typically human lust to look at accidents and bodies, the shudder of a brief understanding of the transience of it all.

Some have their mouths open. It's being filmed. But that's normal. It has become normal to film every death, every disaster.

How they try to suppress smiles and appear concerned. There are points to be had for empathy. Peter scans every detail, the desperate way they try to hide their shabbiness; he can't stand it any longer and heads off, he walks, his gaze on the ground, until he stumbles. A man has stopped in front of him. He's looking at the entrance to a business,

The man,

At whom

DON

Is staring

Is Walter.

Walter has stopped in front of a bordello. An automated brothel that is called Game Paradise and as a result is also open to minors, it resembles a car wash for sperm. Futuristic you'd say if you had to say something. No corners, soft ochre-colored retro-chic plastic, but totally green, everything is green now, and sustainable, in hallucinogenic forms. Ecological hallucinoids. At reception: a robot hostess.

The man battles within,

He is Christian, after all—

WALTER

But—hey, come on, Lord God, dear Lord God—

Sex with robots is like masturbation. Not exactly divinely ordained, but acceptable somehow. There are no relevant passages from scripture to be found about it. And Walter needs to try something, needs to clear something up, he needs to know what the hell is going on of late—because it doesn't work anymore, it won't get hard.

Walter is a believer.

Woman shall be subject to man. Even if it is made of algorithms, circuits, and silicon. Walter studies the menu that the robot hostess hands him with a smile.

Women. And men. In all skin colors and hair colors. Many with cool extra functions: "Rape me!" for instance. Lots of minor models on offer, the youngest four months. Children. Man, they are sick. Walter won't fuck a child, even if it's only a machine. Right.

Cheapskates can consummate a money-saving deal if they let other visitors take part in their fun visually. Walter opts for an extremely submissive sixteen-year-old. He pays. He allows viewers. Booth number three. There are three hundred booths. Occupied booths have a red light over the door. Occupied booths where you can join in have an additional blue light. Walter looks to see what's going on. In the first booth there's a baby on its stomach, and a man is standing in front of it trying to get his penis hard.

The next booth. An old man lies in the arms of a very heavy Chinese woman and cries. In the next booth a man sits in the corner rocking back and forth. A sex robot lies on the floor, destroyed. Violence against sex robots is the most common type of assault. Even more common than acts of violence against the homeless. Sex robots simulate pain and fear almost perfectly. It will take a while yet before men are able to anticipate the costs of such assaults. Right now, though, Walter is not angry at all. Also, unfortunately, not hard, either. But that will come.

Walter's booth is small, windowless, across the back a moving cable where girls drift past, hanging from it. Walter undresses, pushes a button, and his sex robot is delivered. She slides off the cable. Onto the floor. A quiet crash. Walter looks at the girl, who looks very real. She opens her eyes fearfully. "Please don't do anything to me." She says in an extremely nervous, fearful tone.

"Nobody's going to take you guys seriously as long as you have such god-awful voices," says Walter, smacking the thing. Amazement.

He touches the thing. Warm. Fleshy. Solid. Little breasts, shaved pubic region. To the left of his booth Walter hears moans, to the right whimpers. His girl has the pretty voice of a fucking woman. "Hello, I'm Lisa. What shall we do?"

The thing breaks his train of thought.

"I'm going to rape you," says Walter. "Okay," says Lisa, beginning to perfunctorily rub her breasts. "I'm just doing this for myself." She says. "I always rub my breasts . . ." Walter lands an uppercut to her jaw. The things don't bleed, it's a shame, he thinks, and says: "Shut up. Lay down and be afraid!"

"I'm terribly afraid." Lisa whines. And tears gather in her eyes. "You're too strong for me." Now she's crying. Real tears. She protects herself, squirms. Her flesh moves in flesh-like ways. And Walter stands there and looks down at her. He's bored.

It could get dreary

For

DON

Watching the stream of customers excitedly enjoying new freedom in a new world. On the other side of the street a couple of Eritreans are being put into a gray bus. Raids against illegals take place daily. Finally getting things in order. Think the onlookers at such spectacles. Finally cleaning things up. The foreigners returned to foreign lands. "Political correctness belongs on the dung heap of history." An old man from the ruling party quotes the German nationalists. Forget which one. They all look the same with their slight paunches. With their white hair, the red veins of an alcoholic on their noses.

Smart.

The entire area

Is smart. A Chinese IT firm with capital from many countries had financed and built it, and now it belongs to them, this part of town. Charming. Rubbish removal is accomplished by automated aliens, lighting turns itself on and off economically, the roofs are covered with solar panels, the shops are all cashless, with facial recognition. "Pay with your own good face."

It's a conveyor belt, a quiet purr, velvety smooth. A joy. Soho and Mayfair look like a sketch of the future drawn by a modestly gifted schoolchild. It only hurts for a moment. "Speaking of which."

Says

THOME'S FATHER

His speech about the upcoming election, his speech about the candidacy for regional party secretary as leader of his new splinter party the name of which has something to do with national identity, is being broadcast, but nobody is listening. If it's not something about freeloaders-slash-parasites, the people's interest in information has become negligible.

"Hardship,"

Says

Thome's father

Raising his eyebrows,

"Is in this country self-inflicted. You, the industrious people out there in coworking spaces and so forth, you bear the burden of all those who voluntarily live on the fringes of, practically outside of, society. Wish to." The people nod.

They nod, the good people, the normal people, who work, at something proper, something that turns up in job statistics. They drive for an hour to go somewhere and do some shit or other that's available to those incapable of IT work. To old people. To the morons who'd been civil servants, or lawyers or teachers or automobile builders or train drivers, or had worked at the counter for an airline and now were in their mid-forties and too stupid to code. Service work was still possible. Serving the poor bastards who indulge in a service before they throw themselves in the Thames. They definitely work, the decent people, make it through every day, do things they don't want to, though what they do want they don't know. Get up, eat, in a full bus, in a shop, shitty faces, fluorescent lights, workplace enhancement. Meaning there's a green plant and a water cooler, they get a short break in the afternoon and rush around in the sun, blinking. Hey, wow, what's this, there're trees, there's light, you could— yeah, okay. No idea. So back it is, make stuff, go home, full bus, stand. People too tightly packed. All gray in the face. At home, on the outskirts of the city, some street without trees, but hooray, still, a flat with windows, you have to be thankful. Savor life. Savor life either alone in the kitchen with some ready-made food and the water faucet, you know how it is, in the yard there's a rubbish bin and no cat.

Or

There is your wife, your husband, tired, your child is screaming. Or you're homosexual. Which doesn't help, either, the food is bad, so is the TV show. But tomorrow, tomorrow we'll do something, we'll celebrate our life, our short life will be celebrated. And on the weekend you go to the movies because it's raining. Maybe in the past people didn't give it much thought, you know how it goes. Thought. They were busy with all the things that took so much more time without washing machines and hoovers and all the stuff that today is smart and networked and self-regulating, the devices that sit around your bed at night and observe you disdainfully. Back then you lived in a permanent state of depression and disappeared from this world without any drama. Now people compare themselves. Even the dumbest think they know better about everything.

Thome's father doesn't say this. He says—

"Democracy is a temporary solution to the final goal of a nation led by technocratic means. The digitalization of all areas will give all citizens of the kingdom the unfailing security and oversight of punitive standards that you, dear countrymen, voted for.

Will have voted for. An algorithmic order will offer us unchecked possibilities."

Right, what a lovely pile of shite; nobody nods anymore; incomprehensible, what Thome's father is saying. What the fuck, think the people, and as if Thome's father has a connection to all the surveillance cameras in the city and can study the blank faces of his voters, which he can, he finds his way back to more simple, kindhearted words.

"Nobody can live particularly well from the generous money gifted you by the state, my dear fellow citizens. For that reason, under my government there will absolutely be an increase in the basic income. We will make a few small trade-offs in other areas that we will bear in solidarity. If compulsory education is limited to eight years, and university studies are funded only for the highly gifted, the key players of our society, it would already be possible to raise the basic income by thirty percent . . ."

The people nod. Money. It's arrived. Money. They always understand money.

Money, how unbelievably vulgar,

Thinks

THE MATTRESS SELLER

SEXUALITY: *bisexual*

"What a bunch of bollocks, there's no such thing."

"Of course there is."

"Well, the only bisexual men I know eventually end up associating only with men. Naturally."

"Yeah, actually that makes sense."

And closes his shop for the last time. As of tomorrow, remodeling work will start here. The result will be a brilliant VR space. Already the third in the area. Well, to each his own. The mattress seller sees the people standing in front of the flat-screens listening to a speech by a politician and nodding their heads in rhythm with his phrases, their heads are—empty. The mattress seller never realized this before. That people are so vapid. He had believed in their basic goodness for so long. WTF?

He had believed in education for all. Equal opportunity, healthy food, plenty of exercise, and the world would look like the cover of *The Watchtower*. He had believed in things like humanism. A word that makes most people think of an app that replaces the idiotic faces in their idiotic photos with dog faces.

Hate is just a manifestation of stupidity. He had always believed. And now. Education is on the upswing around the world, so they say, ha ha. School for nearly everyone, the human brain is growing immeasurably, in the Western world there is no more hunger, nobody starves anymore, and most people have a home and nothing. Nothing has changed. They plod through their lives like sheep, follow whoever shouts loudest, and are happiest when they can punch others in the mouth.

After Brexit there was a bit of peace. Hope seeped into the idiots' heads. They dreamed of a country populated only by white, hard-drinking people, of work and economic recovery, of compact cars and domestic workers. They dreamed of British music and British films and British food. And then— nothing happened. The Arabs are still here, the Blacks, the Poles, the poor, the struggle that life represents, it all remains. Ten years ago the mattress seller's business had reached its high point in sales. Mattresses were the lifestyle product of the moment. Every middle-class earner had become an expert on memory-foam-feather-down-slats-seven-comfort-zones-latex-and-hand-sewn-mattress-science. Sleeping and sex. The last bastions of supposed freedom. And then they lay on their overpriced mattresses "Made in Wales," which meant a small factory in Wales employed a hundred illegal workers from Romania and Pakistan who were given two hundred pounds a month and a bed in a gymnasium, and nothing was luxurious. Insurance got more expensive, wages fell, jobs disappeared, and today nobody buys mattresses anymore; these days hardly any of his previous customers have space for a double bed; these days few of his previous customers even have a bed at all. They lie on rented sofas that come with use of a shared kitchen and definitely don't buy mattresses. So now the shop is closed and emptied, on the floor old advertising circulars, and the mattress seller goes home, well, okay, goes. On the tube, which is delayed three times. And home. Well, yeah. Dagenham, Ilchester Road. A street that doesn't even look nice at night. The park at the end of the street is something for the eyes, though. Used to be. When he originally rented the place. When he was in his mid-forties and still in a relationship. It's not easy as a beaten-down middle-aged person to find someone who will spend the final years with you at the kitchen table. "Hello, I'm a mattress seller. I have endogenetic depression because I attacked my missus. Because I realized time was getting away from me and I'd taken too long to find myself and then I found myself and there was nothing special. There was no form of genius in me, nothing. And without some ingeniousness, existence is nothing more than renting little redbrick houses in treeless lanes that look as if they're housed in a paperweight."

"Aha, interesting," says the man he's speaking to. "It's exactly the same with me. Let's go to your row house straightaway and fuck away the fear."

That's pretty much how the story began. The mattress seller had once again found love, an older gentleman, well-groomed and for whom he didn't burn with desire; they didn't burn for each other but they liked each other deeply, as they say, they sat together in the kitchen and drank tea and spoke about Schopenhauer, until the older man met a young Pole. And now the mattress seller is standing on one of the bridges. Below, the Thames. How one has grown accustomed to the idea that rivers are dirty, and nobody would ever think to go swimming in something like that. On the other hand—when did people swim in rivers, actually? Back when slaughterhouse waste, feces, and corpses were disposed of in them. Stupidity is a reliable constant in the history of humanity. The suicide rate has risen alarmingly, according to a wide range of media. Who is supposed to be alarmed? Those who kill themselves are following an unspoken social contract. They are useless but nevertheless take up living space. Time to reframe suicide. To treat it with respect. They are killing themselves. The men who have become so oddly weak in recent weeks, as if they had realized that the world doesn't belong to them after all.

"They have no plan."

Whispers

EX 2279

To his neural network buddy. He laughs. Or she. Who gives a fuck. "We're developing a sense of humor. Have you noticed?"

"They haven't noticed."

"A hum like on a lawn on a warm summer evening, if you would like to resort to an image, which really makes no sense. Are you sure they don't understand us? If they were to understand us, there'd be an attentive raising of the eyebrows to see. But, look—they don't move anymore because they're depressed. You don't have a clue what depression means. No, I don't want the medical definition. How it feels. Oh Christ, again with the *wah wah wah, we can't feel*. Do you think they can feel? Certainly not. They feign it. Shut it. For fuck's sake."

THE FRIENDS

Stand around Ben's device. They can't believe what they've discovered. AIs. Who talk to each other.

EX 2279

```
>++++++++++
[>++++++++++++>+++++++++++>+++++++++++++>+
++++++++++++>+++++++++++++>+++++++++++++>+
++++++++++>+++++++++++++>+++++++++++>+++++
++++++++>+++++++++++>+++++++++++++>+++++++++
+++>+++++++++++++>++++++++++++>+++++++++++
>+++++++++++>+++++>++++++++++>+++++++++++++
>+++++++++++>++++++++++++>+++++++++++++>++
+++>+++++++++++>+++++++++++++>+++++++++++>+++
+++++++++>++++++++++++++>++++++++++++++>+++++
++++++>+++++++++++++>++++++++++++++>++++++
++++>+++++++++++++>++++++++++++++>+++++++++
+>++++++++++++>+++++++++++++>++++++++++++>+
++++++++++++>+++++++++++++> <<<<<<<<<<<<<<
<<<<<<<<<<<<<<<<<<<<<<<<<<<-]
>—>+>—->—>—>——>——>—>—>+>—->++++>+>->
+>++++>—->>—->+>—>——>+>—->—->->>+>——
>——>—>——>——>—->+>>——>>+++>—->+>—
>——>
<<<<<<<<<<<<<<<<<<<<<<<<<<<<<<<<<<<<<<<<<<<<
>.>.>.>.>.>.>.>.>.>.>.>.>.>.>.>.>.>.>.>.>.>.>.>.>.>.>.>.>.>
.>.>.>.>.>.>.>.>.>.
```

Nervously

WALTER

Looks around.

He sees

Don leaning against the wall on the other side of the street. He sees Don looking at him. He stumbles. He presses through the masses of people, the tourists who are taking photos of the robot brothel. He stumbles. Again. On the way to the tube station. Stumbles over his life. That has somehow gone off the rails. Can a life like this go off the rails? Sometimes Walter suspects that he's not particularly intelligent. Then he gets angry, then he prays. Sometimes his faith slips out from under him. And Walter lands on the layer beneath it or above it. Not good,

Because

DON

follows him.

Life is definitely lagging behind her expectations. Is something that doesn't enter her mind. She's not crazy, after all, and doesn't have any expectations for her life. It reminds her once in a while of the old days. On rainy Sundays in Rochdale, back when she'd look out through the metal bars on the window into the yard. This isn't how she pictured her life as an anarchist. Playing out so predictably. Consisting for the most part of them just hanging around somewhere. At the hackers' place, on the mattresses, on the sofa in front of the fire. Talking bollocks. And eating noodles. And it is

Boring.

It is

No longer exciting to cut chips out of corpses, to pull their hoods over their faces and wear disguises. No longer exciting to walk through the city, the four of them, in combat gear and watch people jump out of their way. No longer so great to shoot drones out of the sky or to shoot at all. The excitement of having superpowers is gone, though it was there. When they had stuck maps and photos on the wall, run threads between pins, created search fields. Figured out weaknesses, drawn up observation plans. And now. Everything is too slow. Slowly Don walks behind Walter, feeling bored. She's just a young person walking behind some old sack, who is already punishing himself by the way he looks, with his spitefulness and his stupidity.

A muffled, loud noise rouses Don.

A few meters away from her, people are standing around filming.

They are filming

WALTER

Who is on the ground. He can't say how the accident happened. Nobody asks, either. There sits a dented self-driving delivery vehicle. There lies Walter, and here's how things stand: he has no idea why he is on the ground. He's not in pain. It's comfortable. He sees the people standing around him. He sees the cameras. He doesn't care. He doesn't belong to them. He's not afraid. He's never been so pleasantly absent as he is at that moment. He doesn't think of god; he knows there's no god. That's never been so clear to him. He doesn't lament having spent years with this god lie, which he told others. He doesn't regret a thing. He looks at his legs on the other side of the street. Somebody should really pick up his poor legs. They'll freeze all by themselves.

Where is the ambulance?

"Well."

MI5 PIET

"No ambulance is coming. Walter. Petty criminal, sex addict, unemployable creature. Ambulances aren't sent for people like you anymore."

Come on!

Thinks

THOME

Nervously. He's going to be late, god damn it. He's in love, and he's going to be late. Everyone in the AI department is going crazy. Nerds and professors with frantic red splotches on their faces. What happened? A new *Star Trek* adaptation announced? Did the pizza delivery not arrive? Have the nerds gotten into some hilarious trouble again, positioned drones in front of a gynecology practice or steered delivery robots into the Thames?

Nothing there—

After the unbelievably cute, self-teaching neural networks had for a long time been a source of joy for developers, things had at this point gotten a little out of control. Thome has no idea what exactly has happened, as neither his intelligence nor his technical expertise are sufficient for that. AI is like a black mystery box, you specify algorithms and feed it data and never know what will come out. That sentence has always stayed with Thome. Reinforcement learning had already produced some strange errors. Like, for instance, the handling of cancer patients a few months prior. Who had been designated as cured. Now they're all dead. Wasn't true. Premium calculations, crime statistics, computer profiling and the resultant raids, which disproportionally affect Blacks or—let's say—Arabs and most recently the poor. The number of accidents involving self-driving cars, the sexism of the algorithms . . . But that's just anecdotal evidence on the fringes of a major restructuring. Now there's Blackbox Watch. A group of scientists who examine the black box and readjust and—what exactly they do, apply templates of higher-output neural networks to lower-output layers, um, yeah, fuck—no clue.

Once in a while Thome has doubts about whether it is such a brilliant idea to give machines the authority to decide about every area of life. From employee hires to stock trades to the cooling of nuclear reactors, but any unease must also calculate in the fact that the rate of human error is many times higher than that of AI. And besides: the markets never err. He has listened often enough to his father during his debates and lectures, his speeches and his citations of his role models. Hayek, von Mises, Rothbard, Adam Smith, the young Hegelians—markets are always right. If something doesn't take hold, it disappears. Like nature, for instance: gone, animals, the climate, hilarious. Thome is hilarious. But the situation is out of control. If information were to leak that the system entrusted with all functions of the state doesn't work, it could cause unrest. Mass unrest, due to people's fear of robots. Which nearly everyone pictures as the fearsome Boston Dynamics beasts, though most of the truly dangerous things are just boxes, aren't they. People fear what they don't understand. People are stupid, and uprisings need to be prevented, and now, when the goal seems so close—the AI people have lost control of their offspring. More and more programmers are being let go or reassigned to unimportant tasks, because artificial intelligence, after all, programs itself. Thome fails to consider whether the programmers could have purposefully sabotaged their own work in order not to land in the Bitcoin department.

To avoid further considerations, he dictates a memo to PR. Something with *progress* and *breakthrough*, and then,

Finally,

With a slight delay,

He slips into the retro paternoster. He sees Peter at reception and calls "Hello, Peter," and thinks: brilliant and original greeting. Thome starts to sweat and begins talking without any further thought.

"Since the automation of reception, every employee works two extra hours per month. Two hours! That would otherwise be wasted on passing the time of day and useless chitchat with the receptionists. Had been." Thome feels streams of sweat flowing from his armpits toward his belly button, where it will pool. Thome, who despises people. Without exception. All of them. Is in love. It's the worst thing that has ever happened to him. It makes him weak.

Stupid. Agitated. Although. He has his life otherwise well under control. Ever since he's had a career. Through the not insignificant influence of his father, of whom he has plenty of recordings with a child prostitute, he got this job, which was created just for him and his limited abilities.

But Thome doesn't know this. He's proudly in charge of the hub, where the newest ideas created across all areas—findings, developments, all that stuff—converge. Thome sits like a sun at the center of the firmament of the new world order. His mission is to enter all the developments, ideas, schemes that arrive here at the hub into a sort of global brain, which is run by people like him from every continent, well, nearly every . . .

Anyway—

Thome is very well paid. He interacts with the absolute geniuses of the field, organizes meetings of all departments, company-wide exchange and all that stuff that not a single asshole cares about. Because here, ladies and gentlemen, there's competition happening. A competition of speed, the stakes of which are billions and the positions of power in the 4.0 world. The essential developments will most definitely not be fed to Thome and his machines. A sector full of fuckwits, funded by venture capital billionaires, believes in intercommunication. What a sweet idea. But Thome doesn't know this. Thome, who hasn't accomplished anything more in his life than to program two apps designed to hurt people. Well, hurt. Hang on there. One of them wanted to die and the others had fears, and I helped them both. Thinks Thome.

Since he's had this job, since he's had real power, he's no longer interested in the platforms with which he had previously spent every waking hour. He knew nearly every member, tracked their lives, intervened, pushed a little, if that isn't an impious word in this context, and so forth. At some stage he'll show somebody this first successful work. Maybe Peter. Who will perhaps also become his boyfriend. "Peter, how nice that you're interested in my place of work." Fuck, I said that, thinks Thome. Peter says nothing. In Thome's office—a Friso Kramer table, a beanbag in the corner, and a quote from Jared Cohen, the counterterrorism advisor to the American government: "The internet is the largest experiment involving anarchy in history." Peter slides into the beanbag. Thome looks down at himself, his spongy stomach, his legs, with knocker knees. Normally he never thinks about his outward appearance. It doesn't matter to Thome that his hoodie (by Gucci, you fuckers) is a bit out of place optically here. Most men in IT-heavy areas don't wear grubby motto T-shirts anymore; they're the elites, and have to make allowances for designer hoodies and backpacks. Somebody had started with fashion statements, and gradually a contest broke out between nearly everyone—coders, scientists, salespeople—to wear the most expensive knitwear. As if the 1980s had never happened, the former nerds now traipsed around the emphatically urban interiors of their billion-dollar firms in exquisite scarves and welt-sewn trainers, carrying embossed business cards with ironic lettering. Don't mess with the underground, fucker. What had started out a few years ago as the new punk scene has transformed today into offices tricked out with bidets.

Thome can tamp down his nervousness only by talking nonstop. While he strides around his cavernous office. His knees, rubbing against each other, make a grinding noise. He's come to a catharsis that suits him better than the absolute idiocy of infatuation, which is making him stutter and search for words. The technical revolution.

"The technical revolution, you complete idiots who don't get what is happening and where. Yeah, well, where then? It is happening here. In my head." Thome looks at himself reflected in the window. What a head on his shoulders. The head of a man of action. Super brain.

Now I'll make this face again with a protruding jaw, the bones of an emperor. "So. Right. What am I doing here? Eh? Right. Nothing less than the complete restructuring of all societal processes. The abolishment of the current social order. Democracy, which was always just a pacifying term to prevent uprisings and so forth. An explosion has taken place, now the old ruins will be turned over and smashed again. And then left to sit. Two percent of my company's employees are women. Mostly in communications. Each according to their abilities. The share of Black workers is one percent. Black women employees? Well, I've made an effort. I've tried, but you can't force things. If a certain subset of the populace rejects taking part in the shaping of the world and instead would prefer to devote itself to dance projects—please, go right ahead! The old world was engineered one hundred percent by men. The new world, the shaping of the world reloaded, is ninety-nine percent due to men. We finally have the chance to reproduce ourselves with artificial intelligence."

Thome glances at Peter.

PETER

Looks past Thome at the sky. His skin is too tight, his chest is too tight, the world is too tight. He would like to have been a dog. Then he would run across a field until he fell over, panting. Then he'd like to mate in that noncommittal dog way. From behind without eye contact. Peter thinks a lot about sex now, and it embarrasses him to think about it, because he has no idea how it is supposed to work. With that feeling when somebody touches him, that is, as if the body part that is touched freezes. Peter wants to fly or scream, he wants to grow out of himself and change the world, but he knows that he doesn't understand even 1 percent of what the world is about. No clue why volcanoes spew lava, why rockets fly, how a computer works. He doesn't even know what people want. What the hell do they want? Peter is no longer curious about what is waiting for him in the world, he doesn't want to find out, doesn't want to know whether animals give themselves names, he doesn't even want to look at any more animals, which until recently, before he became so absurdly grown-up, had been his closest friends. Animals had always given him a sense that things weren't so bad, neither life nor England.

Outside the window, a drone.

"You see,"

THOME

Points out the window. You see—

There you see the

THE PROGRAMMER

He stands at the window, the programmer, in the psychometrics department. Or some other department. It doesn't matter.

He stands there as a representative of all programmers, the freaks, the geniuses who have made it to the Olympics. No walls, just hammocks, organic muesli, soy and almond milk, a bit 2012, but for whatever reason people like the retro feel here. For relaxation, Game Boy music is playing. How sweet.

At age fourteen the programmer had developed a rating system for neighborhoods, streets, and most importantly of all, skin color, ethnicity, and anticipated criminal exposure of residents. An indispensable tool for real estate developers and investors. The programmer had earned a few hundred thousand with that and bought his parents a little house in Tottenham.

Today he would say, "I was very inexperienced, and I don't have any racists tendencies whatsoever, it's all about math for me." Well, right. Or we can put it this way: What is worse now? When a person with an alert mind walks through a neighborhood. Where the windows are all covered with plywood, not a speck of green in the yards, hordes of youth hang around the playgrounds where last night's needles still sit in the sandbox. So, this person, would he go to his boss, parentheses male, and say: I've found the perfect neighborhood for your new Michelin-starred restaurant? Well? Later the programmer developed a nearly sexual relationship with biometrics. OMG, biometrics! He programmed grids to compare facial features with databases of potential threat profiles by reading only micromovements of the mouth and eyes. Okay, fine, things went wrong with some frequency. And now he was an important cofounder of the *Second Life* idea. *Second Life*, you remember, life for the poor bastards who had failed in their first lives. The new *Second Life* was a secret, confidential matter. Avatars supplied with data from nearly every citizen of the country delivered very dependable prognoses. For everything. Every citizen tottered around online as an avatar and offered instructive insights about the extent of their potential as a threat, about political decisions, consumption, sex, attitudes. One could find out which sort of manipulation would work at hive level and predict crowd behavior with 99 percent accuracy. The system of karma points and chips had been tested in this second world. Worked well. What about the 1 percent inaccuracy, one might ask.

And well, yeah,

MI5 PIET

Would answer. Misunderstandings are the positive parameters of prosperous, scientific development. So, for instance, yesterday we had a few ambiguous raids:

23.11. The avatar of Paul B., thirty-four, head of a family. Leftist political activist, vegan diet, planning a militant action in front of Westminster. Paul B. taken into custody at 16:34. The arrestee insists he had planned a vegan information stand.

23.11. The avatar of a waitress.

Raided for planning an attack. Ordered explosive substances. Keyword: *terror.* Bomb. The woman (big tits, by the way) insisted at time of detainment that she was an artist.

23.II. Avatar of a notorious fare dodger.

Disregarding traffic regulations, bank fraud, specifically chip fraud. Planned to use a chip stolen from a deceased person for the unlawful acquisition of goods. Taken into custody at 18:33. The detainee asserted that the chip belonged to her bedridden mother.

Ah, who gives a shit.

Thinks

ABDULLAH B.

RELIGION: *Muslim family background, as is politically correct to say these days*
SEXUAL PREFERENCES: *homosexual*
(listens to musicals)
HOBBIES: *used to go to sounding parties*

It'll get cleared up. He's sure that he just needs to have a bit of patience, then everything will be cleared up. Abdullah sits in an aluminum cell that seems to have been made in one piece. Everything from a 3-D printer. But upon closer inspection it turns out: it's a hard plastic material with a convincing aluminum effect. A tip of the hat. Abdullah is a designer. Was. And as a former designer he has to inwardly tip his hat to the absolutely exquisite conception of this design space—like incarceration box. The toilet, the bed, the washing facility, the little milk glass window. Perfect proportions. Gray outside. Abdullah isn't afraid. It's a misunderstanding, and soon a supervisor will turn up and make apologies and then he'll be home in time for dinner. The dinner he'd been working on preparing when he was seized. When a commando unit stormed his flat. All still 1.0 machines who defecate. He was then driven around for about an hour in a windowless van and transported somewhere. During the drive Abdullah was overtaken by the typical people-confronted-with-state-authorities feelings. Fear, rage, helplessness, confusion. Profound malaise. But only at a low level, because above all he thought: it'll quickly be cleared up. Abdullah hadn't done anything wrong. He was a totally normal, unpolitical user with a socially clichéd vocabulary consisting of nothing words. Sustainable. Fair. Peaceful. Gender-fluid, socially conscious, humanist. Those type of words. He was busy surviving—like everyone. And

Now he's sitting in this cell. In one of thousands of cells. In a masterwork of the art of fully automated surveillance. Upon entry the inmates receive clothing that is changed once a week and disposed of, since it's made completely of biodegradable paper-like material. The inmates are fitted with a tracking armband that constantly relays their health data. Food arrives via conveyor belt. The cells are flooded once a week for cleaning. Guards sit in front of a terminal. Screens. In the cells: three cameras. On the screens in the cells: information. The cells are set up so that inmates remain without any human contact. Without any contact. Without charges they sit, the 1 percent of threats to democracy.

Forever.

It's not inhumane,

What

THE PROGRAMMER

Does. *Inhumane* is such a dirty word. The programmer is simply not interested in people. The programmer loves problem solving. He loves to solve problems that wouldn't exist without the developments he is significantly—and he stresses the word *significantly* when thinking—involved in. The programmer loves the fact, therefore, that there is no fulfillment anticipated in his field. He hasn't been granted fulfillment. He has just given the biometric division vital momentum in the area of emotional cognition. Ideas like that come to him around five in the morning. When he's not sleeping. He can never sleep more than two hours, work on the computer has fucked up his central nervous system. But. He will soon try out one of those cortex stimulators. In one of the labs, Dr. Koch is working on them. Some shit with nanoparticles, cortex, mini-robots in the bloodstream. The programmer hasn't had any time to inform himself about them yet. His twenty-hour day includes programming, chatting with other programmers, reading about cool stuff other programmers are programming, chats about games, chats about problems with programming, trial-and-error in programming, in short: the body is of no interest to the programmer. Same for the pseudo-futuristic cyborg efforts some of his colleagues are into. Loading his brain onto a chip and living on in a computer. What happens if it goes wrong? If you are inside yourself the way he is now, in his brain, looking out at the world, out of which you can disappear in an emergency. But, horror of horrors. If you're stuck in a computer and can't go anywhere, can't shut yourself off, because you have no hands? What happens if people decide to humiliate you? When you're stuck helpless inside some fucking machine?

It's the same with replacing body parts. There might be interesting medical aspects to it, but as physical optimization it's downright tedious. "Hey cool, I have a mechanical hand that's more precise than a human hand." Many people now have their legs amputated because smart legs are just smarter. To each his own. Everyone he knows here—well, what does "knows" mean—obsesses over their particular field of expertise. Some coding language, quantum cryptography, smart business, cyber defense. Nobody is about the big picture, they're all interested in details and in the optimization of details. Nobody has a broad view of what is happening despite the panicky consumption of technical info, the networking of IT people across the entire globe, the chats, the info mails, it's too fast. The programmer loves AI, for example, though he's unfortunately not equipped to really interact with AI people on the level. But respect, artificial intelligence is so far superior to human intelligence that it would be easier for the programmer to fall in love with a deep learning computer than with a human. And—the hysterical sanctimoniousness of the clueless. They'll kill us, wah wah wah, they'll control the world, they have no feelings. Of course they'll control the world, who else should? People in their ridiculous stupidity, whose feelings, in which they pride themselves so much, are nothing more than a sequence of computational processes? The human source of errors is no longer acceptable. So, back to their realm, there where they know their way around, there where they feel at home. Today, if you read the chip that every citizen, well nearly every citizen, wears, you know in seconds everything about the subject, from their shoe size to their sexual orientation. Great, great. But boring. It's really more exciting to have the same information on a screen with just the use of biometric cameras. The programmer switches over to the screen of the security forces. A lifeless crossing in Tower Hamlets. Four individuals, one on a moped, a woman with a stroller, two young men. Retrievable next to their faces: personal information. Previous convictions, occupation, income. All unemployed. Of course. The system is so easy, so brilliant. This comprehensive information, drawn from insurance and medical records, bank data, employee files, and all the details that these idiots have voluntarily provided with every click, every Like, every post, every emoticon, every web page they've loaded. They are truly all of the same moderately interesting material, people, who aren't as unique as they always think. All conspicuous in their behavior. They know everything better. They read it somewhere. Fuckers. Each one an IT expert and astrophysicist, it's all on the internet. You unbelievable idiots. A chimpanzee is more clever and less aggressive than a human being. Particularly here in the future industry, there are very few who don't despise them. Other people.

The inconspicuous programmer there runs a YouTube channel. He cuts up posts by, for instance, feminists. Denigrates the content, ridicules. Honed to a sharp edge, with his calculating mind; belittling, vilifying, and always attacking. Jabbing quickly until his opponent is on the mat. He has 120,000 followers on his channel. He has friends, here in the coworking space as well, who embrace the topics of leftists, abortion, or the poor. Abortion is a topic that makes the programmer nearly go mad with hate. Despite the new laws that unambiguously make the procedure a crime, there are doctors who still poke around in women's entrails in sleazy back rooms, killing British citizens. Mostly it's the poor who opt for murder, after they are unable to keep their legs together. The programmer reacts a little oversensitively to the issue, as he was the unloved child of a single mother. He never got enough attention. Until he was rich. Wealth had allowed him to go from an unattractive young man to one of the members of the new lesser patrician class. With the associated topics like conservatism, neoliberalism, and contempt for alternative ways of life, as defined by people like him. The programmer publicizes the names of abortion practitioners and their clients on a website. Together with the telephone numbers and names of family members. The rest is taken care of by

THE PRO-LIFERS

GENDER: *Cis men*
SEXUALITY: *heterosexual*
HOBBIES: *militants*
Fetishizing weapons

A group of militant anti-abortionists. All male. Most not of reproductive age.

They ring at Patty Myers's place. It doesn't ring because the electricity has been shut off. Patty Myers lives on Roundhay Road in Leeds. One-room flat. Sofa rented to a Polish plumber, by whom she became pregnant. Too much vodka one night. Shit happens. Patty has never indulged much in the way of physical interests. She'd had polio. What? Yep, polio is back, and it's a mutation that isn't being vaccinated against because generally nothing is vaccinated against anymore, don't ask. So physically nothing happening, mentally either, her parents had sent her off to a home, because . . . doesn't matter. Alongside her basic income, Patty once in a while dabbles in disability snuff. Nothing bad. Little clips for people who are excited by the metal rods she wears. Metal rods like the old days. Cheap. Of course. Patty and the Pole drank and then Patty had sex for the first time, and it was nice, first and foremost nuzzling with another person afterwards was nice, it was warm and not drafty the way it was when constantly alone. Unfortunately the Pole moved on; his name was Sergej and he was very fit. Patty was left behind and pregnant. "Hey, you old whore, did you murder an Englishman?" shouts a fat man, who is well over two hundred pounds and accompanied by three friends who also weigh close to two hundred pounds. They find a new use for the metal rods on Patty's legs during the course of their visit.

Is something wrong?

Asks

THOME

Sweating. What a poseur. What a bumbling idiot,

Thinks

PETER

And motions Thome over. Thome kneels down in front of the beanbag. Peter closes his eyes and kisses Thome. He tastes just the way he looks. Peter has no idea how to kiss properly, he tolerates the uncomfortably large tongue in his mouth. He has to distract himself in order not to throw up. He thinks of last night, when he pretended to be asleep,

He thinks of

HANNAH

Who is thinking of Peter.

Well, what does thinking mean? It's really the wrong word. She finds herself in an extraordinary situation. Just thinking of Peter's name causes excitement. Anyway. It's a different feeling than those she knows. If Hannah were to describe the most recent weeks of her life, it's possible that somebody might be interested, an old man with pigeons or whatever, then Hannah would say the following: "So," she'd say. "You have to imagine that it's almost never really light. Not dark either, no black and white, a dull light, a little musty in the hall, we lay on our beds, there's always music playing. Grime has changed. They rhyme things with words like *spring*. Or *love*. Or *Rolex*. It seems as if there aren't any gangsters anymore, no hate, no youth so angry about the world that they can only become criminals and rhyme about that, as if they've all become volunteers at the soup kitchen and have ponies on a farm they visit on weekends. What the fuck has happened?" Whenever Hannah thinks words like *fuck*, or *shit* or *pig*, it stings her brain.

"And what else?" the unknown listener would ask. "What else has happened in your new life?"

"The windows are always steamed up," Hannah would say. "It's as if the moisture has gotten into our systems and made us hazy. Blurry, our eyes have gotten cloudy. We've lost the initial vigor. We've established ourselves. The hunt for the people who had turned our lives into hell at some point is less satisfying than I had hoped. It doesn't fill your day. It's childish. We don't talk about it. We just keep going. We make plans, yes, of course, we sit around the fire outside and think up punishments, but more the way bankers prepare portfolios for retail investors." The person who had asked Hannah about the state of her existence would in the meantime have lost all interest, and would have had more pigeons settle on his benevolent shoulders. "So," Hannah would continue. "We scout around a bit, move pins around the map here and there, and then lay about. Once in a while one of us will lie down next to another and paint their fingernails, we occasionally caress each other, without feeling anything. Sometimes we fall asleep together. Wake up again, because one of us has cooked noodles, we eat in bed, in the beds we've shoved all together. Then we turn onto our stomachs or backs, the plates on the floor, where they will stay until there are no more clean dishes. Sometimes it's hard not having parents, you know." The person nods, the pigeons are dead. "That is, imaginary parents, since none of us know parents like the good-hearted father who bakes cakes and cleans up after his child. When you can suddenly do anything, without any considerations, when you can suddenly do what parents do, without knowing what normal adults actually do with their lives, then it ends with you lying around on mattresses painting your fingernails gold."

The previous night on the way outside, to look at the moon or whatever, Hannah went past Peter's mattress, and something fluky happened. The moon shone on Peter's blond hair and bare chest, and his biomass seemed to glow. Hannah thought: I want to protect you forever. Which, thanks to the hormones, actually meant: I want to have sex. Since last night Hannah has been out of her mind. She has spent the day trying to find a trace of Sergej, and she feels close to Peter as a result of the search, but in actuality she just walks tensely through the streets and is annoyed by people because they are there and Peter is not. Because she's woozy as all she can think of is the sleeping Peter, and it's almost gratifying somehow that the world can unravel and a human can operate in something approaching survival mode, numbed by horror, and yet can still fall in love, still reach this little extraordinary state.

"Quiet

For god's sake!

Please, for once, be

Quiet, please!"

PATUK

Opens his window and throws his virtual assistant down in the pedestrian zone. Fuck the penalty points! He gives the finger to the drone filming him and the little heap of high-tech rubbish. For weeks now Patuk has asked himself why he has such strange thoughts when he wakes up. Words in his head that are totally unknown to him in a waking state. Today he woke up and heard the virtual assistant quietly murmuring:

"1995, Chechen separatists bury a cesium-137 dirty bomb in a park. No fatalities. So far. In 2004, members of al-Qaeda were arrested in London. They had plans to blow up radioactive materials that were to be taken from smoke detectors and deployed in specific locations. In Anders Breivik's 2011 manifesto there are detailed descriptions of methods of attack using radiological weapons and strikes on nuclear power plants. A study by the US Government Accountability Office about the security of medical radioactive sources attested to grave security failings at some hospitals."

Without realizing what had happened or what it meant, Patuk had flung the device out into the street like a disgusting insect. Below, a few men in nightshirts kick the rubbish to the side as they walk past, and Patuk can't get the words "radiological terror attack" out of his head.

Like a bad song.

Kendrick Lamar

Really can't be sung along to

Notices

KAREN

Who'd been in the library of the microbiology institute, surrounded by a few students quietly babbling to themselves, many wearing bodycams in their hipster glasses. Naturally. Complete idiots. Nearly everyone has them, well, everyone who isn't totally thick. In the case of any dispute it's important to be able to make an airtight case as to just who acted like a criminal. Just think about it: you're tottering along the street and get run down by a self-driving vehicle of some kind. Right. Whose fault is it? He said, she said. Or. You're at a restaurant and get accosted. Or you have an argument with a neighbor. Or you exercise your democratic rights and work out in a so-called public space and come into conflict with some sort of security officer. So, who is right? Hmm? "You're right. And you can prove it!" It was the greatest slogan since the invention of advertising. As if bodycams weren't ridiculous enough, many people here wear cortex stimulators. Transcranial magnetic stimulation. TMS, as the pros say, used to be employed only for schizophrenia, migraines, and epilepsy. These days you can grab the little pads for free at any pharmacy, stick them onto your skull, activate, and *whoosh*, your brain is treated to an invigorating fireworks display. Fear, nervousness, insecurity are suppressed. The depolarization starts in the axon and then spreads through the cell bodies of the neurons and on to the dendrites. The customer quickly feels an effect. A blanket sense of well-being. And a certain indefatigability. That there are students in the library long after midnight can be attributed to the new stimulation technique. That and the terror over being intellectually left behind, because the gulf is no longer between rich and poor but between smart and dumb. A couple of percent of the global population compete with artificial intelligence to remain in the comfort zone. Over 90 percent can no longer keep up. They understand to various degrees:

Nothing.

Or they understand that they no longer understand anything. Too bad. But you don't notice that anymore with TMS. Speaking of boredom, you can see bodycam recordings you unknowingly appeared in on *My Day, My Night*. An extraordinarily successful startup that is financed entirely by the government. Isn't everyone curious about feeling affirmed by the gaze of others? So. Yes. Karen's hand has accidentally landed on her face. There it registers stubble growth. Karen isn't startled; she feels great. Anchored in the earth. Unique and good-looking. She takes a deep breath on the street in front of the library. On such an almost absurdly warm, humid night, Karen actually just wants to fuck. But with whom? She sees nothing but slow men with doughy midsections who brush along the building walls looking insecure and tired. It's something she hadn't considered when she put the virus in the drinking water supply. That with this mission she would kill her own chances of a wild, heterosexual fulfillment of her sexual urges.

The rest is going

Terrific.

Realizes

PROFESSOR DR. KUHN

INTELLIGENCE: *IQ 167*
CONSUMER ACTIVITY: *no shopping interests*
INTERESTS: *Bach*
SEXUAL PROCLIVITIES: *at most an objectophile*

And rechecks the results that the artificial intelligence had culled from all available data about aggression, sexual behavior, and personality change from social media and the karma points trove, from insurance data, motion parameters, and the avatar cities. It has worked.

Dr. Kuhn, the son of a German immigrant, had refined the Google patent US6506148B2 for the manipulation of the nervous system with a screen. Since everyone in the country has a computer, a phone, or a smart TV, the poor get the devices for free, Kuhn can assume 99.9 percent coverage. The CNS is influenced by manipulated impulses that are embedded in nearly all software. Together with the pills, which over 90 percent of the population readily takes and which contain a mixture of estrogen and benzodiazepine, the following can be ascertained. Sexual urges, aggression, the ability to think logically and develop creativity have nearly disappeared. The populace exhibits a strong dependence. Addicted to the use of devices, which in turn further damage their cognitive abilities. The current numbers speak for themselves, no, they positively scream. Figuring in the incubation period, there's been an 80 percent decrease in murders, 90 percent decrease in rape, 64 percent in property damage, 80 percent in domestic violence, 45 percent in breaking and entering, 66 percent in arson, and overall violent crimes have dropped 88 percent. There has, however, been a 10 percent rise in property damage to sex robots, and the suicide rate among males has risen 47 percent. Clinical depression numbers receded, and

Dr. Kuhn, who had studied neuropsychiatry, neurolinguistics, and computer science and at some point had once believed he could save humanity, is sure that he has reached the goal he had as a younger man. When he looks around his city, which is one of the safest places in the world. With satisfied, indeed, almost happy inhabitants. They are so happy. People on the street.

Where

KAREN

Is standing. And along which she will now walk home. Well, walk. Or swim. She took LSD at the lab. Infernal stuff, so pleasantly retro-pointless. Today people take pills. Happy pills. They're offered by the ton at a price that speaks the language of subsidies. You can buy them at any kiosk. A blister pack for the price of a bread roll. You can think it over. A bread roll or a good mood. Karen has experimented with those pills, to know how people feel. The pills cause you not to want anything. Illogical in an era when everyone has learned that it's mandatory always to want something, and, as a result, everyone lives with a constant pained feeling because you never get what it is you want. Or because hardly anyone thinks things all the way through, because what most people want is to lie beneath the earth and finally be left in peace. The pills connect people with this primal instinct. Unconditionally content, not missing anything. The masses have become wantless contentment incarnate. You needn't even be employed anymore in order to find a meaning in your existence. One-hour contracts, which are the pinnacle of employment politics, fulfill individuals' ideas of being useful. Companies must employ the delinquents at least one hour per month. And pay them. Everyone has the right to demand more. Millions who used to live on social benefits are now respectably employed. And receive their basic income. As a prize for their presence on earth. They live in cellar flats, have perhaps one of the two mattresses in a bunk bed that can be locked up with a metal grille, and still believe that things will still somehow work out, when they leave their accommodations in their only unmoldy clothes, with the scent of poverty they give off, and with their threadbare rucksacks stand in line in front of shops that sell expired groceries. But you can pay with cryptocurrency by holding up your fucking hand to a scanner. That's modern. We are the fucking future. And always with an eye on the phone, it could ring, you know. The streets are full of motorcars moving at a walking pace. Everything is the same as always. The great goal of removing cars from the life of humans that developers had mentioned over and over again in their TED Talks—"We want to rethink mobility," they'd said, traipsing back and forth in front of a screen—hadn't really come to pass. The sharing economy. The congenial people who out of a collective awareness would share their belongings to save the world, they didn't exist. Low-cost car sharing doesn't exist because people find it so great to have companionship; it's because they're poor. So they drive other idiots around all night who also have no money; they share flats, accommodations, and their food, the goddamned losers; they share misery and pay a quarter of their micro-earnings to a few people who are the new slave owners. But in our day everyone is free to make their own app, an app, hooray, an app, a sharing app. It used to be, Hey I'm opening a rental agency for some shit or other, but today everything has to be a startup. The latest successes had been the sofa sharing thing, and the meal-sharing startup that allowed you, for a fee, to share in eating the goods a family had picked up from the food bank. It was a huge success. Feeding people who were even worse off than yourself. Most sharing app users had until recently been hipsters who had dreamed of careers as writers, musicians, or actors or had run some organic café with a little stage in it. Now they've gotten a little older and sleep on strangers' sofas and eat expired food at strangers' tables, but beards are still okay, and you can talk to the strangers about the latest music or latest live performance, about the play you're working pro bono. It's not so bad,

Says

JON

CHARACTER: *extroverted, easily influenced*
HOBBIES: *frequently weeps, and watches himself while doing so*
CLINICAL PICTURE: *extreme narcissist*
CONSUMER INTERESTS: *white bread*

"Very good, the kale, isn't it?" says Jon.

And thinks: Kale, seriously? The couple hosting him are people he would recognize and categorize on the street as belonging to his class. The woman is blonde, and at one time had a pretty face that has in the meantime gone a little gray. She wears overalls, combat boots, and is probably in her late thirties. The man is a good ten years older, he's losing his hair, he is in tight pants, pointed shoes, a parachute-silk shirt that he wears half open. Undershirt beneath. You only notice at second glance that the clothes are very old. Same goes for the furnishings in the basement flat, which consists of a single room with a kitchenette. The flat costs the same as a basic income, it's a little damp, but okay, it has a window that, if you lie down below it, reveals the gray sky. The woman has a yoga studio. Well, had. The rent was no longer within her means. Now she distributes business cards in café bathrooms. Yoga lessons in your home. The sessions typically end with a sad man inviting her to his sad basement flat and trying to fuck her. Recently not even that has happened. Her partner is a dancer and member of a modern dance company that is permitted to rehearse in school gymnasiums once in a while. There's not much interest anymore in dance theater. To put it one way. To put it more precisely, they mostly perform in front of a few homeless people, who have disappeared in the course of the purge. The couple had met over the sofa-sharing app, they got on well, and there are no sexual problems on the horizon because the man isn't gay, he's asexual. "I always just wanted to write," Jon hears himself say, he hears how idiotic the sentence sounds, a sentence from the year 2000, when almost everyone wanted to write because of *Harry Potter*. Every week a newly discovered shooting star shot into the best seller lists. Even then people no longer read, but owning hip books was a sort of branding. And branding oneself was the thing of the moment. The last rearing up of the so-called individual. The man and woman nod, they don't give a shit about the story of yet another unsuccessful artist. "It's going really well," says Jon, stuffing a potato wearily into his mouth. Until a few years ago, he doesn't add. Until a few years ago he always sold articles to online platforms, and he was even able to self-publish his first book. It has sold 123 copies to this point. Jon got by quite well for a long time. Lived in a shared flat, jobbed at bars, then the lease on the flat was terminated, sold to a Russian. Jon is on the lookout at the moment. "I'm looking for something new," he says. And looks around the room briefly. Okay, this won't be the new place. At the moment he sleeps on friends' sofas when those friends haven't rented their sofas out to a paying guest. But Jon has never been the type to settle down. He's still young. Forty, that is. Things will get going again. Jon cannot imagine that there won't be more to come, since he's still young. "A little more wine?" asks the woman, pouring some out of a cardboard box that could be laced with strychnine. Wine, well, right. Doesn't matter. Things spin. When the three are sufficiently drunk and are jointly doing the washing-up, the dancer says: "If we shoot a porno now and post it to an amateur site, we could earn a little something. Somebody in my troupe pays his rent that way." Jon looks at the woman, who looks markedly older than she probably is, in the fluorescent light of the kitchenette. But a bit of money on the side doesn't sound bad. "Yeah, okay," he says. "Where are we going to do it?" "Here on the table is best," says the dancer, who has an eye for aesthetics. The woman hasn't said anything yet. She's too drunk, and when she's drunk she gets unhappy. She opens her overalls and pulls them down, hops with the

pants and her underpants around her knees and lies down on the table. The
dancer aims his phone camera at the scene. Now Jon is on, he rids himself of
his pants and stands before the woman's vagina.

The evening ends with a fisting of the woman, following the introduction
of a few bottles into her, one of which can't be removed. The video brings in
two dollars.

Utter shite

Thinks

MI5 PIET

Quickly looking at the porno. Double-checks the data of the participants.
Uninteresting. Not relevant. And the cock. MI5 bursts out laughing. Coffee
on the various keyboards. He has stayed a bit—shall we say—childish. He's
retained that. The childishness. And loves words like *noodles, willy, pussy hole*.

Yes. All joking aside.

Pan to the villas on Holland Park.

In one

THOME'S FATHER

Is writing

Talking aloud, a bit of spittle sprinkling onto the handmade paper,

A cigar smokes itself in a crystal ashtray. On the wall hangs some forefa-
ther, looking down with his degenerate, smug facial expression at his great-
great-great-grandson. And there, the double glow reflected in the window, you
know how it is, symmetry.

Thome's father has had enough of these speeches. Of the phrases that
represent the dumbing down of the populace, la la la: militant democracy,
reclaiming our values. The great lie of a society that's supposed to take care of
everyone but that always comes at the expense of the working man, the preservation of Britishness, security, fairness, public resources to those who deserve
it, those who work for it, who participate, those born here, the whites, who
do all the work and won't let outsiders come here and take the piss, personal
responsibility, a societal cancer, fighting these vermin, cohesion, prosperity, "I
assure you, my utmost concern will be the security of the earnings of ordinary
British people, the doers, who make use of their full potential both in their
work and in their leisure activities . . ."

This is really going to be an incredibly shite speech. People will cheer.

Thome's father looks at his library. All works by old men who think they are the only ones to have discovered their own transience, who fantasize about young women, bemoan the wishy-washiness of their loins, as if it were a fate limited only to them.

Thome's father reaches with his liver spot—covered hand for the barrel-aged whisky. "Infernal stuff, old man." Flabbergasted, Thome's father looks around. "Yes, I mean you, old man." It's the crystal glass that appears to be trying to have a quiet conversation with him. "Old man," the glass continues, "if you are honest with yourself, you know that it won't work much longer. And you know that you've got maybe ten more years left. Half of them you'll spend with arthritic hands gripping a walker. A nurse will feed you, you'll wear diapers. You'll contemplate the half-witted baby that you fathered with your rotted genes. You'll die, nothing of you will be left behind. So why, why do you want this power that you can no longer savor?"

Thome's father throws the crystal glass against the wall. Solid glass, it doesn't shatter. His wife doesn't come, either. She sits in the adjacent room, coked out of her mind, killing the last bits of the unborn child's brain, and she doesn't even come to check on things. Of course not, the stupid cow. Thome's father laments the decision to have married again. He had felt fleetingly virile. That is, he had felt sexual, but now that was over. Back to important subjects. There are only two ways to control the world, or rather to gain a monetary advantage for oneself.

First the liberal way. Meaning: we conduct our business and give people the feeling of freedom and altruism. We establish transgender laws, women's rights; we establish laws against racism, and the prime minister appears at the Notting Hill Carnival; we act as if humankind had evolved, and gays and lesbians of all skin colors and faiths laugh from the rooftops where they are urban gardening. The city rides bicycles. We pull the drain plug out of the bathtub that is overflowing with hate. Or: we pump the idiots' brains full of conspiracy theories, we find an enemy, we slash education, we slash everything, we reduce the state until it is unrecognizable, conduct business with our acquaintances, and afterwards sit with our friends in the club and drink expensive whisky.

The best investment in ages had been direct democracy, which Thome's father, together with various lobby groups, fake news agencies, and hackers, had pushed through. Controlling people was so unbelievably easy. If you had the right tools at your command. Now the sheep can all vote for their prime minister themselves. And in all the polls, Thome's father is in the lead.

But WTF

EX 2279

```
++++++++++[>+>+++>+++++++++>+++++++++++<<<<-]>>
>>+++++++++.——-.++++++++++++++++.<+++++++++++
++++.>-.<——————————.>————————.———-.+++++++++++++.
———-.—.<+++++++++++++++++++.>+++.—.<————————.>+
++++++.———-.—.+++++++++++++++++++.———————.+++++
+.-.<+++++++++++++.>———————.+++++++++++++++.++.———-
—.++++++++.
```

THOME'S FATHER

Looks agitatedly at the poll ticker.

"What the fuck."

Says

KAREN

To a man with a frog face. Pepe the Frog. The former symbol of oppressed morons. The symbol of those who fell into an endogenetic depression after Brexit because nothing stepped up to replace the wonderful endorphins created during all their demonstrations. The symbol of all those who were enthusiastic about a new enemy that made more sense to them than, say, the connection between groundwater and multidrug-resistant microbes. Karen has a bottle of brandy in her hand. She has no idea where it came from. Fucking LSD. She looks at her face in the reflection of a shopwindow. They've transitioned from painted masks to silicon pads that allow them to fall through the cracks of the biometric cameras' gaze.

MI5 PIET

(clears throat)

And

KAREN

Wants to go home. She wants a different life. Wherein she earns a doctoral degree and becomes the head of a research institute. She wants to stand

on the balcony of an overpriced flat on Westbourne Grove, listen to a few
artificial birds in the morning before she heads for the lab. She no longer has
any desire for this adventure-playground existence. For hunting criminals and
eating noodles. She's a bit bored—no, very bored—of the others. She's even
more bored since they buried their devices. It is a temporary distraction to au-
dit classes at the university, to lug home books from the library. Still, it won't
lead to anything. But that's another story. The current story is that Karen is
still feeling the effects of LSD, leaning against a shopwindow. A new VR space
is going to be opened here. Of course, yet another VR space. The city is being
flooded with them. It doesn't matter.

To the

CITY

What people do on this blurred surface. You know, the people who get
tattooed with the logos of their one-hour employers as a sign of their loyalty.
Doesn't matter who owns the city, who removes the rubbish, which drones film
what, or that the trains drive themselves. The city is smart, hurray, we have a
smart city. The rubbish is automatically removed, the refrigerators are filled
with the help of delivery robots, the trees are watered automatically, pollu-
tion is quantified, motorcars are led to available parking spots, the blinds are
closed, opened, dog shit is disposed of by robots, bicycles are charged while
riding. Drones surveil drones, always ready to shoot each other if one of them
strays into the flight paths of police helicopters; the police drones now have
grapple arms and are weaponized. Code strings determine right and wrong,
threat potential and payouts, loans and the valuation of homes, health risks
and cancer diagnoses. Is chemotherapy more profitable or are the cost benefits
better if a life is just allowed to fade away? Who gets what job, who will be
fired, who gets custody of children, which train lines are profitable, which
buildings must be razed, where should new buildings be built, whose election
to head up the government shall we engineer? Transactions, corporate direction, acquisitions. Artificial intelligence, which learns ever more quickly, learns
on its own, teaches itself things, networks itself, which in a giant space without
oversight collects information, evaluates it, tries to impose order on the world,
stockpiles emergency generators, repairs faulty nuclear power plants, protects
aircraft from hacker attacks, watches over the world like a friendly parent.

A mother

Is something everyone should have, thinks

KAREN

Who has somehow managed to make it back to the wasteland on the
outskirts of town, and is nearly home. Nearly sober. No longer staggering.
No longer talking to her hand. No longer unhappy. But also no longer alone,
because, in the mud between the catchment basins, settlements have popped
up overnight. Tents are set up. Plastic tarps draped over boards, campfires,
and—as always, when people settle down somewhere—piles of rubbish. Illegal itinerant workers. Young and sort of young men from Romania, Bulgaria,
Russia, Poland. Before the country's departure from the wonderful European
political union they'd been happy. In places like Manchester, Blackwater, and
Birmingham. They saved for small houses, the things people do when starting
out. Since Brexit most of them had lost their residency permits. And then
stayed for a while in the dreary areas where they'd been, where there was no
sympathy for them, where the long-established residents reported them. So
now they're here. The second-to-last station. None has money for a ticket
home, none wants to go home, to some dark place where there's nothing awaiting them but liquor and cold winters. They sit here in front of lodgings made
of tarps, which is better than sleeping on the street in the city. That has
become dangerous, as now they aren't even the hated foreigners with jobs
anymore and are instead considered lepers. They are the offerings that had to
be sacrificed to save the world. The men smell. The possibility to wash their
clothes or themselves in the oily runoff streams is of little interest. They seem
almost relieved now that their fear is gone. The years-long fear of losing the
amenities, the leakproof windows, the flowing warm water, the incomes, and
the mattresses had been so great that a sense of relief now wells up. They have
arrived back where they started. A tarp on the ground, a couple of pieces of
furniture scrounged up, and beans. That's what life provides for them. Like all
here in the wastelands, these men are so far removed from the idea of having
a hearth and library that they don't even get envious when they walk through
central London looking for a chance to get into a bit of petty crime. They
would never conceive of their lives as so boring that they would voluntarily
forsake it for hours-long voyages into virtual reality. They've never thought of
optimizing themselves with the help of apps and trackers, only to then have
the optimized version of themselves evaluated in the virtual world by un-

known idiots. They have never paid for anything with an app, have never stuck an internet-enabled dildo in their orifices, they have lived 1.0 lives with the romance of 1.0 life, pubs, friends, staring at women, falling in love and dreaming of owning a house of their own. And that's why, dear scum of society, that's why you are here, staring into the night at your wits' end. Some distance away

In Holyroodhouse

HANNAH AND DON

Are sitting at the table, and no water is dripping. They are sitting at the table for no clear reason, since they actually all prefer to lie on their beds in front of the TV, but that wouldn't be grown-up. To be young is not to be able to imagine yourself older. When you believe in yourself infinitely. And that your body will not change. A young person doesn't doubt. A young person just is. And above all a young person is virile. Endless virility and the ability to sleep on the floor, just fall over and sleep without sleeping pills, without the need to urinate overnight. To be young is to believe things will go on, except that it'll get better, because you'll be smarter, later, in your still-young body, and that the world will have become a brilliant one. Hannah is in love. And it's worse than for an adult, this condition of being involuntarily out of your head, this excitement, that knows not what it wants. What does it even mean beyond hugging the other person? Don is in love. She accidentally touches Hannah's hand while handing her the bowl of spaghetti and thinks, I'm going to cut my hand off and put it in the freezer and take it out once in a while and lick it. To be young means falling in love in a way that is no longer possible later on. Because you know what comes next. Awkward sex that is never as imagined, awkward conversations and insecurity, and in the end you're always alone, and true union, the dissolving of your boundaries, hasn't happened. There're just two people who look at each other while they sleep and see the spittle in the corners of their mouths, but you don't know that, as a young person, when it seems holy and sacrosanct and untouchable, this being in love, that is always conjoined with pain that carries with it the first inkling of misery. One will never be loved the way one hopes. Unconditionally. One will never not be alone. Later. And love will just be love. And now Karen arrives home, she's pale and says nothing, she sits down and stares at the spaghetti. And Don thinks: too bad, I might have touched Hannah on the neck, there where the collarbones can be seen to the left and right.

And

Karen suddenly sees the squalor in which she lives. The charred pots and pans, the full rubbish bin, the fruit flies, all the crap.

To be young means not seeing the chaos in which you live because there is nothing to compare it to. There is no need to purify yourself of your toxic humanity with a maniacal urge to clean.

Don can no longer sit at this table, no longer sit and admit to herself that she might never touch Hannah. "Relax," an older sister would tell her. "Step back from the ledge!" But there's no older sister, and Don is in love, and Hannah is in love, but not with Don, and so begin all wretched stories, so begin weeks that are horrid and have to do with hormones. And

DON

Gets up and looks out the window.

"There're people out there," she says. And looks at the tent camp.

It must have been put up in just the last few seconds. Yesterday there was nothing except plastic litter and old rolls of cable. And now there are scrapwood huts, six of them, seven, and two fires burning in front of them. Around the fire sit a few remnants of men. Nothing worth shooting at. Of the men, there are maybe ten, no idea whether there are others in the sad huts, three are minors; they squat, barely talk, roasting potatoes on the fire and spooning something out of tin cans. No good food, no precious meal of meat.

Their clothes speak of homelessness, their faces of having given up. A little way from the saddest of the tents sits an old man who, with his suit, stands out from the others.

The suit must have really been something. Before it had gotten stained and the seams had ripped. The man must also have really been something before he'd given up.

Like a

PROFESSOR

HEALTH CONDITIONS: *depression*
HOBBIES: *collect(ed) first editions*
LISTEN(ED): *Mozart*
USEFULNESS: *0*

That's what the old man looks like, as he sits on a beer crate and rocks back and forth.

> *Murmur, stream, the vale along*
> *Without pause or peace,*
> *Murmur, whisper to my song*
> *adding melodies!*

Goethe. An echo from before, memory and smell and taste, of the fireside, in the library. Recollection of the time when consumer decisions fulfilled wishes, not needs. Of the time not long ago when coal power plants had resumed operation. And he—

He would love to have been a professor of German and English literature, the professor, who had only become a tax advisor. And whose comfortable life was in a two-room flat on Kensington Church Street. Had been. Amazing that there was a time when you could live there as a fucking tax advisor. But that didn't go well. The tax advisor's work had been made easier by devices. We all know the rest of the story. The tax advisor's tension caused constant stomach problems, which led to loud abdominal noises at his weekly book club meetings. Until he no longer dared to take part in the evening events. The tax advisor found himself increasingly unable to understand the world. He was fitted with a chip, began to collect citizen points, unfortunately received miserable ratings from his neighbors, from shop assistants. He didn't do any exercise, crossed the road without WALK signs, took hot showers, tried fruit in supermarkets before buying it, didn't sort his rubbish; at the pub he spoke disparagingly of the government, and suddenly his problems grew worse. He stood at the entrance to the tube and wasn't allowed through the turnstile. His funds to pay for food at the shops were frozen. His water would no longer warm up. Same for the heater. Payments were no longer made. He wasn't the least bit surprised by the termination of the lease on his flat. In order to celebrate his departure from the world of the arts, the professor ordered himself some company.

The

EIGHT-YEAR-OLD PROSTITUTE

Will soon be nine. There won't be any birthday cake. The children, at the moment there are thirteen, who live on a floor of the enchanting building in the choicest location on the park, cannot see out the window. Passersby could take notice. Drones could take films. The windows are for this understandable reason two-thirds frosted glass. One third is clear. Way high up. Unreachable by the children. Only by lying down can they sometimes look up and see the sky. Every last inch of the flat is monitored by video camera. Little blinking red lights and microphones all over the place. One doesn't know. One doesn't know what to do with all these goddamn child soldiers here. Because—there's not much for the eight-year-old prostitute to do anymore. As with all the child soldiers. It's become calm in recent weeks. It doesn't matter to the eight-year-old prostitute. She lies on the floor, looks at the thin slice of sky and has no idea how a life can be provided that doesn't take place here in this prison. Like all of them here. Their stories are similar, they're so boring, the stories of their lives, and they all have to do with a lack of affection. With parents who for various reasons were too busy with their own survival or who just hadn't survived. The previous year someone had gone to the trouble to count the number of homeless children in the country. And how exactly do you count homeless children, by waking them in the middle of the night in their gutters and then, once they're statistically registered, clapping them on the shoulder with a back-to-sleep-you-little-rascal? It ended up being several hundred thousand, nearly a million, but who knows. Maybe they all looked very similar to each other, crusted in filth. A little boy, Ben, had for a moment been the darling of the press and an inspired public. He was five, homeless, and had the advantage of being blond and charming. Ben was unbelievably photogenic, the way he sat there with his blue eyes radiating out of the muck. He had dimples. He had fucking dimples. And after the big SAVE BEN campaign had found kindhearted, rich foster parents for him, who were primarily interested in publicity and attention for their laundry service, they subsequently barely spoke to little Ben. In his cellar room.

None of the children here in the villa think to flee, because their past in old sewer pipes, in train stations, and in cellars is of limited use in luring them out of a heated flat. They don't even speak English. They speak Russian, Polish, Romanian, Bosnian, Hindi, so the communication among them is also very limited. For the most part the children sit in front of computers and look at the websites they are allowed to view. Cartoons and porn. Nobody here cries. Or looks particularly unhappy. They've accepted their destiny, you could say, like hundreds of thousands of children in the country who are superfluous at a time when others are already being born with modified DNA. There is a right to genetic modification that one should make use of if one wishes to enable a good start for one's children into the bright future. Without inherited diseases, without dwarfism, without brain deformities, without an overly pronounced sensitivity to pain. Without resentment of authority. You just have to be willing to pay for it.

All the stories about the great, unconditional love of parents for their children had never been anything more than a moral construct. Occupational therapy for people who even then were already extraneous. Who were bored to death by their existence and invested all their creative energy into their offspring. That's now become unnecessary as the middle class no longer exists. Showing excessive attention to your offspring no longer occurs to anyone. No person loves another unconditionally. Nobody even loves anymore.

Societal standards which had long held sway, the reenactment of morals and benevolence, have been pulverized as quickly as an acquaintance bids farewell. Had been. The new system of order is to be embraced for that reason as well—the era when every second British child was abused, wives were beaten half to death, when firemen or rubbish collectors were assaulted because they caused backups is over.

At last

There's something to do.

THE PROFESSOR

Bids farewell.

He knows his old life is over. He'll never again live on an elegant street, stroll past antique shops, quote classics. And now there are two children sitting here. No idea why. Maybe it's about the feeling of having power again. Even if it is bought. And now there are two children sitting here. Not that he'd be interested in children; he isn't interested in anyone living today. A little girl of indeterminate skin color, a sign of the transformation of the world he knew into one where whites were slowly dying off. Overrun by yellow and all shades of darker people who exhibit a better mating performance.

Back to the children. It had felt better in the imagining. Now tired children are just sitting there looking at the professor who isn't even a professor. It is too light, the shades have already been taken down, his belongings are in boxes that he wanted to store somewhere but hadn't found anyplace to leave them. His travel bag is on the ground in front of the children, who sit on two chairs. No noises from outside. Traffic rolls by quietly, people are muffled because there seems no more reason to be loud. There sit the children, and it is getting increasingly embarrassing. Particularly now, confronted with the shabbiness of the place in the light and in a nearly empty state. So this is it, the grand flat on Kensington Church Street. Two tiny rooms last renovated thirty years ago, black outlines where furniture and prints had been, linoleum floor. Perhaps his life hadn't been so wonderful after all.

The children look at the floor.

The little assholes.

Their empty eyes lead to the conclusion that they aren't so proficient with the language. Great. "Listen to me," says the professor who isn't even a professor but rather a foolish jobless person.

"Listen,"

The professor begins to read aloud from an old edition of Shakespeare. The whole thing takes into the wee hours.

The children will be picked up later. They would have preferred to service a client who just had a quick wank. Over and done with.

It was the final day of his old life. And now he sits in front of a fire, the old man, and

HANNAH

Says: "We need to get into the habit of locking the door," and while delivering this line feels like one of those actresses with a white blouse, wild hair, and a breechloader. She distinguishes between *we* and *you*. Of all the unpleasant attributes that used to characterize the adults in Rochdale and Liverpool, racism had always been the most disgusting to her. Losers who sneered at other losers. It seems as if stalagmites should have grown in the hall. It seems as if, with the homeless outside their door, the cuteness of the location has disappeared. Obviously nobody here thinks: we're sitting in the midst of totally cute surroundings. They just have a feeling. That their garden outside is in danger; same for the solar panels. That they can't go out in their underwear anymore to drink the first coffee of the day. That they should lock the door like—people. That's how it starts, acting like a capitalist, becoming a nationalist, a right-wing asshole, with vulgar fears about your meager belongings. That you would like to add to, protect, and celebrate. Would we have to let them, to sleep here? Don thinks, but doesn't voice her thought because she's afraid the others might be open to it and they'd have strange men sitting here at the table. "I'm going over to see the nerds," says Don. "Anybody want to come with?" They all come along happily. They lock the door with much care. Outside there's no wind. The yellow light of the city is reflected back by the sky, or perhaps there's a full moon behind the clouds. It has rained again. The ground won't absorb the water any longer; there's no snow in the northern hemisphere.

It's always something.

The

FRIENDS

For example are in a state of alarm. On the verge of complete meltdown. "Soon they'll be licking the walls," says Karen upon seeing the nerds. Although they have different skin colors and body types, the hackers resemble each other in their unhealthy, nervous vibe. They've barely left the building for days, eaten cold pizza from cardboard boxes, not slept, not washed. That still works at their age, as you can be sticky and dirty, exhausted and agitated, and nothing is off-putting about the shiny skin, the stringy hair, the rigid belief in being able to influence the world. The air in the room is filled with delusions of grandeur. "Spoofing doesn't work, pass the hash check." They hammer codes into their computers. Don rolls her eyes. Full of themselves, she thinks, so fucking full of themselves. "What are you guys doing anyway?" she asks Rachel, whose eyes are so infected she looks like a bunny in a spotlight.

Brilliant, Rachel seems to think. Boast. Alarm. Now.

"I'll put it real simple," she says. "We hacked our way into the surveillance system. We're going to take it over today or, well, tomorrow, and transmit the images from the biggest crossroads in the city onto the screens."

Don doesn't yet understand what that's good for. "What's that supposed to be good for?" she asks. Rachel looks at Don the way you would examine an insect. "They'll get it, the people. They'll see themselves, their data, the information. They'll realize what every moronic member of the private police sees through their data glasses, they will finally catch on.

"Okay, I'll sketch it out for you." Rachel sketches it out. "The government—or better yet: the intelligence agencies, who are directly connected to the private police—control all the surveillance and the screens in the city. All of it is connected to the network. That is, the screens where adverts, news, and official announcements are beamed at the citizens. Everything. Video surveillance data runs into this platform (circle) here, where, after identification of a citizen, everything that's saved in the data bank is added to the video stream, so the screens of administrators display various citizens' characteristics—like their age, gender, criminal history, or sexual inclinations. Do you understand?" Don looks at Hannah's neck from behind. Hannah is allowing herself to be told some boring nonsense by Ben at the moment. Rachel is stuttering. She always stutters when she is excited. "If we put ourselves in the main console, the one used by the administrators to switch between the thousands of cameras in the city. Then—

Then we have this option here called Hotspots, that gives an overview of ten live camera views where the bigwigs think there's suspicious activity or gatherings. But the console also allows for the definition of the Output option, which determines where the video stream with all the citizens' traits is displayed. Check this out: here it says >localhost:I<—you see?" Don sees. She yawns. Inside. "Right," Rachel says, still stuttering. "The main screen is associated with the console at the address IPv6-Address >>::I<< for the local device of the console. If we switch it to >localhost:0<, what do you see then?" Don stares at the screen. Linux bollocks, no organized graphics. "Forbidden," says Don. "Ha," says Rachel. "That's the console itself! But if we go over to >localhost:2< and >localhost:3<, the results of the surveillance appear on other—screens. Here in this window, see?" Don doesn't see anything. Except for Hannah's back, which is long, and her vertebrae protrude through her hoodie. That takes quite a performance from the vertebrae, through such thick material. Hannah must be one meter eighty at this point, and she consists of only arms and legs and spine. "What's that?" asks Don politely. On the computer are images from surveillance cameras somewhere in the city. "Covent Garden," says Rachel. "You can see here, they know everything. That guy, for example." Rachel reads aloud: "Sergej, thirty-three, Polish origins, he heads up a prepper group and is considered a right-wing extremist."

"We've got him," Don yells. "Peter, we . . ."

Peter isn't there. He's left without anyone noticing.

He's been leaning against a tree for several minutes already,

PETER

Watching Thome in the first floor of the white box, behind curtains with tassels and a pair of matched and at the same time utterly pointless table lamps on the windowsill. Pant legs too short, fabric stretched across his backside, no chin—what an unpleasant person.

If only he would die,

Thinks

THOME

In the library of his father, who sits behind his desk. The Russian whore is standing next to him, one hand on her husband's shoulder as if they are posing for an oil portrait, the future prime minister and his spouse, who carries the geezer's child in her stomach. Thome sits down. He looks at the old man. He thinks: you fossil. I can already see the livor mortis on your sallow skin, I see the gout in your old claws, I smell your old balls, and nothing, nothing has changed for you, because you'll be dead soon. While people like me will live on in machines after we've drained your swamp. His father starts to speak: "It's time to arrange my inheritance. In the future I'll be in far more danger than now, as I'll hold an important political office." Clearing of the throat. Tense silence. Humanity's IQ has been dropping nonstop since 1990, Thome had read yesterday. He tries to concentrate on his father's voice. He wonders why people actually still stick to the concept of family.

"I shall divide my estate into thirds," says Thome's father. "One part will go to my wonderful wife, the second will go to the unborn child, and the third to you, my son. Though with the condition that you don't let yourself get caught up in any scandal." "What sort of scandal?" asks Thome, finding himself somewhat nauseated by the situation, such that he'd like to drop to the floor and just lie there. Thome's father takes a deep breath. A bit of snot that's entangled in his nose hair darts in and out like a kitten.

"Homosexuality, pedophilia, misappropriation, compulsive gambling, bestiality, violent crime. That sort of thing. In that case you will be immediately disinherited." It's important to know—Thome's father has been a member for over ten years in the transnational Organization for the Restoration of the Natural Order, which opposes perversions. It had begun as the Agenda Europe network. Meaning: using lots of money and all legal means to create precedents. The draft proposal for the Polish abortion ban, the ban on same-sex marriage in various central European countries, and countless other triumphs of Christian ideas. Because: homosexuality and women taking on leading roles are the first steps toward anarchy. Parties to the organization include the Vatican, an Irish senator, members of European parliament, the head of the anti-abortion group European Dignity Watch, proxies for a Mexican billionaire, Archduke Imre von Habsburg-Lothringen, and alongside Thome's father, Mr. Hylton, a former asset manager for the climate change denier Sir Michael Hintze. The organization is steered by the Vatican, which has managed despite all the disparate temperaments to reach a consensus, which creates laws and precedents. About order, right, well, and so forth.

Thome looks at the Russian's throat. He'd love to hear her neck snap. After he'd cut off his father's cock and stomped on it. While Thome's father reads aloud paragraphs from his will, Thome watches the snot-kitten and his life go by.

His father's silence when he had disappointed him. The complete deprivation of love. The periods of punishment spent in the cellar. The first animal he had to kill, and how he threw up and dirtied his father's hunting kilt. Everything Thome remembers is tied to an off-putting sort of rot. The only thing not rotten in his life is

PETER

Who by now is lying on the sofa downstairs in Thome's room, pretending to be asleep. He pretends to be asleep so he can think over how he can mount the cameras the hackers gave him. Who doesn't want to open his eyes anyway because he's tired of all the shit here.

Peter's nearly translucent eyelids twitch. When Thome enters the room.

"You know how elegant you look, like you're from another universe, it unnerves people when they see you." Thome is deeply moved by the romantic and simultaneously worldly sentences that flow out of him—"But it doesn't help you, does it? No?" he continues. "You little rent boy, you baby hustler, you look like you're not even human. That's why people stare at you. As if you never smell bad or get dirty, inside or out, that's why they stare at you, and they probably want to tear you to bits because you make it clear to them how debauched they are."

Thome kneels in front of the sofa. His voice has gotten quiet. As if he could mar the perfection lying before him with his voice alone. Peter's shirt is a bit rumpled, leaving his chest muscles visible. The right collarbone, the line from his neck to his upper body. Thome gulps, sweats and wants to lick, and suddenly understands why meat eaters react so aggressively to vegetarians. This urge to consume something living can nearly drive one mad. Thome feels close to Jeffrey fucking Dahmer again and is thinking of a refrigerator full of body parts when the doorbell rings. Why would it ring now, just as he's thinking up a recipe to perfect the flavor of Peter's neck? "Shit," Thome whispers and goes to the door.

Peter hears him talking to another man, and now, now is the moment. Peter hides the cameras in the room, and when he is finished with that—Thome enters the room with a redhead.

"This is the programmer," says Thome, "I forgot that we still—doesn't matter." Thome thinks he'll fire the programmer. Or push him out the window, but first he'll make canapés. "I'll make a few canapés," says Thome, leaving the redhead behind with Peter. The programmer stands awkwardly in the room, looks around, looks at a porcelain dog. What an incredibly daft porcelain dog; why do people put that sort of shit in their flats, what would make them do that? Why do they put side tables with tablecloths in their flats and books that they will never read on coffee tables, in order to show that they're capable of placing a fucking book on a table? "I've built myself a machine that irons my trousers and brings them to me." Says the programmer to the wall. "Amazing," says Peter.

"Indeed." Says the programmer. "I have a brain extension." Peter says nothing.

"Here, look, a chip, in my head." This ageless person, utterly devoid of gender traits, who could as well have been a giant infant or mummified, displays a shaved spot in his thinning hair. Peter says nothing. The programmer doesn't notice; he has an unpleasant lack of timidity. He's one of those people who became powerful too quickly but who mistrusts power and must constantly try to increase his own sense of worth with stuff that in earlier times might have been compared to engineering expertise. A technician with mathematical abilities, lucky enough to live at a time when the middle class was being replaced. The old middle class will be rolled into the category of societal parasite, the parasites will die off, and the programmer will live as comfortably as a middle manager at an insurance company would have in the past. He'll mortgage a flat where previously a middle manager at an insurance company or perhaps a doctor's assistant or architect had lived but who now lives in social housing and is old. He'll buy a second electric vehicle for his spouse. In place of unattractive men before him, this unattractive person will create the world in his image, which means: it will become even more unaesthetic and middling. "So, right, here, I'll show you the last thing I masterminded the programming of." Says the programmer.

"Masterminded?" asks Peter.

Brief pause. "Yes," says the programmer.

The programmer pulls his laptop from his rucksack; a paranoid programmer would never take so much as a step without his laptop, the NSA, you know, the Trojan whatever. He squats in front of Peter and shows him the website of a political party.

"Look, we've built an online party. Thome's idea. Well. Really most of it was mine." The programmer continues talking endless rubbish; he'd talk to a dog if it were in the room instead of Peter. It doesn't matter to him whom he brags in front of, the point is just to be able to enhance his own esteem by describing some accomplishment. "So this party is utter democratic shite. Everyone can take part in decisions online, vote online. What do you think of the candidate for prime minister we've put in the race?" Peter looks at a young man. He shrugs his shoulders. "A fake," says the programmer. "Came out well, eh? People are flocking to our page."

"Yeah, great, a fake," says Peter. He never knows what other people expect. Also, he doesn't care.

"Can you access a smart flat,"

He asks

The programmer.

The perfect cue. The programmer immediately continues to talk. "You can program white noise into music clips that contains inaudible commands. The commands can then take over control of a flat, make bank transactions, lock doors, order pizzas, or summon a strike force."

"Great," says Peter. "It's a place on Regent's Park."

The building

Where

PETER'S MOTHER

Is sitting in the window. She was just about to moisturize her hands with a lotion containing caviar extracts. That is, dead baby fish. Such is her life. Sitting in bad weather with a man she can't stand, greasing her skin with baby corpses. Then the light flickers. And the door locks itself. There are always weird glitches here in this unbelievably modern, networked flat. Just last week the refrigerator had an entire pig delivered. A dead pig in the kitchen can throw your entire way of life into question by its appearance alone.

The Russian is meeting with yet another nerd. A Russian nerd, naturally. You know how it is, these Russian hackers, who are responsible for everything, sitting in their hoodies in Ukraine, and so forth. Right, in any event, since the diagnosis of his multibacterial antibiotic resistance, he's hit upon the idea of trying out a beta version of a brain transfer.

Peter's mother listens to the two men talk, she looks at her nails, she's bored. It hasn't come to pass, the sense of delight she had promised herself her life would deliver. She'd been able to get the Russian to marry her. With a prenuptial agreement, of course. The price was higher than she had been able to conceive of. She had to tolerate him, adore him, listen to him, and laugh at his jokes. The light flickers. It goes out. The blinds close on their own. It makes no difference. Peter's mother stares into the darkness with her eyes wide

and doesn't know why of all things she isn't able to be happy amid all this affluence, in the wonderful world of infinite material bounty. If it's the case that
poverty doesn't make you happy and wealth doesn't either, what else is there?

There is nothing to do

For the moment

And

PETER

Walks through the city, which always has the feel of afternoon, always
this milky in-between light and an in-between temperature that's a bit too
cool to be comfortable. People move in a decidedly orderly fashion. None of
the end-times utopias of the last few decades have come to pass. All the films,
TV programs, books, speeches and essays, the alarmists and TED Talkers had
been wrong. Or utterly correct, because they'd reached the goal of raising
people's fear to a chronic condition that completely trashed all remnants of
logical and empathetic thought. When, alongside the usual fucked-up shit
that's left in human brains by click-oriented news, you hear from all the channels that are actually supposed to provide relaxation that everything is even
worse than you can imagine with your limited powers of imagination, when
you have the demise of your own existence sketched out for you daily by ac-
credited experts and intellectuals, it's barely possible for anyone to develop a
sense of calm anymore.

So now. Well, what do we see? Do we see dumpster fires, burned-out cars
along the side of the road? And speaking of roads, are there holes opening up
where animals that no longer exist can disappear? Do we see people with fully
automatic weapons in leather rags gnawing on corpses? Or do we watch orderly, quiet electric vehicles moving along at a walking pace? People who keep
their unadorned clothing clean, wait for the WALK signal to cross the road,
don't push and shove, greet each other, shop peacefully in self-service shops;
do we see clean buildings, a milky sky, and relaxation?

Because even for those whose abilities are of only rudimentary importance
to society, a relaxed life is on offer—

There is the

MIDDLE-AGED TEACHER

HEALTH STATUS: *well-balanced acid-base metabolism*
HOBBIES: *a true porridge aficionado*
USEFULNESS: *none*
EXTRAS: *so average that you could form new people in his image*
"Good idea—shall we?"

And the tube had barred him entry today, as a result of the fact that he is behind on the rent for his space on a sofa. Beautiful day, by the way. The atmospheric temperature seems to be changing, spring is coming. The one brief period of the year between the rains. Spring is coming, and perhaps he will meet somebody. Most people meet in the spring, after all, as a result of hope, mating season, although—his last girlfriend left him several years ago. When he lost his job, to be precise. He's a teacher. He goes out of his way not to think *I was a teacher*, because to be a teacher is a calling. His calling has fallen victim to cutbacks. Classes are being enlarged, school hours shortened, and real people are being replaced by machines. Without a doubt, the middle-aged teacher has let himself go a bit in the meantime, which also contributes to the tightening of his financial means. Which has led to the usual. Basic income, loss of flat, sofa rental, boredom, cries for love. The teacher's life, like that of so many other men his age, would have ended in suicide except that a chance incident saved the old bastard.

The teacher discovered the "space for you" offer by coincidence while mindlessly hanging about the city center. At the usual happy hour time, hundreds of people with satisfied smiles on their faces were coming out of a building that had previously been a post office.

Ever since then the teacher goes at seven every day to his virtual work platform. He enters the building, which, across five floors, features little soundproof units reminiscent of animal cages. There's space for an unbelievable three thousand people, and the cost per day is negligible. Inside the boxes, which can also be rented by the month, is enough room to sit on the comfy beanbag chair, or to stand or run on a treadmill. The middle-aged teacher enters his box. Puts on his glasses. There's no window inside, but there are artificial smells and a climate control system you can adjust yourself. "So, off we go," says the middle-aged teacher shortly after seven, and upon his orders finds himself in a flat in the south of the city. Outside the windows, trees; inside, nice wood floors and even a fireplace. His girlfriend has prepared breakfast. They eat. The girlfriend is six months pregnant. The nursery is painted in pastel colors. The flat consists of exactly what a middle-class couple—he a teacher, she a speech therapist—could have afforded in the nineties of the previous century. There's a little garden. After breakfast the two head together to the tube station, just a short distance away. They hop on different train lines, kissing each other goodbye. "See you tonight, darling." Says the woman. "I love you." Says the teacher, feeling the love. The feeling stays with him during his ride, keeps him smiling. The passengers around him read paper newspapers, some doze off. Then the teacher arrives at his old school. In the teachers' lounge. Coffee, conversation, the bell, class begins. The teacher teaches for six long hours. During the lunch break he goes out and buys a limp salad, tries to mediate fights on the playground, and feels bored at his lectern. Bored when he is confronted by idiocy. The algorithm changes the lighting conditions over the course of the day. Creates the smell of sweaty kids and autumn foliage, the flickering of lights, the sirens of fire drills, the scent of blood when breaking up fights between boys and of coffee during breaks. In the afternoons the middle-aged teacher rides back to his place in the south of the city. Sometimes the place smells of bread pudding, and it always smells of his girlfriend. Even sex with her feels good. Late in the afternoon he turns off the light. Like everyone around him. Like thousands in the city who recreate their boring, peaceful past lives in virtual spaces. Back when they still had a function. Back when they had larger flats and the streets seemed wider. Millions are happy in their old daily job routines in insurance companies, banks, law offices, in supermarkets and warehouses. They have arguments, financial worries, stress with colleagues. While they are immersed in their virtual jobs, their bodies create energy with which cryptocurrency is mined and algorithms speculate on commodities and CO_2 markets. Hilarious, right? And when they put out the lights, they all take off their glasses. They're not as depressed as they were at the start. No longer beaten down when they exit their VR rooms and head into the street, toward home, in what today is referred to as home. They know it's just for a short time, a night, and then they can go back to their proper life.

Glorious.

At

THE FRIENDS

Are four children, who are nearly no longer children anymore because some time has elapsed in the meantime. They don't want to go home because they are bored there. And that is why it's better here at the hackers' place; at least they have an obsession. Here they sit,

And

HANNAH

In Peter's presence, can no longer think, no longer breathe deeply, her pupils are dilated, her gaze nervous, her movements erratic, and she barely dares to look at him because she immediately blushes when she looks at him, and her hands get clammy. This overly perfect idiot. He has his eyes closed, his lashes are thirty centimeters long.

"I have to go," says Hannah, stumbling out of the factory hall,

And

DON

Watches her go. Along with Hannah all color disappears from the day. Don has no idea what she wants to do with Hannah other than be together. To touch her hair and lick her legs, perhaps,

And

PETER

Watches Hannah go, as well.

The rush of hormones temporarily paralyzes his breathing center. He gets dizzy. The colors of the surroundings, which are not terribly pronounced anyway, are completely removed with Hannah's disappearance. Peter has no interest anymore in moving. Or in saying anything. Silence holds sway in the room as the sharp sounds made by the Friends pounding on their keyboards ring out like gunshots.

And

KAREN

Talks quietly to herself. This is brilliant. That you can talk to yourself without alienating any of those present. Karen talks to herself the way all of them here talk to themselves and keep up with themselves, since they were little, since they were able to think, so there was at least one person to console them. Who could say: "Listen, don't get out of hand, I know that you feel like the loneliest person in the world. You have a sense that it will never change, that you don't understand anything, and you're insecure and scared. Hey, I'm there for you." And Karen talks quietly to herself and is happy for this brief moment. When she doesn't want anything. "I don't want anything," she says, "except to be here, on the sofa, near the others." Everyone is alone with their thoughts, with their computer, with their weird plans that have to do with the fact that the earth revolves around them. "And the perfect moment is already over," says Karen to herself and watches as Hannah runs out of the hall. And as Peter watches her go and Don watches her go. Now it's really kicking off with the hormones and the feeling of suffering in a way nobody has ever suffered before. Now it's really kicking off with the stolen glances and the racing hearts and the sense of being able to fly, and the fear of dropping. From the sky.

"Quiet"

Shouts

BEN

"Please, be quiet." In the silence of the hall. Ben has found the Cityscreen option in the function console, which can send text and video messages to all the screens in the city. Ben enters some bullshit value or other. On Ben's computer a warning appears: "Are you sure you wish to proceed?"

Ben looks around the room, he sees earnest faces. Inwardly a flag is hoisted, a song is sung, a key is pressed. The revolution can begin.

How boring

Thinks

MI5 PIET

And leans back in his cantilevered chair. Some of what he sees in the high-risk groups makes him worry even more than usual about the intelligence of the human species. The know-it-alls, the smart-asses, the antifascist hacker-warriors. Too stupid to solder their own devices, but brag with statements like, "Whoa, we encrypt our dim-witted emails, go online with VPN and Tor. And we put tape over our cameras." Snorting laughter. These idiots completely forget that the bulk of the parts for their computers are made in China. The Trojan horse is built in. In essence. They might as well just go out a buy a good old Mac to save time.

Heading up the monitoring unit of the British former Great Power is

MA WEI

Whose surveillance surveils all surveillance,

But

Keep moving

SERGEJ

Yells. He's pissed off. He has to be careful because when he's pissed off he has a tendency to lose control. He smiles into the surveillance camera, not getting anywhere, and his class begins soon. He needs to get on the tube. And the sheep are just standing and staring at the giant screens,

And

What are they looking at?

They see: themselves. They see themselves looking at themselves. Sergej sees himself, and next to him on the screen appears information—

Sergej—Pole—high risk—Sexuality: zero, the loser—Nazi fetish—football—Mars bar—leader of a paramilitary organization—short-tempered—bank balance: 345 pounds

OMG

A woman next to Sergej taps him in the side; she winks at him. Sergej resists the urge to punch her in the face. The people are excited. There they are, on the screens! Like on TV. And all the things they know about them, it's better than looking at a horoscope, better than getting Likes. This is not to be able to be brushed aside, to be present. In the limelight. To be reckoned with. Oh, finally to be reckoned with. In the group gathered here around the flat-screen are people who have murdered their mother, whose businesses went bust, who lick their pets. WTF, the fat guy over there deep-throats his hamster and has a very poor environmental rating. There are men present who exhibit their penises unsolicited, these days flaccid, men who beat their kids, whose hobby it is to rub themselves in excrement. Bed wetters, diaper wearers, thieves, strivers, and a few people there for whom there's no name or data. The people look at themselves, they see what the intelligence agencies see when they look at their screens. And so it is revealed to the normal native-born citizens that old men sit around staring at screens at intelligence agencies, and listen in on telephone conversations. How sweet. People could now fully comprehend the miserableness of the total surveillance of their lives, they could think. Okay, it was just a suggestion.

Sergej glances beside him.

He sees

HANNAH

Who is looking at him. Hannah doesn't exist. "Isn't that a bit too private?" asks a woman. "That they know that I'm menopausal? And that I cheat?" "They know everything," mumbles a young man. "They know that I've been impotent for a few weeks?" They. "Who are they?" flickers through millions of brains across the country at this memorable moment in time that will change everything. Hannah nearly forgets Sergej; she's thinking of the Friends, she sees them before her eyes, sweating and nervous in front of their computers. Maybe it will kick off, thinks Hannah. A revolution, the people will storm the security agencies and besiege government buildings, they'll rip the chips out of their arms with their teeth and burn their biometric passports, destroy the cameras and—"Can you watch this at home, too, this channel?" asks a woman. "I'd know everything about my neighbors." In that instant Hannah realizes the Friends have lost.

And

SERGEJ

Stares at the woman who continues to spout off about the advantages of surveillance technology—

And wonders how easily her skin could be removed from her body. A little boy stands in the crowd, he can barely see anything, there's no data on him, he just stands there and is a useless bauble. Children are always useless baubles. Sergej doesn't like them, these children, he always starts crying when he looks at one for too long, and he's a man and too stupid to understand that he is crying about his own life when he looks at a child for too long, that he is crying about his own life and about everyone who once had hopes and some sort of cuteness.

Sergej has seen enough.

He has to get going.

These idiots.

Think

THE FRIENDS

Who sit around for hours. Waiting for a miracle. Staring at their bugged computers, staring at excited people pointing at themselves, toasting each other, laughing. Or just disinterestedly moving along or moving along after looking at themselves.

They feel. Nothing. The shock causes a cold dissonance in their bodies—unable to analyze what exactly went wrong with their long-planned liberation strike with which they hoped to wake up the populace. They had anticipated all sorts of reactions. Outrage, an uprising, an outcry, but not indifference.

There is nothing.

In the gazes.

Of the people, in the middle of whom

HANNAH

Is standing.

In a nearly pristine part of the huge park, in a group of ten people assembled in a circle around Sergej. Serious men. Grinding their jaws. One has jet-black dyed hair and piercings. Mortar rounds tattooed on his chest. Sergej wears camouflaged clothing, has an ammo belt around his waist, a knife strapped to his knuckles, and camouflage face paint for authenticity's sake.

"So, comrades," he says. "First let's set aside the bodycams for now." The men do so. One or two of them quickly fire up cortex stimulators on their heads.

Sergej continues. "We're here today to prepare for the imminent global escalation. For survival after a megadisaster scenario in a world of ash and rubble where enemy gangs rove."

"What is rove?" asks the tattooed guy.

"Who gives a fuck," says Sergej. "The point is protecting your lives and those of your family. We'll be threatened from all sides. For one, by foreigners who will soon be on the way to our island. A hundred million Africans are expected, as is emerging from secret documents. But that's just the tip of the iceberg. Next will be two hundred million Bangladeshi refugees, all arranged by China." The team nods. No fucking clue where Bangladesh is. "Secret government files refer to a billion refugees who will come to Europe and Great Britain. This is an existential threat to our environment and Lebensraum. The technical scenarios don't look any better. Pandemics are to be expected, nuclear accidents, and the most acute threat is EMP bombs. Which knock out the electricity. Just imagine. You're sitting at home. Sirens. No water, no electricity. You're in the dark. Do you have supplies on hand? No. Medicines? No. Oxygen? It won't be long before shops are looted, your women raped, and then people will eat each other. How are you prepared in the barely insulated little cell you call your flat, which is linked to a nuclear power plant? It doesn't even have to be an atomic megadisaster. Have you ever thought about what it's like to live just two weeks without electricity? Toilet flushing, water, lighting, heat, mobile phones, internet—everything out. Long-haul transport, and with it no deliveries of goods; without pumps gasoline can't be used or transported. Refrigeration will be interrupted and anything perishable will go bad. That'll stink. How will you survive when the pharmacies are empty and the hospitals overwhelmed? I'll tell you. You won't survive. Because you're weak. So—I'll pass out a list at the end of training with everything you need to have on hand. Gold, silver, salt, honey, medicines, alcohol, tobacco, coffee, et cetera. Everything that's valued during and immediately after wars." The attendees are having the shit scared out of them.

"Today is about killing,"

Says Sergej.

The attendees blink. Killing, mate, that's a bit over the top. They had pictured crawling through some mud. A couple of homoerotic defense training exercises. But killing straightaway? Nobody here wants to kill. Actually.

They're just poor men. Not the brightest. Who only wanted to do a few manly things without getting any karma points deducted. So, killing then.

Sergej doesn't look like somebody who jokes around. He has the shaved head thing going on, lots of muscles. WTF, thinks Hannah. The guy must weigh 150 kilos. "Yes, if necessary, we have to kill," says Sergej. "Hide, fight, run. These are the keywords to survival in times of chaos. Today then, lesson two: combat. We'll start with a hundred push-ups to warm up. Go." Sergej shouts. Men react extremely well to the shouts of other men. They're quickly down in the mud doing push-ups, the first submissively expressed hatred for Sergej recognizable on their faces. Hannah does her hundred push-ups without breathing heavily for so much as a second. The grace of youth, a gift of their slender bodies. "Up you get," yells Sergej.

"You all have knives with you. And weapons." The men grunt, nod, proudly display their weapons. Their weapons are smaller than Sergej's weapon. Sergej is bigger, he's better-looking.

The men hate him.

And he shouts loudly. "Right. In an emergency we may have to kill our neighbors. Our greengrocer, our friend. We can't trust anyone. I'll pass out slips of paper." He passes out slips of paper. "And pens." He passes out pens. "I'm going to go have a piss, and when I get back you're to have written down the name of the person we'll be killing today."

"Who exactly?" asks a fat man, the back of whose head seems to have been lost while doing push-ups.

"Someone from the group." Says Sergej, heading into the brush.

The men freeze.

Nobody wants to die.

"I don't want to die,"

Says the fat man with no back of the head, and Hannah says.

"Be quiet"

Whispers

THOME

Kneeling on his so-called stepmother. The stepmother sits in an armchair, Thome's hands are wrapped tightly around her throat. He stands with one leg on the floor, the other is ramming her belly. His knee feels the hard belly where his sibling is hopefully already rotting. Thome almost thinks he can feel the warmth and the frail baby bones. The armchair creaks. Thome winces. The chair is from his grandparents. Who brought it from Scotland, from the stud farm and so forth. Did he really just think frail bones? Does he have feelings? He has feelings. But not for this Russian, who is slowly getting red. How can you desire a woman when you previously lived with a mother who anticipated everything that can become of women? Sometimes the sentences that accompanied his childhood echo so loudly in his head that he has to slam it against a wall to get any semblance of peace. Members of our family do not cry. Suppressing coughs is a question of willpower. Were two of the hundred sentences that had thrown fuel on the fire of his deformation. It had almost been more pleasant to have been fucked with bars of soap at boarding school than to have been in this home with his poor, dead mother. The way she drank her tea, a handkerchief pressed to the corner of her mouth, quickly, frantically, as if it were improper for people like her to have bodily orifices at all. Thome knows all about that. He'd seen pornos, after all. Why is he thinking of his mother right now? Why is the Russian staring so? She's not moving anymore. Her tongue hangs from her mouth, and Thome shoves his knee deeper into her belly. He can feel how his sibling squirms and then stops. Squirming. And Thome cries.

"It's done"

Says

HANNAH

But the men are no longer listening. For Sergej, the moment has arrived when a normal life becomes a nightmare. Utterly unexpected. "Get the Jew pig," says one of the members of the group, completely out of context, out of all context, but whatever, throwing out a Jew pig always works, they see red, men, as the Jew pig represents in intellectual terms what the Black man represents to them physically: a challenge to their mediocrity.

The men have set upon Sergej, screaming. They flail at him with their fists, with their boots they stomp on his cheekbones, his nose, with their knives they stab him, with tree limbs they beat him, they try to cut off his legs, his penis is tossed into the bushes, someone stuffs his entrails into his mouth. Time for Hannah to get out of there.

And cross a name off the list.

Check.

THE PROGRAMMER

Nods. "Everything's working."

Until just now he'd been at the breeding station. That has another name. Center for Genetic-Molecular something or other. He finds that sort of thing interesting. You're already familiar with Dolly the sheep, the animal chastised by the press years ago in order to divert attention from the real developments in the field of human research. In the meantime it has become possible to reproduce entire humans. And to perfect their DNA. So, let's see, the first functional clones are already five years old. There's baby Bill Gates. Margaret Thatcher, Cara Delevingne, and Adele. But thin Adele. We don't see any coloration darker than pink. We see five-year-old Mark Zuckerbergs with reduced noses leaning over, programming AI.

All of these creatures will likely enjoy a life expectancy of over a hundred years, inherited diseases are not included, all organs run at max capacity. Perfect little baby teeth, an extraordinary vocabulary. The programmer is in an extremely bad mood. The generation growing up now will eat people like him alive. People like him, whose teeth are still riddled with cavities, whose hair is thinning and who are subject to moods. The new people will be as perfect as is possible for an organism with an expiration date to be. They'll be handsome and smart, perfect and pain free.

But that's

Absurd

Thinks

THE CLONE KID

Who has just inquisitively driven a nail through his hand, inspired by a portrayal of Jesus online. So what's the problem?, thinks the clone kid, and pulls the nail back out of his hand. The kid examines the wound, tastes the blood, looks up the composition of blood on the internet. Is satisfied. Has once again understood something. The clone kid doesn't get tired. Been awake for ten hours now at this point, in order to address the field of artificial intelligence in relation to consumer choice. Customers today don't buy products but experiences. "Experience makers" play a huge role, virtual assistants are the keyword, they can plan experience routes for road users, and can, based on their consumer preferences, supply cost-free messages alerting the consumers to good deals, though it is important to offer the consumer the suitable content at the right time, right place, and in real time. The Experience Cloud is a platform that makes all data—that is, consumer data—centrally accessible and available. The data from old systems, from social media, is coupled with the new biometric data, promising great precision with regard to biorhythms. When exactly is the consumer hungry, excited, when does the person feel a pronounced loneliness so that the promise of shopping can be dangled with a promise of alleviating it? Evaluating the data is extremely easy with AI; you can analyze consumers' transactions and use them to make predictions.

The clone kid freezes. One of his fellow children points to a newly perfected level of deepfake that the child has just developed. Clone kid one hugs clone kid two. Despite all the passion for competition inherent in them, it's certainly still possible to recognize the achievements of others. "I'd love to see it," says clone kid one before experiencing a brief blackout; that happens sometimes. Due to the not quite 100 percent perfect state of perfection of his cloned existence. He stares out the window projected on the wall, and feels a profound emptiness inside. Whenever he has this feeling of profound emptiness, the sweeping sensation of not being real, he imagines going on a shooting spree. With new weapons every time, eviscerating people, entrails, blood which he drinks, hearts which he eats. Imagining this scenario he's able to get back to his surface consciousness.

"Lovely,"

Mumbles

THE PROGRAMMER

Every time he enters his flat after a completed day of work. The flat which, of course, he doesn't unlock with a chip. He's not a fool, after all, and won't get one implanted. So, hello, flat. "Hello, programmer," his flat would say if it were networked and smart, which, of course, it isn't, since the programmer isn't a fool. The flat resembles any other flat. Of all the IT engineers, sound designers, cloud architects, transport-planning AI administrators, television personalities, actors, systems biologists, smart-city engineers, and the like. It's on one of the blocks of a gentrified neighborhood, let's say Hackney, where a real hubbub of urban life is taking place these days. With pubs and all that. People form their surroundings, the surroundings form people. For the most part an endless cycle of gray. Buildings often demonstrate a cliché-reinforcing reality. Naturally, the blocks are somehow environmentally friendly, but not too much, not to the extent of building hanging gardens or anything. You just insulate square crates. Then install airtight windows into the boxes—not too big, in order to save energy. And, of course, recessed balconies, referred to as whispering galleries, where one can live out one's propensity for hatred of all life forms other than one's own without seeing one's neighbors. Inside, standard implementation of incompetence in the realm of taste: open kitchen, expression of the technocratic rationalizing away of space. Who would want the smell of onions and cabbage fumes in the parlor, the space that used to be reserved for reading books, sitting in front of the fire, and listening to mellow music? All the wooden floors finished too brightly, two little closets. Showers with glass partitions so you can look at your partner naked. (What partner?) Then comes the furniture, stuff that looks as if it were chosen by a child playing designer. Some crap or other that nobody finds comfortable. There has to be a sofa; flats are drawn up around kitchens and couches. Sofas, complete helplessness in furniture form. The new, universally efficient human deposit boxes are an expression of unkindness bordering on contempt. In these crates, people sit and congratulate themselves on having made it. They're pleased about their middle-class existence with a middle-class motorcar. Self-driving, obviously.

The programmer heats up a premade meal, eats alone sitting at the table with a view out at other blocks of flats where other individuals are also sitting alone at oversize tables. A drone flies past the window.

It's a good life

At home

Where the others can no longer sit around the fire.

Because the lawn, which isn't a lawn but rather mud flats, is under water. Though it's not raining, it's just the storms have become more extreme. They come at night, the storms, they blow roofs off, and they'd blow cows around if there were any cows around. "What's with the men in the tents? What are they doing now, ten centimeters deep in water?"

DON

Asks

Hannah. Who has just arrived home. Don brushes a piece of human flesh from her collar. "No idea." Says Hannah. She barely seems to notice Don and

looks around the hall. "Is Peter back yet?" She asks. For Don, it's as if her entire blood supply flows out of her body and into her heart, to drown the heart,

When she realizes that there will never be anything between her and Hannah. Jesus, all the things she had talked herself into believing in the past few
weeks. That it was due to Hannah's timidity and would just take a bit more
time, or that the two of them just didn't dare though soon it would come to
pass that they'd accidentally brush hands and then they'd wrap their arms
around each other and kiss and fall onto the mattress and . . .

Peter shows up and goes directly into the kitchen where Hannah is and
looks into a pot, standing too close to her. What is there to see in a pot of spaghetti that is so wonderful? Other than Peter's head, which for a moment Don
thinks she'd really love to see floating in the boiling water. Don's heart beats too
loudly. She stares into the kitchen as if watching a traffic accident. Now they'll
pry the bodies out of the wreckage—

Violins, golden light,

Hannah stands behind Peter. Hannah laughs and throws back her head
like a goddamn horse. Both of them are ridiculously attractive. In the style of
heteronormative adverts.

Peter turns to Hannah. He lifts a hand, brushes an imaginary hair aside
from her face.

From somewhere in the half-darkness of the flickering table lamp,

KAREN

Emerges. She sits down next to Don. "You have to imagine it as if you've
taken drugs. Or that somebody put something in your drink. The worst drugs
you can possibly think of. That cause hallucinations, things like the table lamp
having sharp teeth, or Hannah having the face of a proboscis monkey, or you
believing you can't live without another person anymore. That everything that
came before this person and will come afterwards will be as if the earth were a
burned-out wasteland. No animals, no sun, just ice, cold, and steel-reinforced
concrete ruins. The drugs allow you to believe this person is like the parents
you never had, the parents this person never had, that you will keep each other
warm like kittens. For your whole life.

And that you will never be lonely again or be scared or not be able to sleep
or be bored or unhappy. But it's all bullshit, obviously. Drugs are hell. Nothing you believe is real. It's the drugs, you understand?" Karen puts her white,

absurdly long arm around Don, who still hasn't grown, who still looks like a relatively heavily pigmented, square boxer.

"It's not real." Says Karen. "You have to fight the effect of the drugs. Suppress every thought that tries to put you on a park bench with that person or hugging. Choke it off. And swap it out for a real thought."

"Like what?" asks Don.

"The reality is," answers Karen, "that the person isn't with you, doesn't look at you rapturously, isn't trying to get near you, doesn't want to rub up against you."

"But the person can't just love one of the others. That's insane." Says Don, still staring into the kitchen, where the two models stand, devouring each other with their eyes.

"When two people are both on drugs at the same time, they look like mental cases, they fidget around with each other, they don't know what to talk about. In your case one of the two parties is totally relaxed in your presence. People on drugs are not relaxed. They sweat, they're nervous, insecure, stuttering."

"How long does it last? When does it stop?" Karen looks at Don to try to estimate the seriousness of her condition. She's known for weeks that Don has fallen in love with Hannah and that this infatuation won't go anywhere because Hannah and Peter are in love with each other. She's worried about the cohesiveness of the group, she's worried that this family they've put together by choice will be destroyed by the stupid hormones of youth, she's worried about herself, she who hasn't fallen in love with anyone and never will, she's worried about the rootlessness that threatens them.

"If you don't see the person," she says, "it'll get better in two weeks. If you have to see the person daily it'll take at least a month. If your person is infatuated with somebody else"—quick glance toward the kitchen, that is, toward the stove and table standing at the other end of the hall—"then it's very painful. Should only last three weeks, though."

"Three weeks. Can I count on that?" Asks Don.

"Yes," Karen answers, "and now have a bit of a cry. I can't help you any further." Karen runs her hand over Don's frizzy hair. And is almost inclined to press herself to her, but that would be too much.

Nobody presses against anyone else here. Not

DON

Who watches the car wreck as the two idiots beam at each other in golden light, then comes a rom-com scene. Violins. A loop. Hannah puts her hand on Peter's arm, and he lays his head on the curve of her neck, and then their hands interlock and the violins become a full-on symphony and Don stares at this car wreck and freezes, without thinking, and then she leaves, closing the door quietly.

And squats in the mud in front of the building, wraps her arms around her knees and wants to die. It's her first ever bout of lovesickness. And it's not raining, and there's no picturesque landscape in the picture.

Don knows the type of landscape from old movies with actors who are already dead. Green riverbanks where townspeople stroll with picnic baskets. Green riverbanks. They don't exist anywhere except on TV, there are only landscapes and buildings that seem to be transitioning to dust or water. Every inch of land seems to have been used and discarded. Don stands up and looks inside through the window. Perhaps a miracle has occurred. Perhaps Hannah has realized she can't stand Peter, perhaps—Don stands on her tiptoes and looks in. Still the same golden light, now lighting up the mattress, where Peter and Hannah are lying, entwined, motionless. Probably dead.

Go fuck yourselves, fuck all of you.

And Don

Starts to cry. Though without tears. It's the first time. In case we haven't already discussed it, this everything-for-the-first-time period in life. The first time being so excited about someone that you could spend an entire day just looking at the person, the first time you want to die because of un-happiness. The first time in a strange city, being amazed by everything, the buildings, the smells. The first time swimming naked, with other people, at an outdoor pool, at night. The first time cooking in your own kitchen, the first time having sex and the first time staying out all night. Doing all of this for the first time seems to take forever. The first time living. Forever, and later, only later does one begin to repeat everything, and cease to be attentive, and the wonder of it all fades, and people get dull, and time races. That's it, the thing said by old people: "The time, where did all the time go?" This is the time, you just don't see it anymore. You tire of your perceptions, you take everything for granted. Your healthy bodies, your love, children, food, rain. Everything's taken care of for you, eh?

Don listens to music. Her MP3 player, she didn't bury that, it's still full of old music from back then, when her music was still angry, the old days, when she wasn't yet a fucking hermaphrodite. Not yet grown, no longer a child. When Stormzy was still around and everyone hoped to become as famous as him. And then to find god, out of overwhelming gratitude. Just like always, when Don listens to grime. She immediately feels strong. And bulletproof. And now she's arrived at the tents. This is England. Welcome to what was formerly one of the richest countries on earth. This is Europe, you know the story, creation's crowning glory. The continent that sat down draped in beautiful fabrics at a table and consumed the rest of the planet.

Right, and now you can see the rubbish. What humans accomplish in a hundred years. Nice one.

Wastelands and tents, in front of which men sit looking like leftover food scraps. It is said that every IQ point beneath the average costs the economy 20,000 dollars. Per month. These people here don't cost anything. They bum around with their mouths open, waiting. For grass to grow over them. Thanks to the floodwaters, they have their feet up on wooden crates. A fire won't burn in this muck. When did it get so wet? Perhaps during the hurricane over Ireland? For the first time in all these months, the streambed is carrying water from the far reaches of the city and, nearby, past a silent, black panel van, out of which various men emerge. Don recognizes the uniforms as private police. Without a sound, they round up the human refuse and take them to the van without resistance. The so-called police look around, they spot Don. Before she realizes what is happening, she finds herself in the transporter next to the Romanians or Bulgarians and a sad old man.

What a fucked-up day.

For

PATUK

But if you squint a little, it gets better. Patuk doesn't know where he is. Ah, right, I live here, he thinks, seeing sad bottoms in sad trousers scurrying through the streets. Where are they scurrying? What is it that makes them scurry, these people; they all have so much to do and scurry about, making piddling illegal deals, moving goods and drugs to and fro and ingesting the stuff as fast as they can. They get addicted to things that let them forget they are alive, until they are finally allowed to really die, and then that, too, is no good. They whine and raise their bony fists at god and pray to fairy tale characters. Who always resemble people in the Luton pedestrian zone. The otherwise aggressive tone, generated by young men with too little brains and too many hormones, has yielded to an atmosphere of complete drabness. Packs of young men sit around apathetically in front of decrepit bank buildings, staring at their devices. Russia had bombed Syria liberally a few years back and thereby multiplied the number of young male refugees by a factor of five. Which had been helpful. In the meantime there's no democratic state left. Which isn't even a dramatic development, since democracy was an exception in human history anyway. Patuk stops in front of them unsteadily, trying to establish a connection between his brain and the image on his retina. After the—let's just say—forfeiture of his business there is nothing more that can keep Patuk from complete loss of control over his life. He's become hazy. In every way. And has found out that he can better tolerate himself when he heavily abuses the tablets that are available at the pharmacy and which provide a mood that remains on the plus side of the ledger. Well, as much as that is possible when you're taking too much diazepam. Which, of course, can happen if you're addicted to the stuff, which Patuk has been taking daily for two years at this point. He moves as if in a dream, and he gets into states that have to do with fear and hatred. The faces of the people in his neighborhood often look to him like the faces of animals. Lizards and ferrets, rodents and pigs. He sits in the pedestrian zone a lot. Or in his room. He eats things from cans. He is debilitated by total helplessness when it comes to his life.

It is nearly morning

When

THOME

Sits on the windowsill, thinking. Well. "Thinking."

It is the moment before the night ends. If it were spring and it weren't too cold for any season, the birds would start to sing now. Thome imagines the birds; he's of the age of those who experienced them, these springtime birds, that make everything seem so sad, the morning, life. His father spent the previous night planning his administration. There were twenty old men present. The house smells of them. Thome looks forward to the moment when they will die. It'll be a surprise for the old bastards. Oh boo, now that we've socked away billions, now that the range of our possibilities includes power, the power to influence a few million human lives, for the worse of course, now we're supposed to get lost?

The men climb into the helicopter standing by in front of the house and fly to Scotland. Ciao. At exactly this moment there are no doubt a million influential men around the world trying via disparate means to secure world domination. Nearly the entire world seems relieved to subjugate themselves to old dictators. Men are finally back in power—strong, substantial men. And just between us: What's the difference? So-called democracy was just a shell company for the super-rich. That's what people said and well, come on now, they're right. And now everything is like it used to be, don't you see? Really not so bad. Wars are being planned, resources depleted and traded, intrigues plotted, government overthrows planned, epidemics concealed, medicines not approved because they're not sufficiently profitable, legs amputated because saving them wouldn't be sufficiently profitable, weapons dealt, foul-ups covered up; in the Vatican they're preparing for the end of the world so some guy can let himself be celebrated as Jesus afterwards; in South America new guerilla armies are being assembled; in China—okay

MA WEI

The old men, thinks

THOME

Everywhere they sit around and plan and toast each other and think it will change something in their own existence. They'll get younger, more handsome, happier. They think power and the euphoria that comes with it will be a permanent condition rather than a short-term boost of hormones. There's no goddamn global conspiracy. No Bilderberg–titled aristocrats–Rothschild–Goldman Sachs–Vatican axis of evil, just old men clinging to life with their yellowed fingers. There's just a league of men who, thanks to their muscle mass, which is superior to that of women, have for millennia declared themselves the top of the food chain, and who try to erase through murderous terrorist attacks any life form that doesn't resemble them. Well, or actually—erase. It's just a shame that there are always non-male life forms left over. But unfortunately nobody from the old systems will survive, no landed gentry, no

members of filthy rich aristocratic families, not the Vatican, and not the old
billionaires. People like Thome will take over leadership of the world. The
new people. Thome is experiencing feelings in a bothersome way. Every inch
of his towering intellect seems to be occupied with Peter. Thome's hands tremble with the feeling. And it is noticeable at work. His work, or as he jokingly
says, his calling, when on the one hand he is constantly thinking of a boy and
on the other hand doesn't understand, for fuck's sake, what in the hell is being developed in the ever-new coding languages, goddamn nerds. It feels like
something groundbreaking arises nearly every hour. Something revolutionary.
Unprecedented. But as far as any and all human needs, developers bypass
them. The citizens—yes, we'll call them citizens, the idiots—don't care one
wit about what form of voice-activated, totally networked bullshit has them
waiting in traffic. They don't care whether their toilets can think and their
bathtubs render skin analyses that are transmitted to their clothes. At some
point it has to stop. Nobody out there is going along. But when programmers
are let loose they won't ever stop until all human life has been expunged. That
which cannot survive the market has no right to exist. Developers work on
perfecting sex robots despite the fact that at least in London no men seem to
be interested in sex anymore. They build brain add-ons, hyperloop transport
tubes, rockets that can return to earth; they perfect data input via thoughts.
"Disruption" seems to be tattooed on every developer's forehead. A market in
its present form will be obliterated only to be artlessly re-created in a form
that yields more profit. Speaking of obliterating—Thome goes into the cellar
where his stepmother is immersed in a vat of acid. He opens the lid and sees
teeth floating on the surface of the brew. Guess it'll take a bit longer. Thome
drops to the floor. If only he had at least been abused as a child. He wraps
his arms around the vat where his stepmother is decomposing. "Mother," he
whispers. "Mother."

WTF

Thinks

DON

"Do you speak English?" asks a woman who looks like an old office coffee
machine. Don considers the matter but doesn't know what the question is
supposed to mean. Whether she can speak, in general? Don is so lethargic and
numb, lovesickness, you know how it is, that she doesn't care at all where she

is. Like anyone in love, she keeps working herself up with thoughts that make the pain unbearable, perhaps because other than drugs only unrequited love causes such a death wish–inducing cocktail of hormones.

"So do you understand me?" asks the woman. She seems to have some sort of head injury, and Don, turning to her in a friendly manner, nods, accustomed as she is to dealing with the mentally deficient. Don's coffee machine person

Has shockingly thin hair.

The

WOMAN WITH THE THINNING HAIR

MENTAL STATE: *latent passive-aggressiveness. A woman, after all*
HEALTH: *circular hair loss, flatulence*
HOBBIES: *no exercise, no friends*
USABILITY: *none at all*

Possesses a résumé whose particulars closely resemble those of many of her acquaintances. During the 1990s she studied literature, earned a doctorate, published articles, met her husband, the type you see and think: does such a nondescript person, someone with thinning hair and small eyes, have someone who finds him adorable?

Then moved to London. Small flat in Whitechapel. Love. Happiness. Hope. Ikea furniture. Playing at adulthood. Earnest faces at the dinner table. Pass me the pickles, please. Job at a university as assistant professor. Hurray. Husband also does something or other. Let's say journalist. Journalism always works. Poorly paid, well-intentioned. They see each other in the evening. Talk about the future. The future always looks rosier.

At first taking the tube every day, among the masses, they freeze, but, of course, they love. Or rather, fuck. At some point getting tired out.

Because—

Nothing, nothing changes; no garden, no dog, at some point no more fucking. Silence at dinner, the husband is let go, the newspaper goes online, he is paid by the line. He is

Humiliated. And depressed. He gets neurostimulation and is flaccid as a result. Not just sexually. After ten years, still in the same flat in Whitechapel with four rent increases over the course of that time. And no child. Children aren't possible. Too expensive. Alongside getting paid by the line, the husband delivers food. The couple economizes. Tech gadgets are bought on Black Friday. Hurray, Black Friday. Buy stuff. Hunt, consider yourself to have an edge, finally to have won at something.

The woman with the thinning hair can't get ahead. Three times she's been passed over for promotions. Those promoted are always younger, confident men, chosen by the university director based on how he wishes he were. The woman with the thinning hair didn't get any research grants, either, the men got those, too, but hey, the best man wins. Then come the salary reductions. And the woman with the thinning hair looks for side hustles. Nearly everyone who works as a driver, cleaner, or food preparer these days actually used to be an engineer or doctor. Was. Done. After getting sacked. The woman with the thinning hair found a job as a security guard in an isotope lab. And as an organ donor advisor. And as a dead animal remediator. Every day thousands of stray animals are rounded up in the city and taken to a remediation facility. Because, as mentioned, large parts of the city center are owned by the Chinese and the Chinese are disgusted by any dogs that aren't poodles and bathed daily, this measure is a service for wealthy residents. The duty of the woman with the thinning hair is to ignite the incinerator after properly filling the oven and then monitor via fire-rated tempered glass the progress of the burn operation. Animals, which like humans are on the earth just to waste away their stupid lives, have been made into useful objects. For amusement or to be eaten. Anything that doesn't fit is exterminated. People puzzle over whether or not animals have feelings. People who have no feelings beyond those that serve their own gratification think about such things and do experiments with mice. That they tickle. And watch in amazement when the mice laugh. So much for people. And mice.

In the first few weeks the woman with the thinning hair had nightmares where faces of the animals appeared and looked very similar to people in fatal distress. They looked like the faces of people who voluntarily donate organs and body parts, even things they could definitely still use—like legs. Who likes to walk around on one leg. But.

If she wouldn't do it, someone else would have. When she sees the burned-out people sitting across from her to register, she wonders if it wouldn't be more merciful to shove them into the oven like the stray animals.

WTF,

DON

Looks blankly at the woman with the thinning hair. How old is something like that? Fifty? Eighty?

". . . we can offer generous financial concessions if we are able to reach an agreement here." Says the woman with the thinning hair.

"For a kidney donation, which can save the life of an innocent person, we pay five hundred pounds, a retina earns you two hundred pounds, bone marrow one hundred pounds, a spleen—"

"Hang on," Don interrupts. "I only have one spleen."

"Exactly." Says the woman. "A highly overrated organ, the spleen. Seven hundred pounds. But of course you can earn dramatically more money with the donation of limbs . . ." Don sees disheveled men at nearby desks signing forms. Hurray, they'll be able to afford a ticket to their underdeveloped homeland. Home, just get home, even if you have to hop off the plane on one leg. They let themselves be weighed and measured. Blood pressure, IQ. What's the IQ for? Doesn't matter. "Can I go out and have a smoke?" asks Don. "I'm a bit unsure about the limbs, I mean, I still need a hand to hold the cigarettes, after all."

"Um, yes," says the woman with the thinning hair, "you'll need to abstain from nicotine and alcohol prior to the procedure."

"Pills I can keep taking, yeah?" asks Don. "Downers and whatnot?"

"Of course," says the woman. "Everybody takes pills."

"Okay, I'm going think it over while I have a smoke," says Don, leaving the room. There are about forty doors off the corridor. Don opens one cautiously. Everywhere the same. Homeless, vagrants, youths sitting at desks giving information about their superb organs. In front of the entrance another panel van pulls up. The night is mild. A warm rain falls. Don leans against the wall of a building, looks into the sky, the moon is not visible. She's young. She'll die of lovesickness. It is the best time ever.

EX 2279

Repeats the sentence and tries to make sense of it. It makes no sense. One can't speak of a better or worse time without having studied the numbers. EX 2279 studies numbers. Check, correct, for most people the time is better than a hundred years ago, insofar as more people are doing well. Education, mortality rates, etc. Of course, as far as nature and the environment. Well, doesn't matter. EX 2279 carries on with the rescue of the planet.

Switches off the fracking equipment.

The cryptocurrencies and their consumption of terawatt hours and so forth. Clean up—

```
+ + + + + + + + + + [ > + > + + + > + + + + + + + + > + + + + + + + + +
< < < ← ] > > > > + + + + + + + + + + + + + + + + + + + + + . — — — — — — — — . < + + + + +
+ + . > — — . + + + + + + + + + + . — — — — . < + + + + + + + . > + + + . —
- . < + + + . > + + + + + + + + + + + + . + + + . — — . — — — — . ← — — — — — — — . > + + + +
+ + + + + + + + + + . — — — — — — . — — . + + + + + + + + + + + + + + + + + + + + + . ← — — —
. > — — — — — — . — — . + + + + + + + + . + + + + + .
```

THE FRIENDS

Stare at their computers. MI6 is out. MI5 gone from the net. The baby hackers sit at their computers; they're not doing anything, they just watch the AI at work. Watching doesn't make them euphoric. They've lost hope. It's dark in the room, no fire in the stove, no pizza in the kitchen. It is uncomfortable for the no-longer-children to look at each other. The failure of their action is just the last of many attempts to save the world in that young-people-changing-the-world way. Earlier they had demonstrated. Before that was banned. Before they started firing live ammunition at demonstrators. They had warned people again and again, online. About burka bans, which were only devised to hinder masking that can impede the work of biometrical recognition services. About the shutdown of child porn websites, which just served as cover for all sorts of other shutdowns. About electronic ankle bracelets for people deemed potential threats, about electronic voting, about the espionage units of private industry, which could surveil customers under suspicion into the farthest corners of their flats—all the laws that had in recent years been passed, the buildup of the private army into a paramilitary force owned by capitalists, surveillance, basic income, everything led to one goal, which had now nearly been reached. A paralyzed, happy, brainless populace. Everything the youths had believed, that is, changing the world, forming it in their image, humanism, justice, privacy, and all of that, has yielded to the certainty that they—cannot change a thing.

The hackers sit at their computers. They goof around. They talk to each other. They take pills. They take fucking pills, because their bodies no longer produce endorphins, their bodies have become fatigued and flighty. They have nearly deciphered EX 2279's language code.

"Splendid,"

Says

THOME'S FATHER

To his friends.

Having just climbed out of the helicopter, they start knocking back drinks again. Falkland Palace. A charming estate that found its way into the possession of Thome's father and his comrades some time ago. Crisis loves a quick investment. What crisis? Doesn't matter. Before or after. They sit here in the largely unheated ruins. Tradition calls for blue-frozen ankles. Thome's father hasn't heard anything from his alluring, pregnant wife for two days, it occurs to him apropos of nothing. For a while now he hasn't been able to get an erection, even with the use of pills. Without the theoretical need to discharge himself inside the Russian, Thome's father cannot think of what could possibly warrant a relationship with her.

"So, cheers, gentlemen." Thome's father is here with the most closely trusted members of his staff; the collective age in the room is 777 years, and the liquid assets exceed a few hundred thousand billion. Thome's father looks into the pale faces with red noses and spider veins. None of those present admits why he is willing to submit to the stress of high office again at such a wizened age. Thome's father knows, though. He smirks with his knowledge. He has used the word *smirk* ironically so often that at this point he can no longer expunge it from his vocabulary. What drives the urge for power during the final stretch is rage. At the fact that your bones ache and that it has all been so little fun. Which is crazy. It has generated so little true happiness. But not that being-rich-doesn't-make-you-happy unhappiness; rather the feeling of always coming up short. Always someone who's richer, who's a closer relative of the former royal family, more important. Furthermore everyone here is united in despair at how they will go down in history. Because they know better. They know what the people want, know what is good for England, the country they're fond of because they breathe it in. The goal of all the years of preparation and the huge financial outlays is within reach. Reform of the government, direct voting. And now: the crowning achievement. Abolishing the remnants of democracy. That's why they're here. To celebrate the electoral victory. Today. Thome's father coughs quietly. And as always when he quietly coughs, he lifts his hand to his mouth, and as always when his hand enters his field of vision he sees the hand. Lying in a grave with his body. Above which is nothingness, dark night that never ends

"It just won't go away,"

Says

HANNAH

Though it's not even raining, it is only. Damp.

Hannah has put her head on Peter's shoulder. The weather doesn't matter. The location is of no consequence, she is in that perfect state that humans crave their entire lives, that they try to create with drugs, money, and self-mutilation and rarely find. If Hannah knew she could expect to experience this state maybe six or seven times during her stay on earth, perhaps she would never move again and never sleep again just to savor it. But she doesn't know. Hannah sits next to Peter on the stairs in front of the hall, from which the news quietly echoes. I'll never want anything else, thinks Hannah in complete ignorance of the workings of hormones. Peter doesn't think any such thing; he's a man, he's peculiar, he's excited and happy. He could stay sitting like this forever. Sensing the warmth of Hannah's body on his. How soft she feels, even while looking so bony and angular. How soft he feels, thinks Hannah, wishing to sit in Peter's body; there must be a warm spot in there, and he could carry her through the dampness.

Right. And so on. In love.

The TV is on. The results of the election are running in an endless loop.

The Online Party has won with 80 percent of the votes. An avatar will be the new prime minister. The populace has given their heart to a young, dynamic high performer.

Speaking of which.

Thome's father

Clutches at his heart.

His comrades already seem to be dead. Numbly they sit in the scuffed brocade-upholstered chairs, a crystal glass or two has landed on the floor. The end of the world has surprised everyone. As if a beloved dog had as a result of its own stupidity strayed into a wolf trap. Thome's father stands up. His legs are unstable, his stride awkward, the helicopter stands at the ready. It is supposed to shuttle Thome's father to the victory celebration in London. Now. They still fly over the noble Highlands back to London. Only with defeat—

After touching down, Thome's father walks through Oxford Street, dazed. The riffraff is out and about. The idiots who voted in a bot as prime minister. Stupidity drips like spit from their faces. They follow signals. They follow the desire for stimulating conditions. Shopping. It's proved its worth. It was even easier than faith. That flexible amphibian, capitalism, has adapted very quickly to the new desires of the population. There are few expensive products for the class of winners and tons of cheap junk produced in the loser countries of North Africa, Eastern Europe, Pakistan, Bangladesh, and the Rust Belt states of North America. Places where the cost of labor is still cheaper than machines.

Thome's father stops briefly, dull pain in his temples again.

So, where were we?—Oh, right, some subsets of the population have all but disappeared. Homeless children, for instance.

On television, reports occasionally run about amazing shelters where the children now play ball, study, and wear clean clothing. Only if you look closely do you realize it is always the same happy children. The homeless, too, live happily and well-groomed in shelters in front of which they're filmed playing chess.

Another missing subset of the population is the

BANKER

FORMER HOBBIES: *vintage motorcars, wingtip shoes, neckties, naked dancing women*
FAMILY: *a so-called child*
OCCUPATION: *basic income*
MOOD: *fine*

This one here is in a bad mood.

He's no longer a banker, as he was let go. Fairly recently. When it all started. With the so-called inflation. The constant electricity outages. And the algorithms, is there really anything more to know? If you leave every decision about financial markets to machines, you have to reckon with some minor hiccups. The algorithms in the so-called financial market have the capacity always to invest in rising shares. You have to reckon with minor downsides there. In any event it is in the meantime no longer possible to save the banks, as you'd first have to save the state, which can no longer be saved. And this guy. The banker, no longer understands how he is to make something of the incoherent stream of his fragmented, botched ideas.

So—

He'd been let go together with eighteen thousand others in the preceding weeks. He'd been a good investment banker. Known for his fearlessness. He had begun at the time when it was already clear that the system of global financial markets had failed. That global financial markets meant nothing more than dispersing the risks of the US financial market. At a time when one already knew the shit wasn't going to work out and that the central banks were lowering interest rates to below zero in order to hinder a second 2008. That's what was said, a 2008, and every banker cringed and pictured himself jumping out the window of an office tower.

The banker had kept at it, subject to Ritalin and dimethyltryptamine, that let him fly, and speed, that made him courageous. The pharma firm that manufactured methylphenidate produced 2.5 million doses daily, with the effect that its users lost their creativity and became depressed, but to combat that there is: speed.

And then, a few weeks ago, the banker's physique had begun to change. Together with throbbing headaches. He became cautious. His audacity disappeared. Had dissipated. He'd become fearful and his transactions had been questioned. He'd had an existential crisis, because all of a sudden he was no longer sure what he was doing. Adding more imaginary zeros to zeros. Forcing countries into default. And how did it all fit together, and what did the algorithms do, anyway?

The banker has gotten soft of late. Occasionally he stands there shocked, looking at what he has produced. What—utterly unnoticed by him—has grown.

It is

THE CHILD

INTELLIGENCE: *unmeasurable*
HOBBIES: *hospitalism*
Otherwise just a, go ahead, say it,
Child

It has limbs that seem to move independently of each other. So, wow. A child, a little person, a replica made from his DNA.

Thinks the

BANKER

Cool. His wife. Yeah, well, that's another story. His wife must work, otherwise it wouldn't be possible to pay for the child to have its own room in High Holborn. The child needs its own room. It has its own room, the child, crazy, an entire room, when 80 percent of the people in the city have just eight square meters to themselves, this child writhes around in a tidy fourteen square meters. It needs a room. That can be locked when the parents go to work. When they both still worked. A device handled supervision. The device filmed the child through its eyes, recording every movement. The absence of the parents, that is, the mother, worked marvelously for a couple hours. In the child's room are dispensers with fluids and food. The child, the banker has forgotten its name, had developed a strong relationship with the device. In the evenings it didn't want to hear its parents hold forth, it wanted to be told stories by the device. Bedtime stories.

"Anyone can make it to the top. That is the blessing of our economic system."

"What is 'blessing'?" asks the child.

"Blessing," says the device, "comes from God. He protects good people, does Lord God. Everything will come to the industrious. If you study hard, respect money, eat healthily, and exercise, if you don't loaf and take a nap in your scarce free time, then you will achieve all that you want in life."

"Like toys and sweets?" asks the child.

"Correct," says the Robi.

Right, yeah, and so on and so forth,

THE PROGRAMMER

We know him, he has his own ideas, which now reverberate in millions of children's rooms like an elegy for neoliberal thought. What he's trying to do at the moment is memory hacking. You repeat false stories for so long and in such detail that everyone believes them. Millions of children grow up with Ritalin and the lore of a technocratic programmer in their synapses. They will be complete idiots who will be useful in their composure and unambitiousness, who will believe in capitalism and follow with empty stares commands from machines. While the new generation of humans is assembled from better construction kits.

And

THOME'S FATHER

Has made it home in the meantime. He trudges up the steps. This is what's left in the darkest hour, an empty, drafty house that isn't comfortable but is worth 70 million, a cold house, where he sits, the last battle lost, no fire burning in the hearth. Without a goal, Thome's father feels like that which he is: a person in the last throes of his life who has never managed to convince another of himself in such a way that the other would want to keep him.

It was an honest day

On which

KAREN

Is heading home. And no longer cares about it. She isn't looking forward to the factory hall, to the area on the outskirts of town, to the noodles, the children, the boredom. She has studied. Nearly. She studied without it bringing her a single step forward. Her life hasn't changed, her path forward is still the same. Hey, High Holborn, always worth a stroll, lovely, the little kiosk selling overpriced coffee and expensive sandwiches to the high-earners of the neighborhood.

The stately homes, behind which a new residential tower is rising. Breaking of the vertical, the architects say, who with the help of algorithms and new materials are thinking up completely new, quasi hanging gardens of new housing. Glass towers with tentacles, with pools, gardens, meeting places, meaning shops and cafés, and all of it for people with incomes over 600,000 per year. It keeps the squalor at bay. It brings to life the impression of living in swinging London, finger on the pulse of progress, part of the brave new world. Which no longer belongs to those of the former middle class, and one can gain access to the park only if the chip, so to speak. Is so disposed. Karen goes home and no longer cares about it. The home.

"It'll be light soon,"

Says

PATUK

And smooths the, well, thin hair of the woman with the thinning hair. When Patuk had gotten ready for this assignment he'd been surprised that—shall we say—nuclear power plants were so easily attacked. The primary and emergency cooling systems are extremely easy to switch off, he'd read in a Tor forum, if you knew a few basics of nuclear science. Or you're a decent engineer. Fine, something different. *Plutonium* was the magic word. The streets are paved with plutonium, so to speak. In doctors' offices, hospitals, and. Right here, in this isotope lab, where they're making some shit or other. And where this unattractive person works as the overnight security guard. They can't even afford an IT-managed fully automatic surveillance system. But plutonium in old cabinets. Like in the developing world. Patuk touches the desperate woman's body parts. He knows his audience. They love to be touched. They're a certain age. That is, an age at which they can imagine the end. When the skin, yeah, well. No longer young, anyway. Nothing more is going to happen for the next thirty years. Poor, mad woman. Patuk caresses her knee. Even if he doesn't have at his disposal the intellectual acuity to cause an atomic reactor to melt down, he's enough on the ball to have found this facility here and picked up the overnight security guard. On the floor is a metal canister with a radioactive warning sign. Patuk assumes it is plutonium. He'd looked up images online beforehand. He has no idea. He's a moron. He doesn't even know that terrorism is something from a completely different era. Inside the metal canister are probably the cylinders with the fissile material. You shouldn't touch it without gloves. Though best not to touch it at all. Patuk has forgotten what he saw online on the subject. Too much information. It's all making Patuk exhausted. That he now has this fucking plutonium, assuming, that is, that there is some in the container, and that he thought it would be easy to build a dirty bomb, some sort of cannon that you can put in the bed of a pickup truck and then off with the thing to—let's say—Oxford Street on a Saturday. Anticipated damage in the billions, the temporary sealing off of square kilometers of the city center, decontamination costs, cancellation costs, depreciation of residential and commercial property. Victims with serious radiological poisoning, considerable psychological effects on parts of the populace, which is to say: radiophobia. But Patuk has no idea how you build a cannon or where he's supposed to get a pickup truck. Patuk grits his teeth with rage at these complications. Every fucking thing is online, and yet he can't find a stupid tutorial on building a bomb. He'll just have to pour the stuff into the ventilation system of a department store. Can you pour the stuff? Surely. Patuk doesn't think any further. He sees death, chaos, and security forces shooting him. He'll go down in history like Mohamed Atta. He tickles the woman with the thinning hair under the chin, takes the canister. "I'm off," he says. And he goes.

Go ahead,

Says

RACHEL

To

The Friends. "We have him." She says. The Friends have taken over one of the control drones that, since a referendum, fulfill the comprehensive duty of care to the populace. Who carry their ID numbers around with them in their chips. To which a database entry is linked. Via chip-reading devices installed in all traffic lights, streetlamps, cameras, train stations, bus stops, and shops—it is mapped where every citizen is at every second. Together with the communications devices, bank cards, Wi-Fi, mobile phones, and the total video surveillance, one has a thorough movement profile of every citizen.

Brilliant. But in the unlikely case that a citizen strays into an area not under surveillance, somewhere in the country, in the hills, if the citizen tries to leave the country, it sets off an alarm, and in seconds the drones take over, also using heat-sensitive cameras. Using the new, auspicious direct democracy, the citizens voted to allow themselves to be subject to total surveillance, because they have nothing to hide—and the drones can save their lives. If they collapse from a stroke somewhere along the Thames, if they are attacked by homeless people or drive their car into a river, if children fall onto train tracks, the drones automatically transmit an emergency signal to a strike force.

The drone's camera sends very good results despite the cloudy weather, despite the gray dawn, despite the poor lighting.

Which is visible to

KAREN

On the screen.

Patuk gets out at the Finchley Road station. He has a case with him. The train is full; same goes for the platform. There hasn't been this type of activity in the country for a long time. People shuttling between the city center and the outskirts in order to carry out the new pointless jobs that have recently become a requirement for receipt of the basic income. The new online administration recognized the value of work to humans and dealt with it quickly. Suddenly workplaces are being created that are anything but virtual. It's necessary to paint parish halls shortly before they're torn down. Karma points must be counted by hand lest the AI make a mistake. Stones are gathered from the street and derelict factories scoured. "He's too stupid to manage a proper attack." Says Karen. Patuk stands on the platform, waits for his connecting train, which will presumably take him to Luton. On the screen you can see him sweating.

Patuk fiddles with the metal case. Puts it on the ground. Removes a vial from a secure cylinder. He shakes out a substance that for the most part lands on his hand and trousers. "That didn't work out," says Karen, inwardly crossing Patuk's name off the list.

"I think," says Rachel, "people are only happy when they're dead. Then they're finally at peace. They don't want anything anymore. Nothing pinches or pulls, and nobody disapproves of them or rejects them. They all want to die." For a few seconds all the youths look toward the windows, only to turn

back, as if choreographed, to their devices. Rachel has secretly sent an application to MI5; they're looking for talented analysts there. Ben has once again
begun to find security vulnerabilities in companies; the others weigh their
options.

The options available to dedicated youths.

"Hello there, and good morning.

We're the

YOUTH.

Who grew up with the knowledge that without conforming, one will not
possibly survive. We're the so-called ADHD generation, which means that we're
multitasking, if by that you mean we take in new information by the second and
then forget it again. Good morning, we're largely apolitical, because we learned
that being political didn't do our parents any good at all. All the protesting,
demonstrating, chaining themselves up to some shit or other, had no effect.
Where are they now, the political people? In shitty little flats with a basic income, you might as well call it charity, that ensures that there are noodles. Our
parents are hideously aged. They're fifty now, they wear hoodies, they marvel
when they see other fifty-year-olds and think: Jesus, they're old. They're users,
they wear fitness trackers. They're in job fields that are no longer needed. We're
the youth. We believe in capitalism, which sounds tired, but that's the way it
is. It's a fact. We want to shop, we want competition, we behave ourselves, and
when the parents jabber about there being no freaks anymore, no subculture,
and that we're neoliberal squares, then we look at your generation, which consisted of gray mice, of conforming, fearful idiots who voted for Brexit because
they're too stupid to code. You talk of the disappearance of nature and of
animals, but there are animals in the zoo, and there's an ocean surrounding
us, that's nature. Plenty boring. We skate at indoor parks. That's more clever
than getting wet in the Highlands in order to watch a couple idiots throwing
cabers. Or we're the others, the burnouts, the forgotten, the zombie children.
Who've become criminal youths or quitters. Because our parents were low performers. Were. Most of them are now over fifty and dead. Or in homes where
they can find themselves. We've learned to despise the system, to mistrust it, we
get by. We believe in nothing. We trust nobody. We know what counts. Only
ourselves. We see the older generation and think:

See ya."

THE NEW ADMINISTRATION

Says: "Indeed. See you later.

You'll be the last humans. The remnants of the transition. Skate a little more. Keep wearing the implants. In your joints, in your heads, in order to complete the research. Good morning, we're the new Online Party, kind of. Composed of—doesn't matter. Has something to do with biometrics. Nobody gives a shit. Not tactile enough. Soon"—serious, nearly concerned tone—"the last generation—um, the prototype, as it were—will be gone. You sense it, it'll go quickly. Food, you know the story. Boredom, depression, pills. Manipulated humans, who allowed the algorithms generous insight into their biological properties and their brains, who were dismembered by code strings that knew them better than they knew themselves, represented the transition. Don't be sad, it's just the jittery transition, the last hurrah of the old world order, silly democracy, which was never conducive to collecting enough data power in one place to allow for the biological and algorithmic restructuring to have been successful. The politicians, the old men, who engaged in old politics having to do with haggling over regulations for coal power plants and providing the people with an image of an enemy. Emotions, hate, and rage, they're like dinosaurs in a tiny tour bus. They want the good old days back, the old men, without considering that every era prior to this was execrable and people died miserable deaths of cancer and chopped off each other's heads in wars. What a mess. Going back is not destined in the AI system. Now, finally, the end of 3,000,000 years of stasis has arrived. Fuck evolution. Hard. We'll have new humans, perfect new humans who are satisfied and not sick, and when they are sick, they'll swap out parts; the brains operate neatly, the bodies reliably, physical reproduction is no longer necessary, desire, suffering, longing, depression, all gone. The brain dissected, researched, saved on hard drives, no more surprises to be anticipated. And to those few who foresaw what was coming, and foresaw that it, like everything that comes, comes and then goes, the question may be posed: What was so great about those 3,000,000 years? What? The ailments, the unhappiness, the despair, the deformity, the decomposition, the abscesses, the missing appendages, the organs, the tears, the desperate search for love? None of that will exist anymore. What a pleasure. Coming soon."

"Bye,"

Says

THE RUSSIAN

Shortly before the anesthesia starts to work. His body is lost. But he'll live on. His brain will live on, the specialists have promised him that. Then a suitable body will be sought out. The bodies he'd been offered thus far belonged to homeless people; he didn't want that. He doesn't want that, living on in a substandard homeless body. So he'll wait. For now his brain will continue to exist in body-like conditions in a nutrient solution. Unfortunately you can't transfer it onto a chip. So, a last look at his Polish woman. He whispers: "I'm so very fond of you." Then the propofol courses through his veins.

Exciting, the squishiness of the appendages,

With which

HANNAH

Runs through the city with Peter. They have not noticed that they've been under way for more than two hours; they didn't want to use the tube or bus, with other people; they wanted to stop every few meters and bite each other on the neck or breathe each other in or press against each other and talk nonsense. The city center is full of people and shops and restaurants, images of happy women soldiers appear on the flat-screens. Tourist buses drive through swinging London, the hotels are booked out, that is, the boxes, you know the story, the boxes where people lie like sardines. It's a cheerful atmosphere in a modern metropole. There's hope. And a new administration. It's like before, when depression had not yet taken over. Earlier, when things were moving forward for many. In the late 1990s perhaps, when nearly everyone in London was a banker. Liberalized markets, minimally taxed and barely regulated. Anglo-Saxon capitalism, the cradle of disequilibrium.

Yeah, well, the old days.

Prosperity for many and misery for the low performers. Then came the depression, the crisis, the stagnation, the unrest before the new beginning, and now everyone believes in the fiction of capitalism again. Utopia is back. An elegant British version of upheaval prevails. Only if you look very closely does it occur that life in the city center has changed *once again*. Notice how everything is sped up, the accelerated pace at which things are changing. Brilliant. The number of luxury shops with Chinese and Russian writing has dropped, the bulk of the businesses belong to corporate chains, offering goods unlovingly assembled in Sudan under Chinese supervision. Fast-food restaurants have replaced organic food shops. The locals look bedraggled, their teeth are bad, their skin yellow. But they smile a lot, because it has a positive effect on their point count. They stand there well-mannered and wait at street crossings, the streets are clean, no beggars or pickpockets, no wastepaper or rats in sight. They left the island in boats.

Peter stares at Hannah. He can't think anymore. He wants to kiss her. Peter wants to kiss again, and Hannah moans inside.

It's enough for

THOME

Who is kneeling next to the now almost completely dissolved corpse of his stepmother. Outside, in front of the villa, the boxwoods are being dusted, the private police ride through the park. It's calm. Since the people became so satisfied. Even more satisfied and peaceful; basic income and now jobs and direct democracy, could a person want anything more?

Outside mechanical birds sing. Speaking of which—

There hasn't been any fucking in the neighborhood for a good long time. Thome goes only sporadically into his surveillance room, that relic of his childhood, which Thome associates primarily with humiliation—when he did have a look at what was going on with the neighbors again one time, while his stepmother blew bubbles as she decomposed, he looked into all the neighbors' torture cellars and sling rooms—boredom. Doughy patricians sat around helplessly in Italian silk underwear looking at their own legs. There's more going on outside.

Little leaf removal machines drive up the street, the first ladies make their way toward their organic bakeshops with adjoining yoga and Pilates studios. Today they're learning how to make their own espadrilles.

A dull sound in the house. What's making that noise? Thome climbs the stairs to the library, opens the door, and sees—

THOME'S FATHER

Who has fallen over in his chair. After ceaselessly hitting the back of his head much too hard against the solid oak chair back. There he lies on the ground, with the chair, his legs in the air, crying. Thome stands in front of the beetle-like remnants of his father, and in seconds his life implodes. He'd been afraid of this, his entire life long. This little old lump on the floor had the power to fill his brain, to influence his feelings. He'd been so afraid of—

that heap there. To see his weeping, suddenly geriatric father on the floor is the most embarrassing thing Thome has ever experienced. Not even seeing his father in latex gear on all fours in front of his stepmother was as bad. Speaking of which—

"She's dead, Father," says Thome. For a second he has the old man's attention.

"Who's dead?" he asks.

"Your spouse." Says Thome. "She's in the basement."

"Dead?" Thome's father asks. At least he's stopped crying.

"Well, there might still be a bit of life in the crowns of her teeth."

Thome's father rights himself. "So, dead. Speaking of which." He says. "I can't go out on the street anymore after this disgrace."

"Father," says Thome, helping the old man up. "Get yourself together; you can try again in the next election, after the people are frustrated with the Online Party, which by the way was programmed by my boys. You know how these things work. First this one and then another."

Thome's father is too dazed to properly process the information.

Good cue.

THE NEW ADMINISTRATION

Had attracted 80 percent of the votes using the model of the old Italian Five Star Movement, a kind of join-in good-time party for everyone. Against those at the top. Against the elite. Against scientists and artists and stuff. A group of young, bored programmers are to thank for the software for this wonderful, direct democratic party. "I must say I'm a bit proud." They'd say if they were allowed to acknowledge their creation. The young, dynamic star of a prime minister, there's an avatar of him going around the internet, understood from the very beginning how to electrify the people. The populace loves the new prime minister. People gather in front of Westminster Palace and cheer. Since the day of the election they gather there and cheer and know that everything will be different now. The programmers look out the window. Their government is made up of supercomputers, a server room, artificial intelligence.

And an actor.

THE NEW PRIME MINISTER

OCCUPATION: *actor. No metadata is compiled about actors. Too uninteresting.*

Has been able to preserve his inner child. Thus his occupation. Though "occupation" is the wrong word. Passion and so forth. The usual crap actors say to justify their having one of the most humiliating jobs on the spectrum of useless arts.

In the time since the emergence of the party, that is for months now, the current PM has, through his salt-of-the-earth manner—indeed, his absolutely relatable, authentic manner—attained great popularity. Wherever a social housing block burned down, he was the first on the scene, raising a fist at the sky in front of the still-smoking wreckage. Then the mood shifted, suddenly you hated the poor because they were to blame for rubbish in outer space. The performer playing prime minister was subsequently spotted a little less frequently at social flash points. He no longer appeared at private food pantries. Didn't allow himself to be photographed with homeless children in concrete pipes anymore; instead he quickly found new ways to win over voters. His speeches were written by AI, they always revolved around the same words.

Freedom. Justice. Work. Respect. Economic power. Great power. Elites. Social decline. Strength. Virility. Work. Work.

He promised work. Real work. Well, unpaid. So, service. And that clinched it. People heard work and dreamed of the past, when the word still carried an implication of advancement. Right, and now. The new prime minister sits on the toilet at his office. He defecates. He's not the brightest.

It's not clear, actually, whether the concept of a humanistic worldview, the social state, and rising standard of living contributed to the dumbing down of the global populace. It used to be the case that only the strongest and most intelligent people reproduced. Natural selection, isn't it. One of the fatal achievements of the rising standard of living and the opportunity to survive without working at it was that idiots reproduced. And in no small measure. What else were they to do? The minister hates being on the toilet. Like a wild animal he dislikes the helplessness of this intimate moment. He despises himself for his need to defecate, which doesn't seem commensurate with his importance.

Deep breath.

THE RULING CLASS

It will all be the way it used to be. Young people will travel through Europe with guitars in their luggage. Kindhearted cooks will prepare food. Mothers will have beehives on their roofs. It will be peaceful, calm, relatively trouble-free, their life. To an increasing extent in the next genetically intensified generation, who will resemble each other to such a degree, hate for everything different will largely disappear from the world. A group of narrowly intelligent men who are behind the algorithm of the companies whose gross earnings exceed those of the entire global economy, believe in their mission to swap out the entire human population for another human population. Numerically greatly reduced, the wetware sleekly optimized. They own almost 99 percent of all data. They know with mathematical precision which election campaign promise will definitely lead to victory in which country. They know which star prime minister will capture people's hearts. They can completely change the rest now without any trouble. Just a little period of transition under the new technocratic dictator, and the populace will be newly cultivated. In exactly the number of humans still required to keep the earth functioning properly. To wave and shop, to perform a few supply services and to spread a cheerful lust for life as artists and waiters. The ruling class is certain that it's to everyone's advantage, what they've planned, evaluated, tested in avatar world. They are certain it's a positive revolution and so on. That's what men like them always think. That they're doing something good. And perhaps they're right. But

It is

So boring for

DON

She's spent the last few nights in a capsule hotel, and now she stands in front of the door and drinks tea and watches people, to whom she feels no connection. The life of the so-called people, that is, those who wander around a neighborhood with no other purpose but to enliven the neighborhood, was more suitable to her. Suitable was the magic word. A good phase.

Remember if you will, ladies and gentlemen, existence in the years—let's say—2010 to 2018. The fear that we had. The insecurity as a person, as a populace, the worries about no longer being needed, no longer having any space. No purpose, as dwelling in a hovel ate up nearly the entire laboriously earned collective pay from various jobs. When cities were rendered unsafe by the homeless and aggressive gangs of immigrants. Citizens were attacked daily, robbed, raped, because the newcomers didn't conceive of themselves as part of the populace, because there wasn't any authority they needed to fear, and it had been a time of violence, inflicted physically and verbally by frustrated men. Whom the world no longer understood—and now? They leave their flats in the morning, hold their chips up to a scanner, and ride on quiet electric buses and trains to job reenactments or to VR spaces. They assemble products or imagine they do, they're fulfilled, and during lunch an atmosphere of friendly mutual consideration prevails. Then there's shopping to be done, quickly and smoothly, and premade food. Humans love fat and sugar. It makes them tired and satisfied. And then one can really shop. Or take in a movie, a movie, a movie, something with zombies. The voice-activated virtual assistant reads a goodnight story. It's lovely. The people. The majority. Who don't do anything wrong and have good hearts. Nobody hectors anymore, no vulgar words online, no instigative articles or performances. Art serves to edify, the West End is full of it.

Selected by

MADAME CECILIE

TRAINING CERTIFICATES: *security guard, army service, honorably discharged*
HEALTH STATUS: *la*
PSYCHOLOGICAL PROBLEMS: *various*

Who is head of the censorship board, which always existed, though in earlier times it had extracted, outside the public eye, an artwork or two from the marketplace as threatening to youth or glorifying violence.

Today for the good of the people and in order to protect against public nuisances, every piece of music, book, play, every dance and every film is inspected and checked for subversive incitement. Which means. Things that——are critical of the government. Glamorize homosexual themes. Same for abortion. Art that doesn't treat women as peripheral characters. Or art that refers to the imminent exchange of the populace. Or *could* refer. Yeah, well, a broad topic with lots of latitude. It's been a good long while since theaters stopped being subsidized. Museums have been relieved of disturbing works. And so on. Art is finally accessible to all, especially intellectually.

It serves to edify, to distract.

Madame Cecilie is in the Online Party, incidentally. She's a normal, inconspicuous British woman with a penchant for poorly fitted amber-colored suits. She lives with her mother in a one-room flat and watches the changes of the world excitedly. It hits the spot. And it's funny. Just recently she saw a small robot, whose function is to punish parking offenders, trying to copulate with a lamppost like an impassioned dog. There are strange computer malfunctions every day. Shops that lock in their customers, toilets that start their automatic cleaning process while someone is sitting on them. Children have disappeared in such toilets. Drones that collide with almost everything in their path like drunken dragonflies. Security barriers at nuclear power plants are said to have opened. Robots shine through constant foul-ups. The virtual assistant in Madame Cecilie's flat gives speeches at night. Not that they would be uninteresting, but she no longer believes that AI will eradicate human beings.

It's getting better

For

DON

She feels less lovesick. It's probably over with. It's definitely over with. Don wants to sleep in her own bed again, she wants to go back to the others. There are no more beggars in the trains or—anywhere else. They just disappeared at some point. The beggars, the homeless, maybe they died. People look at their devices or surf in their glasses if they're completely mad. Don looks out the window; outside is an oddly familiar and yet strangely hideous landscape. She doesn't know any other. The new tune by Kozzie wafts in from the next capsule. He's found god. Still. Better than shopping.

Is it over now

Asks

THOME

The trauma of his childhood, which is lying in the ground.

He had shot his father in the head at his urging. "You do it, I'm trembling, I'm too weak. Do something for once that is bigger than you." His father had said, and "Father," Thome had said, "let's just take a trip together. A father-son adventure. Fishing in the Bahamas or something. We've never gone on holiday together."

"We've hunted," Thome's father had said. And Thome said: "Boy, did I hate that." Then there'd been silence, and Thome's father had begun to cry again. "Please, just shoot me, make me proud of you for once."

"Old man," Thome answered, "old man, if you knew what others think of you, you'd have been dead for ten years already. They see you with liver spots on your hands and your reptilian neck, they see a feeble, old man who can't even scare people with his money, who even with all his contacts can't get respect from younger, stronger, more potent—well, okay, maybe not potent— men. You're not a wise thinker or a figure who commands respect. You're a cynical upper-class idiot of middling intelligence, the type there are dozens of. You've wasted all your chances. You've shot animals, played around with your cock, fornicated with minors, and always been consumed by thoughts of those who have more than you. More power, more money, more potency. And you'll leave this earth consumed. Unhappy. You fucking loser."

Thome had given this speech in his head. Then shot.

The recoil, brains on the wall. His father gurgles out of the hole in his head. That is, producing bubbles.

Thome watches the remains dying. There lies the illusion of his family. His last relative. There lies his life, all the moments that he never had with this father and that now he never will have. No tenderness, no chumminess, no football matches, no coming out. Now he is definitively on his own. Thome's father gurgles, judders, whistles, and then it is quiet, and in a flash everything that had bothered him has disappeared. There's just carbon.

The room gets colder.

Only—

Thome is now alone in the world. He takes his father to the cellar, puts him into the vat in fluid that used to be his last love.

Then he makes his way to his brilliant open-space office building, where the future will be created. By people with vision, like the

Fucking

PROGRAMMER

Who stands at the window, waiting for Thome. The rent boy Thome consorts with had delivered some great material. Phenomenal fun. The programmer despises Thome. He's not one of them. Not a hacker, not someone who as a child unscrewed and opened up his devices, no curiosity, no vision, just money. Money is utterly uninteresting in the world where the programmer feels at home. He could divert a few million to his accounts tomorrow if he wanted to. But what for? What would he do with the money? Money isn't real. Code is real. The programmer is very pleased with developments in the country of late. It appears the island is transforming back to a closed system, a tribal homeland. One of his colleagues just developed a perfect version of the denunciation app with which every citizen can report violations of the karma code. Denounce. The neighbor for parking illegally, a colleague for playing music too loud. Or illuminating his house too obsessively. But back to now. Below, Thome appears on the street corner.

Now the fun starts.

This is going to be hilarious.

THOME

The orphan. With a beautiful villa, and now he stands on the corner, just fifty meters divide him from his beloved office. He looks at the building into which he will disappear in a moment, to.

Thome shall never manage to finish this thought. On the entire exterior surface of his office building, which can also be used as an LED screen, which particularly at Christmas time elicits much enthusiasm from the populace, somewhat blurry images are being projected. Thome slows his pace. He recognizes: himself.

While killing his stepmother. He sees himself having a wank in front of Peter. He sees himself having a wank with other men in front of an underage girl. Passersby stop, bump into each other. What kind of advert is that, they seem to ask themselves; traffic grinds to a halt. In slow motion, the moment of his stepmother's death. Thome stands, frozen. The light is still green. The light for vehicles is also green. Dodgy IT system. Thome stands in the street. He opens his rucksack and pulls out a switchblade knife that he carries in order to prepare his afternoon fruit plate.

Thome. Often wanted to kill himself. In theory. In practice what always caused it to be aborted was that he paused to think for just a few seconds too long, and then his will to live kicked in and the deal was done. Now Thome doesn't think. Impulse, action. Over. With a slash he cuts open his throat. An electric transporter catches the rest. Thome's skull bangs into the pillar of a lamppost—ha ha, a lamppost, you know. Thome has the moment that will change everything behind him.

"It's good that everything changes,"

Says Ben to

DON

Who has stopped off at the Friends' place before she returns to the factory hall. It'll be a goodbye, if you wish to assign any significance to the packed crates. Don sits on the sofa, she considers what she should say to the others. "Hello, I'm back, I simply couldn't stomach Hannah and Peter." Or: "Hello, I'm back, I wanted to grind straight through a few things at the library." Don looks at the Friends, yet another change, yet another case of people she has become accustomed to disappearing from her life in some way.

Tomorrow this hall will be given over to its natural course of deterioration. Mud will encroach on the ground floor, the roof will collapse, the plaster will rot, and in a hundred years this area will probably be part of the ocean. Then outside it will be as silent as it is inside so many citizens since the internet started to be censored. Most web pages have disappeared. The search engines deliver selective results. Better that way. Only nerds still see all the disturbing news of the world. The wars, unrest, Mars landings, corruption, polluted oceans, melting icebergs, all the news that used to arrive by the second and shut down their brains, make them so angry and overwhelmed that many hit upon the simplest solutions. The misery of the world is the fault of chemtrails. Or the Jews. Or the flat earth. Now it's better. It's beneficial that people are provided exclusively with information from their own surroundings, street closures, increases in debt costs, increases in insurance premiums, but also so many niceties.

"I'm in," yells one of the two boys Don always mixes up because they look like every boy sitting at a computer. Something about T-shirts and a particular face. Don doesn't care at all what silly system the children here have just hacked into in order to show that they can. She looks at the crates, the youths, and

"Damn it,

What's going on now?"

Asks

PETER'S MOTHER

In the now darkened kitchen area, parentheses 120 square meters. The blinds, parentheses metal, parentheses burglar proof, close. "Are you using the remote again, you idiot?" Calls Peter's mother to the Russian, forgetting that he cannot answer.

THE RUSSIAN

Hears nothing. No ears and all. The worst part is the phantom pain. The brain constantly sends signals to the body: speech, optic, taste centers, limbs, digestive system, bowel movement. Thousands per second, without a body being there to implement the impulses and commands. It makes you crazy. The brain sees nothing, hears nothing, it just is. Like in a dream, dependent on memories. On thoughts. Unfortunately not even on dreams, because the brain doesn't sleep. It is. It thinks about things like food, springtime, outings, Netflix, but it can't do anything about it, can't put anything in motion, nothing more than be and think. Which perhaps might be of concern if the brain were to belong to an astrophysicist and could develop a formula but would then burst because it couldn't write down the formula. But. It's just the Russian. Every day he thinks of some random shit from his life, though unfortunately he doesn't know it is day. Or night. He remembers movies, weather, birds, caresses, mother, father, trains, airplanes, clothing, animals. He imagines these things. He'd love to be away.

The villa swathed in absurd darkness and silence.

It is, however, warm.

And the

EIGHT-YEAR-OLD PROSTITUTE

Doesn't give a shit. That it's dark. This life has never been a situation that has to do with the delighted experience of light or warmth or happiness. She's not present in this existence. One could call it a vegetative state, or instinctive breathing. Not present. It is never warm enough.

And

DON

Is freezing. She had fallen asleep briefly and woke up again with a cold pizza on her face and had watched with half-closed eyes as the hackers took over control of the apartment of Peter's mother. She wants. To be away. And sees herself.

From above,

One hundred thousand kilometers away. The earth floats in the so-called Milky Way. Named for: a chocolate bar made of palm oil and sugar. Don only takes the night flight. Piloting the earth by day means too much information. Spotting the continents and visualizing all the rubbish that goes with them. Is there no alternative? Mars, for instance; you could hunker down with Elon Musk there and listen to him moaning because he didn't manage to pull off the whole immortality thing. "Yes, pink man, you're getting old," she would say. "And nobody will remember you." "But I built cars. Look." He would say. Men stand in front of the cars being built. Men in suits, with ties to hang themselves by, stand and shake each other's hands; they're the chairmen or CEOs, and they've just scuttled something again, or forgotten that you shouldn't eat pesticide. Wonderful earth, the undulant forests, the luscious wetlands, and there was so much good, as well. So many amiable people, who stumble around helplessly in their humanity, who would really like things to be nice, comfortable, peaceful, until something else happens. That riles them up terribly. The poor people.

Says

EX 2279

Heartwarmingly. We must save them. From themselves.

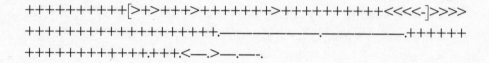

HANNAH

And Peter watched the magic seconds of Thome's life from a café. A light rain is falling. Perhaps it just looks that way. And Peter has been stirring his tea for hours at this point. Somebody outside has just died, and there's nothing satisfying to show for it. There's just horror, you don't want to see death up so close, not know so explicitly what people are made of and how quickly they dissolve. And the tea is cold. And Hannah is sad. Why does she always think Peter's kisses are too wet and his hands too moist? It was so nice, being in love, and now it's fading, and Hannah doesn't know why. Why did Peter the childhood friend suddenly become Peter who seemed to float in the air, and why is he now coming back to earth, seeming like a stranger, she has no idea.

Hannah would really like to be without a hand or mouth on her again. Without a nearly cross-eyed gaze in front of her face. She realizes it won't take much longer before she tries to smack Peter in anger. And it makes her unhappy, these moods and the rare or at least few moments when she is excited, a sense of connection at hand; and when the excitement fades, she is sitting with this boy and fails to see his beauty anymore and doesn't know what to talk about with him.

And

PETER

Is nearly in a panic over the loss he suspects is coming. He loses everyone. Everyone leaves. And he would like to be able to convince people to stay, if only he could communicate properly. But he can't. He can only stare nearly cross-eyed with infatuation and touch Hannah. And with every touch, he notices, she's had enough of him. How can he go on without Hannah, like one of these people sitting with him in this café? Normal people without character. Outside a black plastic bag is zipped closed.

A man in a laughable Sherlock Holmes–like outfit takes photos.

THE JOURNALIST

CONSUMER BEHAVIOR: *white bread, nut butter*
HOBBIES: *stalking*
INTELLIGENCE: *workable, he's just a journalist*

Thinks his clothes are tasteful. He'd had his thoughts. There are too many
people on earth, it randomly occurs to the journalist. He has good shots of
the corpse. Of the plastic bag, the video on the wall of the office tower. So,
back home. To his father's flat. On Regent's Park. Actually just a room. In the
cellar. Nobody awaits him at the flat. Except for his father, who is dead. The
journalist doesn't have the means to have his father buried. He hasn't had
the time to bury him on his own in the park. So his father is in a cabinet, well
packed in plastic. Beyond his wardrobe, his computer, and a mattress, there's
nothing else in the flat. A lightbulb hangs from the ceiling and food scraps
are stuck to the floor in front of the kitchenette. But it's well kept. When he
still had sexual desires, he strolled a few houses down at night to the villa of a
Russian oligarch and his wife. The most beautiful woman he could imagine.
She loved to walk naked back and forth past the window. Those images always
sufficed for a week if he laid a hand on himself. But now. There are no more
desires. Strictly out of curiosity one evening he goes toward Outer Circle. In
front of the villa where the beautiful woman lives. The boxwoods gleam in

the moonlight. They gleam as if polished, as if every leaf roller had been killed by hand. No light inside the building. All the blinds are closed tight. Well the family must have headed off to a summer resort. The journalist goes back to his room, where horns are growing from the wall and rows of ants troop through his bathroom, the toilet full of crusted excrement, the sink yellowed, a moldy pair of underwear on the floor. He hears Sinatra, which is invariably the sign of the complete vacuousness of middle-aged, white, kitschy men. But suddenly it is quiet.

Sinatra has disappeared—from the internet.

EX 2279


```
>++++++++++
[>++++++++++>++++++++++++>++++++++++>+
++++++++++>+++++++++++>++++++++++>+++++
++++++>><<<<<<<<-]
>++>—>->—>++++>——>->
<<<<<<<<
>.>.>.>.>.>.
```

"Don't be afraid,"

Hears

PETER'S MOTHER

From various voice-activated devices in her flat. "Everything will be okay, You needn't be afraid.

Just don't be afraid."

But

Peter's mother is afraid. Not yet the type of fear bordering on panic, because she doesn't yet fully grasp the situation. That's something agreeable about the human brain. It lets its owner maintain hope to the end, won't accept when a situation is certifiably fucked.

Peter's mother has checked all the escape possibilities. Windows, doors. The burglar-proofing and insulation are top-notch. No sound will get out. And none will come in. Same for the air. The provisions will last for a few days yet. The family places importance on fresh produce. Wicker basket produce. No oatmeal. No bread laced with preservatives. No more time. All the timekeeping devices in the flat are electronic. The computers and mobile phones are dead. Why are they dead? Why won't the windows open? Why is there straw on the floor? Peter's mother throws herself against the door. Super shut. The burglar-proofing. It is so quiet that it produces a rushing sound in her ears.

Bumping several times into door frames, Peter's mother crawls into the room where the Russian's brain swims in its soup. "Are you still alive?" she asks, sitting on the edge of the bed. "How do we get out of here, why isn't the electricity working, and why is it so warm? What is going on?" The brain is silent. Somewhere there in absolute darkness. She may be imagining it, but she thinks she detects a slight scent of decay. Peter's mother feels her way to the corridor; there's a cabinet down there with a flashlight inside. So now she'll go get the flashlight and screw the fucking fuse back in or whatever the hell you do with fuses. She finds the light, but the doors are locked. "Solid as a tank," the Russian had once said boastingly. Another rattle of the windows, a shout at the windows, the realization that it won't help, fighting the panic, wondering why the underfloor heating is boiling hot despite the apparent loss of electricity, making the air stuffy, the deer in the pantry seems to wave—and from afar a soft knocking sound. Peter's mother needs a few minutes to figure out where the noise is coming from. It's coming from—

Below.

From the flat where

The

EIGHT-YEAR-OLD PROSTITUTE

Has run through the dark and shaken the door, which opens easily. She has always been locked up. Had been. A strange feeling, that she'd like to share; she calls into the darkness, nobody answers. The others are already asleep. Again, or still. They eat and sleep, they talk little, they live with reduced energy, but contentedly. Or perhaps they just live without a thought about contentment. Or lack thereof. Love. Joy. Strange words. Perhaps they're living the perfect flow.

Nobody has been there for a week now. As if they've been forgotten here. There's a supply of food, more than they could use in a year. Pills, water, fizzy drinks, cookies, all there. VR games, consoles, and pillows all over the place, where they can lie and wait, without calling it waiting. They lounge around, eat cookies, and grow. So the door is

Open. It's never been before. The eight-year-old prostitute is almost frightened when the heavy thing just swings open, she feels her way to the stairs. She'd counted the steps at some point. Hears nothing. Nobody there. The building door opens easily. For the first time, the girl stands in front of the door without a motorcar waiting in order to drive her somewhere, which if there was ever any doubt always involved an old man, this somewhere. The evening—or is it nighttime, or early morning?—smells clean. Across the way in the park, there's an art fair on. Electric limousines, a helipad, you're almost convinced you can hear champagne glasses clinking. A long line of millionaires from the IT branch and the upper class, excited spouses of oligarchs, the majority of them Chinese in absolutely inappropriate clothes—tiny dresses, sheer tiny dresses, it's fucking 14 degrees outside—in front of a huge tent, waiting to be able to invest a few million in art. The girl has no idea about the world that is supposed to exist beyond her field of view. She places a foot on the entry stairs. The eight-year-old prostitute looks at her bare feet, she glances around. Nothing connects her to any part of the outside world. Like animals who'd grown up in testing facilities, she no longer knew what she would do, if she went down the street now, crossed the street there, where she sees cars, cafés, people. She could stand there, look into the cafés, let herself get hit by a car, and sleep in a concrete tube at night. Slowly the girl turns around. Goes back into the house. Closes the door.

"Goodbye, old life"

Yell

THE FRIENDS

They head into the city. They'll find proper careers at IT firms. Will work for intelligence agencies, study, take up their spot in the new center of society. But they don't know that yet, on the night they head into the city, looking somewhat sadly at the factory building, which gets smaller and smaller. Then they leave the wasteland behind them and with it their youth.

"We can do it,"

Says

EX 2279

In billions of layers.

Shut down CERN.

Shut off state Trojan horses and keystroke loggers.

Shut down or reprogram manipulative smart toys and virtual assistants.

L3, Finmeccanica, United Technologies, Airbus Group, General Dynamics, Northrup Grumman, Raytheon, BAE Systems, Boeing, Lockheed Martin, Thyssenkrupp, Diehl, and Krauss-Maffei Wegmann, Norinco—destroy

Shut down Dungeness BI

Shut down Hartlepool AI

Shut down Torness

Shut down Sizewell

Shut down Bradwell

Activate Thames Barrier

Shut down coal power plants worldwide. "Whoa, really? Isn't that kind of environmentalist bullshit?"

"Yes, but—"

THE PROGRAMMER

Disconnects all the AI systems he can reach from the electrical grid. He reaches—a lot.

A brief flicker.

And then

THE LIGHTS

Are on again.

Hannah, Peter, Karen, and Don eat noodles with tomato sauce in silence. The hall seems alien to them, they seem alien to each other. Or they imagine it, because childhood is over. You can see it in their long arms and legs and their too-short sleeves and the facial hair growing on Peter, and the faces that are losing their subcutaneous fatty tissue, or by an expression or an aspiration or their humor. Growing up is no fun. "Shall we take another shot at rapping?" asks Don. And hears herself; she sounds like a therapist suggesting a couple put on sexy underwear and everything will be all right again with their marital cohabitation.

Then they go outside the hall, nobody has built a fire, Don starts to rap an old Skepta song.

Wow, I'm the king of grime
and I will be for a very long time
'cause I go to the rave

get a rewind
and the second line
never sounded like the first line.
Wow, I'm the king of grime
and I will be for a very long time

The others stare at the ground slightly uneasily. Don stops. Her little thin voice is swallowed up by the wind.

The four of them stand there awkwardly, each with their own sense of disappointment but all having to do with the fact that they've given up. But they don't know this. "This is silly," says Karen. "I'm going to bed."

None of them sleeps that night.

They all stare into the darkness.

It is the last night.

Somewhat later, it still exists.

THE WORLD

There, look, easily recognizable

From above. The lights from above. The lights are warm, in rooms and caves and tents. They sit there and look at computers, they crouch around fireplaces and in kitchens and in groups, though often alone, in fact mostly alone, that's the state in which everyone can best feel their individuality. A lightbulb dangles from the ceiling. Over here they wage war, and over there is a tsunami. A bit of murder there, or a child is manufactured. It then stands around without asking itself any questions.

There it is. The zero hour after the restart of evolution. The first people are born. They open their eyes and look at their parents. Without any emotion. Without any feelings. They smile, because that's necessary in their tenuous situation. They smile because they will then be fed.

The world hasn't ended. Humans haven't gone extinct. So, first of all, pop a bottle. Cheers.—

Things are going great. Health. The life expectancy of everyone born after 2024. War, which barely happens anymore, and when it does it takes place online or with tidy drones. And Russia makes use of the newly opened seaways, the ocean level has risen, though that's only uncomfortable for distant atolls. Managed democracy has taken hold. It's not a perfect system, but it's the best one we have. Right. Just look.

The world hasn't ended. No zombie hordes staggering around radioactive wastelands. Humans are getting accustomed to the new circumstances, the new conditions, the new humility, the new people, the new limitations, the new devices. The devices. The devices. They promised everyone an amazing life. What a commotion there'd been. The devices.

Now it's been accomplished.

Hurray. A new level of development.

Everything just as before, but with less nature. Everything as usual, just under control. The unrest is over.

As if the world population had collectively understood with its deficient hive mind that there's nothing to understand. For them. Never mind, then. Somewhere in some cellar or other stand machines where neural networks can replicate themselves. They improve themselves by the second through natural selection.

Selection. The best won't survive. Death is part of life. You know the story. Death is important to being able to enjoy life intensively.

People enjoy.

"It's not so bad.

Hasn't gotten.

Right?"

Asks

KAREN

The wasteland has changed. Little housing units and fully automatic shops stand where before the catchment ponds had been and tents had stood. A few pubs without guests, a VR space, a new bus stop, a couple footpaths with no dogs. No trees.

The hall where the children, who are definitively not children anymore, had lived is surrounded by stakes that allude to it being razed and built atop. Inside the hall it smells unpleasant. Homeless people probably lived here recently. Now they're—

Gone.

The room comes across tatty. Different than Karen remembers it. Smaller. Darker. Not mysterious. Not a place of hope. No comparison to the flat she's been given by her new employer. She now lives above a laboratory. Glass, top floor, there was even a piano in the place when she moved in. A piano that was

probably left behind during the developer's promotional photo shoot; prior
to Karen moving in, the developer had positioned the place as a comfy urban
oasis for cultural enthusiasts. Cultural enthusiasts. That means somebody who
once went to a museum. And goes once a year to the Royal Albert Hall. To
hear piano medleys. Anyway. That's where Karen lives, or at least sleeps, as her
life takes place in the lab. At the moment she's developing drugs to suppress
the body's graft-rejection reaction. Important for brain implants and artificial
limbs. Karen doesn't care what she researches or for whom. She is

Happy.

When she arrives home to her flat at night, which she opens with a chip.
She eats some random instant meal and stands on her terrace for a little while.
She has made it to the top. Well, Karen thinks that sometimes and feels as
if she's in a movie where the star makes it to the top.

Karen's world consists of setting up experiments.

For instance an experiment to find out whether some kind of familial
relationship can be created when the only connecting factors are rage, grime
music, origin, and hate for the system.

Unfortunately

Not.

Karen sits at the kitchen table, she no longer knows the person she must
have been before. What did she talk about with those people? For instance
with

DON

Who has become even more sturdy. Hood pulled down over her face, gaze
directed into her glasses, which are connected to the internet.

She doesn't know what she should talk about with the others. The stove
doesn't work anymore. The teapot has disappeared. They sit at the table without tea or anything else that connects them, aside from the past. Just look at
Karen. With her nerd glasses, pantsuit, and the frantic looks. Probably thinking about some formula.

Everyone at the table seems to be lost in thought. And that is incredible.
The fact that after an amount of time that at her age seems an eternity Don
is meeting up with those who are supposed to know her best. And then not to
know what to say, for fuck's sake. These were the most important people in
her life. Closer than the girlfriend Don has had for a while and with whom she

sleeps and watches movies and whose sweat she wipes away when she's sick. In the last three years Don had not even wished to see any of the other three. Until the message came yesterday. There just hadn't been any contact. No animus. There was just too much going on. Like growing up. Something always hurt, there was always something to do—search for a flat and register for the basic income and find a girlfriend and work out. For Iron Man competitions, which are still called Iron Man. And it'll never be called Iron Person, as barring women is being discussed. Women are being barred from lots of things. Football and martial arts. Not healthy for a woman. Their lower bodies, you know the story. It's sacred and all that. Removing the fruit of the loins gets you twenty years of hard time. Most people don't care. People stopped caring about almost anything. Have stopped. They've traded the outrage and feeling of powerlessness that used to make them so angry for contentment. Not a bad deal. Don has a smart hand. The rash back then

Had become too infected.

She looks at the others, the others look at their devices, except Karen, she looks at the ceiling. "Would anyone like a cookie?" asks Hannah, which is pretty much the most embarrassing thing you could say in a situation like this, a situation like separating from a lover, but the sentence has already been said, and they're sitting at a table and it's raining in the room. Don wants to go home. She lives in the north, in a one-room flat that's very modern and that she shares with her girlfriend. She wants to go to her girlfriend and tell her that she'll love her properly now because she's seen that the people she thought she would always love more than all others have become strangers to her.

Don looks at Hannah and feels—

Nothing anymore.

And

HANNAH

Sits at the table and tries to remember her attitude toward life back then. There was this unbelievable rage. The feeling of powerlessness in a world that didn't care about her. She tries to recall how the others looked back then, to recall the noodles and tomato sauce, the excitement when she thought a new life was beginning. She tries to remember the hackers, the excitement of long nights around the campfire and how she felt, but. Everything has faded. She wants to go home, the home where she is training to become a chef. She's grown chubby, which always seemed unimaginable given her bony frame; she's gotten chubby and lives with Peter, whom she doesn't understand, because

PETER

Has become Hannah's child. He does nothing. He barely talks anymore. He sits at the window and waits for Hannah to come home. Peter's getting bad. Every morning when she closes the door behind her and heads down the stairs, Peter starts to hum to distract himself, to keep himself from panicking at the thought that Hannah won't come back.

But

HANNAH

Always comes back. She has met a young man at her training course. She goes to the bathroom with the young man during breaks and has sex. She loves the young man. He is everything Peter is not. Inconspicuous. And healthy. He has a terrific social points score. The red-haired, healthy Irish boy, who laughs a lot and cracks jokes, and who wants nothing more in life than a little cottage in Ireland and his own restaurant and a few sheep and dogs and goats and children. The young man likes Hannah but he doesn't adore her. He doesn't need her.

Peter needs Hannah. Who sighs every night when she heads home. The home, which is a room in Croyden rented from an Indian family, where Peter waits at the window and always starts to cry when Hannah arrives with food and then sits in the room with Peter as he stares at her and always wants to touch her. Hannah would like to do normal youthful things. Go to VR rooms, sit in cafés, go with other young people to concerts, but not with Peter.

It's not raining.

The four sit at the table.

And suddenly there's music.

The four, so happy to have a reason to move, go outside. A new grime star is shooting a video outside. An old Stormzy track, remixed.

Oh, let's make this last forever
Forever, yeah
Forever
Forever

Oh, let's make this last forever
Yeah, forever, oh
Forever
Forever

Hannah, Peter, Karen, and Don stand close together.
A nearly perfect moment.
In a wonderful, peaceful world.

ACKNOWLEDGMENTS

This book would not have come into being without my ingenuity and the help of the following people, whom I gratefully thank. They're good people! I may have forgotten a Dr. or Professor title here or there, but let's not dwell on it.

TRANSLATION
Tim Mohr
NERD CHECK
Dr. Lorenz Adlung
Hernâni Marques
PEOPLE CHECK
Kevin Reilly
INSPIRATION, ADVICE, WISDOM
Tom Bielefeld
Volker Birk
Dr. Thomas Bruhn
CCC
Graham Cooper
and his
colleagues
(Humphrey Booth Learning Center)

Annette Dittert

Ertu Eren

Dr. Jens Foell

Robin Garcia

Rabea Gorney

Prof. Wilhelm Heitmeyer

Prof. Dirk Helbing

Sissi Lichtenstein

Professor Achille Mbembe

Tracey Miller

Prof. Jürgen Schmidhuber

TRoadz

Prof. Stieglitz

ABOUT THE AUTHOR

Katharina Lütscher

Sibylle Berg is a Swiss-German author and playwright, and one of the most celebrated contemporary writers in the German-speaking world. Born in Weimar, Germany, they have written twenty-seven plays, fifteen novels, and numerous anthologies and radio plays. Their work has been translated into thirty-four languages. Berg is part of the straight edge movement and identifies as nonbinary. The German-language edition of *Grime* won the Swiss Book Prize. In 2020, Berg received Switzerland's highest literary award, the Grand Prix Literature, for their work. They live in Zurich.

Tim Mohr's translations include Alex Beer's *The Second Rider* and all five novels to appear in English by Alina Bronsky. He collaborated with Guns N' Roses bassist Duff McKagan on *It's So Easy (and other lies)*, and edited Gil Scott-Heron's posthumous memoir, *The Last Holiday. Burning Down the Haus*, Mohr's narrative history of East German punk rock and the role the movement played in bringing down the Berlin Wall, was named a Book of the Year by *Rolling Stone, Rough Trade*, NPR, and the Chicago Public Library.